ACCLAIM FOR
APOLOGIZE, APOLOGIZE!

"Part *Grey Gardens* and part *The Royal Tenenbaums* . . . beautifully written . . . Kelly is a gifted writer . . . Collie's quest is worth reading for the elegant prose alone."

—*Publishers Weekly*

"Wacky and smart and ambitious . . . marks Elizabeth Kelly as a formidable new storyteller, one to put on your Must-Read list straightaway . . . This novel takes risks, jumps off cliffs, throws caution to the wind, and takes us in directions we don't expect."

—*Buffalo News*

"Laugh-out-loud funny . . . Kelly is a clever, witty wordsmith . . . Meet the Flanagans, a quasifunctional family that might give Jonathan Franzen pause."

—*Library Journal*

"These are people you can't imagine living with, but can't resist reading about . . . Good enough [and] witty enough to make us want more from Kelly."

—*Washington Post*

"Dave Eggers fans should enjoy Kelly's rambunctious first novel about the guilt-ridden scion of a super-rich, eccentric Martha's Vineyard family."

—*Kirkus Reviews*

more . . .

"Very entertaining . . . Kelly takes a big gamble by letting most of her novel unwind through a male character . . . Her character Collie carries it off. Good for him. And good for Kelly."

—*St. Louis Post Dispatch*

"Kelly displays an unrelenting quirkiness that begs comparison with Daniel Wallace and John Irving . . . Even the dogs and pigeons have personality to spare in this story . . . slightly surreal . . . whimsical . . . will appeal to lovers of the offbeat."

—*Booklist*

"The language shimmers, and the cast of characters is unforgettable . . . rich in imagery—Kelly has a gift for lively figurative language. And all the characters have lacerating wit . . . There's so much leaping off the pages that you'll want to read it more than once."

—*Vancouver Sun*

"This novel starts with an enjoyable Celtic kitchen brawl of one-line put-downs in the heart of a family, and then moves its gears, through malice and disaster, to a quiet tone in which the protagonist finally learns to live with himself. It's a tour de force of energy and spirit."

—Peter Pouncey, author of *Rules for Old Men Waiting*

"A warm and wonderful tale with smart, sassy, yet gentle sensitivity. Elizabeth Kelly writes with an original, rhythmic style that ushers us in as we turn the first page of this magnificent story of family ties, devotion, understanding, and acceptance. I loved this book!"

—Daryl Roth, producer of *August: Osage County*, *Proof*, and *Three Tall Women*

"[Kelly has an] ability to fashion sentences that conjure wonderful images and descriptions, to combine factual details with fancy, and to do it all in elegant style."

—*Martha's Vineyard Times*

"When I read this novel, I didn't know whether to laugh or cry; so I did both—as the graced and disgraced life of Collie Flanagan came roaring at me, all mad comedy and pure grief with the brio of an Irish pub at closing time. And then I bowed my head, because this fine a story told this well doesn't happen every day or every decade. With the linguistic mastery of a Carol Shields or a Julia Glass, Elizabeth Kelly's debut novel comes down hard and strikes the bell."

—Jacquelyn Mitchard, author of *The Deep End of the Ocean*

"Every page is meaningful, every line vital. And Kelly's language is always deft and occasionally breathtaking; the pure, stimulating beauty of her words leaves no need for apologies."

—*Rain Taxi*

"An imaginative and energetic triumph . . . What you hear from the onset of APOLOGIZE, APOLOGIZE! is the delicious sound of a gifted novelist taking flight for the first time. (Think of Dostoevsky on laughing gas.)"

—David Gilmour, author of *The Film Club*

"Jarringly lovable, alternately hilarious and heartbreaking, and, afterward, challenging to talk about: a perfect book club book . . . Funny, sometimes shocking, this astonishingly readable and memorable first novel contains disasters great and small, poignant introspection, the antics of dogs and pigeons, and the fierce and tender bonds of love. Elizabeth Kelly is an author to watch."

—wowowow.com

more . . .

"The startling and painful wit of Collie's voice makes Holden Caulfield sound like a kindergartner, and lays waste to the acres of banalities and clichés that usually accompany stories about redemption. Rich with moral nuance and narrative surprise, this is a book as delightful as it is moving."

—Elizabeth Frank, author of *Cheat and Charmer* and winner of the Pulitzer Prize for *Louise Bogan: A Portrait*

"For all the novel's considerable comic brio, Kelly achieves something deeper and more unsettling, depicting the distortion of values that extreme wealth can cause and showing, without getting heavy-handed about it, how fun is often something pursued as a distraction from deep pain."

—*Montreal Gazette*

"In this unflinching and funny debut, Elizabeth Kelly deftly paints her tale in alternating shades of lush whimsy and hard-won ferocity. APOLOGIZE, APOLOGIZE! reads as if Padgett Powell's Edisto had a first cousin from New England who was wealthier, more eccentric, more gothic, and more drunk."

—Mark Winegardner, author of *Crooked River Burning*

"Well-written and clever . . . brims and bubbles with the effervescence of Kelly's hard work."

—*Ottawa Citizen*

apologize, apologize!

ELIZABETH KELLY

New York Boston

To my father, Arthur J. Kelly

Twelve
Hachette Book Group
237 Park Avenue
New York, NY 10017

www.HachetteBookGroup.com
Twelve is an imprint of Grand Central Publishing.
The Twelve name and logo are trademarks of Hachette Book Group, Inc.

Printed in the United States of America

Originally published in hardcover by Twelve.

First Trade Edition: March 2010
10 9 8 7 6 5 4 3 2 1

The Library of Congress has cataloged the hardcover edition as follows:
Kelly, Elizabeth
Apologize, apologize! / Elizabeth Kelly. —1st ed.
p. cm.
Summary: "A novel about the triumphs and tragedies of the dysfunctionally rich"—Provided by publisher.
ISBN: 978-0-446-40614-7
1. Rich people—Fiction. 2. Massachusetts—Fiction. I. Title.
PR9199.4.K448A66 2009
813'.6—dc22 2007049531

ISBN 978-0-446-40615-4 (pbk.)

Book design by Charles Sutherland

CHAPTER ONE

I GREW UP ON MARTHA'S VINEYARD IN A HOUSE AS BIG AND loud as a parade—the clamor resonated along the entire New England coastline. Calliope whistling, batons soaring, trumpets bleating, everything tapping and humming, orchestrated chaos, but we could afford it. My mother was rich, her father's money falling from the sky like ticker tape, gently suppressing the ordinary consequences of all that noise.

We lived up-island on several remote acres on the south shore of Chilmark. I'm still shaking the sand from my hair and scraping it off the soles of my feet, the sand from the beachfront filling every crack in the aging floorboards of our large, faded, shingle-and-clapboard captain's house.

The private saltwater shorefront of Squibnocket Beach made up our front yard, rugged surf pounding away, monster waves obscuring the skyline. On turbulent days the surfers almost landed in our kitchen, my uncle Tom chasing them off, using epithets as his broom.

Tom was my father's older brother. I'd call him the resident lunatic, but he faced tough competition for the title. Skirmishes abounded in our family, where arguments and opinions were as profuse as the tracks left by sandpipers along the shoreline.

A sparrow couldn't fall from a tree without eliciting wildly divergent commentary from Ma and Pop and Uncle Tom, who made up the adult members of my immediate household. Looming in the distance, constant and reminding, was my maternal grandfather, Peregrine Lowell, a man of expansive wingspread we called the Falcon, who roosted at great heights, poised to fly in and finish off lesser birds in midplummet.

My younger brother, Bing, and I were raised with the dissonant sound track of their collective insurgency playing continuously in the background—not exactly a tune anyone could whistle.

Those fantastic Flanagans, they exist just outside the door leading to me, Technicolor characters in what seems like a separate cartoon-strip version of my life. Plain as a line drawing by comparison, I was the domestic equivalent of a moderate voice in a divided Ireland. According to Pop, my Flanagan blood—Catholic as Communion wine—was corrupted at the cellular level by an infusion of Protestant DNA courtesy the Lowells, my mother's northern Anglo-Irish tribe.

Memories of home follow me wherever I go, chewing at my heels, panting for attention, as unyielding as all the dogs my mother accumulated over the years. Wet dog and the salty brio of surrounding sea air—my past hangs on in great olfactory waves, dragging its matted tail. That broke-down house and its thronging packs of dogs, it was like a reenactment of the fall of Saigon just trying to get from the entranceway to the living room.

English mastiffs, Neapolitan mastiffs, Tibetan mastiffs—those guys will bray at the moon until your soul shakes—and Jesus, that goddamn bull terrier, Sykes. My mother presided over all of it like some sort of mad, curly-haired, Celtic fairy queen. Her operatic wants and rants, feral hatreds and lavish affections, clanged like a lighthouse bell.

My name is Collie Flanagan. Ma chose the name Collie after rediscovering the books of Albert Payson Terhune, the guy who wrote *Lad: A Dog*.

Pop swore she read him throughout the pregnancy, hoping to

give birth to a puppy. During my baptism, a fight broke out at the altar when the priest objected to me being named after a breed of dog, saying there was no St. Collie, and Ma told him there damn well should be and Pop announced that maybe I'd be the first.

At Andover they called me Lassie. That was fun.

My mother always wanted a daughter. The day I was born, November 22, 1963, was otherwise known as the worst day in Ma's life, the disappointing birth of a son coinciding with the death of her hero JFK. She commemorated her epic fury by building a bonfire on the beach and setting fire to Pop's beloved record collection, the smiling faces of Jo Stafford and Perry Como melting onto the driftwood. She even threw in a can of Raid just to hear the sound of her own anger exploding over the skyline.

Nine months later, on August 3, she had another boy, named for an Irish setter, my brother, Bing, who, lucky for him, shared a birthday with her other idol, the British war poet Rupert Brooke. Even so, before she carried Bing into the house for the first time, she paused to rip out all the pink geraniums from the front window box. Ma, it must be said, had a gift for making even flowers tremble.

She was the only female, the requisite bitch, according to Uncle Tom; otherwise it was an inelegant masculine settlement—even the dogs were male, the toys pissing on pillows, the giants drooling thick ropes of testosterone.

It's safe to say that my mother and my grandfather had a curious relationship. She loathed him, and he coolly financed her contempt. Sometimes I think he stuck around only in the hope of unlocking the secret of their estrangement. Hating her father was my mother's life's work and study, her daddy doctorate. She'd been accumulating data on him as far back as I could remember, research piled on chairs, in stacks of paper high as the dining room table.

There were charts and graphs pinned to the walls, filled with the grousing of ex-employees, former friends, and jealous business rivals. There were black-and-white photographs, secret testimonies, and endless lists of her personal grievances handwritten in red ink and block letters, a perverse tapestry smeared across the walls of her office, all in support of a roman à clef she claimed to be writing entitled *The Bastard*.

The protagonist, an enormously wealthy and powerful newspaper mogul, murders his wife and gets away with it. Then he devotes the rest of his life to destroying his daughter's happiness.

My grandfather always assumed a wry and world-weary tone when referring to his only child. Whenever Ma's name came up, I half expected him to ask for a last cigarette while waving off the blindfold. Ma raised us to believe that she was interesting, in the same way that Stalin's family was no doubt encouraged to think of him as an eccentric. It took me a long time to realize that my mother was crazy, her baseless vendetta against the Falcon one of the ways she told us the true tale of all that churned around inside her.

Pop was a stray, a drinker, and a womanizer, professionally Irish, a guy of mixed pedigree that Ma plucked off the streets because she was mad for his hair color, the same shade as a ruby red King Charles spaniel.

"There's not much that money can't buy," she used to tell us. "I knew the moment I laid eyes on him, his hair glowing like the sun and the moon and the stars, that I'd give over my whole fortune for the privilege of waking up next to that glorious head each morning."

Ma never sounded so in love as when she was waxing in the abstract.

The first time she saw him was late at night. Pop was drunk and dressed as Carmen Miranda, clinging to a streetlamp for support, having come from a costume party. She was leaving a meeting of Marxist sympathizers. Ma collected Commies the way other women accumulate Tupperware.

Uncle Tom insisted that Pop married Ma on a dare. Said Pop was out on the town with the infamous Dolan brothers, otherwise known as "the Corrupters," when he announced to everyone at the costume party that he'd marry the first woman to pass him on the street. Stumbling outside in his Carmen Miranda getup, barely able to stand, Pop looked up and there was Ma. Stretching out his hand, he offered her a banana from his headpiece and the spell was cast, according to Tom.

"Peachie 'Pittsburgh' McGrath almost beat her to the punch. What a wagon that one was—drawers the size of Cork. She'd just turned the corner and was lumbering up behind your mother. Charlie told me had it been Peach, he would have gone through with the ceremony to appease the Dolans and then killed himself right after. Married and buried on the same day."

"Pop, is it true you married Ma on a dare?" I asked him, nine years old and starting to wonder about such things, staring down at my new running shoes from my spot on the stairs of the veranda. It was twilight, a summer night, deep in August; the beach was empty except for the ever-present purple martens darting in search of insects as the lap of the waves made a buttery soft sound.

"I married your mother because I loved her," Pop said as if from a distance, not looking at me, but watching the water from where he sat still in a high-backed rocking chair, red hair shining like his personal sunset. For all of himself that he offered up—he was a torrent of words and emotions—I never felt as if I got to know Pop all that well.

I knew what he wanted to talk about, there was no shortage of topics, but I never really knew what to talk to him about.

Ma and Pop, despite their compulsive vividness, might as well have been partners in an accounting firm when it came to public demonstrations of affection. Bingo and I always knew, even when we were little, that a certain unresolved tension existed between them.

Pop would disappear for a few days, and Ma would grow quiet. She used to run the water in the upstairs bathroom so we wouldn't hear her cry. We'd stand outside the door, waiting, using our fingers to chip away brittle strips of cracked white paint, and we'd look at each other until she turned off the tap and then we'd scatter.

When Pop finally showed up, he'd bring Ma an amaryllis bulb. Terra-cotta pots filled with amaryllis lined the iron shelves in the greenhouse next to the stable. There were so many of them, Ma finally ran out of room and reluctantly started keeping them at my grandfather's conservatory.

One time Pop went away to New York for a weekend, claimed it was a business trip—"dirty business," Ma said, showing us his empty briefcase. Pop was always taking so-called business trips when we were little. As we got older, they relaxed into overdue vacations.

"So what? Pop's always carrying around an empty briefcase," I said, shrugging, earning a mild cuff on the back of the head. It wasn't until I was twelve that I finally realized what the amaryllis bulbs signified.

"Pop's trying to make up for going around with other women. He's got a guilty conscience," I said to Bing, who looked unconvinced.

"This is interesting," Ma said to Pop late Sunday night as Bingo and I eavesdropped in our pajamas from our hiding spot on the second-story landing. "Two amaryllis bulbs."

"Yeah, well." He kissed her—we recognized the significance of the little silence. "I know how much you love them."

Ma loved to proclaim her need for beautiful things, as if it put her in a special class of elite human beings, the rest of us content to be surrounded by irregular profiles and sidewalks. She had three ideals of male beauty: Pop, Bingo, and Rupert Brooke. She even became president of the Rupert Brooke Society and made occasional pilgrimages to his grave in Greece. She'd come home dressed in black, swaying back and forth and clutching her heart.

"Jesus," I once heard Pop mutter, "I swear there's more than a little Italian in that woman."

Bing and I grew up in the only house in the modern world where a long-dead poet was a daily source of tension.

"Why can't she just have a crush on Tom Jones like all the other mothers?" I asked Bingo, the two of us peeking around the door as she sat by the hour at the pine desk in the library—Ma had a thing about pine, called it the people's wood—staring at his photo, when Pop spotted her and hit the roof, shouting:

"How'd you like it if I took up with Virginia Woolf?"

What did my parents see in each other? In Ma's case, I think it was a simple matter of aesthetics and disorder. Pop was a good-looking anarchist who appeared to believe in everything and nothing at the same time all the time.

Of course, I might be overthinking the matter.

"It's good to have a man around," she said. "In case the sewage pipe ruptures."

They used to get into fistfights, Ma and Pop, for Christ's sake, Uncle Tom taking bets from Bing and me on the outcome—collecting on them, too, once threatening to kneecap me if I didn't pay up. But I spent a lot of time studying them, watching them, searching for clues, and they had a way of looking at each other.

In addition to his improbable Irish beauty, talent for canine coloring and marrying well, Pop had one other minor gift: He knew a lot about magic. Before he met Ma, he used to perform as Fantastic Flanagan at fairs, second-rate nightclubs, and nursing homes. Afterward, he pretty much confined his act to our living room—it took me until puberty to figure out that these were *tricks* he did. His greatest illusion was convincing Bingo and me that he was some sort of special being endowed with extraordinary powers. We made an exception for him. To us, the drunkenness was a form of penicillin, his way of coping with the burden of an ordinary existence.

"Ah, boys, I wasn't meant for this world," he used to tell us as we helped him up the stairs and into bed, me under one shoulder, Bingo holding up his half. "Charlie Flanagan sentenced to life on earth without parole. It's a cruel fate for a man such as I."

Then I'd catch him pissing in the driveway after a night on the town, and I'd wonder.

Uncle Tom used to tell me, "The thing of it is, Noodle, they're all dense as bottled shite, even Charlie. Thank God every day that you and Bingo have got me, or Lord knows what would become of you."

Tom lived with us, took care of us, cooked and cleaned and fought with Pop on a daily basis—Pop referring to him as our "maiden uncle." To witness one of their foaming encounters was to contemplate a small boat on a collision course with Niagara Falls—every brawl a kind of helpless plunge.

So many fights, and Bingo and I were like turkeys in the rain, standing around helpless, tail feathers drooping, watching in wonder as they crashed through the railing of the upper-story balcony, Pop's hands around Tom's neck, Tom's arms flailing, fury seeming to suspend them in midair. The whole murderous time they'd keep arguing, talking, always talking, a wall of sound and temper, how many times I just wanted to scream at them, "Shut up! For Christ's sake! Shut the hell up!"

The end would arrive with a big thump, them landing in a mangled heap at our feet, Bingo grabbing my arm in excitement, thrilled by all that mayhem, while my circulation was grinding to a shuddering standstill.

Brawling came naturally to the Flanagan brothers.

"Your grandfather never backed away from a disagreement," Pop told us. His father's penchant for fighting was one of Pop's favorite topics when we were growing up. Pop had a fairly narrow measure of manhood and used broken noses to chart masculinity the way scientists recruit tree rings to chronicle age.

"He got into a terrible flap with the parish priest back home one Sunday after Mass."

"What were they fighting about, Pop?" I asked him, already familiar with the answer by the time I could tie my shoes.

"The fighting skills of the American army, of course—how he

loved to hold forth on that subject. I well recall your grandfather talking to me about the glories of the American fighting man in my high chair. 'The Americans couldn't lick their own lips,' says Father Duffy to your grandfather the moment he sees him—this is before the Yanks entered the war. Well, you might just as well pour gasoline into hell . . . the eruption could be heard from miles around. Let me tell you a little something about your grandfather, God bless him, you wouldn't want to stand next to him and light a match."

Whenever Pop talked about his old man, I could smell something burning. Hugh Flanagan was a firestorm, according to Pop. "He left grass fires where he walked. He burned down barns with the ferocity of his judgment."

He sure as hell knew how to piss off a priest.

"May your sons never have any luck," Father Duffy shouted, slamming the door behind him. Soon after, Hugh and Loretta Flanagan left Ireland with their family, three boys, Tom, William, and Charlie, and two girls, Brigid and Rosalie, and immigrated to Boston. It was 1940. When it came time for the United States to enter the war, Hugh wanted his two older sons, Tom and William, in American uniform. Pop was too young to enlist.

"Your grandfather never recovered from the disgrace of your uncle Tom trying to join up wearing ladies' underclothes," Pop told me. I was eight, standing across from him in the living room, where he sat parked in his favorite morris chair, voice booming as I flinched.

"That's a goddamn lie, Charlie Flanagan, and you know it. I wanted to serve. My flat feet kept me out of the action. Name one veteran, dead or alive, that's suffered as much as I have," Tom hollered from the kitchen, where he was chopping onions for stew.

"Oh, so that's what they're calling cowardice these days, a matter for the podiatrist, is it? Next you'll be telling me had you only been born with balls, you'd be the boys' uncle instead of their aunt." Pop, never happier than when he was producing friction, approached me playfully, shoulders hunched, assuming a classic boxer's stance, punching the air, one-two-three, narrowly missing my chin.

"Your uncle Tom single-handedly put the personality in disorder," he said.

Uncle Tom was my mother's sworn enemy. He referred to her as the Female B—his obtuse way of calling her a bitch. He was always doing funny things with language, mangling words, making up crazy expressions, being deliberately provocative, saying schedule as if it were pronounced "shek-a-dool" and then daring you to correct him. Tom never outgrew the desire for negative attention, a trait he shared in common with Ma.

Ironically, considering their mutual hatred, there wasn't much to give or take between their views. Tom and Ma were against just about everything everyone else was for, yet year in and year out, they circled each other, glaring like rival warlords.

"And thank God for it," Pop proclaimed. "Jesus, Collie, can you imagine what might happen if they joined forces?"

"Move over, Abbott and Costello," I said.

I suspect that my mother underwrote every postwar revolution undertaken by Marxist insurrectionists from one end of the globe to the other. Anais Lowell Flanagan was writing checks for her pet causes all through the 1970s when we were growing up. Nothing Ma enjoyed more than the incendiary overthrow of established order.

Uncle Tom lived for the pleasure of infiltrating and disrupting her political gatherings. He used to call everyone on the guest list and tell each one there had been an outbreak of impetigo at the house, leaving my mother to fume when no one showed up.

"Some revolutionary he turned out to be . . . scared of a little fungus," he'd report to Bingo and me, receiver to ear, as he knocked them off the list one by one.

He raced for the phone whenever it rang, and if he didn't approve of the caller—he never acceded to anyone—he'd shout into the receiver, "Gotta go. There's a squirrel in the house!"

Once in a while, someone would call back.

"Hello, this is Denny the Red. May I speak with Anais?"

"I'm sorry, there's no Denny the Red here. You've got the wrong number."

"No, you don't understand. I'm Denny the Red—"

"Are you deaf as well as dumb? I told you there's no Denny the Red at this number."

He used to put Bingo and me through the same crazy routine. Dialing home was like trying to get God's private line. When I was in grade six I broke my arm at school, and the hospital called, trying to get permission to operate. I was going nuts from the pain—it was a compound fracture—everyone, including the surgeon, was standing around waiting to go, and a nurse walked in with a bewildered look on her face and announced there appeared to be some emergency at my house.

"Something about a squirrel?" she said.

CHAPTER TWO

PEREGRINE LOWELL, MY GRANDFATHER, WAS PRESIDENT AND SOLE owner of Thought-Fox Inc. A big wheel in the Democratic Party, he owned hundreds of newspapers and magazines in dozens of countries, including some of the world's most influential dailies. An aggressively merciless proprietor, he had a reputation for being hands-on when it came to editorial content, viewing the op-ed pages of even the lowliest community publication as his personal soapbox. One time, he got so inspired by the proposal to ban outdoor cats in some little town in Iowa that he wrote a guest editorial championing the rights of songbirds.

Not content simply with interfering in the grinding minutiae of his empire's daily operations, he also considered it his duty to despise and denigrate everyone who worked for him, reflexively pointing to his signature on their paychecks as evidence of his superiority.

My grandfather both demanded and deplored compliancy, which meant he posed a unique set of challenges for the people around him. Fortunately, working for him was generally a temporary condition. He set some sort of industry record for firing people, a distinction he welcomed, saying, "Good people come, and good people go," and sounding a whole lot like a raptor that's just decapitated a goldfinch.

Nicknamed the Falcon by Bingo and me—seemed clever when we were kids—he sat darkly in the tops of trees, sleek and straight, eyes like stones, defined from all angles by his remote habit of trenchant surveillance. An Anglo-Irish Protestant on loan to New England from Ulster, he was bored by the conversation of field mice, and it showed.

It's safe to say that he terrified and intrigued me. Stuck for a moment alone with him in the butler's pantry at his sixty-third birthday party when I was ten, I weakly inquired what kind of icing he liked best, chocolate or vanilla, feeling as if I were interviewing Dracula about his preference in blood type.

"What *are* you squeaking about?" he asked, looking down on me, his contempt a talon, snapping my neck with the power of his disdain.

"Never mind," I said, temporarily unable to swallow. I had asked him a question. For years, I never asked him another. A distinguished Dickens scholar, he'd published several books on the subject, but ornithology was his true passion, part of a family tradition that extended to the naming of male heirs. His old man was named Toucan by his father, Corvid, my great-great-grandfather, an unchecked eccentric from an aristocratic background—nicknamed Cuckoo Lowell by all who knew him. He bizarrely practiced ornithomancy, a form of divination using flight patterns.

The Falcon wanted us named after birds—Larkin and Robin were his choices—but Ma infuriated him by naming us after dogs instead.

"It could have been worse," Bingo said. "She could have called us Sacco and Vanzetti."

The Falcon lived on a century-old estate called Cassowary, a few hundred choice acres of woodland, marsh, and open field tucked into the New England coastline and within spitting distance of Boston. A black wrought-iron gate at the entranceway had this cheerful, biblical admonition engraved across the top, his idea of a welcome mat: "For what is your life? It is even a vapor that appeareth for a little time and then vanisheth away."

My grandfather wasn't big on small talk.

Cassowary was formally landscaped with topiaries, walls, and hedges. Four life-size elephants constructed of metal frames and filled in with a cladding of dark green English ivy paced round and round a large ring outlined in yew, their inertia like an airless memento of Pompeii. The big, Georgian-style gray brick house was covered in an ancient flowering wisteria; its winding stems were thick as tree trunks, a momentous sight in the spring, with thousands of lavender blossoms hanging like lanterns.

An outdoor aviary sat beneath my bedroom window, filled with ring-neck doves that made a pretty opiate sound in the mornings. Their cooing reminded me of Uncle Tom's racing pigeons, a hobby he'd retained from boyhood.

Bingo and I loved to play in the rose garden, where there were two life-size limestone sculptures of English mastiffs, one sitting, the other one standing. We used to chase fireflies and feed the koi in the fishpond, hide in the tall grasses. The koi we fed as children still inhabit the pond, swimming back and forth in those same mysterious geometric patterns, pausing as always to bask in the sunlight as it feeds through the waterfall.

Cassowary was famous for its heritage rose gardens; hundreds of varieties bloomed all summer long, tended to by a battalion of English gardeners who handpicked them for every room in the house. Leave it to the Falcon to take a thing of beauty and turn it into a military operation. White roses in the living room, red roses in the dining room, pink roses in the library, orange roses in the conservatory, yellow roses in the kitchen, blue roses on the mantelpiece overlooking the wintry fireplace in my grandfather's bedroom.

Cream-colored roses sat atop the desk in my mother's old room, next to a framed portrait of Rupert Brooke, whom she discovered as a young girl. Ma's likes and dislikes remained pretty consistent over a lifetime, as I can personally attest. To this day, the rose is my least favorite flower—I think of it as a scented hand grenade—although

I still maintain the gardens. Their history outranks any preference of mine.

The Falcon, a widower, lived alone except for staff. I never saw him with a woman in a romantic way, although he was very social in the old-money sense of the word, frequently entertaining and being entertained, making it difficult to reconcile the charming public performer with the private contrarian.

My grandmother Constance Bunting was sole heir to the Ogilvy fortune and died at the age of fifty-one the year before I was born. Cassowary was her family home. My grandfather approached her father in the early thirties wanting to buy the estate, and when he refused to sell, the Falcon set out to marry his only child in order to get what he wanted.

Cassowary was a wedding gift. As for Constance: "Let's just say that your grandmother was the price I paid," the Falcon remarked tersely after I discovered their wedding photo buried underneath some old clothes at the bottom of a trunk tucked away in the attic.

My mother's feelings about the marriage were slightly less discreet. "He never loved my mother. He hated her. He set out to get his hands on the estate, and once he achieved his goal he decided to get rid of my dear mama," Ma told Bingo and me when we were little, her arms flailing as she paced frenetically around the room, pinging from one corner to another, her consternation as jarring as a slot machine.

"Sounds like an episode of *Bonanza*," Bingo said, grinning over at me, flicking baseball cards against the kitchen wall, fiddling away as Ma burned.

Faced with Ma's sketchy mental archives, I got in the habit of consulting outsiders when it came to trying to discern the facts of my family history. The general consensus among the Falcon's biographers is that a few years into his marriage he fell in love with a champagne-and-caviar socialite by the name of Flora Hennessey and planned to leave his family for her. All that changed when Flora's small plane disappeared at dawn somewhere along the eastern seaboard.

It might be true. I remember one time Bingo and I were snooping around in the library at Cassowary when we found the key to the Falcon's desk. After unlocking its narrow drawer, Bingo pulled a small, black-and-white photo of a young, dark-haired woman from inside the pages of a slender notebook.

"Who's the babe?" Bingo gleefully asked the Falcon, whose sudden entrance surprised both of us. Rather than conceal the evidence of our crime, Bingo, eleven years old, bravely held up the picture while I felt my scalp smoldering.

The Falcon walked toward us in soundless fury, seized the photo with one hand, and with the other slapped Bingo across the face so hard that he left a bright red handprint that glows in my memory to this day. Bingo tumbled backward off the chair and onto the ground, his hand to his cheek. Jumping to his feet, he met the Falcon's angry stare and then watched in silence as the old guy spun around on his heels and vanished into the hallway.

"Wow, I've never seen him so mad," I said, feeling weak in the knees, slowly sidling up alongside Bing.

"He's always mad about something. Who cares?" Bingo answered, rubbing his eyes through clenched fists, trying to conceal an involuntary surge of tears.

"Not me," I lied.

The truth was that I cared deeply about everything my grandfather thought and said, though I would have surgically removed my liver with a jackknife rather than admit it to anyone—in our family, it would have been less dangerous for me to confess to eating dog meat.

"Are you okay?" I asked Bing, unable to make eye contact, embarrassed by the sheer honesty of what had just transpired. I felt paralyzed, as if I'd been given a shot of pure unfiltered emotion directly into my spinal cord.

"I'm fine. Leave me alone," Bingo was mumbling into the shirt collar he'd pulled up around his face. His hands were shaking. I thought about hugging him, but in the end it was easier to hide my sympathy than it was to show it.

"What was Grandma like?" I asked my mother a few days later as I lay on my back stretched across the bottom of my parents' tarnished brass bed. Bingo and I didn't dare tell Ma about the slapping incident. The repercussions would have demoted the assassination of Archduke Ferdinand to the status of a minor irritant, a stray lash in the eye of history.

"She was a saint . . . ," Ma said, her large, almond-shaped eyes a dilute blue watercolor as she stared beyond me and somewhere into the distant past. She was sitting at the head of the bed, legs extended beneath the covers, perfectly erect, narrow shoulders square as a military parade. The pillows at her back were purely ornamental—Ma never needed propping up.

The buttercup yellow wall behind her was bathed in late afternoon light. I was fascinated by the shadows cast by her chestnut brown hair, so wild and wavy that it could have supported teeming jungle life.

"Constance Lowell was skinny and mad, a veritable vibrating hairpin. . . ." Next to her, naked and ruddy, covers pulled up to his waist, Pop rubbed his face in disbelief and interrupted with a hoot. "She fell off her horse when she was thirty-five, sprained her ankle, and went to bed for the rest of her life claiming she couldn't walk. Except that the servants used to hear her up and moving around all night while the rest of the house was sleeping."

Laughing at the memory, he leaned forward, his big hand on my knee, and I felt the infrequent thrill of his undivided attention. "You should have seen her, Collie. She had long brown hair that hung in waves to her waist, all done up with satin ribbons. She was white as a ghost from being inside all the time, and she wore white lace nightgowns and collected ivory figurines, with a somewhat ironic emphasis on elephants. Her bed was covered in silk and satin. She was crazy as they come."

"Don't you dare ridicule Mama!" Ma's long upper lip disappeared, her lower lip protruded like a boxing glove. "The most wonderful woman that ever lived, and he poisoned her a little bit every day. She warned me. She told me he was adding things to her food. He's a monster." The circles under her eyes darkened.

"For heaven's sake, Anais, according to every medical man short of St. Luke, she died of stomach cancer. You throw around accusations of murder as if they were rice at a wedding. For years you've been accusing Tom of adding plant fertilizer to your coffee." Pop looked over at me and winked as Ma's escalating fury caused the room to spin. I hung on to the blanket out of habit—I knew where this was going.

"My mother did not have cancer. She was poisoned. He killed her, and he paid off the doctors. And as for Tom, you tell me why does my heart beat so erratically every time he serves me something he's made? I enjoyed perfect health until he moved in with us, and since then I've had one ailment after another." Her voice lowered to a whisper as she glanced fleetingly toward the door, as if Uncle Tom were poised outside with ear to glass—not an entirely far-fetched idea, by the way—and would up the ammonia content in retaliation if he overheard.

Ma never had a prosaic thought or justified suspicion except in the case of Uncle Tom's eavesdropping, which fell into the same category as birth, death, and Lawrence Welk. She painted pictures in blood and tears and secret passions, everything intensely fragrant and wildly overgrown.

"Like most aesthetes, she's a barbarian at heart," Pop once confided to Bingo and me, the two of us nodding silently, chins bobbing in unison, though at the time we were barely able to write our own names and didn't have a clue what he meant.

She threw back the covers, the fringe from the chenille bedspread covering my face, and launched herself from the bed as if it were a catapult—Ma always seemed poised for takeoff—her worn cotton nightgown reaching below her knees as she yanked open the top dresser drawer and began rooting strenuously through dozens of mismatched socks.

"Tell you what, Collie, the Lowells and the Buntings are all nuts, every one of them," Pop said agreeably, settling deeper into the pillows, cozying up to one of his favorite topics, the shortcomings of my mother's family, gesturing broadly, mellow as honey. "Do you know that the only time your mother and grandfather ever saw eye to eye, they accused your batty old grandma and me of having an affair? They might just as well have accused me of carrying on with an opinionated coat hanger."

At the time, I had only the vaguest notion of what constituted an affair—if you'd asked me for a definition, I would have said it was something that my father did.

"Ha! You did, and you know perfectly well you did." Ma banged shut the drawer and spun around to face Pop, who was visibly enjoying her anger. "And you got off easy. My mother paid for her vulnerabilities with her life, while you're pensioned off courtesy her fortune."

"Is that why Granddad hates you, Pop, because you did an affair with Grandma?" I'd taken up Ma's position next to Pop on the bed.

"That's one of his many phony excuses," Pop said, examining his nails. "The reality is, Collie, your grandfather hates everyone. In my case, he holds me in particular contempt because I'm poor, I'm Catholic, and I refuse to mind my place. The worst crime you can commit in this life is being broke, and God help you if you don't dress the part. Always dress well, Collie, it drives the Four Hundred mad."

Ma laughed, a pealing sort of ringing bell sound I'd come to dread. "Please, Charlie, your personal vanities are nothing more than a symptom of moral vacuity. They are not any sort of challenge to established social order," Ma said, opening the door to Pop's elaborately endowed closet, bespoke suits of every color on irresistible display.

In Pop's view, clothes absolutely made the man—the sight of a baseball cap and a sport jacket made him apoplectic. "The windbreaker crowd," he'd mutter, erecting a bridge of contempt between himself and anyone in a sweatshirt. If Pop had been born a woman, he would have walked around the house fully accessorized, struggling down the laneway to pick up the mail in nylons and high heels.

He shot me a merry conspiratorial glance, inviting me to join in on the joke. I smiled nervously—if Ma was a seismic rumble with occasional release of acidic gases, then Pop was a full-scale volcanic eruption. Everything was funny to Pop until he lost his temper for reasons apparent only to him, and that's when the sky opened up and the wind blew round him in brilliant shades of magenta, the world erupted and lava flowed in the streets, and everyone started running for their lives.

"Tell me again why we hate Granddad?" I asked.

"It's a sin to hate. We don't hate anyone in this family," Pop said, taking a serious tone.

"Oh, yes, we do!" Ma said, practically producing sparks as she pulled on her blue jeans beneath her nightgown. "We despise your grandfather because he represents all that's wrong with this world. He cares for nothing and no one. He despises the poor and denigrates the helpless. He thinks that poverty is a character defect—all that matters to him is accumulating wealth and power and setting himself up as some sort of pasha to be worshipped and obeyed."

I could feel the pulverizing effects of my mother's personal radioactivity as she stared me down. I averted my gaze and pulled the blankets up around my chest.

"You can't hide from me, Collie. I know that you like him."

"No, I don't," I said defensively while Pop looked mildly embarrassed, as if some unpleasant family secret were about to be revealed.

"You can't fool me," Ma said, triumphant expression on her face, her voice crackling with bitterness. "You think he's so wonderful, then why don't you go live with him? I'll pack your bags and put you out the door myself. I'm sick of your betrayals."

It was a familiar threat. I glanced over at the corner of my parents' room, days of clothing heaped high as a small mountain range, two little dogs curled up on its summit, Ma agonizing over the laundry—how to do it, when to do it, why do it at all—the way international think tanks dwell on questions of war and peace.

"It's nice there, at Granddad's house, I mean," I said, finally daring to look at her. "It's quiet. I like the way the sheets smell."

"That figures," Ma sneered. "You're so typical, Collie. I can hardly believe you're my son. You want everything tied together in a nice, neat little potpourri package. Well, the world is a filthy, stinking place. I'm so sorry if I don't conform to your narrow idea of what a mother should be, cooking and cleaning and pressing your sheets and starching your shirt collars. Life is not a goddamn dance recital!"

"Well, it's not a bunch of dirty socks, either," I said as Ma's face contorted into a fixed expression of silent rage. She stared at me. Ma was always giving me the stare, aiming her eyes at me like loaded weapons.

"Charlie," she said finally, "are you going to allow him to speak to me that way?"

"Don't talk back to your mother," Pop said, not paying attention, his eyes drooping, fingers tapping out some tune on his bare chest that only he could hear.

"Get your suitcase, Collie, you're going to your grandfather's. Make it fast," Ma ordered, bouncing from the bedroom without a backward glance and banging down the stairs, big dogs and little dogs, their nails clicking against the hardwood, bounding forward to greet her.

Ma was a total hypocrite when it came to her old man, offering me up to him on a regular basis in the same way that primitive tribes would try to ensure good times by feeding virgins into the village volcano to appease the local gods. I used to spend most school holidays at Cassowary and went there at least one or two weekends a month, and Ma was right, I did like it there. My dark secret—I guarded my love for Cassowary as if it were a cache of dirty magazines under my mattress.

My grandfather was a tall man and a long road, formal and austere, but when you're surrounded on all sides by clashing cymbals and blowing horns, it's nice to occasionally find yourself with an oboe. Cool, cavernous, and resonant as a concert hall, Cassowary was a place where I could sit in peace and listen to the music of my own thoughts, free from the aural warscape of home, where I used to sneak off and climb on the roof of the stable to try to obtain some relief.

I'd sit with my arms wrapped around my legs, my forehead pressed against my knees, ocean breeze skimming the top of my head, and I'd empty out my brain, pour out the contents in one smooth flush as effortlessly as if I were tipping over a basin of water. Not thinking can bring its own pleasures, but it could cost you your life if Ma suspected even for a second that your insides weren't rumbling away like the neighboring Atlantic on a stormy day.

Cassowary presented its own difficulties, but at least they were peacetime challenges. And unlike Ma, who could go from love to hate to indifference before brushing her teeth in the morning, the Falcon was consistent in the ways he was impossible to get along with. Still, I suspected that he liked me, though perhaps not very much, liked me in a vague, unloving sort of way—for one thing, we both shared a deep and abiding devotion to Cassowary. It was a quiet bond between us that even he understood and welcomed.

Ma made it pretty clear that the only reason the Falcon took notice of me was to annoy her, while Pop figured he was out to manipulate and subdue the magnificent Flanagan spirit, "spattering paint on the *Mona Lisa*," he called it. In their combined view, Bingo was a tiger, primeval and exotic, a beautiful savage hovering way beyond the Falcon's corrupting influence, while I was a less glamorous, more pliable species—something that liked to dig, an armadillo, maybe, something that could be housebroken.

Uncle Tom had various theories as to why the Falcon demonstrated an interest in me; one had to do with his bird preoccupation.

"Let's see: Life gave you wings, but you can't fly. What kind of a bird is built for running?" He stared at me. "Did you know that the ostrich's eye is bigger than its brain? Hmmn . . . Your grandfather told me when you were born, he thought you had tiny eyes. Well, say, that's not good. He had you pegged as an imbecile from the get-go."

Who knows? I had enough trouble trying to understand my own crazy feelings, let alone achieve any real insight into what my grandfather thought. Why did the Falcon persist in involving himself with people who appeared to hold him in contempt? Maybe it was simply the desire for connection, the yearning for family, that drove him, and he couldn't overcome the outlandish tics of personality that prevented him from achieving his explicit longings.

One thing is certain. It was easier for him to declare his intention to take over the world than it was for him to ask me to join him on his morning ride before breakfast, though he never enjoyed riding alone.

And then there was Ma's epic distaste for both of us that forged an unspoken, if creaky, alliance. Being mutually despised wasn't much, but it was something, and it had the good effect of making me think that maybe Ma was the one with the problem.

No matter how anyone looked at it, I wasn't exactly Ma's cup of tea. Her distaste for me constituted a kind of psychic birthmark, a port wine stain that resisted fading. On the few occasions that she felt constrained to give me a hug, it was less a soft show of maternal tenderness and more a memorable lesson in force physics, like tripping and falling face-first onto an ice rink, her affection wounding as a cold, blunt object.

In the first hours and days after my birth, she tried to convince everyone that I was suffering from Down syndrome and needed to be institutionalized, pointing to my vaguely almond-shaped eyes as proof, the baffled doctors concluding she was suffering from a hormonal balance. Ma never would say die—all the time I was growing up, she continued to refer to the "Oriental cast" of my eyes as evidence there was something wrong with me.

Pop used to argue with her, armed with his own hyperbolic skill set: "Anais! The boy's a genius. Look at his school marks! Right off the charts—and what about his language skills? He was only two years old and it was like talking to Sean O'Casey. If he's an idiot, then he's an idiot savant."

"Well, you've got the idiot part right anyway," said Uncle Tom, not bothering to look over at me but continuing to whisk a bowl of pancake batter.

Pop ignored him. "And let's not forget he's left-handed. Everyone knows that being left-handed denotes incipient genius."

"Well, if that's the case, then Princeton better start recruiting from the Arctic Circle," Uncle Tom said. "Show me a polar bear that isn't left-handed."

As a kid I spent a lot of time trying to understand why Ma hated me, figuring the reasons were psychologically complex, mostly beyond my grasp, and maybe even a bit flattering. It wasn't until I got older that I realized my greatest sin was that I looked like my grandfather.

Right from the start the resemblance was apparent, and it only increased over time. I was like a living portrait of the Falcon through the seven ages of man. Still am. Tall and narrow—Pop called us "the matchstick men" on account of our long limbs—I inherited the Falcon's wide cheekbones (he could have passed for a Russian model), full lips (he could have passed for an Italian porn star), curly black hair (same again), mortician's pallor, dark blue eyes, and permanently clenched jaw. Bingo took great pleasure in pointing out that I even inherited the Falcon's girlish ankles.

The Falcon kept an Old English mastiff called Cromwell, his habitual companion. When one Cromwell died, he was immediately replaced with another, which he also named Cromwell. The Cromwells represented the only living creatures to which he showed affection, feeding each one a constant stream of shortbread cookies and carrying on long, complex conversations with them alone in the library when he thought no one was listening.

I once overheard him asking a Cromwell what time he'd like to eat, which seemed a very lonely question to ask a dog. I slipped away, not wanting to hear any more.

I was ten years old and staying with my grandfather for a weekend when one of the Cromwells died suddenly of a heart attack. I came down the long, winding stairs to the hallway, where he lay on the black-and-white floor tile surrounded by my grandfather and various members of the household staff.

When I realized what had happened, I quietly began to cry. My grandfather, in his indigo housecoat, silver hair falling over his forehead, turned sharply at the first sound of my sniffling.

"Oh, Lord," he said. "I suppose this is what we have to look forward to for the rest of the visit."

Feeling embarrassed and ashamed, I wiped my tears and watched as Cromwell the fifth or sixth, I'd lost track, was wrapped in a white cotton sheet by two of the housemaids and carried off by the cook and the groom to be buried on the grounds of the estate, a secret location only the Falcon knew.

Bingo and I spent many days looking to no avail for the Cromwells' burial grounds. I suspected the Falcon paid frequent visits, but I never had the heart to follow him.

Even now I have no idea where the Cromwell collective lies buried, nor do I look any longer. Like my grandfather, it represents a mystery I'm content to leave unsolved.

Later that night, I awoke to the sound of pacing on the floor beneath me. I got up and crept partway down the stairs, stopping and concealing myself in the darkness in the curve of the banister railings. My grandfather was at the end of the hallway in front of his bedroom, pacing back and forth, back and forth, illuminated by the light from the moon as it shone through the windows in the landing. He was wearing his dressing gown and plain black slippers; he was rubbing his hands and crying.

I sat in the shadows for a long time, feeling almost paralyzed with the cold, my feet achingly exposed, until he went into his bedroom and shut the door. I waited for a moment, and then I did the same. It was my first indication that there was more to the Falcon than he was prepared to reveal to a ten-year-old boy.

Two days later the new Cromwell arrived, a three-month-old British import, an identical fawn-colored match to all his predecessors.

The Falcon greeted him indifferently. The next morning, I saw him offer the new Cromwell a shortbread cookie, and as the puppy wagged his tail and took up his place alongside him in the library, the door closing behind them, shutting me out, I heard the Falcon ask his opinion about the condition of the walls.

"I've no interest in changing the color, but I think maybe the room needs a fresh coat of paint. What do you think, Cromwell?"

CHAPTER THREE

BINGO DIED TWICE BEFORE HE WAS NINETEEN. THE FIRST TIME HE was five years old, pale as the moon and small for his age, "no bigger than a beer bottle," as Uncle Tom would say. Bing coughed when he laughed, he was always coughing, sand and grit in his voice, scratchy as Pop's old record collection. It was spring 1969, the air blowing cold and dry. All it took was a sudden shift in temperature and Bing would be in trouble.

"Why didn't you wake us?" my mother screamed at me, standing next to Bingo's bed in her nightgown, teeth chattering uncontrollably, her body shaking so much that she was a blur, coming at me in waves of hysteria as I squinted against the sudden sharp injection of light.

Bingo, lying on his back, struggling to speak, reached out for Ma, but her focus for the moment was on me.

"For Christ's sake, Anais, it's not Collie's fault," Pop said, grabbing her by the shoulders. The words were hardly out of his mouth when she lashed out, wound up, and slapped his face. *Whack!* I marveled at her speed; there was no palpable distinction between cause and effect.

He didn't miss a beat, but shoved her against the dresser, her head wobbling like one of those dashboard ornaments. Way to go, Pop! She rebounded, took another swing at him, he ducked, and for a moment I thought he was going to hit her back, and I was right!

I was only six years old, I should have been horrified, but I was thrilled. Ma forever accused me of leaping to my feet, the mattress a trampoline, and clapping my hands in glee when Pop struck back. *Wham!* Right across the kisser, it was the joyous sound of a hundred angels getting their wings.

"It's therapeutic! It's therapy!" he shouted, trying to explain why he had my mother in a headlock. "It's medicinal, Anais. I'm sorry, Collie, but your mother's gone right off her nut!"

"Jesus, what's all the fuss about?" Tom wandered in, wearing boxer shorts and a white T-shirt, his gray hair standing upright as quills, the familiar smell of booze trailing him like one of Ma's wiener dogs. Eyes rheumy and face muscles slack, he was trying in vain to impersonate alertness. His eyebrows rode up his forehead like a couple of struggling elevators.

"What do we do? What do we do?" Ma wailed, throwing her head so far back that it was practically sitting on her shoulders. She'd broken away from Pop and stood in the middle of the room, seeming to generate her own spotlight, her legs spread apart and arms thrown skyward in a pose so dramatic, I felt convinced the hand of God was going to break through the ceiling like some sort of cosmic crane operator and spirit her off, Ma's unbearable intensity finally propelling her into another dimension.

"Someone call an ambulance!" Pop hollered as if he were in the midst of a crowded dance floor.

"Daddy! Daddy, where are you? Help me. My baby! I want my father." Ma just kept shrieking, her feet planted, arms pinned to her sides, eyes squeezed shut, mouth wide as a cavern, calling for the Falcon, a scenario that had me, young as I was, completely flummoxed, since she was popularly known to hate his guts.

Tom, weirdly calm and self-involved, nudged me and bent over, whispering, "Oh, listen to that. The proof we've been wanting all this time. I told you, Noodle, the Female B is father-fixated. It's love-hate—that's what makes the world go round. What did I tell you?"

By now, Bingo was quietly smothering, making only the weakest croaking and squeaking sounds in a last-ditch effort to attract some meaningful attention.

"What about Bingo?" I asked finally, fully awake and mildly exhilarated, standing up in the middle of my bed. "Who's going to save Bingo?"

I pointed over to his bed, where Bingo was lying on his back, still and staring, one hand resting on his chest, the other hand at his throat, the mechanical sound of his breathing whirring and clicking.

All three of them stopped and stared at me until Ma let out the biggest scream I'd ever heard.

"Jesus, she's gone Crazy Horse on us!" Uncle Tom said in amazement, scratching his cheek, his fingers noisily scraping stubble.

Fortunately, I remembered that Ma's cousin George was visiting. A mild, quiet-spoken veterinarian, he was as ordinary as a crew cut, but that night he was our only hope. Jumping to the floor and running from the room, I shouted his name as I ran along the hallway.

"Help! George, help!" I banged on his door, turned the knob, swung into the room, and flipped on the bedroom light.

"What the hell?" he said, instantly alarmed, popping up to a sitting position, squinting, hand at his forehead, struggling to understand what was happening.

"It's Bingo. He can't breathe. Help me. Please." I dragged him by the hand, rushing him toward the room I shared with Bing.

"Good God!" he said, pushing through the dumbstruck audience of Ma and Pop and Uncle Tom, all of them looking down into the bed as Bingo, ribs shuddering, struggled for air, hissing and whistling like a steam kettle.

I looked on expectantly. It was the first time I'd seen George without his black-rimmed glasses, and where once he'd seemed bland and concave, now he seemed positively inflated with dynamism—the only thing missing was the cape. He didn't hesitate for a second, picked Bingo up, cradled him against his chest, and issued calm instructions. His voice was as steady as a piston. He said, "Let's get him to the hospital for emergency treatment," and clearing a swath, he headed outside—I sat back in my bed, stunned to encounter an adult capable of decisive action—Ma and Pop following behind him, shrieking orders at each other.

I watched from my window as they climbed into George's car and took off, George holding Bingo close, Pop driving wildly, and Ma screaming into the night.

"Is Bingo going to die?" I asked Uncle Tom, who'd been rendered almost sober by the night's events. He rolled his eyes in exasperation as he slid next to me on the bed.

"I thought you were smart. That's just about the dumbest question anyone has ever asked in the history of the world since the beginning of time. Now, if you're so intelligent, spell 'Mississippi.' You can't, can you?" he said, complaining all the while about having to sleep with me, even though it was his idea, not mine.

"At your age! Say, it's nothing short of a national disgrace. When I was your age, I was the financial mainstay of the family, selling newspapers in the predawn hours on the corner of Newcastle and Abbey. How old are you, anyway?"

"I'm six," I said.

"Six! I had no idea. I thought you were five. Six! Why, I was a corporal in the army by the time I was six and thriving on a steady diet of boiled Spanish onions and raw shrimp. So, what about it? Let's hear you try to spell your mother's middle name, Termagant."

"T-e-r-m-a-g-a . . ."

Uncle Tom covered his eyes with his hands, pretending to beat on his forehead with clenched fists. "Haven't I had enough to contend with tonight? I don't have time for your nonsense. This is why no one with any sense likes children. They haven't a thought for anyone but themselves. Mangle the English language on your own time for your teacher. At least she's paid to pretend she's interested. Good night and good riddance," Uncle Tom said, gathering his pillow into a ball, shifting onto his side, his back in my face.

"Aren't you going to get under the covers?" I asked him.

"And have you infect me with some intestinal parasite or ear mites? Your father picked up fleas from your mother on their honeymoon. . . ."

"He did not." I giggled—the idea of my mother suffering from a plague of vermin had definite appeal.

Then I remembered. "T-e-r-m-a-g-a-n-t," I spelled aloud, gazing at the back of his head, stubbornly finishing my assignment, though Uncle Tom pretended not to listen.

The spelling bee was a classic device Tom used to shut me up. But I was reading by the time I was four, and I was a pretty good speller, which frustrated him no end. Eventually, he resorted to making up words to stump me.

"Spell 'auntiefrankensteinestablishmentitarianism,'" he said, his voice full of sarcasm.

He was prepared for me to get it right, which I often did.

"Wrong," he said, carrying on with his housework, avoiding my eyes. "The first part is spelled 'auntie,' not 'anti.' Even the village idiot knows that."

"It's not a real word."

"Oh yes, it is. I wouldn't expect you to know with your limited intelligence and lack of sophistication."

"What's it mean, then?"

"It refers to the sweeping powers possessed by a catastrophically ugly female relative."

"Use it in a sentence."

"My sister, your maiden aunt Brigid Flanagan, is a classic example of the terrifying phenomenon known as auntiefrankensteinestablishmentitarianism, whereby children, at seeing her hideous visage, instantly turn into turnips. That's why they're known as turnips, by the by, just one more thing about which you're abysmally ignorant."

"Uncle Tom . . ." I crawled onto my knees and touched him on the shoulder. "Why can't Bingo breathe?"

"I don't know. Maybe someone like you put a pillow over his face. Now that I think of it, I don't much like the malignant shape of your head, and you've got the shifty eyes of a murderer."

"I do not," I said, unaffected by Tom's accusations, which were as regular as rain. All the time I was growing up and anytime there was a homicide anywhere in New England, he used to demand that I produce an alibi or he'd threaten to turn me in.

"Well, what about the incident with the boiling water last summer . . . the attempt on your brother's life . . ."

I lay back down beside him, the back of my head flat against the pillow. "I never did that, Uncle Tom. . . ."

"So you say—that's what they all say."

"Uncle Tom, you know I didn't do that."

"Maybe I'm just covering for you so you don't wind up in the penitentiary with all the other desperadoes. Now for heaven's sake let me alone—and remember, I sleep with one eye open."

I rolled away from Uncle Tom, putting distance between us, so far from him that my face was pressed against the wall, the plaster cool against the bare soles of my feet as they climbed up along the window frame.

"You're not funny," I said.

"All right, Noodle." Uncle Tom lifted his head and looked over his shoulder in my direction. "I'm only teasing."

I wasn't talking. I didn't want Uncle Tom to know I was crying.

Outside the window, an owl called.

"Parliament's in session," Uncle Tom said. I didn't respond.

"Oh, Jesus," he said suddenly. "Fine, have it your way. I'll get under the covers."

Soon he was snoring away, but I couldn't sleep. I was afraid that Bingo would die and Ma would tell the police that I had killed him. It wouldn't be the first time. Ma was having one of her famous political gatherings. It was a bright afternoon the previous year, in June, and Bingo and I were put in charge of the dogs. With everyone talking, gesturing, making points, conversation coming at us from all directions like pockets of small-arms fire, the dogs quickly got out of hand. Giving up on trying to control them, Bingo and I went into the kitchen, where Ma was making tea. I watched as she poured boiling water into several mugs, and then, interjecting loudly, she rushed to rejoin a gathering of three or four people at the end of the room.

I caught sight of one of the missing puppies and bent down to call him over, and at the same time I was looking around for something to eat, when there came this long gasp and a crack, something shattered and then quiet, then a little kid's sharp scream, then a fulsome silence, all of it seeming to happen at once—and then all hell broke loose, and Bingo was crying in explosive spurts the uncontrollable way that he did when something was really wrong.

Steam rose from his bare arm, scalded a deep red color and soaked. The skin seemed to melt and then bubble up into a transparent bag that filled with fluid. One of Ma's guests was a doctor, who took a quick look and volunteered to go with her to the hospital since Pop was officially nowhere to be found.

Ma gathered up her stuff and was so unhinged that she was filling up her arms with crazy things, *The New York Times*, a loaf of bread, a tea towel, until she spotted me over by the window seat, and then she was all focus as she swooped down, grabbed me by the shoulders, and shouted in my face.

"What did you do? What did you do?"

"Nothing. I did nothing," I said, shrinking into the corner, the hushed murmuring of all those strangers hovering like smoke, settling in like guilt.

"You poured that boiling water on your little brother, didn't you? He couldn't have reached it on his own. What did you do?" She shook me so hard that I couldn't answer.

Uncle Tom appeared and started arguing with Ma.

"Say, you let him alone. I saw the whole thing from the doorway. Bingo climbed up on the stool, and before I could stop him he reached up and pulled the cup off the counter. He lost his balance. Collie wasn't anywhere near him."

"No . . ." Ma spat out her words and releasing her grip on me stood up straight as Bingo wailed in the background. "Impossible. You're lying, sticking up for him when he doesn't deserve it. I set those cups back far enough from the edge of the counter so nothing like that could have happened. If that's what you saw, then Collie deliberately moved them."

"I suppose he kidnapped the Lindbergh baby, too," Uncle Tom said. "You've got a screw loose, lady. You should be ashamed of yourself, accusing Collie to cover up your own carelessness."

"For God's sake, I haven't time to fight with you, Tom Flanagan," Ma said, pausing once again to bend down, her face next to mine, so close that her hair fell against my cheek. I can still smell the woodsy fragrance of her shampoo.

"This isn't over. I'll never forgive you for what you did today to your little brother. Never!"

She told everyone at the hospital what I'd done, and someone, a man in a suit, came to speak to me and Bingo—Ma told me it was the police and to expect a long sentence—and I never knew the outcome of his visit. I was too scared to ask. When I didn't go to jail, I figured it was an oversight.

After the burn healed, Bingo was left with a white scar shaped like a half-moon on his inner arm beneath his elbow joint, so just in case Ma was ever tempted to forget, she always had his disfigurement to remind her, confirming her view of him as a serious hard-luck case, unlike me. She looked at me in my playpen and saw the president of the World Bank and not the future president, either. The whole time I was growing up, in every conversation between us, Ma acted as if she were sparring with John D. Rockefeller about the merits of socialism.

Bingo was different. He looked like Pop, though he had Ma's chestnut hair. Everything seemed to go wrong for Bingo, which only increased his irresistibility factor. Nothing Ma loved better than a beautiful victim, since it played so well into her own image of herself.

She used to talk about how people should never stop with one child since it was important to have a basis for comparison, gives a much-needed perspective, she would insist, leaving most people to wonder what the devil she was talking about, though I got the message loud and clear.

Her adoration for Bingo was exclusive, but she made me a critical part of their relationship, casting me in the role of his malicious persecutor. I could never separate her love for Bingo from her contempt for me.

"Your little brother died last night," Pop said at first sight of me in the doorway the morning after the asthma attack. Hearing him and Tom, the sun rising and rosy, I hopped from my bed and went down to the kitchen, where the two of them were sitting at the table drinking coffee and eating fried-egg sandwiches.

"But like Lazarus, he was brought back to life," Uncle Tom said, telling me how Bingo turned blue in the hospital, pure Irish blue, he said, "an exotic mix of Himalayan poppy, antifreeze, and the eyes of a Siberian husky."

"Lazarus, my ass, that low-rent bastard," Pop said. "Bingo rose up like Jesus himself. Come to think of it, he did better than Jesus. It took Bingo only three hours to resurrect himself. It took Jesus three days!"

"Match that, can you, Noodle?" Tom asked me. "Start by spelling 'unremarkable.'"

"Where's Ma?" I inquired, making my way to a plain wooden stool, which I dragged from the counter to the table, one of the poodles tugging at the bottom of my pajama leg.

"She had to be admitted—it was the reaction. She had a heart arrhythmia, according to the doctors," Pop said casually, sifting through the mail.

"I wasn't aware she had a heart," Uncle Tom said.

"What about George?" I persisted. He'd just arrived for a week-long visit.

"Oh well, he's been called back home. Some kind of problem at the clinic," Pop said.

"May I have an egg sandwich?" I asked, trying to extricate myself from the dog's playful grasp.

"Oh, my Lord," Tom said, sighing, shoulders collapsing, his face an anguished mask. "Look here, Noodle, I'm melted after all I've been through these last hours. I'll make you some tea and you get yourself a couple of lovely pieces of fresh bread with butter."

"That's not a proper breakfast," Pop said. "He's not on death row, you know. Surely he deserves better than thieves and murderers."

"Fine. Tea and toast, then, the act of toasting adds nutrients to the bread, same as if it were a bowl of oatmeal."

"What nutrients, Uncle Tom?" I asked.

"Zinc."

"Well, you know what I think?" Pop said. "There's nothing like a miracle to make a man crave a drink."

"There's no one to say we didn't earn it," Tom said.

"Bartender!" Uncle Tom snapped his fingers in my direction.

I jumped down from my stool and ran to the cellar to get them their beer, startling the mostly sleeping dogs, who leapt from their spots, barking, wondering what all the fuss was about. Uncle Tom and Pop watched silently for once as I carefully set out two immaculately clean, tall and skinny, cylindrical glasses.

"Why do they represent a better choice for drinking beer?" Tom quizzed me.

"Nuance," I said, whispering, concentrating on the pour, tipping the glass on a forty-five-degree angle, focusing on the slope. I poured with confidence—I'd been doing it for half my life. The bottle half-empty, I shifted the glass to ninety degrees and kept pouring down the middle, creating a perfect foam head.

"Beautiful, Collie!" Pop said. "You're the champ."

"Not bad," Tom said. "You'll do until someone better comes along."

I handed the drinks over without so much as inhaling. Pop made me take the pledge of total abstinence when I was three years old, and which I've maintained to this day, with the exception of one adolescent slip.

"Here's to Bing Algernon Flanagan," Pop said, raising his glass in salute. "Died and rose again on April 7, 1969."

"So, Collie, what do you say?" Uncle Tom jabbed me in the ribs. "Can you spell 'thaumaturgy'?"

CHAPTER FOUR

WITH HIS SLIGHT BUILD AND HABITUALLY UNDONE SHOELACES, Bingo, despite a kind of slouching natural elegance and balmy rich-kid veneer, was as wild as if wolves had raised him. Perpetually on the prowl, he was always looking to mess around and make trouble, always changing shape and challenging the people around him to keep pace.

Bing had a kind of heightened vibrancy, as if he'd emerged intact from Walt Disney's imagination. His chestnut-colored hair, the same rich shade as Ma's, hung in his eyes—he had an annoying way of constantly shoving it off his forehead and tucking it behind his ears. When he was younger, Uncle Tom used to grab him every few months, catching him for an impromptu trim on the way out the door. "The virgin accountant," Uncle Tom dubbed the result, an ear-skimming Alfalfa cut with a slick center part.

With his spooky green eyes and translucent white face, he was a freckled landscape, like an animated Jackson Pollock, with big brown spots wall to wall—I swear Ma must've shacked up with a Dalmatian.

He was always in some kind of jam, mostly arising out of his sense of humor, which overran him like a form of Tourette's. The nuns and priests had his prison cell picked out by the time he was ten years old, though Ma waged guerrilla war against anyone attempting to discipline him, including Pop, who had a special talent for throwing up his hands.

When Bingo was twelve he started to throw snowballs at the altar boys as they arrived to serve Mass at St. Basil's on Sundays, me yelling at him to cut it out, both of us forced to attend church by Ma because she knew how much it annoyed the Falcon. I'm sure the only reason Ma converted to Catholicism was to bug her old man—meanwhile she so scandalized the priests with her views during obligatory marriage classes, they canceled her wedding to Pop the day before it was to take place. Despite his opposition to the marriage, the Falcon reluctantly went into secret negotiations with the bishop, and things went off as planned.

"After some discussion," he told me, "the bishop and I both concluded that your parents deserved one another."

The nuns warned Bingo over and over to stop tormenting the altar boys, but he wouldn't listen. He loved it—the nuns' wrath, scolding, and threats were like fuel supplying his incorrigibility. Finally one of our teachers, Sister Mary Ellen, out of patience, grabbed him by the collar of his jacket, gave him a push, made him kneel down, and ordered him to bury his face in a freshly shoveled bank of snow.

"Fuck off, Sister," he said, kicking snow up into the air, so high that it reached the treetops, landing lightly like a dusting of icing sugar. He grinned over at me and, running, cleared the iron fence in a single leap; then, whooping, he left the churchyard and disappeared down the street. He vanished into a shower of snow and rebellion, and when the priest came later that day, we were told to pray for his soul.

In a lot of ways, Bingo was a chip off the old block. Every night was devil's night as far as Bing was concerned, the clergy his favorite target and toilet paper his weapon of choice, toilet paper streaming from every tree in the churchyard. He got into big trouble when Father Woodward, setting up for morning Mass, and after discovering that his vestments were missing, fell to his knees at the sight of Jesus on the cross wearing a T-shirt, "Too Fuck to Drunk" emblazoned across the chest.

His stolen vestments were found by a hiker later the same day, floating in the ocean, seagulls circling, swooping in closer for a better look. I think the most outrageous thing I ever did as a kid was drink Pepsi before ten o'clock in the morning.

After the vestments' prank, Pop was summoned to an emergency parent-teacher conference, where Sister Mary Ellen delivered an impassioned review of Bingo's crimes.

"The prosecutors at Nuremberg were indifferent by comparison," Pop said, standing in the middle of the kitchen, unbuttoning the jacket of his navy blue suit, and loosening his tie as Uncle Tom and I looked up from where we sat together at the table, drinking hot chocolate.

"And you let her spew this nonsense unchallenged?" Ma demanded, appearing in the doorway at the first sound of Pop's voice. "What kind of a father are you?"

"Well, according to the teachers, the same as the one who raised Charles Starkweather."

Pop pulled a chair out from the table, scraping it along the floor and into the middle of the room. He sat down with a thump and, preoccupied, began tapping his foot. Brightening suddenly, he gave me an admiring glance. "On the plus side, Sister Mary Ellen raved about our Collie. Said he was the smartest and the finest boy she's ever taught."

Ma made a noise like a car backfiring and ricocheted out the room and down the hallway, announcing that she was pulling us out of the school. I wasn't concerned. Ma never followed through on anything—saying it was the same as doing it as far as Ma was concerned. Uncle Tom poured some Murphy's Oil Soap on a cleaning rag and started to polish the table, his hands moving in vigorous circles. He claimed to have worked for a traveling circus when he was young and told Bingo and me that he used Murphy's Oil Soap to clean the elephants.

He looked over at me, and then just as quickly he looked away.

"Well, I'm not convinced. That nun must have worked a crop of lemons over the years to put you at the head of the class. I'd like to know one thing that you've ever done that makes you so smart." Pausing to apply more oil to the cloth, he turned around and confronted me. "Say, did you know there's a species of crab that can climb a tree? Top that, Socrates."

"Tom, for God's sake, you're eroding the boy's sense of self-worth," Pop said, heading for the fridge to seek out his daily consolation of ice cream.

"You can't possibly be referring to this cathedral of conceit? I'm doing him a great favor, dismantling his vanity piece by piece. It's the work of a lifetime. Answer me this," he said, focusing his full attention on me. "What do you call a gathering of ravens?"

"A murder," I answered, staring back at him. I knew this game.

"All right," he said. "That was easy. What about a group of goldfinches? Hares? Goats?"

I shook my head. "I don't know, Uncle Tom. Who cares?"

"A charm of goldfinches, a drove of hares, a trip of goats. Well, it seems your reputation for brilliance notwithstanding, you've been exposed as an imbecile in less than thirty seconds. I rest my case." He resumed his cleaning.

"I thought this was supposed to be about Bingo," I said, mildly exasperated.

"You rang?" Bingo popped his head through the open kitchen window as Pop jumped up to let the dogs out onto the veranda to welcome him home.

"Hey, take your shoes off, you slob," I spoke without thinking as Bingo came in through the door, his running shoes leaving a trail of oozing black footprints on the floor.

He looked baffled. "Why?"

"Look at the mess you're making," I said as Pop finally took notice of Bingo kicking off his running shoes.

"What are you doing removing your shoes at the door?" Pop asked.

"Ask Collie," Bingo said, fighting off the dogs.

"I've told you boys a thousand times, removing your shoes at the door brands you as a hopeless member of the middle class. Next you'll be clipping coupons and asking questions about the state of the eaves trough."

"Don't forget to rake the lawn, Pop," Bingo contributed in good-natured fashion as he drank from an open carton of orange juice. Pop didn't believe in raking leaves. "That's why they call them leaves," he used to say.

"What's going on?" Bingo said, taking quick measure of the room's temperature.

"I've just come from a meeting with your teacher. I hope never again to hear a child of mine talked about as you were talked about tonight," Pop said, straining for solemnity.

"Sister Mary Ellen's had it in for me since grade four," Bingo said.

"And why is that?" Pop asked as I looked on incredulously.

"Because I told her I didn't swallow all those stories about the lives of the saints—all that junk about flying around on magic carpets and stuff. . . ." He glanced over in my direction, squinting, his lips pressed together as he tried to conceal a grin.

"Oh, that perpetual nonsense! Is that what this is about?" Pop was instantly galvanized. "Did you mention St. Euphrosyne and her penchant for cross-dressing?"

"Yeah, and St. Uncumber, too," Bingo added as Pop characteristically pumped the air with his fists.

"Good for you! Did it shut her up?"

"Yeah, but she still smacked me on the back of the head with a ruler," Bingo said.

"Bullshit," I muttered.

Pop was obsessed with debunking the notion of sainthood—from the time we were babies, he used to read aloud to us the lives of the saints and loved to deride church claims of miracles. St. Uncumber was a personal favorite of his. She took a vow of virginity, and when her father tried to force her to marry the king of Sicily, she prayed to God to make her unattractive. She appeared one morning sporting a full beard and mustache, putting an end to the marriage plans. Her father was so mad, he had her crucified.

"This changes everything," Pop said. "I forgot my cardinal rule. Never trust a nun."

Uncle Tom was searching through the cupboard, pretending indifference.

"You over there, the one with all the disfiguring marks on your face," he said, turning around to face Bingo. "What's the collective for a group of pheasants?"

"A bouquet," Bingo replied, zinging me in the cheek with an elastic band he'd picked up off the floor.

"Good. What about woodpeckers? Rattlesnakes? Hawks?"

"A descent of woodpeckers, a rumba of rattlesnakes, and a kettle of hawks," Bingo said, rattling off the answers, reveling in my earned contempt.

"A perfect score so far," Uncle Tom said, staring over at me. "It seems as if there is some confusion as to who is the real genius in the family."

Ma laughed so loudly, we heard her from the living room.

"Ignore her," Uncle Tom instructed Bingo and me, lowering his voice to a whisper. "It's a biological fact. Try as they might, witches can't conceal their delight."

Later that night, I awoke in time to see Bingo climbing out of the open window of the bedroom. We shared a room until we were in high school and I finally rebelled and claimed one of the empty bedrooms as my own.

"Hey, where do you think you're going?" I asked him as he dropped out of sight. He'd just started sneaking from the house at night, a practice he kept up all through his teens. By the time he was sixteen he'd often stay out all night, climbing in and out of my bedroom window because it was easier.

On the weekends, he used to head out around ten and would come home just before daybreak, me listening for him in the dark, the snap of wisteria signaling his return. I'd wait for the sound of the first broken branch, hyperalertness fixing me in place. I could hear his jeans scraping against cedar shingles as he scaled the ivy-covered trellis to my bedroom window, dark hair poking through lace curtains. Ma hung lace everywhere, her only concession to domesticity.

"Shit!" he'd say as he dropped his keys, which hit the ground with a metallic clang, followed by a tiny avalanche of gravel and dried sand from the soles of his shoes.

I'd tell him quiet, shut up, you asshole, they'll hear you.

"Ma and Pop don't give a flying fuck," he'd say. "Why do you care, Collie?" He'd be panting gently, gripping the ledge with his fingers, their tips livid with exertion, hoisting himself inside, dusting himself off, careful not to make a sound as his toes touched the floor, but not for long.

He'd leap into bed beside me and tell me everything, let me in on all of it: the lawlessness, the girls, the booze, the fun. And Christ, the guiltlessness! I envied the remorseless pleasure he took in being Bing Flanagan.

By dull contrast, the only time I ever got drunk I was sixteen and made it an exercise in earnestness, hooking myself up to an intravenous of vodka. What a soppy fucking drunk I was. Bingo told me I made out with Eliot Harrigan, captain of my swim team at Andover.

"You lying sack of shit," I said to him, propped on my elbow, leaning over him in the partial darkness, moonlight casting its silvery glow.

"Maybe," he said, eyes laughing, "but then again, maybe not."

A few weeks after Pop's meeting with Sister Mary Ellen, Bingo got kicked out of St. Basil's for the remainder of the school year. The caretaker, a creepy guy named Mario who had yellow teeth and pretended to eat worms to scare the girls, trapped a small stray dog in the yard, pulled off his belt, snapped it as if it were a whip, and ran after the little mutt, flaying him with the belt, terrorizing him and us, the black-and-brown dog howling, the little kids crying, the older kids, my friends and I, standing around shocked and numb, looking to the nuns to intervene, expecting the priest to do something.

Nobody moved. The nuns and priest went on with their small talk; only Sister Mary Ellen looked upset, her hands fidgeting with her rosary beads.

"You bastard!"

I turned around at the sound of a familiar voice as Bingo ran across the yard and lobbed a rock at close range at Mario, hitting him hard on the shoulder. Mario stopped and let loose a profusion of profanity so fluent and expressive that I thought he was speaking a foreign language. Then all hell broke loose as the nuns chased Bingo down and the priest, who reached him first, grabbed both his shoulders, and Sister Rosemary, her cheeks red as a geranium, pulled a strap from inside her habit and whacked him across the face, hitting him with so much force that her feet left the ground and her glasses fell off, cracking on the pavement.

For days afterward, Bing walked around with the shape of a strap imprinted on his cheek, his face black and blue and red and swollen, his "valorous palette," Ma called it, "the colors of courage." Predictably, Ma turned into a human tornado when she got the news, boring a hole into the ground with the spinning velocity of her fury.

She showed up at the school the next morning with our Caucasian Ovcharka, Lenin—or Lennon, which was what I told my friends he was called—a fierce Russian dog best described as Khrushchev-on-a-rope. She turned him loose on Mario, who had to scramble onto the church roof to escape.

I never again felt quite the same about the Catholic Church or about Bingo. Though I thought the world of Bing, I took pains to conceal it, resenting him for his bravery as much as I admired him for it.

It's not easy coming to terms with your shortcomings. I was just an average grunt—not so pathetic that I was the movie cliché in the prison camp who loses it and throws himself into the barbed wire trying to escape his frenzy of fear, but more like the guy crouching in the dirt who sees something of himself in the aberration. I was always more of a chicken than I would've liked to acknowledge, but I was saved from full egg-laying status by my habit of taking my cues from the hero.

Ma knew.

"Run for your life, Collie," she used to say to me. "The creek's gone dry."

CHAPTER FIVE

Between Pop and Uncle Tom, and the sheer quantity of alcohol they consumed, most of the time our house was something lost at sea, aimlessly floating and drifting, rocking gently back and forth like a cork in a bathtub full of gin.

It was an unholy baptism, Tom getting grotesquely drunk every month, submerging himself body and soul in the stuff, a full immersion, evangelical in its fervor, part of a weeklong ritual, passing out, coming to, drinking some more, passing out, drinking until his small government pension money ran out.

He kept his cash in a discarded peanut-butter jar under his bed surrounded by a moat of mousetraps, a familiar sequence of snaps, in quick succession, signaling his deposits and withdrawals. It was an intense operation. He used a cane to trigger each one, going in like a demolition expert. Bang. Bang. Bang.

"Tom must be doing his bang-king," Pop said to Bing and me, eyes rolling upward in the direction of each tiny blast. It was early evening. We were in our mid-teens, sitting around the kitchen table eating a meal of vanilla ice cream, the only thing Pop knew how to cook.

"Look out, the world's about to get shook. Bingo, there's no choice, you're going to have to sneak in there and take what's left. You're the only one allowed in the inner sanctum. If he insists on getting sloshed the way he does, he's going to kill himself."

Bing was trying to squirm out of it. He didn't want to steal from the old reprobate even for a good cause.

"I don't know," Bing said. "It doesn't seem right. He trusts me."

"So you do have a conscience after all," I said.

"I do not." He frowned and, giving me the finger, headed up the stairs. Bingo resented any suggestion that he might possess character or integrity.

"You'll need to stay hidden in the stable for a couple of days," Pop said when Bingo, looking paler than usual, handed over the dough. "He'll be gunning for you."

"Here he comes."

The stable was located on the acreage behind the house. I was perched at the window, eyes peeking above the ledge, as I caught sight of Tom and his drinking buddy Swayze heading in our direction, the pair of them making up an arthritic posse, not quite two men, more like front and ass ends of a donkey costume.

Before she married Pop, Ma was an equestrian, competing internationally, specializing in three-day eventing. She rode a big black Irish draft horse called Lolo, pidgin for crazy. He used to try to come in the kitchen, Ma encouraging and coaxing him all the way. No one else could go near him. Bing and I grew up thinking of him as a psychotic older brother, his teeth marks decorating my ass well into adolescence.

Bing, giddy, scared, and excited all at the same time, scrambled to hide himself under a pile of straw in Lolo's box stall, Lolo mulling over a course of action, pawing the floor and snorting, tossing his head, thinking about turning in Bing for the reward. Lolo was staring at me, and I was staring back at him, hoping for the best—that horse had no moral center.

"Where is he?" Tom said, his face inches from my own, eyes taking on the color of malt liquor. "We're here to perform a citizen's arrest. He stole my money. He's going to jail and he's going to make full restitution."

"I don't know where he is," I said, stepping away from him. "He's probably with friends."

"How would you like me to arrest you as an accomplice?" Tom said, grabbing the collar of my shirt.

"Uncle Tom, for crying out loud . . ."

"Swayze." He turned to his tipsy deputy. "Cuff him."

In the final analysis, there wasn't much to choose between Pop and Uncle Tom when it came to their old buddy booze. "Those damn Dolan boys got me drunk," Pop used to say to Bing and me—one way of explaining what happened on my fourteenth birthday when he crawled into a neighbor's chimney, where he got stuck and passed out. He'd still be there except that Sykes, his white bull terrier, refused to come home and barked for hours at the roof in a high state of excitement.

I was the first to figure it out. Bingo scrambled up the eaves trough, waving madly when he reached the chimney, choking with laughter, shaking so he could hardly stand, and hollering that he'd found him.

"Pop says to call in the army," he shouted. "He says he'll need expert extraction. He doesn't trust the locals to perform such a delicate operation."

I argued for leaving him there permanently, but the nice old lady who owned the place wouldn't be persuaded.

"It's not right, Collie, he's your father, and besides, think of the smell."

"You've got me there."

A few days later, Pop, a man of pure inspiration with a sanctimonious aversion to self-reflection, decided that Bingo and I were culturally deficient and needed exposure to the work of some of the great Irish playwrights. He also wanted to reward us for rescuing him from the chimney, so he took us into Boston to see a production of *The Plough and the Stars*.

For some mysterious reason, Pop hated restaurants. He loathed restaurants but loved hotels and longed to take up permanent residence in one.

"I could live in a hotel. As a matter of fact, I intend to retire to the city and live in a hotel suite, and then it's a steady diet of plays, concerts, horticultural shows . . . no more homemade meals and nights in a rocking chair. Your mother is free to join me if she chooses," he told us as Bingo scrunched up his face and looked at me, puzzled.

"Huh?"

"Crazy," I whispered.

We roamed the old-world lobby of the Steinbeck, Pop turned out like the Prince of Wales, heads swiveling to look at him, everyone trying to figure out who he was—people always said he looked like a movie star. He was winking at every attractive woman in the place. We had dinner at Heliotrope, a formal dining room, where he got exasperated with Bingo for insisting on having a giant steak and nothing else. He just wanted one big, juicy steak on a plate. After we finished eating, Pop left us to our own devices in the lounge while he disappeared into the bar for an hour or so, looking like the Red Planet when he finally emerged, spinning wildly on his axis, his disheveled hair the victim of crazy weather patterns, toxic vapors spewing into the solar system.

Once at the theater, the other patrons cleared a path as Pop, leaning to the left and teetering to the right, attempted to find us our seats, loudly losing his temper with one of the ushers. It was at that point I began to scuff the carpeted floor with my shoe, focusing all my attention on the vast sea of cabbage roses under my feet.

The play was set to begin at eight o'clock. By quarter past eight, Pop stood up and hollered, "When will this performance begin?" as Bingo, thrilled at the commotion, looked over at me and giggled, field of freckles glowing against his pale skin, while I quietly burned away on a pyre of mortification.

At eight-thirty, Pop, radiating impatience, rose to his feet, shining like a beacon, and began to sing the Irish national anthem, his clear tenor voice ringing out like a church bell as stunned members of the audience shifted in their seats to stare, one giant set of eyes in one huge head on one enormous craning neck. Bingo was incandescent with joy and excitement, gasping and laughing, and me, well, I was somewhere on the ceiling looking down on the lifeless body I'd abandoned, pupils fixed and dilated, respiration and heartbeat ground to a skittering stop, skin the color of chalcedony, inner voice a dying squeak.

Bing adored Pop. As for me, well, Pop had a way of testing the fragile limits of my humor—there's something about being a teenager and bringing your friends into a house where they're met by a middle-aged man sunning himself in the living room window in February and bragging about his tan. All the while he's wearing a skimpy bathing suit and scuffed black brogues with no laces, his ample stomach glistening, and he's making elegant, expansive gestures with his long, perfectly manicured fingers, sporting sunglasses and a wide-brimmed lady's straw hat, big turquoise chiffon bow tied under his chin.

"So much for the so-called experts who say you can't get a tan through glass, well, I'm living proof the experts don't know what they're talking about. Everyone asks me if I've just come back from Florida. An hour a day in front of a sunny window is all you need to give Nat King Cole a run for his money."

We were back at home—the embarrassment I endured at the theater days earlier still working its way through secondary skin layers—and I could hear Pop in the next room delivering one of his famous daily affirmations.

"Oh, my God, look at that," Ma said. "Charlie, please stop talking such nonsense and step away from the window. Tom, come here quick before you miss it. Collie, you too."

Ma got up from the sofa and stood next to Pop, who had his back to the window, as Tom slowly ambled in from the kitchen, feigning annoyance. Curious, I abandoned the TV in the study that adjoined the living room and joined the crowd gathered around the window.

Bingo and one of his favorite dogs, a young Leonberger called Mambo, were playing a game. There was a small tree near the stable with a single branch that extended for a long way and hung about seven or eight feet off the ground. Mambo was running to the tree and leaping into the air, twisting midway through his jump, a giant, growling, furry corkscrew. He clamped his teeth into the branch and hung there for a couple of seconds.

After repeating the same jump sequence five or six times, Bingo joined him, and then the two of them would take turns snarling and spinning and hanging from the branch; sometimes they'd even perform their little trick in unison.

I could hear Bingo laughing and Mambo barking, and for a moment it felt like fun, the four of us assembled around the window to watch, the sun pouring in.

"Say, this is better than a fireworks display," Uncle Tom said as Pop chuckled and Ma agreed. Agreed! Ma!

"The woman is an aphid," Ma said, interrupting the moment, confusing me with her remark. "She was born pregnant."

It was then I realized that we were looking at different things. Ma and Uncle Tom were deep in discussion, enjoying a rare conviviality, sharing their mutual contempt for the woman down the road. The Conceiver, Tom called her. She had seven kids under the age of ten and was expecting her eighth. I welcomed her pregnancies since they tended to produce a *sitzkrieg* in the war between Uncle Tom and Ma.

"That creature sets the cause of women back by generations," Ma said, leaning forward, squinting to get a better look.

"The size of her, she looks like a Guernsey," Uncle Tom said. "It violates the laws of natural science."

"Have a little respect," Pop said. "She's doing God's work. What else are we good for except to repopulate the world? I consider the boys to be my greatest achievement."

"I know, Charlie. I know. You are an absolute bore talking about it," Ma said wearily.

"Having kids is nothing. Chimpanzees have kids by the barrel. I once found a toad inside a hailstone," Uncle Tom said. "Now there's an achievement."

"Wow," I said under my breath as Mambo and Bingo jumped, soaring so high that they seemed to touch the edge of the sky, Bingo's triumphant hoot blending in with the noise of the seagulls and the calls of the blackbirds as they scattered from the adjacent trees and circled overhead.

"What's that, Collie?" Pop said distractedly, looking my way. He and Ma and Uncle Tom were still focused on the Conceiver.

"Oh, nothing," I said. "You missed it."

CHAPTER SIX

I WAS SENT TO ANDOVER FOR HIGH SCHOOL—SENTENCED TO Andover, was how Bing put it—a concession to my grandfather's conviction that his financial support meant he could institutionalize any of us at will. By age sixteen, I was well established at school. It was 1979, and I'd grown accustomed to living away from home as a residential student, where I was a three-year upper, which is prepspeak for being in the eleventh grade. Reluctantly, I used to come home one weekend a month at the insistence of my parents. Trying to get back to school after any holiday was a recurring nightmare. Pop was always encouraging me to relax and forget about school.

"What's it matter?" he'd say. "Good Lord, Collie, you're due to inherit a bundle. Take an extra day at home. Jesus, if I had your situation, I'd live like a lawn chair."

Ma held prep schools in particularly low esteem, labeling them capitalist propaganda outlets. The main reason I was at Andover was that the Falcon threatened to cut her off financially if she didn't give in to him on the critical issue of our education. When it came to self-preservation, Ma could be flexible.

"The priests had them for the first eight years. Now they're mine," he said.

Although I pretended some consternation in an attempt to appease my mother, I was quietly thrilled by the Falcon's edict. As usual, Ma saw right through me. She referred to Andover as "Collie's folly."

Like a salamander that's found its rock, I basked in the warm sunshine of Andover's conventions and certainties, ceremonies, clean sheets, and Latin mottoes. At Andover, life was reduced to a series of rituals ruled by an unwavering sense of assured outcome. Samuel Phillips, school founder, despised idleness. In 1778, he had a beehive engraved on a silver seal along with two mottoes: *Finis Origine Pendet*—The End Depends on the Beginning, an admittedly scary thought in my case—and *Non Sibi*, which means Not for Self. My home life, in contrast, was a paean to the cult of narcissism.

Andover had pretty definite ideas about what constituted ideal young manhood, and I made an avid study of all of it. Like most prep schools, Andover was big on fostering excellence in all things, yet for much of the time the whole experience seemed to me like a protracted sigh of relief. Occasionally, though, alternating between Phillips Academy and home could feel a bit like trying to outrun schizophrenia. Every day a different voice whispered in my ear, competing for my loyalty—the inveigling voice of Samuel Phillips kept urging me to get out of bed at the crack of dawn to run five miles and still have time to practice the cello before breakfast.

Sometimes all that striving for excellence could get on your nerves, particularly when your roommate is Kip Pearson, son of the Canadian ambassador, and he never quits talking about his collection of edible underwear. And gradually I was discovering that a little Latin in the service of an epic sense of obligation goes a long way.

That's when I'd begin to feel a twitch from another direction, like an embarrassing itch signaling the recurrence of a secret rash. I used to wait until Kip went out for his nightly troll, then I'd reach for the phone and dial home, just wanting to hear the sound of Pop's mutinous voice.

But first I had to get by Uncle Tom.

"I'm going to spell a word, and I want you to pronounce it for me."

I groaned.

"Cholmondeley," he said, emphasizing each letter.

"Chumley," I answered.

"Finally, I have it, the proof you're a snob. That's something only a snob knows. And you fell for it. Collie Flanagan, the so-called brain box, isn't so clever after all."

"You knew about it . . . so what does that make you?"

"It makes me a Renaissance man."

"Let me speak to Pop. Is he there?"

"Charlie!" Tom hollered into the receiver. "It's your long-lost son."

"Collie?" Pop said into the receiver. "It's grand to hear from you. Will you be coming to see us?"

"Sure I will, Pop. I've been busy with school, I'm sorry."

"No need for apology. Everything is understood. But listen, Collie, hear me out. Slow down, don't work so hard, and learn to take it easy. What do I always tell you? School would wear a mighty sour puss if it weren't for recess."

I hung up and sat for a while, staring and tossing a tennis ball into the air, and then I went back to gathering pollen to make honey for the hive.

When I was in my final year, the Falcon hand-delivered Bingo, freshly ejected from St. Paul's School in Concorde, to the admissions office, where he enrolled him in the tenth grade—a random choice, since he hadn't achieved a legitimate promotion since kindergarten. Holding him at arm's length, the oval tips of his long fingers hovering in the air just above Bing's shoulders, he was as squeamish as if he were scraping gum off the sole of his shoe.

Bingo cut into my bespoke existence at Andover like a serrated edge through fabric. I didn't want him there, and he knew it. I resented him for insinuating himself into what felt like my secret life. There I was, all laid out like a pair of gray flannel pants, and in he came—a set of shears ready to rip me apart at the seams.

"Just stay far away from me. Don't even look at me," I warned him, knowing it was an exercise in futility. The more I threatened, the more he glistened like early morning grass, his eyes taking on a familiar green gleam. I might as well have thrown popcorn at an advancing tank.

I knew he was going to start it up. Bingo always insisted on going right to the seditious heart of things. In no time, the school was churning with him.

He smuggled a girl into his room, and when he was found out, he claimed she was our sister. The first week of school and already he was threatened with expulsion. The only thing that saved him was the Falcon and the universal terror he inspired. For punishment, he was supposed to clean the windows in the downstairs floor of his residence. Later that night, he and twelve apostles removed all the glass from the windows and in the morning offered up the air for inspection.

"They're so clean they're invisible," Bingo said as the headmaster did a double take.

Bing insisted that he didn't have anything to do with the missing window glass but reluctantly confessed that he knew who did, describing where they could find the proof right underneath my bed.

"Don't worry. I wasn't born yesterday, Mr. Flanagan," the headmaster said as I sputtered inelegantly about my innocence.

A few days later, Bingo rigged up a dummy to look like a student and then waited until nighttime, when he and the boys laid their jerry-rig corpse in a pool of ketchup in the middle of the road leading into the school and lingered in the bushes for their hapless victims to arrive on the scene.

It took a pile of the Falcon's dough to save him from that one. Mr. Fadras, the biology teacher, called Fat-Ass by just about everyone, including his colleagues, swerved into a ditch at first sight of a bloody corpse in his headlights and damaged the front end of his car.

When a cheating scandal erupted in the early fall—someone

stole the answers to the second-year math midterm—Bingo was a natural suspect and spent hours undergoing the third degree.

"Let me get this straight," I confronted him in my room, where he was collapsed on the bed, both exhausted and invigorated by yet another grueling interrogation. "You stole the answers to the exam and you still failed? That must be some kind of a world record for dumb. Or, don't tell me, you were too lazy to memorize them."

"I didn't steal the answers."

"Then who did?"

"Teagan."

"Mark Teagan stole the answers and sold them. . . ."

"Yup."

"But he says that you did it."

"Yeah, well, he's lying. His old man will kill him if he gets turfed from the school."

"So what? He's an asshole. His dad is his problem. For once you didn't do it. You've got to tell them."

"No." He shook his head. "I'm no rat."

"Are you insane? This isn't the Cosa Nostra. Why are you protecting that little creep? He sure as hell isn't worried about you. Come on, Bing, you don't want to get expelled for cheating. Stuff like that follows you. . . . It's one thing to shit on the roof of Fat-Ass's Toyota . . ."

He laughed at the memory. I couldn't help it, I started to laugh, too, both of us side by side on the bed, so close we were touching, our shoulders adhering through the glue of habit, both of us staring up at the ceiling, laughter gradually subsiding, not looking at each other. In the end, my tone was pleading.

"Come on, Bing, save yourself. . . ."

But he wouldn't, and I knew he wouldn't because he was so goddamn unrelenting. I felt my throat pound and constrict. Bingo's stubbornness was its own desolate country. Sometimes trying to navigate that barren landscape, I thought my heart had altered its geography, relocating to my feet, throbbing away inside my shoes.

"Why does it always have to be like this? What's wrong with you? Are you missing some crucial chromosome? Even Ma and Pop will make concessions when it suits them. Why is everything a crisis with you? Can't you ever just stand down?"

"Hey, Collie, just because you lack conviction . . ."

"Lack conviction? Holy shit! You terrorize everyone with your behavior, and then you peddle all these moral absolutes. . . . Fine, get expelled, get branded a cheater . . . what do I care?"

"You know what your problem is, Coll? You're obsessed with what other people think."

I pulled myself up into a sitting position and looked down at Bing, who smiled back up at me. He didn't have a clue.

"No. You know what my problem is? My problem is caring about what you and Ma and Pop and Uncle Tom think. That's my problem."

"You don't give a shit what we think. You're too busy sucking up to the Falcon to care about us. Anyway, we're all nuts, isn't that right, Collie? It must be hell to be so sane in a crazy world."

I couldn't sleep thinking about what to do. The next morning, my insides tossing and turning like a washing machine, I went to the headmaster and told him that Mark Teagan stole the answers. He looked thoughtful and thanked me for coming forward. As he spoke, I glanced down at the tiny crack between the closed door and the floor, feeling small enough to crawl underneath.

At lunchtime I was standing around outside my residence, scuffing the recessed ground with my running shoe, digging a deeper hole, surrounded by a bunch of guys, friends of mine, who were reassuring me that I'd done the right thing by ratting out Mark.

"Teagan is a little prick," somebody said.

"Yeah, well, so is Bingo," I said, staring down at the ground.

"Yeah, but he's a likable little prick," someone else chimed in. "And he'd never hang your ass out to dry to save himself."

"Uh-oh, here comes trouble," said my friend Crunchie, whistling, glancing up and nudging me with his elbow, nodding in the direction of Bingo, who broke into a run at first sight of me.

I stepped out from inside my circle of friends to confront him, but before I had a chance to speak, he threw down his knapsack and let me have it, socked me right in the eye.

"You son of a bitch!" he said as the other guys, scrambling, reached in and dragged him away. I fell down on one knee, momentarily stunned, trying to get my bearings, feeling as if the world around me had exploded.

"Christ, Bing . . . ," I muttered, tears streaming down my cheek. I watched out of my good eye, my hand forming a patch over the other eye, as Bingo reached for his knapsack, turned, and walked away.

"Jesus," Crunchie said, concerned but a little titillated, too. "Are you all right?"

I nodded, though my eye hurt like hell. I stared after Bing until he vanished into a crowd of admiring girls who parted like the Red Sea to let him through—it looked as if I were his free pass to getting laid that night.

"If that was my little brother, I'd kick his ass," Crunchie said as we headed back to my room.

Bingo got expelled from Andover for giving me a black eye.

"Say," Uncle Tom said when I called home to give my side of the story, "it's about time somebody took a poke at you."

After he got tossed from Groton for wearing a hand buzzer, the next stop for Bingo was Upper Canada College in Toronto, where he distinguished himself by failing every course he took. His overall percent was 1, which intrigued Pop and Tom as they speculated forever about whatever he did to earn one mark.

"It doesn't seem mathematically possible. You don't suppose it was something to do with carnal relations?" Pop voiced his worst fears.

"No, surely he would have earned a passing grade in that case," Uncle Tom said, looking thoughtful as the two of them sat on the front porch rocking, nodding, sharing a beer. I could hear them from my bedroom above, the sounds of their conversation floating upward through my open window. Finally I couldn't stand it anymore.

I stuck my head out the window. "He got one percent because he only wrote one test and he scored one out of a hundred on it, that's all. It's not a great mystery."

"I say it was the pomegranate. I gave him a pomegranate to give to his geography teacher, who'd expressed an interest in tasting one, that's the source for sure," Uncle Tom said, oblivious to my intrusion, his voice holding steady and full of knowing.

"Oh, that would be it!" Pop exclaimed. "The pomegranate, of course! Jesus, you can't beat fruit! The tales I could tell about what I achieved with a little help from an apple and an Olympian sense of timing."

Weirdly, despite his academic record, they liked Bing in Toronto and expressed hope for his future. Equally inexplicable, he seemed to like it there, too, and was making plans to return in the fall.

"Canadians have a high tolerance for eccentricity," the Falcon said when I indicated amazement at the turn of events. "For morons, too, apparently," he continued, adding his trademark sprinkle of cyanide.

Bingo had a more direct explanation. "I'm making it with the headmaster's daughter, and she's got her old man wrapped around her little finger."

"Nice," I said to him, but he just laughed. Bing's attitude toward sex could probably best be summed up in a single word, "Woo-hoo," and that's when he was feeling pensive. For some bizarre reason, Ma found his promiscuity oddly charming, though she didn't extend the same latitude to me. When it came to my love life, Ma assumed the role of disgusted adolescent being forced to contemplate her parents "doing the hoob," as Uncle Tom referred to intercourse, insisting it was a proper biological term. Thanks to him, I got the strap in grade five for referring to coitus as hoobalah in sex ed class after Uncle Tom "corrected" my terminology.

Unlike Bingo, who lost his virginity at thirteen to the island's official deflowerer, Melanie Merrick—he had to scramble around the kitchen, emptying cupboards to find Saran Wrap to create a makeshift condom—I was a late bloomer, relatively speaking, struggling to catch up with my younger brother. When it came my turn, I was sixteen and I told Ma I was spending the night at a friend's house.

Instead I pitched a tent in the conservation area near home, and that's where I lost it to Eleanor Parrish, who undid the zipper on my jeans as casually as if she were pulling her blond hair into a ponytail.

Her parents found out and went nuts, though their response was mild compared with Ma's reaction. She let out one long scream when she saw me the next morning, and gathering up my shirt in her fists, twisting it into a noose around my neck, she pinned me against the nearest wall.

"How dare you take advantage of that innocent girl," she said. "Animal! You have no idea what you've unleashed! Girls are very emotional about sex. She may never recover from you exploiting her."

Pop looked at me as accusing and disappointed as if he'd caught me trying to set fire to him while he was sleeping. He and Ma grounded me for three months.

Years of Catholicism burning a hole in my conscience, I crawled into the study and stretched out on the sofa and stared up at the ceiling and thought about how much I loved Eleanor Parrish.

"Say, what were you thinking?" Uncle Tom appeared in the doorway.

I don't know who was more horrified, Uncle Tom or me, when I began to cry. I covered my face with my hands.

"I just wanted to see what it was like," I said, sobbing and unable to stop. I hadn't cried in front of anyone since I was a little kid.

"Well, I could have told you that you'd like it," he said, wandering over to the sofa. He sat next to me and took my hand.

"It's all right," he said. "And you're not grounded." He reached into his pocket. "Would you like some peanut brittle?"

"No thanks," I said, starting to regain some composure, rubbing my eyes with the sleeves of my shirt.

Uncle Tom and I sat together in silence, the only sound the persistent buzz of a circling fly.

"I've been listening to him for the last few minutes. It's true what they say about flies humming in the middle-octave key of F. And it's a good thing they do," Uncle Tom said, pausing, inviting the question, refusing to continue unless he was satisfied I was fully engaged.

"Why?" I asked him, powerless after so many years to resist.

"Think about it. The possibilities are staggering. You wouldn't want a common housefly with a magisterial high C. Say, he'd have the power to break your heart."

CHAPTER SEVEN

I WAS SEVENTEEN, JUST ABOUT TO GRADUATE AND TRYING TO decide what to do after Andover. Ma wanted me to organize migrant workers. I wanted to go to Brown with my friends.

"Friends! Hah!" Ma shrieked. "What friends? You don't have any real friends. They're all a bunch of vacuous social climbers, and you're the worst of the lot. Just once I'd like you to express a single unconventional thought. I'm surprised you weren't born wearing a tie."

"You get that from your grandmother McMullen," Pop said to me after the long weekend at home. He was talking about my conservatism, a family preoccupation generally referred to as if it were a disease or chronic condition, like syphilis of the soul.

"How I detest conservatism in a man," Ma said as she lit the gas stove.

What passed for conservatism in our household, however, could get you arrested anywhere else.

Pop was more accepting of my flaws than Ma, since in his quixotic but definite view of things, you were the preordained sum of all your parts. My mother was simpleminded over Bing, but according to Pop, it was in the DNA.

"She gets it from her mother. The Buntings are fixated on good-looking people to the exclusion of all other considerations." He paused for a sip of spiked coffee, the full cup raised to his lips. Lovingly, he inhaled the steam. I intuitively took two steps back. You could have gotten drunk on the fumes from his coffee.

"When it comes to looks you've got nothing to apologize for, Collie. You're a fine-looking lad, Jesus, you look like an Irish prince, and more important, you wear the clever pants in this family, and that comes right from your cousins the Hanrahan twins—"

"I know, Pop. You've told me about those idiots a million times. . . ." But it didn't stop him. His chin hit the floor.

"Idiots?" he thundered. "They graduated from the university when they were only fifteen years old. They were the smartest boys who ever lived. The only thing is they weren't practical, and it cost them their lives. They hadn't a clue about water and electricity. Who would ever have thought a plugged kitchen sink and an old toaster could wreak such havoc? Always be practical, Collie. To paraphrase the great Mr. O'Brien, pragmatism's your only man."

Probably because he was so hopelessly inept, Pop viewed practicality as if it were the mother lode, a treasure as elusive and fulfilling as the Holy Grail. This was a guy with an unreasonable reverence for duct tape, which he deemed a discovery of enormous cultural significance surpassed only by fire and archery. He once backed Ma's car out of the garage in a drunken stupor with the passenger door wide open, nearly tearing it off the hinge. The next day, he proudly showed me how he'd fixed it using miles of duct tape.

"Now that's pragmatism," he said.

I'd never seen so much tape. The whole side of the car was sealed up so tight you could have used it to safely transport the plague. Ma drove around for months with the car door sealed shut. I don't think she ever noticed—all that money, and we were some can of piss.

Ma and Pop used to stay up all night and sleep all day, stumbling into the kitchen to make coffee, her hair wild as the wind, sleeping mask worn like a necklace, his eyes watery and red.

"It's the circadian rhythms," Pop would say. "Each man is a prisoner of his internal clock. God help the man who won't make peace with his circadian cycle."

"What are you doing up? Washed and dressed. Have you already eaten?" my mother asked. I was teetering back and forth on a swivel chair in the corner near the window, the bad-humored ocean bubbling and hissing in the background.

"Ma, I've been up since seven. You were supposed to take me back to school, remember? I should have known. Next time I'll get to the ferry myself."

"Oh, I know. In bed by eleven, be up at seven. The drivel they espouse at that school of yours. You know, of course, nothing interesting ever happens before one o'clock in the afternoon. You and your pasty face and your banker's hours."

"What am I supposed to do? I've got school! I need to get back."

"And God knows we wouldn't ever want to miss a day of school. Aren't you the good little comptroller."

Her conversation was turning into one long protracted sneer. I could feel something warm glowing at the base of my skull. The years away at school spent among teachers who liked me for my ordinary urges and common interests had made me bold with Ma. It must have happened somewhere between all those weekend trips from the house to the campus and the campus to the house. I finally had decided I wasn't going to want her to love me anymore.

"Leave the boy alone, Anais," Pop said, speaking up from the other side of the room, where I could see him pouring more brandy, like cream, into his coffee. He sighed. "He can't help himself. It's right in him."

I got up and stared out the window; the skyline and the waves were an identical slate color, the greater world a stark monochrome, the frayed white curtain blowing, one of the little dogs standing on all fours, trying to catch the fluttering lacy edges in his teeth.

"Did Tom feed the dogs? Did Bingo get something to eat?" my mother asked me.

"Yes," I said with no small hint of frustration as I turned away from the window to face her.

"Is that exasperation I detect? The nerve of you."

Oh, I can still feel the rising tension in my shoulders, my neck tightening, my veins constricting, the flow of blood roiling to a crimson standstill, me silent and growing taller and straighter with every weighted word, vertical with the sheer breadth and scope of her.

And somewhere in the background, a million fleas were hopping from dog to dog to dog and back again, an invisible flea circus, full of the sounds of scratching, heads shaking, collars ringing, and paws thumping. To this day, I'm still coughing up hair from hundreds of dogs. A dog is curled up in every chair my inner eye surveys, every sofa draped in dogs, dogs piled on dogs like firewood from the floor to the ceiling. I drag a dog by my shoelaces across the uneven floor of my daily life; there's a dog tugging on my pant leg, refusing to let go, pulling me back when all I want to do is go forward.

"Hey, Collie, look smart!" Pop said, grinning as he pulled a coin from behind his ear and tossed it. I caught it between my fingers and nodded. He laughed. Charlie always figured there wasn't an unhappy moment that couldn't be redeemed by a flick of the wrist.

"Darling, darling, how is my precious darling?" Ma was diverted from her impending tirade by the sight of Bingo coming through the door after a long, lively day of truancy, feeding chocolate-chip cookies to his favorite dachshund, Jackdaw, looped round his shoulders like an inflated inner tube, ready to burst at the seams.

"Look at him, just look at him, Charlie, standing there as beautiful as if he'd stepped from a bandbox. Look at him, Collie. Isn't he a picture with the sun in his hair?"

"You're going to make him conceited as a corpse with white teeth, Anais. Let him be a man. No man worth his salt ever gave a hoot about his appearance. Back me up on this, Collie. When's the last time you washed your hair?"

"I don't know . . . a few days ago, I guess. . . ."

"There's the man. Jesus, I've never been more proud," he said, squeezing my shoulders, as I tried to shake off the implications of being the son so without distinction that his erratic personal hygiene was cause for celebration.

Bingo looked over at me and grinned, opening up like a tulip under the sunshine of Ma's blinding adoration. Bingo liked everyone, and everyone liked Bingo. He knew Ma was crazy, but so what? She was crazy about him. He sat back and enjoyed her, reveling in her insanity as if she were a recurring character in some sketch comedy. Parody Ma, he sometimes called her.

"Shut your mouth, Coll," he said. "You're catching the flies your hair is attracting."

"Don't listen to them, darling," my mother said, pulling Bing into her open arms, hugging him until he begged for air; she was kissing Jackdaw on the top of his head, the other dogs crowding excitedly around them. "What else would you expect a couple of run-of-the-mill fiddles to say in the presence of a gleaming Stradivarius? They're forever stuck at the barn dance, but you, Bingo, my love, you're going to the ball."

And then she swept around the kitchen with him in her arms, loudly singing her dissonant Sondheim tunes, the dogs going crazy.

CHAPTER EIGHT

A COUPLE OF WEEKS LATER, I GRADUATED FROM ANDOVER. IT WAS a hot day, and the air-conditioning broke down just before the ceremony, the hall hazy as a sauna. I stepped up to receive my diploma, my hands slippery with sweat, and glancing down, I saw my mother glowering at me from the front row, she and the Falcon separated only by the presence of Pop, heavy-lidded and bored, the smell of whiskey filling the air around him like incense. Ma's right fist was clenched inside a black leather glove. Her version of a tennis bracelet, it was intended to express her solidarity with whatever injustice currently engaged her imagination. That day, she was pretty worked up about the plight of coffee plantation workers in Brazil.

Bingo got ejected a few minutes later for causing a disturbance with his coughing—based on their experience with him in the past, the staff was convinced it was a deliberate disruption, but this time they were wrong. The intense heat kicked off an asthma attack, the first one he'd had in years.

Two men, their voices turned down low, discreetly tried to escort him away, but Ma, who never missed the opportunity to make a scene, reacted as if Bingo had fallen into the hands of a military junta and were about to become one of the disappeared.

"Get your hands off him!" she yelled, reaching for Bingo's arm as the men tried in vain to calm her down, audience members craning for a better look, my friends laughing, my nervous system experiencing a series of rolling blackouts.

"I'm afraid we're going to have to ask you to leave, Mrs. Flanagan," one of the men said firmly but soothingly, as if he were trying to talk down a mental patient from the ledge of a high-rise.

My mother spun around to face me on the stage. "Are you happy now?" she yelled up at me.

Pop, who had up to this point shown unusual restraint, jumped to his feet, wavered a little, and announced, "We're leaving." Taking Ma by the elbow, pushing his way past the two men, cheerful Bingo in the lead, he headed down the center aisle. Ma kept noisily resisting.

"Do you have any idea who I am?" she screamed as she vanished from sight, her voice echoing in the corridors, a slight smile crossing the Falcon's face, his eyes locked briefly on mine, his arms crossed over his chest.

He relaxed his posture, stretching out his legs, and I heard him chuckle. I couldn't believe it. I was as astonished as if I'd stumbled across a saltwater crocodile giggling over something a giraffe said at the local watering hole.

I stared at him, and then I laughed, too, a little apprehensively, maybe, but it seemed the impossible had happened. The Falcon and I were sharing a laugh.

A few days passed before I managed to work up the courage to confront Ma with my decision about the fall. I may have given up on winning her affection, but I still feared her wrath.

"I've decided to go to Brown," I said, fan whirring overhead, my hand gripping the collar of Bachelor, our two-hundred-pound St. Bernard. He was sitting next to me as I stood in the middle of the kitchen, his dense fur pressing against my bare legs. Panting and grinning, drooling in the early summer heat, steam rising from his dangling tongue, his tail banging, he was leaning into me, and I was leaning back, grateful for the support.

"Oh. And what do you intend to study?" Ma paused at the open refrigerator door, her back to me, then closed it slowly and turned around to face me, a tray of ice cubes in her hand.

"I don't know exactly . . . I guess maybe I'll get a liberal arts degree to start. . . ."

She dropped the tray with a bang. It hit the black-and-white checkerboard tiles, ice shattering, shards spraying across the floor. The little dogs attacked like fire ants, scrambling and bickering, competing for the spoils, crunching loudly on the frozen fragments.

"To what end? Film studies? Theater arts? My God, is this about going into show business? You're going to be an actor? You want to be in the movies, is that what this is all about?" Her voice had a pinging quality, like the taut quiver of a bow.

"No. No. Ma, jeez, here we go. . . ."

"I'm expected to bankroll an Ivy League education so you can churn out crap? Does it occur to you that the world does not need yet another aspiring creative with no talent? Next you'll be telling me you want to write comic books. Are you looking for fame? Is that it? Is your life nothing more than one enormous vanity project?"

Her hair was getting curlier by the moment, each serpentine tendril coiling into a series of minitornadoes blowing wildly, the room seeming to swirl and spin. I held tight to Bachelor, watching helplessly as the world around me took on a deep indigo blue color, Ma's eyes flashing like heat lightning.

"You with your bristling bourgeois ambitions . . . Why not just be an orthodontist and be done with it? Proclaim to the entire world: 'I am a bore. I think only of braces and bruxism and accounts receivable and slender blondes with bobs! Nothing else matters!'"

"Ma, what are you talking about? You never listen. Would you listen for once? You just go off on these crazy tangents of yours. . . ." I was standing there out in the open, Bachelor licking my knee, his watery spit running down my leg, as I shoved my hands through my hair, ducking flying objects coming from the other side of the room.

"He has to ask, my God, he just doesn't get it. Charlie, do you hear this? Are you paying attention? Your son has just announced his intention to become a movie star."

Pop was sitting on a wooden chair, reading yesterday's *New York Times*. He was always two or three days behind the rest of the world, his bare legs tucked under a long pine table, Bing's initials carved into its scuffed surface.

"I thought we discussed this, Collie," he said, sapphire blue eyes peering over the top of the page. "We decided you were going to become a mechanical engineer and design bridges, don't you remember?"

"Pop, that's your idea. I don't want to be a mechanical engineer."

"Well, that's ridiculous. How could anyone given the opportunity not want to be a mechanical engineer? A man can do nothing finer in his lifetime than build a bridge."

"The real question is, how can anyone submit to all those years of Westernized education yet emerge knowing absolutely nothing about what truly matters? The world hovering on the precipice of revolutionary social change, and you want to wear makeup and chase starlets," Ma said, getting warmed up, practically eating coal, she was that stoked.

"All well and good, Anais, but your revolutions and the men of mysterious angers that spearhead them are small potatoes compared to the timeless achievement of building a bridge," Pop said, turning his divided attention back to the op-ed page.

My heart sputtered, every nerve ending sparking and shorting. I felt as if I needed to loosen my tie—I wasn't wearing one. I put a figurative gun to my forehead and fired several times. I missed. Most times, dealing with Ma, I knew better than to jump into the fray, but not this time. This time, I was just plain angry.

"What makes you such a revolutionary?" I walked toward her. "You're a joke. You shoot your mouth off about the poor, but you don't have any idea what it's like to be poor. You don't even know what it's like to be middle class. When's the last time you were even in a grocery store? Uncle Tom does all the shopping and the cooking and the cleaning. What do you do? You think because you don't wear lipstick that you're a social maverick? You claim to despise Granddad because he's some sort of evil oligarch, but meanwhile you use his money to live like a member of the royal family.

"If you were serious about what you say you believe, then you'd give up everything and we'd live among the kind of people you claim to love so much. But you won't do that because the truth is that you hate everybody—you just want to annoy everyone around you and establish rules for them that you don't follow. If we moved into some public housing unit, you'd be parading around in a tiara and bragging about your silver spoon. How can you stand being such a hypocrite?"

Whenever Ma was confronted, which wasn't often, she'd inevitably react with a preternatural calm, swallowing her furies and reimagining her anger as a state of Zen, heightened tolerance her favored tool of torture. She smiled over at me, a doctor's wife sheathed in silk and sarcasm, exuding the kind of painful predatory pleasantness usually confined to social encounters among strangers who instinctively dislike one another.

"What is this? Some kind of teenage tantrum? Upset because you can't get a date to the dance, Collie? Yes, I use your grandfather's money. You bet your ass I do, because it suits me. I like the fact that I'm committing enormous amounts of his fortune to destroy the system that helped create him and protects and sustains everything he stands for—and believe me, Collie, I make things happen with that money. I serve my causes well." She leaned back against the fridge, arms folded in front of her, self-satisfied grin on her face.

"Oh, please, you're always intimating that you're some kind of international outlaw when all you do is hand over money to a bunch of homegrown Marxist phonies who've learned how to work the cocktail circuit. Granddad has a party and you show up in work boots and start insulting everyone, and you think it means something, like you're on the front lines of battle—when all it really means is that you're a jerk who enjoys making people uncomfortable and belittling them."

"Here, here, Collie, your mother deserves better than that. She is your mother, for goodness' sake," Pop interjected.

"Don't remind me," I said.

Ma laughed. "Spoken like the spoiled adolescent you are. Oh, let him talk, Charlie. I don't mind. Only a fool argues with a fool. And anyway, it's good practice for when he's acting out scenes in his little movies, helps him get used to all that second-rate dialogue he'll be spewing for the rest of his life. Is this an audition of some kind, for one of those beach blanket movies?" She looked at me with utter contempt. I was fighting with all my heart the urge to let her have it, wishing a giant anvil would drop from the sky and turn her into a scrambled grease spot on the floor.

I glanced around at the sound of the kitchen door opening and banging shut once and then again, a warm, sudden gust of salty sea air lifting up the corners of the curtains and scattering the newspaper. Tom and Bingo returned from a walk with so many overheated frothing dogs, they flowed like lava into the kitchen.

I struggled with the urge to pant.

"Collie says he's going to be a movie star," Ma said as if she were announcing I was suffering an outbreak of genital herpes. Bingo rolled his eyes.

"For the last time, I don't want to be a movie star."

"It's the only way he'll ever get the girl, Ma—if it's in the script," Bing said, reaching into the fridge for a bottle of soda.

"I think you're aware of my feelings on the subject," Tom said, removing his straw boater and sitting in the chair across from Pop. He stared at me.

"Oh no," I said.

"Oh yes. I have only two words for you."

"Not again."

"Pigeon coach."

"For God's sake, Tom, how many times must we go through this?

He's not going to coach pigeons." Ma threw her arms into the air and then, bending over, pulled Marty, one of the poodles, onto her lap and buried her face in his curly topknot.

"And why not? Racing pigeons are the thoroughbreds of the sky. Owning a flock of racing homers is the same as owning a professional sports team. Even the damn Royals keep a flock of racing pigeons."

"Would you stop talking about pigeons? Leave it to you to champion a public nuisance," Ma said.

"Oh, and I suppose GI Joe is a public nuisance, is he? The most highly decorated pigeon in American history, was he being a pest when he saved the lives of one thousand British soldiers?"

"To say nothing of Captain Lederman, Jungle Joe, and Blackie Halligan," Bingo said from his spot in the doorway as he sipped his Pepsi. "And don't forget your own Michael Collins, Uncle Tom. Boy, there was a glorious bird."

"Thanks, asshole," I said, eliciting a frown from Pop.

"I'm not likely to forget that bird in a hurry. He disappeared on a five-hundred-mile journey. I looked for him for days, weeks went by, and I'd given up. Broke my heart to think a predator had claimed him. Six weeks later I went out to the loft and there he was, bless his noble heart, his wing broken. He couldn't fly, so what does he do? He walks."

"And he wouldn't have made it but for the Brooklyn Bridge now, would he?" Pop said.

"For God's sake, Tom, don't be absurd. Why do you say such preposterous things?" Ma said. "You fill the boys' heads with utter nonsense."

The old lady, sighing deeply, decided to put an end to the conversation—it was an argument that diffused into a conversation as opposed to a conversation that escalated into an argument, both standard progressions in our family. "Well, if you're determined to be a teen idol, you can get the funding from your grandfather."

"No, I can't. He wants me to go to Yale and study international law. But it doesn't matter. . . ."

"Really? He doesn't want you going to Brown? The nerve of the bastard. Who does he think he is? How dare he tell one of my children what they're to do."

"Ma, I don't need anybody's money, especially yours. I've been offered a full scholarship."

"What?" She sprang forward in her seat, Marty scrambling to remain in her lap. "What is this, the final days of the Apocalypse? You can't be serious? You come from one of the wealthiest families in the country and you're offered free access to Brown? Meanwhile, children of the inner city are left to their own impoverished devices, even at the elementary school level—"

"Ma, for Christ's sake, a scholarship is based on academic merit, not need."

"Bullshit! Academic performance is skewed to socioeconomic background. . . ."

"Oh, the Ivy League, is it? Bingo, don't look at him. No one can have eye contact with him now he's a Brown man. And don't talk to him. He'll only converse in Latin, hadn't you heard?" Tom said, cast-iron skillet in his hand, preparing to make his habitual late lunch of bacon and eggs—singing to himself every afternoon, "Tom Flanagan's makin' himself some eggs and bacon."

"Didn't you tell me you wanted to get your doctorate? What was it you said? Something about being attracted to the academic life . . . ," Bingo said unhelpfully.

"That's a lie and you know it." Along with everything else, the old lady despised academia.

"Dr. Fancy-Pants needs to go to Brown to learn to ask people to pee in a cup," Tom said provocatively—deliberate misunderstanding was his favorite form of interaction—while cracking the first of several eggs against the edge of the skillet.

"Not that kind of a doctor, you jackass," Ma said, finally about to lose it, squeezing shut her eyes, her lips whitening, anger pumping through her bloodstream in incremental surges—like a balloon receiving helium, she was about to burst.

"Now that you say it out loud, 'Dr. Flanagan' does have a nice ring to it," Pop said, chin in hand, newspaper bent, staring dreamily out the window; then, frowning, he abruptly interrupted his own reverie. "For heaven's sake, Collie, promise me you'll not become a pathologist . . . God knows what they get up to."

"I'm not sure what I want to do . . . I'm just thinking. . . ."

"Remember, back home, the case of Annie Mulroney's boy?" Tom interjected. "He was a pathologist and got caught photographing dead people's genitalia. Turns out he had quite a collection, claimed it was an innocent hobby and educational. . . ."

"I was thinking of him," Pop said. "Wasn't there some problem with him performing prostate exams postmortem, alleging it was research done in the service of science? But you know, I still say curing athlete's foot in Africa isn't worth one-two-three compared to the building of a lovely suspension bridge."

"If you mention bridges one more time . . . honestly, Charlie, you'd think you lived under a bridge, the way you romanticize them—" Ma was starting to sputter.

"Say," Tom interrupted, using the same tone people typically reserve for sudden revelations. "Let me go on record as saying I'll take you out and shoot you myself if you go ahead and become a priest."

"A priest! Jesus, Lord, Collie, you're planning on the clergy? Your grandfather would turn over in his grave," Pop said, a look of horror on his face.

"Who said anything about being a priest? I've never even thought about being a priest. I don't want to be a priest."

"That's not what you told me," Bingo said, lifting himself onto the window seat in the dining room, his legs dangling playfully, his eyes shining.

"Collie, I'm begging you. I'm on my knees to you. Don't waste your life in a Roman collar." Pop finally put down *The New York Times*, signaling his level of commitment to the conversation.

"He's going to wind up just like Francie Sherlock," Tom said, expertly scrambling a pan full of eggs.

"Who the hell is Francie Sherlock?" I said.

"Language. Watch your language," Pop said, frowning. "Anyone can curse, you know."

Pop liked to compare swear words to termites. "They'll bring down a man's character in the same insidious ways as a termite works in secret to destroy a building."

"Our first cousin, he was your second cousin," explained Uncle Tom. "When he was little, the nuns warned him against biting into the Communion host, said it was the literal body and blood of Christ. Francie didn't believe them, and when he was twelve he was showing off for some girls and he bit into the host and wound up with a mouth full of blood. I say he bit his tongue, but it made quite the impression on him, and he joined the Benedictine order. He was killed a week after getting his first parish, hit by a car while he was heading off to give Agnes O'Connell extreme unction."

"I don't get it . . . what's it got to do with me?"

Tom sighed in exasperation. "Do I have to spell everything out for you, Noodle? He was abusing himself in the rectory when one of the ladies from the Catholic Women's Society rushed in to tell him about Agnes having a heart attack. She screamed at the sight of him, and he was so flustered that he ran wildly out into the street, and that's how he got killed."

"Collie, please, masturbation is a sin of vanity, it's a terrible waste of time, a drain on your manhood, and once the pedal and crank takes hold of a man . . . ," Pop said.

Bingo shook his head from side to side. "Too late, Pop. Why do you think I screamed when I walked into Collie's bedroom last night?"

"I'll go mad if I have to listen to any more. Must you go on and on about this, Collie? Such narcissism—is every discussion in this house to concern only what you want? It's too much. I can't handle any more." Ma clutched her head, her hands a helmet compressing her skull, which was threatening to explode.

Most conversations with Ma concluded on a similarly theatrical tormented note. Implicit in every encounter, however banal, was the threat of her suddenly evaporating, vaporized by the ubiquitous self-centeredness of others. The world, according to Ma, had nothing better to do than think up ways to drain her blood, a little bit every day.

"Fine," she wailed. "Have your own way. Do whatever you want. I haven't the strength to fight you on it. I'll pay for it, if it will just put an end to your interminable whining, but only if you go to Brown. You must go to Brown. You let me handle your grandfather," Ma said, rising to her feet in a swirl of rising tides and cloudy consternation. Brushing past Bingo, patting him on the head as if he were a puppy, fluffy pick of the litter, she ducked into the hallway, Marty following her up the stairs.

"What's her problem?" Tom asked as Pop shrugged.

"Girls only," he said, raising an eyebrow, the unfastidious specter of female problems resolving the discussion.

"Hey, Collie . . ." Bingo stopped me at the door as I headed down to the beach to drown myself.

"What do you call a guy that fucks models all day long?"

"Bing Flanagan."

"That's who I want to be."

CHAPTER NINE

THE NEXT WEEKEND, THE FALCON AND I WERE IN NEW YORK CITY, alone at last, a kind of nightmare honeymoon in June, just the two of us. A couple of times a year, he swept in and spirited me away to shop for a "decent bloody wardrobe." The Falcon took clothes and appearance seriously, a characteristic he weirdly shared with Pop.

"The face you present to the world," the Falcon called it. "Where the exterior eye leads, the inner eye will soon follow."

It was ninety degrees, or maybe it just felt that hot. Rivulets of sweat ran down the back of my neck. I glanced into the mirror in the dressing room and tried vainly to batten down the curls. Jesus, the only thing missing was a Pan flute.

I took a quick appraising look and groaned—when it came to informal wear for young men, the Falcon was all about Barbour jackets, varsity cardigans, cashmere scarves, and moleskin trousers. I looked like an effete fugitive from Wallis Simpson's id.

"What are you smiling about?" he demanded, standing at ease in a cream-colored suit, slim and straight, the salesman fluttering around him like a butterfly when I emerged from the dressing room.

"Nothing, I guess."

"Do you always walk around grinning about nothing?" He seemed to be making an effort at levity, but his voice betrayed an arctic edge.

"Well, actually, right at the moment, I feel as if I may never smile again."

"No one likes a wise-ass, Collie," he said, moving toward me, adjusting the lapels of my jacket. I stood my ground, but psychologically I shifted a couple of steps to the side, unaccustomed to such intimacy with the Falcon. That kind of proximity to my grandfather made me feel as if I were stranded in the most isolated pocket of the earth and trying vainly to scale the volcanic cliffs of Tristan da Cunha. I took a deep breath—if good taste were a scent, it would have smelled like the Falcon.

"Hmmm . . ." He paused to consider, narrowing his blue eyes. "Stand up straight . . . there now. That's better. I must admit, you do wear clothes well," he said, both hands lightly dusting my shoulders. "You've got me to thank for that. You're the image of me at the same age. It's like looking in a mirror." The Falcon shook his head as if he were trying to comprehend the idea that nature could be so generous, not once, but twice.

"Too bad about Bing—oh, he's cute enough, but that's the problem, isn't it? Unfortunately, your brother is too diminutive to make much of an impression. That mop of hair and all those freckles are damned undignified for a man." He patted me on the arm before stepping back to take a better look.

Appearing satisfied, he summoned the salesman with an all but invisible gesture—as if he were carrying around a silent dog whistle that only the pathologically subservient could hear. Despite daily exposure to high-profile types, the salesman was so intimidated by the Falcon that he performed an involuntary half-bow on approach.

"We'll take the lot, and I want him measured for a couple of suits," the Falcon said, his demeanor communicating a sort of generalized impatience, as if he had places to be and people to see.

"Thanks, Granddad, I appreciate it, but when am I going to wear this stuff? I'm going to be living in Rhode Island, not eighteenth-century Glasgow. I look like somebody shoved a skeet-shooting rifle up my ass, as if I should be hunting pheasants on the Scottish moors or something."

The salesman gasped and erupted into a hiccuping fit of

pedestrian conversational tics; visibly panic-stricken at this mild insurrection, he measured my inseam as my grandfather stared out the window and onto the street below. From his jacket pocket, the Falcon retrieved a silver cigarette case, which he slid methodically between his fingers before turning his full attention to the man on his knees in front of him. Terrified, the salesman started blithering.

"Young people today have their own ideas about how they want to dress. Blue jeans, T-shirts, and baseball caps seem to be the order of the day. Oh well, youth will out, I suppose. I can remember wearing some pretty offbeat stuff myself, all part of the rebellious age," he said cheerfully, his lips trembling.

"If I was interested in your theory concerning the apotheosis of adolescence, I would ask for it," the Falcon said to the salesman, who appeared to be shrinking before my eyes. "Do you always insinuate yourself in the private conversations of clients?"

"Oh, I'm sorry," the salesman responded, laughing uncomfortably, clicking into instantaneous robo-servant mode. I felt my liver shut down, my insides shuddering in response to what seemed like an obnoxious historical extract—it was like being present the moment before the start of the French Revolution.

"Yes, well, enough of your fumbling exegesis. Just do your job. Does my grandson look like some teenage street riffraff? Don't waste his time with your silly chatter." The Falcon strode past me, pausing just long enough to tell me he was going down to the first floor to speak to Michael, his driver.

"Hurry up. I don't want Collie waiting any longer than is necessary," he ordered the salesman as he left.

"Sorry about that," I said to the salesman, who politely dismissed my concerns.

"Some of this stuff isn't that bad," I said, trying to make amends. "I like the pea coat, and you can throw in a couple of pairs of cords, too, with all the other stuff, while you're at it."

Although I'm not one of those rich guys who assume that everyone

I meet is after my fortune, I learned early that when you're loaded, money is the only form of apology that matters to most people.

"Certainly, whatever you'd like," he said. "Thank you."

After that, we both relaxed a little and wound up talking about baseball, until the Falcon reappeared and the salesman began to struggle with his train of thought and we both lapsed into an uncomfortable quiet.

The silence persisted most of the way home in the car, until the Falcon finally spoke:

"I'm going to make a prediction about your future, Collie, and you won't like it. I regret to say that you're not going to amount to a hill of beans. Do you want to know why?"

"Why?"

"Because you suffer fools gladly."

"It wouldn't kill you to be a little nicer to people," I murmured into a cupped hand.

"What did you say?" the Falcon said, leaning forward in his seat, his hand on my knee.

"Forget it," I said, unwilling to elaborate.

"No, I won't forget it. You made an accusation, now you must defend it."

"Well, I don't think that money and power entitle you to treat other people badly, especially people who lack privilege. I don't notice you being unpleasant to the people who attend your parties. It's obvious what you think. Someone has to have a lot of money before you take them seriously."

"How much money do you think that salesman back there makes?" he asked me.

"I don't know. Maybe twenty thousand. . . ."

"That's right. Think about what type of person would be content to settle for so little. What in God's name would such a person have to offer someone like me? Why would I be the least bit intrigued by anything such an individual would think or say?"

"Not everyone is interested in accumulating wealth and power. People have other priorities. . . ."

"Like what? Watching hockey games?" Sometimes the Falcon demonstrated an almost demented aptitude for belittlement.

"I've met a lot of famous people and important people. I've gone to school with their kids and been in their houses, and most of them are pretty disappointing."

He sighed. "Well, of course they are. Who would argue otherwise? There is an old saying, Collie: 'Get a reputation for rising at seven and you can safely sleep until noon.' It's only by acquiring wealth and position that you can truly derive the benefit of reputation—it's a form of protection against the vagaries of life. I'm not interested in life's victims."

"You know, you and Ma come at this stuff from opposite extremes, but you're really not that different in the way you view things. I'm starting to think that it doesn't matter what people believe in—it's the way you treat people that counts."

The Falcon settled back into the leather seat and looked straight ahead.

"Collie, if a mockingbird can change its tune dozens of times over the course of a few moments, surely you can find a new song to sing."

I started classes at Brown that September unsure about what I wanted to do, so I kept my options open by taking mostly arts courses and a few science courses. Unimpressed, Uncle Tom told every tradesperson, merchant, and deliveryman on the Vineyard I was majoring in hieroglyphics. Even now, more than twenty years later, I occasionally run into someone who asks me how long I think it will be before hieroglyphics catch on again.

Bingo, finally kicked out of Upper Canada College, went from there to Exeter, but not for long. He wasn't exactly focused on schoolwork or issues of character building. First semester, he and a bunch of friends sneaked home and hijacked the Falcon's vintage Bentley—everything the old guy owned was vintage; Bingo once semi-innocently asked him if he drank vintage milk—and drove it off the pier and into the Boston harbor.

A few months later on a school-sponsored skiing trip to Colorado, he entertained his friends by ducking behind a tree, stripping off all his clothes, and flying naked down the slope in subzero temperatures. He was promptly sent home and suspended for the rest of the semester.

"Not to worry. I understand that when Lenin was a young man he liked to do the same thing in the Urals," the Falcon commented dryly to my mother, who had no sense of humor.

Bingo got the boot from Exeter on Holy Thursday. My second year at Brown, Deerfield sent him packing on Thanksgiving Day. My third year, the Falcon enrolled him at Rugby in England, where he achieved an A plus in swinging from chandeliers—they gave him the heave-ho just before Valentine's Day.

"I'm like my own special occasion," he joked as he alternated studying from home with brief erratic stints at a local high school.

"There's nothing left," the Falcon said, sounding helpless for the first time in his life. "We've run through every good school and several countries."

"There's always Miss Porter's," I joked, but he didn't see the humor.

Bingo celebrated his expulsion from Rugby by making headlines—the name Bing Flanagan was splashed in crimson like a bucket of spilled paint all over the English tabloids. They delighted in pointing out his relationship to the Falcon, which made Ma giddy with happiness. Reports were he'd had sex with some girl in a public place.

I called him from a phone booth on the beach in Rhode Island.

"Hello," I said, my voice conveying a whole lot more than simple greeting.

"So?" he said.

"So? So, interesting headlines."

His silence was a shrug.

"Bingo. You rogered some girl in a bar?"

"Yeah. No. We made out. It's gotten so exaggerated." His offhand manner was designed to deflect my accusatory tone. "Anyway, it's not like it wasn't consensual."

"That's hardly the issue." I couldn't believe what I was hearing. "Come on. What are you, an animal? Thanks, by the way. It's really been a pleasure fending off all my friends."

"Oh yeah, I know how easily offended the Andover and Brown crowd is," he snorted.

"Give me a break. You sound like Ma. You don't need to have a trust fund to be disgusted by what you did."

"You couldn't even tell. We were standing up. We were at the bar. Anyway, it didn't go that far."

"Well, apparently you weren't quite as discreet as you thought."

"Look. I'm not happy about it, but I'm telling you, nothing major happened. I was drinking. Things just got out of hand. I can't help it if people in England are uptight about sex." I couldn't believe how casual he was being. Jesus, he didn't even have the grace to be embarrassed.

"So this was a socially motivated act of civil disobedience? Score one for the revolution. . . ."

"In a way. Yeah." He was obviously warming up to the idea—I envisioned him curling up in the nearest fuzzy armchair.

"Then it's a proud day for the Flanagans. . . . Don't you think maybe you're pushing the irrepressible factor a little?"

"How's the Falcon taking it?"

"Well, publicly he's not dignifying the matter with comment, but privately he's ready to dip you into a vat of burning oil. He summoned me to Cassowary, and I had to spend the whole weekend listening to him rage. Why don't you come home and deal with him yourself? Why should I have to take all your flak?"

"Really? He's that pissed?" Bingo wasn't sounding quite so chipper. "What about Pop and Uncle Tom? Are they mad, too?"

"Well, it's really fun listening to them review the teachings of the catechism by the hour. The two of them are hung up on the premarital sex part. Pop says it's a venial sin—Tom's arguing it's a mortal sin and you need to go to confession or you're going to go to hell."

"What do you think?"

"I think I'm sick of listening to them tell me off instead of you. I'm not the one living like some low-rent playboy. Is this how it's going to be for the rest of your life? It seems like every time I talk to you it's because you've pulled another stupid stunt. Why can't you just do what you're supposed to do? You can start by coming home."

I got off the phone with Bing, and first thing I did was call Pop.

"Pop, don't you think something should be done about Bingo? He's completely out of control. Where's it going to end?"

"I agree with you, Collie. But what can I do?"

Faced with the throbbing bass line of Pop's obliviousness and the perverse pride Ma took in Bingo's antics, I decided it was up to me to talk to Bingo about his future. I was pretty earnest in those days.

It was midmonth, one of the warmest March days on record, and he was just back from England. We were on the beach with the dogs, and Bingo was riding Lolo, walking him along the shoreline, cooling him down. I was on foot, trailing alongside them, chirping ineffectively, struggling to keep up.

He was wearing jeans and sandals with work socks, miscellaneously topped off by a white T-shirt with a red plaid flannel shirt over it and Uncle Tom's crazy old wool sweater tied around his waist. Bingo practiced a wayward form of cross-dressing—one part tony frat boy, the other part a jumbled paean to the nursing home.

Finally, ready to knock him off his perch, I reached for the reins to slow them down, Lolo's ears flicking dangerously.

"I want to talk to you about something," I prefaced as Bingo stayed silent, making it plain he wasn't interested in what I had to say.

"Hey, would you listen?" I said, stopping and standing still.

"Why? So you can start your usual crap—"

"Jesus, Bing, you're not even nineteen years old and you're totally fucked. You've got no education. You haven't even finished high school. You don't take care of yourself . . . you're drinking a lot . . . you'd screw a cabbage if there was an opening. You're going to wind up like Pop and Uncle Tom. . . ."

"Don't worry about it. I've got plans, big plans, I'm going to be a dental hygienist," he said, slipping his sandals from the stirrups, letting his feet dangle. He was a good rider, natural, like Ma.

"It's not funny. You're not funny. You're an idiot." I had vowed this wasn't going to degenerate into insults, and there I was frothing at the mouth—moron, shit-for-brains, asshole—I was rabidly trying to come up with an insult big enough, but it didn't exist.

"Hey, what's your problem? Relax. I've got things under control. I've got a plan," he said as I pulled on the reins, Lolo coming to a halt and Bingo swinging his leg over and sliding onto the ground beside me as we resumed walking, Lolo in between us, the dogs crisscrossing back and forth in front of us, racing on ahead, playing in the waves.

"What kind of a plan?" I asked him, neatly sidestepping Lolo's failed sudden attempt to separate my right cheek from my face.

"I call it the Man Plan," Bingo said, Lolo's big head blocking my view of his face.

"For Christ's sake . . ."

"It's my manhood project. I'm going to implement it in stages. I figure I'll start when I'm twenty, begin with small stuff, you know, doing up my shoelaces, quit drinking out of the milk carton, put my laundry away, and then I'll gradually progress to some of the bigger stuff. . . ."

"Why does everything have to be a joke with you?" I was shaking my head, trying to hear over the din of barking dogs.

"I'm not kidding. By the time I'm twenty-five I plan to own stocks and have a subscription to *The Economist*. . . ." He was enumerating points with his fingers.

I started to laugh. "Now I know you're hosing me."

"No, I'm serious," he said, grinning. "I've got it all worked out. My only rule is that for every step forward, I can't take a step back."

"What about school? What about getting an education?" I stopped and stood in front of Lolo, who was pushing forcibly against my chest with his head.

"Well," he said, not looking at me, focusing on Lolo, "that's the beauty of the plan, that's why I don't want to start too early. I want to get this whole school thing behind me, otherwise it'll just mess up the plan. Pop's right when he says that too much education erodes your intellect."

"And the Falcon is right when he says that annuities were invented for guys like you. Bingo, you can't make a plan to become a man—it's like deciding to be generous or smart or funny sometime in the future. You either are or you aren't. Life is a process," I concluded, sounding as if I knew what I was talking about.

"Lord, make me a man, but not yet," he responded, unfazed by my wisdom.

He signaled me to give him a leg up. I linked my hands together, and he used me to hoist himself back into the saddle, its leathery smell mingling with the breeze off the ocean, the dogs leaping around us excitedly.

"All I know is that I've got better things to do with my life than conjugate Latin verbs and try to figure out where the Phoenicians went wrong," he said, leaning forward slightly in his seat, encouraging Lolo with his heels, pressing them lightly into his flanks. He didn't apply any pressure, just kind of urged things along.

The beach stretched for miles, not a soul in sight as Bingo vanished into Lolo and cantered off along the shoreline, beating up the sand, dogs forming a moving line behind them, leaving me far behind, arms dangling helplessly at my sides. Bing had perfect carriage, a motionless seat, straight, graceful, weightless, and effortless. I was a good rider, too, but I had to work at it, and the effect was more studied.

My little black-and-white dog, Eugene, paused in his pursuit and pranced back to where I was. I crouched down on my knees, and he stood up on his hind legs, his front paws in my lap as I stroked his head, and we both watched Bing until he was no longer visible.

You could have dropped Bingo from the sky onto the back of a horse and he'd land in place like a waterbird skimming the surface of the ocean.

That night, temperatures hovering in the high sixties, Bingo and I went to a party on the beach, everyone home for spring break, giant bonfire set up along the dunes, beer on the night's breath, a moonless night so dark that everyone was invisible, like Ma's black dogs, her Labrador retriever, Harry, her Great Dane, Jesper. People vanished quietly into the tall grasses, then reappeared softly without notice, brushing up against you to signal their presence.

"Let's go," I said, bored and indifferent, stumbling over couples laid out in the sand. I flipped on the flashlight, the sudden bright light announcing my intention to head home. Bingo wasn't listening. His attention was on a group of guys heading off the beach and into the trees. Laughing but purposeful, they were not carefree.

"Hand me that flashlight," Bingo said, taking it from me and shining it after them. I could feel his intensity from where I stood next to him and saw him in silhouette outlined by the flashlight's narrow beam, up on his toes, staring after them.

"Was that Mandy with them?" he said, referring to the younger sister of a friend of ours. The Lindell sisters were notoriously easy, the kinds of girls Uncle Tom referred to as "streetcars."

"I don't know," I said, feeling uneasy. "It might have been."

"When I saw her earlier she was drunk out of her mind," he said, turning back around to face me. "We should check it out."

"I'm sure it's okay," I said, knowing he was right but needing a moment or two to talk myself into investigating. "Gimme a break, Bing, this is Randy Mandy we're talking about. . . .

"What are you doing?" I asked him, but he ignored me and took off jogging, then broke into a run as he headed into the woods after them.

"Bingo! Hold on!" I hollered after him, trying to navigate the blackness using the leftover light laid down from the flashlight.

He disappeared and with him the light, so I was left to follow the sounds of muffled male laughter and drunken murmuring as I groped my way to a small clearing concealed by tall trees and thick bushes, individual flashlights glowing in random jarring sequence.

There were about a dozen guys clumped together in twos and threes, unwholesome excitement like the sour smell of algae in the air, and Bingo was pushing through them to the head of the line, where Mandy was half sitting half lying on the ground, her shirt hanging around her neck like a lasso.

He reached down, grabbed her by the hand, and pulled her to her feet to lead her, weaving and uncomprehending, out of the clearing and back down toward the beach.

"Hey, what the fuck do you think you're doing, Flanagan?" One of the guys stepped in front of him, so drunk that the motion almost sent him spiraling off his feet.

"Get out of my way," Bingo said, not stopping, hand in hers, pulling her along next to him, so out of it that she might as well have been in a coma. There was a collective shout of anger from the others as they moved toward Bing and Mandy.

I stepped from the darkness, Bingo's flashlight blinding me, my hands in front of my face as I headed toward him and Mandy, taking her by the elbow and urging Bing to pick up the pace.

"Let's just get the hell out of here," I said as we broke into a sprint, our backs to the wolf pack, their overheated indecision one long, loud pant rivaling the background noise of the waves and the wind.

We walked home in silence, Mandy stopping occasionally to heave into the bushes, me methodically going over what had just transpired and trying in vain to cast my reluctance to intervene in a better light, Bingo navigating the blackness with ease. We left her to sleep it off on a chaise longue in the screened-in summer porch at the rear of her house while we made our way back down to the beach, the shoreline constituting the most straightforward way back home.

"Thanks, Coll," Bingo said, a disembodied voice that I had to strain to hear over the wind and the water. The waves rushed up onto the beach and pooled around my feet. I could feel the drag of the riptide.

"For what?" I asked him.

"Following me, backing me up."

I didn't answer. My insides were burning, embarrassment warming my core like a gastrointestinal blush.

"Hey, will you slow down a little?" I finally complained.

"Don't be such a wuss," he said as I came up behind him.

"Hey, asshole, does part of your Man Plan include leaving me behind?"

"Catch me if you can," he said, and kept on going, breaking into a jog.

I was thirsty. My throat hurt, my breathing was ragged; I couldn't keep up with Bingo, he was moving so fast, and he knew it was getting to me, yet he had no intention of slowing down. If anything, he picked up the pace and was amused by my stumbling efforts to tail him. I was having trouble keeping my bearings with no light to guide me. Son of a bitch, why wouldn't he slow down? He just kept forging ahead while I tried to stick to the path he made.

"Come on, Bing. Slow down. I can't figure out where I am. What is your problem?"

"You're the guy with the problem, Collie, not me," he said. "You should be able to walk this route blind. Quit thinking so much."

It was different when we were kids. When we were younger,

Bingo followed me everywhere as if I were the one to lead him on a great adventure.

"Get lost, you freak," I told him whenever I spotted that white face and those sea green eyes peering out at me from behind the trunk of a century-old copper beech.

"Come on, Collie, can I come?" His hands were pleading.

"No!" I turned my back and moved on.

"I'm coming." I could hear him behind me in steady pursuit.

"Beat it!" I faced him, anger surging, fists clenching and unclenching.

"Bingo, please, go away. Leave me alone." Threats of violence were ineffective, so I was frequently reduced to begging. I'd finally drop to my knees and he'd get down on all fours and crawl forward tentatively, like one of the dogs. And I'd sit slumped with my back against the old tree, the bark rough against my shoulders, and he'd nestle next to me, the winner, the champ, as if nothing had transpired, as if he were perfectly welcome, as if I wanted him with me.

"So what do you want to do?" he'd ask, wriggling with friendliness, practically wagging his tail, and I'd bury my head in my hands. It was a ritual that never wavered, me resisting, him persisting, and me giving in. So why wouldn't he ever give in to me?

We walked along the rest of the way without saying a word, my pace slowing as Bingo's picked up until I was trailing way behind and he was practically sprinting for home. It was four in the morning as we headed up the laneway. I heard the muted thud of his footsteps on the veranda, the bump of the old screen door as he went inside.

He flicked on the light. I used the golden glow from the kitchen to pick my way through the darkness.

CHAPTER TEN

A few months later, and Bing and I were together again, both of us home for the holidays. It was late spring 1983 and I was almost twenty years old, reasonably happy at Brown, still trying to figure out what to do with my life and looking forward to enjoying the humid pleasures of summer inertia. I had my first real girlfriend, Alexandra, whom I liked well enough. Her father was a producer, bankrolling shows on Broadway and in London's West End. He was thrilled by proximity to the Falcon's money and influence and encouraged sleepovers.

"Dad, Collie and I have something to tell you," Zan said as the two of us stood outside the door to his home office, whose lined walls and overstocked shelves paid homage to his career. We were visiting her home in Connecticut for the weekend.

"Are you pregnant?" His eyes glistened, quavering.

"No! Honestly, Dad . . . the things you say. We were thinking about going to the house in Palm Beach for spring break."

"Oh, well, of course. Whatever you'd like," he said, shrugging, the light in his eyes flickering out, cataracts forming, things growing dim.

A swirling series of spring storms that year had cut the beach in half. On fierce days, the ocean banged away at the front door, the wind raging, Uncle Tom getting doused from the spray, hollering and shaking his fist as if the encroaching water were a neighbor intent on selling him a magazine subscription.

Bingo and I spent most afternoons digging our toes in the sand and body surfing, the bigger dogs wading into the foamy waves alongside us, the smaller dogs pacing along the shoreline, barking.

It was a beautiful day near the end of May, and I was back from an early morning sail and hauling the boat onto shore when I saw Pop's great shadow darken the sand around me.

"Hey, Pop," I said, squinting up at him, hand covering my eyes as I reached into my pocket for my sunglasses. It quickly became apparent that Pop was in no mood for summery salutations.

"The tennis club just called. The fellow on the other end said you didn't need to come in this afternoon but they'd need you for tomorrow morning. What in heaven's name does that mean? Do you have a job? What's going on here?"

"Pop, it's just a part-time job, chasing balls and . . ."

"And what else? Helping bored society ladies improve their serve?"

I looked at him incredulously. "You've got to be kidding."

"Why would you go behind my back this way and get a job, and at the tennis club of all the places on earth? What is this secret life you lead?"

"Secret life? Pop, do you have to be so dramatic all the time? It's no big deal. It's a dumb job. What am I supposed to do all summer, sunbathe and avoid Ma?" I'd been wrestling with the idea of getting a part-time job for a while—kind of a half-assed attempt at making myself mildly useful—but Pop wouldn't hear of it.

"Wherever did you get such an idea?" he said, looking at me in astonishment, as if I were wearing a different face. The slightest whiff of industriousness was an insulting glove to the cheek as far as Pop was concerned.

"Who's been encouraging you to take up the horse's harness? Is this your grandfather's influence? Have you learned nothing at all from my example?" Pop said as we began walking back toward the house, where he resumed his spot on the chaise longue. He'd spent the morning in his bathing suit, sunning himself outside on a small patch of overgrown grass. He peered at me from behind his sunglasses, the stems covered in silver duct tape, an overzealous attempt at repair.

"Pop, it's not like I'm planning on becoming a sharecropper. The tennis club was looking for someone to help out a few hours a week. . . ." I sat on the ground under the white oak tree and braced for the explosion to come.

"Have you lost your mind? No son of mine will ever work for a tennis club. Why, I'd just as soon you went to work for a radio station as have you become a professional tennis bum." Pop had a noisy aversion to all kinds of people—chiropractors, cheerleaders, folk dancers—he especially disliked tennis players, whom he lumped in with on-air radio personalities, despising them for their "commonness. To think they're proud of themselves, the great belches."

"Look at that boorish brute, spitting on the court! You're scraping the bottom of the barrel with that profane, stringy-haired crew," he used to say whenever he caught us watching a match on TV.

Wimbledon coverage was an annual nightmare.

"Who's talking about playing professional tennis? I'm just helping out around the courts and clubhouse." The dogs had discovered me on the ground. Pushing them aside, I felt as if I were cutting a swath through the rain forest, hacking through endless resistant curtains of undergrowth.

"And isn't that how it starts? Next thing you know, you'll be answering me back with your middle finger. No. Sleep until noon, play in the water with your brother, soak up the sun, and forget about the rest. You'll get a bellyful of the rest before life is through with you. I've higher expectations of my sons than to see them flinching under the lash of menial labor." He was staring skyward, hands extended over his chest, fingers waving elegantly in midair, like a maestro of leisure directing some inner symphony.

"Pop, I want to do something and I've got to start somewhere. I don't want to just coast through life."

He sat up and removed his sunglasses. "And why not, for heaven's sake? By Jesus, if I could attach runners to the soles of my feet, I'd do it, and you and Bingo, you two boys were born wearing roller skates and you have the temerity to turn your back on such a gift—"

"Say, if you're so anxious to make yourself useful, then how about making yourself useful to me," Uncle Tom interrupted, appearing from inside the house, stopping briefly to speak to Pop and me, Pop almost naked and glowing red from hours of exposure to the sun; and me in shorts with Sykes panting between my bare legs.

"Eavesdropping as usual, Tom, I see," Pop said, putting his sunglasses back on and resuming his prone position.

"Surveillance, more like it," Uncle Tom said, a reference to what he broadly termed "matters needing expert attention." Once invoked, that entitled him to violate privacies and usurp personal liberties, listen in on telephone conversations, read journals, open letters, upend drawers, and go through pockets.

"I need you and what's-his-name-the-green-eyed-devil to come with me to the lighthouse first thing in the morning," Uncle Tom said. "It's time to release the youngsters, same as always."

"How about I take a rain check?" I said, leaning the back of my head against the old tree trunk and staring up at its heavy branches resting along the roof.

"Oh, I forgot, it's the Kublai Khan. Never mind, the nuisance and I will do quite well on our own," Uncle Tom said as he stepped off the veranda and headed round to the back of the house. "We've outgrown you, anyway."

"Okay," I hollered after him. "You win. I'll come with you and Bing. I can always call in sick at the club."

"No, I wouldn't think of disturbing your schedule," he answered as he turned the corner.

I jumped to my feet and headed after him. Despite the heat he was wearing his uniform, a red-and-black-checked, long-sleeved flannel shirt and oversize tan slacks.

"Do you want me to come or not?" I was talking to the back of his head.

He shrugged and kept walking. "Suit yourself. Well, it makes no difference to me what you do, but since you're so mad to come, then prepare for an early start."

The next morning around six, Uncle Tom, Bingo, and I set out on our bicycles, six young pigeons in release baskets—two to a basket—strapped to the backs of our bikes, making the journey, part road, part sandy beach, to the lighthouse, where we'd toss the birds skyward and then pedal back home to await their arrival. It was an annual event signaling the start of preparations for the racing season.

Uncle Tom had been racing pigeons since he was a boy, and although he considered himself a leading international authority on the subject of raising and training homing pigeons, he'd never enjoyed much success in competition. Never one to let the greater world cloud his personal skyline, however, he continued to espouse and develop his own theories, oblivious to the ideas or opinions of others.

Uncle Tom was like Mount Everest, daring you to climb to the top of him and take in the view.

The conversation on these expeditions to release points all over the island never varied. Year in and year out they followed the same pattern, like a familiar song you know by heart.

"Uncle Tom, how do you think pigeons are able to find their way home?" Bingo always got things under way. He and Uncle Tom had an established, comfortable conversational rhythm, a sort of call-and-answer routine they both enjoyed. Bingo was like Tom's prompter, the official facilitator of his eccentricity.

"Multiple factors," Uncle Tom said as we rode along, side by side, taking up half the road, swerving briefly into single-file formation to avoid the occasional car.

"The sun, the earth's magnetic pull, and common sense are key. Then of course they follow the roads same as we do. A homing pigeon will observe a stop sign as diligently as any traffic cop. Why, I once had a pigeon called Brendan Behan that would even yield right-of-way at a four-way intersection."

We were laughing and pedaling, but not too fast, keeping up a nice relaxed pace—Uncle Tom was opposed to speed, considered it the province of nitwits—and Bingo and I were exchanging confederate glances as Uncle Tom carried on talking.

"But then, what do you expect? The pigeon has character, guts, intelligence, and heart—the very things you two brass tacks lack in abundance."

The three of us stood close to one another in the early morning sunlight, breezes blowing gently, and we tossed the birds high into the air, watching until they disappeared over the treetops, and then we cycled back home and climbed to the top of the stable roof, where we sat and waited for them to reappear. Bingo kept checking the stopwatch while Uncle Tom, lying back, eyes closed, the sun beating down, pretended not to care.

"They'll be along," he said. "In the end, it's the people they come home for."

"I think you're romanticizing their motives, Uncle Tom," I said, squinting in his direction from my spot where I sat on the roof's crease across from Bingo, elbows resting on my knees. "Where else is a pigeon going to go? The Cannes Film Festival?"

"Oh, is that cleverness you're practicing? Well then, if that's what Professor Collie Flanagan thinks, then I'd better revise the experiences of a lifetime and reconsider every thought I've ever had."

"You're wrong, Collie. You're forgetting about Gabriel," Bingo said to me, hand at his brow, jumping in quickly to back up Tom.

When Uncle Tom was ten years old and living in Ireland, he had a little white homing pigeon named Gabriel that he found by the side of the road struggling to survive with an injured wing. He spent the summer nursing him back to health.

"I had a ruptured appendix and had to be rushed into surgery," Uncle Tom said, taking up the story Bingo and I knew by heart. "I was recovering at my grandmother's house, and on the third day I hear this tapping on the window and there's little Gabriel perched outside my room on the windowsill. My grandmother and aunts were all so impressed, they let him spend the next few days with me until I went home. Even the local priests and nuns came in to view my miraculous bird."

"I love that story," Bingo said as Uncle Tom stood up and moved to the other side of the roof, trying to catch sight of the birds.

"You would. He's making it up, you moron," I said. "It's bullshit pure and simple."

"No, he's not. I believe it. Even Pop says it's true."

"Oh well, if Pop verifies it, then that's different. Pop believes in leprechauns, for Christ's sake."

"Why do you always have to be a prick?" Bingo asked me.

"You get like the people you share parents with," I said.

"How come you never go anywhere, Uncle Tom?" Bingo asked, changing the subject and rechecking the horizon.

"What do you mean, never go anywhere? Are you referring to the fact that unlike the rest of you, I don't have ants in my pants?" Uncle Tom asked.

"Well, I mean you grew up in Ireland and then you came to Boston and then you moved to the Vineyard and that's it. I can't even remember you ever crossing over to the mainland," Bingo said as I looked on with something approaching interest.

"And where should I go, according to you? And why would I want to go there?" Uncle Tom asked us.

"Travel is good for you, Uncle Tom," I said. "You can't say it isn't."

"Oh, can't I? Well, as far as I know, Aristotle never made it to Puerto Rico, and he was smart enough. Why, look at you two nitwits, you've been plenty of places and neither one of you knows which end is up."

Bingo looked over at me and grinned as Uncle Tom pulled his hat farther down over his forehead and continued.

"In the interests of advancing your education, I'll tell you something else that happened to me when I was a boy. . . ."

"Oh no," I groaned in an aside to Bing, who lay back down on the roof, eyes closed against the sun. "Here it comes—death by anecdote."

And then Uncle Tom, ignoring me, told us about an annual spring ritual at his school conducted by the nuns and priests.

"They used to round up all the boys, including your dad and me, and force us to march in prayerful procession to the outer boundaries of the parish, where they'd beat us with a strap."

"Why'd they do that?" Bingo asked.

"So we'd never forget who we were and where we came from," Uncle Tom said.

"Typical Catholic pathology—parochialism as an excuse for sadism," I said with a high degree of personal satisfaction and drawing a derisive snort from Bingo.

"You're such an asshole," he said.

"That's Professor Asshole to you," I said.

"I'd expect just such an obtuse remark from you," Uncle Tom said. "I should have taken a stick to you when I had the chance." He stood up and pointed skyward. "Here they come. Look at them. Now there's an intelligent creature. Pigeons know that home is the only place worth traveling to."

"See! Look! There they are," Bingo shouted, pointing to a distant spot in the sky, and we glanced up in unison, watching as the birds, all six together, came around a big copper beech tree near the loft and made a smooth hook to the left, dipping the trailing edges of their wings downward before landing.

Each day after that, we took them a little farther than the day before, and each day, no matter how far we took them, they made their way back home, the signal flap of their wings stirring me in ways I took great effort to hide. Not Bingo, who was so unconcealed that he might as well have been a goat.

"Here they come! Collie, look at them, they're coming. Son of a bitch!!" He was shouting, his arms thrown wide over his head.

"A racing pigeon's heart is bigger than the Parthenon," Uncle Tom proclaimed, and then he began whistling the tune to "Bye, Bye, Blackbird," ordering us to do likewise. Pigeons, like dogs, respond to whistling, according to Uncle Tom.

"Jesus!" I yelped as the returning flock passed overhead and one of them shit on my upturned forehead, much to Bingo's delight. Ignoring me, Uncle Tom, continuing to look skyward, never missed a beat.

"They're opinionated, too, with a talent for punditry, just like you, Collie. I never knew a pigeon that didn't have a gift for summing up a man's character in a single eloquent gesture."

CHAPTER ELEVEN

THE LAST WEEKEND IN MAY THERE WAS A LAVISH ROCOCO AFFAIR held in New York City to honor the Falcon for his various measured philanthropies, an event that generated not a little discussion around the table at home.

"Next they'll be pinning a medal on Pol Pot for his humanitarian work," Pop said.

Obsessed with opera, the Falcon was practically a parody in his violet Napoleon-tie cravat—he always seemed to be financing some new skylit performance of *Tosca* in exotic international locales. When he developed diabetes in his sixties, a mild case controlled through diet and exercise, he got all fired up about finding a cure, donating millions of dollars to research.

"Self-interest is a perverse foundation for charity. For all his wealth and power, your grandfather lacks humility and perspective. Always seek the panoptic view, boys," said Pop, who was committed to the notion that check writing begins at home.

The Falcon issued an embargo on Pop and Uncle Tom—they were forbidden to attend the party.

"I've no problem with the banning of Tom, but what will I say when people ask me where my husband is?" Ma asked him.

"Believe me, no one will inquire," the Falcon said.

The big night arrived, and I was in my room getting ready—we were flying out of Boston in the Falcon's jet. Ever the control freak, he had suits made for Bingo and me just for the occasion. The fabric of my dark blue jacket was so soft, I felt as if I were plunging my arms up to my shoulders in rainwater.

"You're a cheap date," Bingo said from the doorway, spotting from a distance my willingness to be sartorially seduced.

He was wearing jeans and a T-shirt, his face burned red from an afternoon in the sun. "Why aren't you dressed?" I asked him.

"I'm not going."

"What do you mean, you're not going?" I stopped buttoning my shirt midway through and looked at him.

"Pop and Uncle Tom aren't invited. If they're not going, then neither am I."

"Come on, in our crazy family, what the hell difference does it make?"

He shrugged and leaned into the door frame. "It makes a difference to me. Anyway, I'm going to San Francisco for the weekend with Peter Holton and his family. We're leaving tonight."

"The Falcon's going to be pissed if you're a no-show." I pulled on my pants.

"That's all right. He's always mad about something." He was tossing a tennis ball in the air and catching it.

"I suppose you think I'm wrong for going."

"I didn't say that." He caught the ball and held it for a second before sending it soaring. It made a loud mechanical thump on the tin ceiling overhead.

"You don't need to say anything. It's implied." Slipping on my shoes and bending over to inspect their shine, I deliberately avoided looking at him.

"Oh, it's 'implied,' is it?" He was making fun of me. "How's it implied?"

"Well, you're sticking by Pop and Uncle Tom. I'm betraying them, choosing the Falcon over them—anyway, that's how it will seem if I go and you don't. Thanks for making me the bad guy." I stood up, turned around, and confronted him.

"That's your problem." He let the ball go, and it bounced across the bedroom floor and under the chair.

"Look, Bingo, even Ma is going . . . what's the big deal? Pop and Uncle Tom don't give a damn. Stay or go . . . all of them will have something crazy to say about whichever option either one of us chooses. It's only a party . . . can't anything in this family just be simple? I want to go. Why do I need to feel guilty about it?"

"Who's making you feel guilty? I'm doing what I want and you're doing what you want. Like you say, it's only a party. I don't feel guilty about my choice. Why do you feel guilty about yours?"

"I don't." I put one arm into the sleeve of my jacket. "Shit." I reached for a lint brush sitting on the dresser top, a skein of dog hair making faint layers on the suit's dark fabric.

"Well then, forget about it. You do what you want and I'll do what I want."

"Great. I intend to."

"Yeah, well, have fun," he said as he stepped backward into the hall, "you treacherous, disloyal, star-fucking sack of shit."

Even Ma was persuaded to attend the tribute to her old man, despite the banning of Pop. She claimed it was so she could buttonhole some of the world's most influential people—you know, wave her index finger in their faces, shriek abuse, and make them change their minds about the importance of boycotting lettuce.

But from the way she fussed over her hair—by the time she and her team of gardeners were finished, she looked like an enormous hydrangea—it was clear to me her real purpose was to meet Robert Redford, which isn't to say that her entrance was any less reminiscent of a Bolshevik charging the palace on foaming horseback.

"My kingdom for an ice pick," the Falcon muttered as I stood next to him, watching in dismay as she chased down a prominent CEO, running him through with her verbal pitchfork. Before the night was over, just about everyone in the place had sprung leaks, blood and champagne spurting from all those glamorous human fountains.

Several senators, the usual Hollywood actors and industry players, media personalities, big Democratic Party donors, and a smattering of international philanthropists were among the guests, old money and new money chatting warmly, patting one another on the back, and kibitzing—you could lace up your ice skates and slide across the burnished ease of it all. Then Ma plowed in among them, making war and sport, hip checking and high sticking and smashing everyone into the boards.

Ma turned especially vicious whenever she found herself in the company of men who liked to proclaim their uncompromising belief in excellence, a propensity for which she reserved special loathing and contempt.

"Spare us from two things," she said, her zealotry so out of place that she might as well have been a plumber wandering around looking for a drain to rescue. "Spare us the community-minded and their zealous pursuit of excellence."

"I'd like to add a third item to that list, if I may," the Falcon said, recognizing an implicit insult when he heard one. "Lord, spare us your perplexing and relentless juvenilia."

Champagne—Ma was drinking a lot of it that night—inevitably made her susceptible to one of two courses of action, fomenting revolution or launching a direct frontal assault on her old man. On this occasion, she decided to go for broke and attempted to do both.

"Hey, Perry . . ." She leaned forward and poked the Falcon in the chest with her index finger as the group around him cleared a space roughly the size of Manhattan.

I closed my eyes and braced for the worst. Whenever Ma referred to her father as "Perry," it was a signal to release the flying monkeys.

"I'm not a member of your fan club. I'm not looking for a donation or an endorsement. I'm not some mandarin on the make. Don't confuse me with one of your groundlings. Save the Pliny the Elder crap for someone who actually needs your self-serving approval."

"You've all met my daughter, I presume? The jewel in my crown." The Falcon glanced around at the shining assembled, who stood dumbfounded, too shocked to respond.

Embarrassment washed over me, so gangrenous that I felt as if skin tissue were dying systematically, starting at my feet and burning upward, devouring every last living part of me. Sometimes I think my real life's purpose is to refute the cliché notion that you can't actually die of embarrassment.

"Do you know 'Long Ago and Far Away'?" I asked one of the musicians who was passing by, touching him on the forearm, reaching out in desperation, anything to shift the attention away from Ma and the Falcon. It was one of Pop's favorite songs and the only thing that came to mind, and as the first familiar notes sounded, I nodded in the direction of the orchestra, offering up quiet thanks, and then, like everyone else, I stopped to listen, impelled by an urgent hollering that was coming from the direction of the room's entranceway.

Pop, impeccably dressed and manifestly drunk, had apparently decided to crash the party and was threatening to take apart anyone who tried to interfere.

"What's he saying?" one of the guests asked while I watched, aghast and disbelieving, as Pop, shouting and red-faced, spewing spit and rage, trumpeting and heaving like a rogue elephant, wrestled with security. He was bent over at the waist, his stomach straining against three sets of arms, hotel employees trying vainly to drag him back outside.

"Peregrine Lowell . . . something . . . I can't understand him. . . ." The woman next to me shook her head in bewilderment.

"Sounds like 'Peregrine Lowell . . . please.' Please what, I wonder?" her friend asked.

"Beats me."

Peregrine Lowell, he was saying Peregrine Lowell, that part was terrifyingly clear.

"What the hell?" a combined murmur went up, accompanied by barely suppressed laughter as the message finally emerged with mortifying clarity.

"Peregrine Lowell pees!" Pop was screaming to the heavens, claiming his bizarre revenge. "He is not a god! He's a man with a complete set of human frailties. Peregrine Lowell pees!"

Trevor Boothe, grandson of Senator Avery Boothe—we went to Andover together—came up behind me and tapped me on the shoulder. I made a half turn and was taken aback by his horrified expression. In Boothe's world, my parents were enacting a chain-saw massacre. I touched my hand to my cheek, thinking I was developing a nervous tic. Trevor was so white that he shamed the linens.

"Oh, my God. Sorry, Collie, how embarrassing for you," he muttered, shaking his head, his hair not moving—funny, the small things you notice while you're being cremated.

"Embarrassing? You think this is embarrassing? You don't get it, Trevor. Embarrassment is my business. It's my only business," I said, inexplicably merry, convinced I was having a nervous breakdown. I was giggling the same way I did when I was seven years old and Uncle Tom licked his fingers and used spit to clean off my dirty face in front of the whole congregation before Mass one Sunday.

I felt Trevor's hand press fleetingly against the hollow of my back, as if he were extending comfort to a stray dog with fleas. Then, as he was slipping away, trying to put subtle distance between us, I instinctively looked over at the Falcon, who appeared momentarily transported to another realm, some wonderful place where Fantastic Charlie Flanagan had just been pronounced dead after choking on his own rum-soaked vomit.

Cognizant suddenly of the spotlight, and as Ma rushed to Pop's side, the two of them disappearing noisily into the corridor outside the ballroom, Ma's scream of "Murderer!" threatening to shatter the crystal, the Falcon took immediate remedial action and, apparently fully recovered, started to laugh and then went on chatting as if nothing were wrong, and the room heaved a huge sigh of relief as the band played on, the singer launching into a hypercheerful version of "Fly Me to the Moon."

My eyes burned, and I felt a familiar ache deep in my throat. Ma was certifiable, but Pop . . . well, Pop spent his whole life snapping towels.

Bingo would have loved every moment of the performance Ma and Pop put on. I was wrong about the Falcon being mad about Bingo not attending the party in his honor—the truth was, he didn't even notice that Bingo was missing. But I did. Without Bing, it felt as if I'd shown up without my teeth. I spent the entire night grinding my gums, half listening, imaginary conch to my ear, the evening's low, reverberating party talk mimicking the insistent roll of the tide back home.

CHAPTER TWELVE

THE NEXT DAY, BINGO CALLED FROM SAN FRANCISCO TO commiserate with Ma and Pop about the events the night before, which were being played out in the New York gossip columns, and to announce that he was staying on for a few more days.

While Pop had no memory of the party, or pretended not to, anyway, Ma was as triumphant as if she had single-handedly brought down the Bastille, spending so many hours on the phone being celebrated by her activist cohorts that she developed situational laryngitis.

"Your brother wants to speak to you," she whispered in deadly fashion, handing off the phone as I smiled weakly and thanked her—she'd been giving me the long stare ever since we got home. I felt as if my neck were being measured for the guillotine.

"Poor Pop," Bingo said.

"Well, I don't know about that. Poor Pop put on quite a public performance last night. It was pretty humiliating," I said.

"I wish I'd been there," he said, voice full of longing.

"Yeah, I wish you'd been there, too," I responded, though my tone wasn't quite so winsome. "When are you coming home? Ma's looking at me as if she wants to sacrifice the fatted calf."

"I promised Pop I'd get him Karl Malden's autograph. I wanted to cheer him up. It may take me a few days."

"How can you make such a stupid promise?" I asked Bingo. "You're not going to meet him."

"Yes, I am. Why are you always so negative?"

"Being negative has nothing to do with it. Would the outcome be any different if I was acting like a cheerleader? San Francisco is a big city with tons of people. You might as well say you're going to meet the queen because you're in London."

"Collie, you're not going to change my mind, so you might as well quit trying. I'm gonna meet Karl Malden and get his autograph for Pop. Why else do you think I'm staying on?"

"You're crazy. I give up," I said. But I didn't give up, the whole situation induced a kind of temporary madness in me. I kept calling and arguing with him about it.

"You're not going to meet him," I said, gripping the phone as if I were hanging from the ledge of a cliff.

"Yeah, I am," he said.

Pop loved the movies, fancied himself a bit of an authority and a discerning critic. His favorite actor was Karl Malden, which meant that Karl Malden assumed a disproportionately large role in our lives—between Ma and Pop and their mutual obsessions, we might as well have hung separate Christmas stockings for him and for Rupert Brooke.

Pop would argue his merits to anyone, always concluding his carefully prepared defense of Malden's performances by insisting that his looks were underrated, at which point you could always depend on Uncle Tom to say, "What you see in that thin-lipped proboscis on legs, I'll never know."

"If I hear the name Karl Malden one more time, I'll go mad," Ma would chime in right on cue.

"I still say he was cheated out of the Oscar for *On the Waterfront*," Bingo would say, clever enough to know the events he was setting in motion.

"Don't get me started . . . ," Pop would say, nicely getting started.

Bingo and Pop never missed an episode of *The Streets of San Francisco*, starring Malden.

"Hey, Pop, our show's on!" Bingo used to alert everyone five minutes before the starting credits.

"I'll spontaneously combust if I see that man's face staring back at me from the TV screen one more time," Ma would say, using her fingers to make tiny revolving circles at her temples.

"It's insane to think that Bing is going to get you an autograph—you can't will these things to happen," I said to Pop, who looked at me with pity as he prepared a place of honor on the mantelpiece in the living room.

"You most certainly can," Uncle Tom interjected, sticking his nose in, emerging from the kitchen in an apron and carrying a dishrag. "And by the way, I take umbrage to your tone," he continued, his hands red from water so hot that it would practically peel flesh. He took pride in his ability to withstand scalding temperatures. He turned around to face me where I was sitting straddled over Mambo sleeping on the floor. Out of the corner of my eye, I saw Pop hastily slip away—he didn't have much tolerance for Uncle Tom's digressive pronouncements.

"Conventional expectation has no sway over me," Uncle Tom said, pausing for a moment as he sat on the sofa across from me, squeezing aside Bachelor, waiting out the cutlery, still too hot to handle even for him.

"When I was fifteen years old, I was struck by lightning. They found me in a field still smoking hours later. It turned me into a kind of good-luck charm and a talisman to boot. Some say my powers are even greater than those attributed to the Miraculous Medal of Mary."

He pointed his finger at me—his certainty poking me hard in the chest.

"Who are you to challenge life's great mysteries with your dourness? All I know is that I can cure a toothache if I put my mind to it."

Two days later and Bingo arrived back home, rushing from the cab and in through the back door, hollering for Pop from the kitchen, Ma actually tripping over her trailing housecoat as she rushed from the study to greet him. Something deep inside me recalibrated as I watched Pop proudly hang a framed sheet of lined paper torn from a spiral notebook that said "To Fantastic Charlie Flanagan, with warmest wishes from Karl Malden, June 2, 1983," dated the last day of Bingo's trip.

"Oh, my God, you're a marvel. Isn't he the most amazing boy!" Ma was exclaiming all over the place. "And you said he couldn't do it," she said to me, watching with evident scorn as I approached the fireplace to have a better look.

"How'd you do it?" I asked Bing, who was busy fending off the worship of the mob.

"What's the collective for killjoys?" Uncle Tom asked me as he spit into a cloth and wiped a smudge on the glass of the frame that contained Pop's greatest treasure.

"I don't know, but I'm sure you'll tell me," I said.

"A Collie of killjoys," he responded with exaggerated blandness.

Bingo launched into an elaborate explanation for how he got the autograph, Ma and Pop standing arm in arm, looking as if they were on board a moonlight cruise swaying to the smooth musical styling of Bing Flanagan.

"I tried everything. I went to every hot-spot restaurant and hotel in the city. I checked out nightclubs, made some calls, even conjured up the evil specter of the Falcon to try to find Malden, but nothing was working. I had some tough moments, believe me," he said, laying it on thick but careful to wear the mantle of his greatness lightly as I shook my head through the whole protracted tale of his triumph.

"I was almost ready to give up. It was the last night and I figured that I'd failed, but I couldn't understand it because I was so sure it would happen. I could see the outcome in my head, so why wasn't it happening? I couldn't believe that I'd been so wrong. It didn't make any sense. I had to catch an early plane, so I was certain it was over. I left the hotel room to go to this little store on the corner—it sells that drink I like, you know the orange one?"

Pop and Ma are nodding—you couldn't move in the mudroom for the boxes of Bingo's favorite orange drink.

"Anyway, I'm on the elevator feeling depressed and defeated—now I know what it feels like to be you, Collie," he said in an unamusing aside, though Ma let out a howl of appreciation that caused Lenin to leap up from his spot in the dining room and attack poor Bachelor.

"The elevator stops on the eighth floor, and I'm so dejected my head is hanging, but I summon up the interest to look as this guy with great shoes steps aboard, and it was him. I couldn't believe it!"

"It was Karl Malden?" Pop said, as stunned as if he'd been visited by God in his sleep. "What are the chances?"

"Slim to none," I said.

"He was a wonderful guy, Pop, a real powerful presence, just the way you imagined he'd be. . . ."

"What did I tell you?" Pop said.

"Charlie, let him finish," Ma said, exasperated.

"When he heard the whole story, he was as excited as I was, and when we reached the lobby he stopped some high school kid walking by and asked for a piece of paper from his notebook and signed it. He said I made his day."

"I'm sure he's still talking about it," Pop said. "I wouldn't be surprised if it's made the rounds in Hollywood and Kirk Douglas is entertaining his friends with it."

"It's a miracle, someone should notify the pope," I said.

Pop never questioned the authenticity of the autograph or the veracity of Bing's story. He believed in Bingo's ability to conjure up Karl Malden like a rabbit from a hat—as far as Pop was concerned, life was a series of magic tricks.

I didn't know what to think. I still don't know what to think, though my thoughts about it have evolved a little over the years. Eventually the autograph just seemed to disappear, got lost as treasures sometimes do.

I wonder where it is. It would be nice to know.

CHAPTER THIRTEEN

A FEW NIGHTS AFTER BINGO'S CELEBRATED RETURN FROM SAN Francisco, some record company executive in Boston called to say he was having a party. I'd met him casually a couple of times. He was the older brother of some guy I went to school with at Andover. Bingo knew him through a stepbrother he'd shared a room with at Upper Canada College. With the big shiny presence of Peregrine Lowell uppermost in everyone's minds, Bingo and I could get into anything—concerts, book launches, opening nights, parties.

"There's going to be all kinds of people here," he told Bingo over the phone. He was so loud, I could hear him from across the room. "Not just musicians, but writers, artists, journalists, editors, lawyers . . . There's going to be lots of great conversation . . . you'll enjoy it."

"Hey, Coll, he says there's going to be great conversation," Bingo said in a clumsy attempt to get me to go with him.

Jesus, who did the guy think he was talking to? Sartre? I was flipping mindlessly through the pages of *Spin* magazine.

"Come on, Collie, let's go," Bingo was begging me. "Stevie Nicks might show up."

"Oh, now who's asking for a favor? Maybe I'll just tell you to go pound salt the way you told me the other night on the beach when I asked you to slow down. And let's not forget the way you left me to fend for myself at the Falcon's party."

"Can't you take a joke? Come on. Let's go."

"Why is it so important that I go? Why don't you go by yourself?" I asked him.

"Let's go together," he said. "It'll be fun. I'm just gonna bug you till you say yes."

What the hell? It occurred to me I had nothing better to do.

We got there, we were barely inside the door, and right away Bingo was ensnared by some woman with an enhanced prey drive—women of all ages went crazy for him, for reasons that generally eluded me. So there he was, trapped in a corner with an overweight feminist writer in her twenties, signaling me with his eyes to come rescue him.

His braless pursuer was wearing overalls and a pair of rubber boots, an outfit that I previously thought existed only in the minds of sitcom writers. She had a thick torso, and her hair was coarsely chopped off above the ears, with tiny bangs that formed a sparse, workmanlike hedge across her forehead, the centerpiece of a familiar banal landscape.

"The premenopausal power helmet," Pop called it.

"It's fucking torture to have to look at her, Collie," Bingo whined during a rare reprieve.

"Man, you're just like Pop," I said. "Anyway, you can handle her. You're the expert with women."

"You handle her."

"What's wrong, Bing? Not enjoying the great conversation on offer? If you'll excuse me, I think I'll plumb the psychic depths of the redhead in the corner."

I was enjoying the mess he'd got himself into and left him to his own devices while I continued fighting with a music critic who'd flown in from California, who said Mick Jagger was the best front man of all time. I was arguing for the sake of arguing on behalf of Robert Plant.

We were right in the middle of it when she walked in. Her name doesn't matter. Believe me, you know her name, just another cinched waistline and diverting décolletage at the heart of a scandal. A twenty-eight-year-old juvenile delinquent, onetime beauty queen, wicked drunk, reluctant former heroin addict, she was a convicted drug dealer, desiccated groupie, and tawdry professional girlfriend.

She was out of jail after serving eighteen months in medium-security for her part in the drug-related death of the son of an internationally renowned rock singer. He was young, maybe eighteen or nineteen. She liked them young.

"Ooh, don't tell me, let me guess, cold hands, warm heart," she cooed, making a beeline for Bing, taking his hand in hers, undoing the top button of her blouse, holding his hand in her hand, and laying her other hand on top of his hand for just a moment longer than was necessary or even polite, long enough to cue his faulty wiring. He leaned into me for support. I could feel his knees buckle as we both watched her hip-check the feminist writer, who retaliated by loudly proclaiming her contempt for the cliché appeal of a cheap woman with a long neck and a short skirt.

The target of her scorn laughed. She knew. I knew. I knew more than she did. But Bingo didn't have a clue. She had him and was aroused by his adolescent collaboration. It wasn't complicated. She was a pro, able to open an artery without detection.

We left the party with her around midnight. What was I thinking? I was just going along with this thing, partly because of inertia and partly because it let me indulge all my worst thoughts about my brother. One half of me wanted to bear witness, the other half of me thought this was a journey he shouldn't make alone.

I played chauffeur as Bingo clambered into the back next to her, and they were whispering and giggling and carrying on while I was trying to figure out how I could bring the evening to an early end.

Fifteen minutes later, we pulled up in front of a decaying, sunken low-rise whose only exterior illumination came from a streetlight. The front lawn was scuffed bare and littered with ripped and shredded green garbage bags whose rancid contents spilled out onto the sidewalk. A dry wind lifted the open end of one of the garbage bags. Rodent eyes stared out blindly from inside the bag. A poinsettia in a red plastic container sat on a downstairs window ledge.

The lobby's interior was covered in graffiti, the walls were pockmarked, and the linoleum floor, orange and brown, was heaving.

"What apartment are you in?" I asked her.

"The third floor, apartment 306," she said as we approached the elevator.

The doors struggled open to reveal an older guy—he had to be sixty—fondling a young girl—she may have been eighteen.

"You going up?" he growled. No teeth.

"We'll take the stairs," I said, eyeing the circle of vomit in the corner of the elevator.

"Holy shit," I exclaimed, repulsed, as Bingo, captivated as a kid at the zoo, neatly navigated a pair of denim cutoffs abandoned on the bottom steps of the staircase.

Her place smelled of cat, the air stale as the indiscriminate crackle of TV noise. She asked us inside. I started to refuse, I'd had enough, but Bingo overruled me. I glared at him, but he just glared back, unmoved.

I was watching from a broken La-Z-Boy as she rooted through her cupboards, a consumptive gravel-voiced raconteur in a micro leather skirt.

"It was too bad. He was a nice guy," she said insincerely about her notorious conviction, offering me a coffee, which I declined with thanks. Cracked CorningWare.

Bingo, on the sofa across from me, eagerly accepted what I rejected. I watched disapprovingly as he casually added spoonful after heaping spoonful of sugar to his cup.

"Don't get too comfortable. We're out of here in five," I whispered as she left the living room to go into the bedroom. He made a face at me. I rolled my eyes in exasperation.

"Fuck off, Collie," he said quietly but good-naturedly as she came back into the room and sat beside him. She was right next to him. Their shoulders were touching. She kicked off her shoe and rested her stocking foot on his running shoe. He was humming offhandedly. Singing softly to himself.

I recognized it. He was singing "Beat Out Da Rhythm on a Drum." Pop had been singing that song for years. She didn't notice.

She was too busy simulating intercourse. He caught my eye. He was so pleased with himself, he might as well have been tingling. She started playing with his hair, winding it through her fingers as if it were long grass and she were an evening breeze. She was sending ripples through the long grass and out into the room.

He grinned over at me. He kept singing, full of mischief . . . I ignored him. He loved that.

"I admit I was an enthusiastic recruit," she was acknowledging huskily, referring to her choice of work, knowing that to say no was to risk a lifetime behind a cash register.

"Initially, I slept with the guys in the band, who were happy to supply me with dope, then when they got bored with me, our roles were reversed. If I wanted to remain part of the entourage, I had to supply them. So that's what I did." She shrugged.

"How old were you?" I was asking all the questions.

"Sixteen. In retrospect, I think that I was a stupid, selfish girl, looking for trouble, craving a way of life I hadn't earned but felt some entitlement to." She had obviously availed herself of counseling in the Big House.

"I was mixed up, but they . . ." She inhaled lightly, exhaled deeply. "They were evil."

I didn't respond. I was thinking. I glanced over at Bingo. She ran her finger crudely along his pant leg, from his knee to the top of his inner thigh. "Just like you—"

"Let's go, Bing," I interrupted as he sank deeper into the fraying foam back of the sofa. "It's late." I reached for his arm, grabbed, and pulled him forward to emphasize my point.

"Hey," she interjected, pulling him back down, abruptly beseeching Bingo, who was preparing to argue with me. "Can you loan me a hundred bucks? I'll pay you back. I just really need it—like yesterday."

Bing looked mildly surprised and hesitated before answering. She had nothing to worry about. All anybody had to do to get money from Bing was ask for it. She reached for her drink, impatiently crushing a cigarette into the puddle of coffee pooled in the bottom of her cup, and lashed out. "What do I have to do?" she demanded angrily, looking at him. "Fuck you, is that it? You want me to blow you? 'Cause that's no problem."

He caught his breath, the way you do when someone comes up behind you and shoves cold hands under your sweater. Then he looked at me and laughed. A real teenage boy's guffaw, it had no nuance. No secrets, either, at least not from me.

I stood up, fingering the car keys in my pocket, their jingle a reassuring signal.

"Why don't you go on ahead, Collie?" Bingo said, grinning up at me.

"No, we're leaving." I had this tight smile on my face.

"No thanks. I'm all right." He turned away as she leered at him.

"Bingo . . . you can't be serious. . . ." I shifted my weight from one foot to the other, my arms extended in a gesture of disbelief.

"Beat it, Coll."

My first instinct was to knock him out, but I struggled for indifference, and almost instantly it enfolded me like a warm blanket.

"Fine," I said, flush with self-satisfaction, convinced this was the last time I'd see him, and good riddance. "I really don't give a shit how this love story ends."

"So long, Coll." He waved me away, the door closing on the sound of her boozy laughter.

By the time I got to the lobby, I knew I was going to hell if I didn't go back for him. He was in way over his head. While I can't say my first instinct wasn't to let him get his ass kicked, fortunately I'm the prince of second thoughts.

I took the stairs, took two steps at once, gripped by a sudden bad feeling, afraid for him in a way that made my insides shake; I reached her apartment in record time, thumped on the door with my fists, my heart banging away in my throat. By now I was almost hyperventilating, thinking I was going to find him fried on the floor from an overdose of her and whatever she was peddling. I was hollering for her to open up or I'd break the door down—pretty corny stuff, but I wasn't kidding.

Finally, the door opened a crack, I shoved my foot inside, shouldered her aside, and dragged him the hell out of there; she was screaming at me, whacked me on the head with a carton of milk she grabbed from the coffee table, sour milk spraying my hair, my face, the front and back of my shirt. He put up a fight, mildly swearing and digging in his heels, but it wasn't that much of a fight.

On the way home, I was at the wheel and he was sitting slumped in the front seat next to me, silent and staring out the window. I kept looking over at him, willing him to say something. I like to know where I am. I always want to know what the other guy is thinking, and I couldn't get a read on him. Finally, I kicked him in the ankle just to get his attention.

"Collie."

"Yeah?"

"You're an asshole."

"You're welcome."

"Next time, wait ten minutes before barging in. . . ."

"Oh, here we go. . . . What do you mean, next time? I'm not a goddamn St. Bernard, Bingo."

"Yeah, you are. I knew you'd come back for me."

"Well, you knew more than I did, then."

"Yeah, yeah . . ."

"Yeah, yeah, is right. I'm serious."

He wasn't listening. He leaned over and licked my cheek, like one of the old lady's big, slobbery mutts. I was covered in sour milk and spit.

"Jesus Christ." I used my jacket to wipe my face, grabbing for him, nailing him in the upper part of his leg, all the good it did. He was laughing.

I started laughing, too. We were laughing, and we could see no end in sight to the hilarity.

CHAPTER FOURTEEN

I WOKE UP EARLY THE NEXT MORNING, COULDN'T SLEEP, ROLLED over, and first thing I saw was the date on the wall calendar. It was June 7, 1983. Ma and Pop and Uncle Tom were still sleeping, wall-to-wall dogs snoring noisily in every room in the house. I stopped Bingo as he was heading out the door with Mambo.

It was eight o'clock.

"What are you up to today?" I asked him.

"Nothing. Taking the tour. See who's around. Why?"

I had just finished speaking to Huntington "Rosie" Ferrell on the phone, my friend since we were little kids. I woke him up. His father was heir to a steel fortune and owned a summer home on the Vineyard. Their principal residence was near Boston. I told him I was bored. He was bored, too. We kind of made a profession of boredom in those days.

Overnight it had turned unseasonably cold, and we were looking for something to do. We put together a haphazard plan for a day trip to Dead Canary Wet Caves on the mainland, a poetically named system of river caves.

It was something we'd done before. It wasn't a particularly challenging project, especially for a couple of young guys who weren't overly preoccupied with details and had grown up around the ocean.

"You want to come?" I asked Bing, who cocked his head and raised his eyebrows. I was kind of surprised myself.

"You're kidding, right? Is this a joke? You want me to go along with you and Rosie?"

"Why not? Look, if you don't want to come . . ."

"Sure I want to come. I'm coming. Count me in. Let's go." Unlike me, Bingo was never bored. He was up for anything. He was already on the porch and heading for the car. "Hey, Coll, is this 'cause I gave you tongue last night?"

"Keep it up. I can always take back the invitation."

"Sorry. You're stuck with me now."

"Don't remind me."

"Can he come?" Bing asked, casting a sympathetic glance back at Mambo, who was doing a series of jumping jacks off the porch, aching to be included.

"No way. Come on, Bing, just once can we do something that doesn't involve a dog? You've got five minutes to get your shit together or else I'm gone."

"Sorry, Mambo," Bing apologized to him as he led him back into the kitchen, Mambo drooping and resistant and then watching from inside the house, through the screen door. Bingo reluctantly pulled shut the big wooden door, Mambo disappearing behind it—he'd gone through one too many screens in pursuit of the car.

"Poor Mambo," Bing said as we headed toward the driveway, and then he stopped and, facing me, pulled on my elbow, focusing on me with those spooky eyes of his.

"He'll live," I said dismissively, unreasonably annoyed by his expressions of sympathy.

"This isn't some kind of trick, is it? Are you trying to get back at me for last night? You and Rosie aren't planning to drag me off somewhere just so you can leave me behind, are you?"

"You're already starting to be a pain in the ass. If you don't want to go . . ." I stopped in the middle of the driveway and threw up my hands, accidentally tossing my car keys into the air, Bingo lunging for them as they hit the damp sand, stained brown from an overnight rain.

"I want to go. I just don't want to wind up stranded in the middle of nowhere again and you guys thinking it's funny." He stared at me meaningfully, fingering the keys, as I laughed at cherished memories of his recent abandonment at a gas station outside of Framingham after a concert.

"No . . . Jesus . . . come on . . . get over yourself. I've got better things to do than hose Bing Flanagan."

He shrugged and let it go, light and easy, as if he were setting a kite adrift in the wind. I felt a tiny bit ashamed as I watched him, noisy and chattering, hop into the convertible, swinging his legs up and over without opening the passenger door.

I made a quiet deal with myself to do better, be a better brother. I was always trying to give him the brush-off. I was vowing to improve when my good intentions took a sudden detour.

"No way are you driving," I said as he slid into the driver's seat and inserted the keys into the ignition, the car rumbling to a start.

"Why not? To the ferry . . ."

"No. You're not driving my car. Forget it."

He hesitated, and I gave him a shot in the ribs. "Jesus," he said, clutching his side, grimacing and laughing at the same time as I used the opportunity to shove him aside and into the passenger seat. He bent over and grabbed the remnants of a half-eaten doughnut on the floor, then turned around and whaled it at me, jelly dripping down the side of my face and sticking to my hair.

"You asshole," I said, scraping the doughnut off my cheek and throwing it back at him, his hands held up defensively in front of his face, both of us laughing.

Before we cleared the driveway, I was already devising ways of giving him the slip.

"Hey," Bingo said, touching me on the shoulder. "Listen."

I pressed the brake. I heard a low keening sound coming from the house, mournful and sad. Mambo was crying.

Bingo shifted in his seat to face the house. "Collie, look at Mambo."

Turning my head, I caught sight of Mambo standing on all fours on top of the kitchen table. He was staring after us, watching from the big kitchen window—it was an unsettling picture, an enormous, wolfish black-and-red dog, poised and unmoving, intense and straining for one final look, his amber eyes vanishing into his black face.

"Crazy dog," I said, and then louder: "I'm so sick of crazy dogs and crazier people!"

"What the hell's your problem?" Bingo asked. "You're getting more like Ma every day."

"What are you, nuts? If there's one person in the world I'm not like, it's Ma."

"Whatever you say, Coll." He burrowed into his seat, sand-encrusted running shoes up on the console. We bumped along the narrow gravel road, and he looked away from me and out over the sky and ocean, both a dark sable color, lines of division blurred as brown-and-gray waves rolled in only yards from the road.

I kept sneaking intermittent sideways glances, which he pretended to ignore as we swung onto the main road, canopy of trees blowing overhead, fishing boats rocking in the choppy bay, wind blowing back the hair on our foreheads.

"Hey, Coll, look out!" Bingo sat up suddenly and pointed to the side of the road as a giant snapping turtle made his way slowly across. I applied the brake, and even before the car screeched to a halt, the door opened and out he leapt, rushing to the turtle's side. He picked him up, hands gripping either side of the banged-up shell, and stopped at my side of the car, pushing the turtle toward me, its mouth open and hissing, the overwhelming smell of stagnant water filling the car.

"For Christ's sake, Bing," I said, recoiling as he dashed across the remainder of the roadway, released the turtle into the water, and then jogged back to the car.

"Great, you stink worse than usual," I complained as he reached over and wiped his hands on my shirt. "Fuck off. . . ." I stepped on the accelerator, the impetus jerking him backward as we zoomed down the road leading to Rosie's place.

We were clipping along, the wind fresh and moist and vaguely fishy. The radio was cranked, it was too noisy to talk, so we settled back into our separate compartments, the silence between us punctuated by a smack here, a jab there, and the soundless thump of Bingo's fingers on the leather seat, tapping in rhythm to the music.

The ferry crossing was cold and damp, and the water was rough. Once we were on the mainland, a sudden morning storm almost canceled the trip, but then the sun shone through, and because he was bugging me about it, we decided to go in Rosie's new car, a Mustang convertible. I left my car parked in the driveway of Rosie's "winter" house.

Twenty minutes down the road and Rosie's new car got a flat.

We made Bingo fix it as we sat by the side of the road and issued profane instructions. Then we shoved him back into the cramped backseat, where we piled our stuff on top of him.

"Jesus, Coll, I can't feel the lower half of my body," he said. "Can we trade places for a while?"

"What? Are you kidding?" I said, taking one last bite of an apple before I tossed the half-eaten core behind me, beaning him on the temple.

He scrambled for it and mashed it on the top of my head. A thin stream of fruit juice ran down the side of my cheek. I lunged for him, and the car swerved. At 90 mph, you don't want too many distractions.

"Hey, assholes, fuck off," Rosie said, overcompensating, steering the car back onto a straight course, rattling my neck.

"Ouch," Bingo said without much passion, hitting his head on something back there.

"Fuck you, Ferrell," I said, grabbing Rosie's Red Sox cap and tossing it into the wind and onto the road. It's the kind of eloquent exchange that passed for polite interaction in the rustic world of young manhood, all three of us the knuckle-dragging, shiny-haired by-products of the best education privilege can buy.

"So I hear you met Collie's girlfriend, Zan. What do you think?" Rosie said to Bingo as he turned the car down a long, narrow country road.

"She's pretty. She's smart." He was staring out the window.

"Why does 'smart' always sound like a pejorative whenever you use it to describe a girl?" I said, looking back at him through the rearview mirror.

I shrugged as he turned back to Rosie. "She's kind of WASPy."

"She's a Catholic. What the hell are you talking about?" I said.

"Um, I don't know; she just seems kind of stuck-up or something."

I snorted. "Any girl with a library card and clean hair is a WASP as far as you're concerned."

"What's that supposed to mean?"

"It means that you're an idiot when it comes to girls."

"And everything else, too, right, Collie?" He was leaning forward and directly behind Rosie, but I wouldn't turn around to face him.

"Come on, you guys, don't start," Rosie said, intervening.

"Girls are more than a cup size," I said, wanting the last word.

"Must be nice to always be morally superior to everyone else," Bingo said, shooting me an accusing glance, which I caught out of the corner of my eye.

"Would you two shut the fuck up already?" Rosie had had it.

We rolled into a little hick-town gas station around ten o'clock and picked up breakfast—Gatorade and jelly beans—and waited around for Bingo to reappear.

"Where the hell did he go?" Rosie asked.

I swore. He was always vanishing. "Let's give him five minutes and then we split," I said, giving the whole matter about ten seconds' thought.

"Hey! Wait! . . . You guys!" Bing broke into a run at the sound of the engine turning over, appearing from around the corner of the convenience store building, a smiling, dark-haired girl in a short black skirt behind him, his hand in her hand pulling her along.

"Holy shit!" Rosie said, eyeing them through his rearview mirror.

We exchanged annoyed glances. Bing, despite his field of freckles and wobbly intellect, got laid more than any guy I knew. It wasn't as if he came on like Pepé Le Pew, either. Unlike the rest of us, who were running around with our tongues hanging out, panting for attention, all he ever had to do was show up.

"Not all relationships boil down to love in an elevator," I told him, knowing I was delivering my lecture to an empty room. I once saw him emerging from a confessional at St. Basil's with a cute girl and a big grin on his face.

"One for the road. I'm giving up sex for Lent," he said.

"Jesus, Bing, that's sacrilege."

He laughed. "Not the way I do it," he said. "The way I do it, it's pure sacrament."

"Can she come?" Bing said, dragging his new friend, Erica, by the shirtsleeve.

"Where will she sit?" I asked, smiling at Erica through clenched teeth.

He hopped into the constricted space and pulled her onto his lap, cheerfully making introductions.

"I love your car," she said as Rosie nodded in courteous strained acknowledgment.

Just what we needed—another girl impressed by a car.

"You're not exactly dressed to go caving," I said by way of a hint.

"I just live down the road a mile or so. Bing said you wouldn't mind if I ran in and got changed. . . . It'll only take me a minute. Is that okay?"

"Sure it is," Bingo said. "Collie and Rosie don't mind a bit. Do you, guys?"

We exchanged a murderous glance, my fist clenching and unclenching.

"No problem," Rosie said.

"Wow," Erica said, taking in the whole picture, settling deeper into Bing's lap, her arm around his neck. "Are you guys rich? It sure seems as if you are."

"Oh yeah," Bingo said. "Ain't life grand?"

Rosie laughed. It was a classic Fantastic Flanagan remark. With his soft features, slight build, and breezy manner, Bing, upper-class inflections intact, looked and sounded as if he'd just stepped off a yacht docked for the social season on the Italian coastline.

I turned around and glared at him. He didn't care. Only I knew there was more than a little of Pop, percolating like an alchemist's blend of bargain-basement charm and a handful of cheap tricks, beneath that glistening surface.

As it turned out, Erica worked at the convenience store, was saving for college, was planning on becoming a physiotherapist, and was chatty and transparent as hell but pleasant enough. Nothing I liked better than being mad and exasperated with Bingo, so it suited my ongoing agenda to have her ruin our plans.

I glanced in the side mirror. She and Bing were making out. Nothing so graphic it would offend the Junior League, but just obnoxious enough to make me wait until she was out of earshot, tripping up the steps to her family's nice little brick house, rushing to get changed, before I took the opportunity to smack him upside the head.

"Man, you're such a puritan, Collie," he said, rubbing his ear. "Pop told me it's genetic. You're a certain kind of Irish Catholic. . . ."

"That's bullshit," I said. "Typical Fantastic Flanagan horseshit."

"Admit it. You are a bit of a puritan, Coll," Rosie said. "So it's not all horseshit."

"Next to Bingo, the Marquis de Sade would seem uptight," I said. "I just like a little decorum, you know. A bit of restraint might be nice. I know it's a foreign concept in our house, but it's something to consider."

The front door opened, and Erica, in shorts and sweatshirt, said good-bye to her mother, who smiled and waved at us from the porch as Erica ran down the steps and toward the car.

You've got to be skinny to go caving. You never know when you're going to run into a tight squeeze. We had a couple of flashlights among the lot of us, no headgear, and we decided not to worry about the rain. Rosie and I had been through the caves in the past. I was familiar with one route in particular and was confident we could make it a pretty straightforward excursion. We talked about bringing ropes, but in the end we thought forget it, we don't need them, we're going on a lark, we aren't Stanley and fucking Livingstone, for Christ's sake. Parents took their little kids on excursions through those caves.

We got to the cave entrance—a narrow opening in the limestone—and right away we had problems. Bingo was slim enough, he could pass through the eye of a needle no sweat. I wasn't as slender, but I was pretty lean, so it was no problem for me or Erica, but Rosie had put on a little beer weight, and he couldn't make the cut.

Even with Bing pushing down on his shoulders at the surface and me pulling his legs from below, we couldn't budge his fat ass.

"You guys are gonna kill me," he said, his face getting redder with each passing moment.

I was so disgusted, I was all for leaving him wedged in there for the rest of his life.

"Well, this was a total waste of time," I said, hoisting myself back up to the surface, unkindly poking Rosie in his soft gut with a long stick I picked up off the ground.

"Let's look around for another entrance," he said.

"No," I said. "It's too dangerous. We didn't bring any stuff with us. And I only know my way from here."

"Come on, Coll, where's your sense of adventure?" Bing said mischievously, eyeing Erica. It was plain to see his reasons for wanting to go belowground. She smiled back at him.

"Adventure's got nothing to do with it," I said. "You don't know what's down there. If we get into a jam, we've got no way of getting out. I don't want to be one of those weekend spelunker dorks they have to rescue after they've spent three days wandering around in circles in the dark."

Bingo started squawking like a chicken.

"That's mature," I said.

"I've come all this way. I'm looking for another entrance. Are you coming?" he asked the others.

"I'm in," Erica agreed, pointedly looking at me. I shifted involuntarily.

Jesus, I thought, outclassed by a girl.

"What the hell? Come on, Coll, we've come this far . . . ," Rosie said, hauling himself up and dusting off his jeans, stained a rich brown from the earth.

"Jeez, we've driven for a couple of hours. You guys make it sound like we trekked for days through the Himalayas," I said, bringing up the rear as the others scrambled out across the limestone, searching for another way in. But no one was listening to me. The momentum, clearly, was for going in.

Everything was telling me it was wrong. I felt my uneasiness spreading as if it were poison ivy. My skin itched with reluctance, and still I went ahead. What is that? Every part of me covered in hives, my whole body screaming out an alarm, and I ignored it? Even after years of thinking about it, the only explanation I have is that those whom God would destroy He first makes itchy as hell.

"Over here!"

I looked up. It was Bingo. I heard him whoop delightedly. I

saw the top of his head, and then he disappeared. The others were laughing.

"Jesus, Bing, you asshole!" I said as I stood looking down at him in disbelief.

He shone his flashlight in our direction from where he stood in the darkness about eight feet below. He'd found an opening in the limestone and he'd jumped, without thinking, without discussing it with anyone, he'd just leapt in. I couldn't believe it.

"It's awesome down here," he said.

I was bent over the hole and staring down at him.

"Come on. Jump," he said.

"Are you crazy? How do we get back out?" I yelled down. "How the hell are you going to get out?"

"Oh, Collie, there are a million ways out of here. What are you so worried about? I can see light way down at the end of this big cavern. At the worst we can always just follow the water to the river opening. Come on, Erica, I'll catch you. You can do it. Jump."

Erica hesitated for a second, giggled nervously, closed her eyes, and let fly.

"One, two, three . . ." Rosie followed, landing with a loud thud.

"Hey, I felt the earth really move for the first time," Bingo joked. "Come on, Collie. It's fine. There's light streaming in. I can see it down round the bend."

"Bingo's right," Rosie said, his flashlight illuminating his face. "You know how porous these caves are. There are openings all over the place."

I hesitated. I was thinking about something, and for the life of me I can't remember what it was. I've gone over every moment of that day a thousand times in my head, so thoroughly that I can account for every second, but no matter how I try, regardless of what tricks I play on myself, I can't remember what I was thinking at the precise moment before I jumped.

Mostly I remember following the trail laid down by Bing's laughter.

"Are you finished?" I asked as Bing emerged from the darkness, his knees covered with mud, yellow dust in his hair, his eyes shining like an oil lamp, Erica trailing him, this ever-loving girl, this obliging mattress he'd found somewhere on the way and insisted on dragging along.

"I think I'm in love," he said, full of high spirits. Clapping both hands around my head and dragging me into him, he kissed me as Rosie and Erica hooted in shock and delight.

"Come on, Collie, let's fuck!" he shouted, and even amid the ensuing hilarity, no one was more amused than he was.

"Yeah, yeah, hey, Shecky, let's get going." I gave him an impatient push. "We've got to find a way out of here in the next couple of hours," I said, turning away and starting the meandering trek around the bend and toward the light glimmering somewhere off in the distance.

It was then I noticed Bing limping.

"Are you okay?" I asked him.

"It hurts," he said. He had twisted his ankle in the jump.

"What a fucking asshole you are," I said. "What are you going to do if we have to climb? Damn it, Bing."

"You'll help me," he said matter-of-factly. "It'll be fine." He said it as though he meant it, as if he knew it was true, as if he could count on me.

We were navigating a long, narrow pitch down to the level of the streamway. There was a squeeze in the middle that gave us a bit of trouble. Bingo slipped and fell a couple of times as we carried on our journey downstream. Three hours into our trek and his ankle was swollen and bruised and his toes felt cold.

"Ouch," he said, jumping, grabbing my forearm as I gently felt my way around his foot in the semidarkness.

"Jeez, Bing, I think it might be broken."

"Nah. It's just a sprain," he said, looking over at Erica, pretending to be brave, trying to impress her.

"Oh, and you'd know, of course," I said. "I'm telling you it's broken."

"Poor baby," Erica said, kissing his forehead.

I reached out and, taking his hand, helped him to his feet. "Put your arm around my neck," I said.

We hobbled along for a while, Bing making the odd joke, but for the most part he was uncharacteristically quiet, not singing or whooping it up or cracking wise. It was a bit disconcerting, him being so silent.

"How you doing?" I asked him.

"Just leave me here to die," he said. "I can't take another step. You guys go ahead and save yourselves. If I get hungry, I'll gnaw on a limb."

"Shut up, you idiot! Here . . ." I bent over and gestured for him to climb aboard. "Get on my back."

"Thanks, Coll."

"I wish you were my big brother." Erica looked over and smiled at me.

"No, you don't," I said.

Just ahead, we heard the muffled roar of water. We came around the bend and saw a deep pool fed by twin waterfalls—tall, explosive cascades of surging water feeding the plunge pool, the water, unusually high from the rain, sweeping in a strong, circular motion, a series of complex currents competing. At one end, the pool narrowed and opened up into rapids phasing into a fast-moving current that by the look of things—I could see light sparkling on the water's surface off in the distance—eventually led outside the cave and onto the wider river.

There was a huge boulder near the base of the waterfall. I felt uneasy.

"Rosie, do you remember anything Mr. Morrison said about

aerated water?" Mr. Morrison was our geography teacher at Andover and had led us on a few caving expeditions.

"I don't know what the hell you're talking about," Rosie said. "What's aerated water?"

"You can't swim in it," I said, struggling to recall the details of Mr. Morrison's warning. "You need to be careful in a pool like this where there's a waterfall. Especially when there's something like a rock or a log—see the big boulder down there? Something about the currents making a hole in the water and you just sink to the bottom. Remember he told us the story about the guy in Australia who tried to swim out of a cave, but he drowned because it was aerated water?"

"No," Rosie said. "I remember something about staying away from dams. Who ever heard of water you can't swim in? Where the fuck do you come up with this stuff?"

"Tell me about it," Bingo said, sliding off me and back onto the ground. "Collie, you're like the Grim Reaper or something. Don't be such a downer all the time."

"Pointing out legitimate danger isn't a character defect," I said. "You guys are acting like Curly and Larry."

"I guess that makes you Moe," Bingo said as Rosie laughed a little too appreciatively.

I ignored them and looked around, trying to decide whether we should go forward or head back and wait until someone else came along who could help us.

It didn't look good. The only way to avoid the pool and waterfalls was to go up to the source of the light shining on the water. Above us was a narrow limestone ledge, covered in moss and slick with water and wear. It wrapped around the tops of the waterfalls, gradually ascending to what seemed to be a series of openings beyond the rapids in the cave's ceiling that I hoped were wide enough to take us aboveground.

But there was no way in hell Bingo could make it across with his injured ankle.

He read my mind. "To hell with it, I'm gonna swim out of here."

"Are you crazy? You can't take the chance. It might be that weird water," I said. "There's no buoyancy. You'd sink like a stone."

"I can swim in anything," he said, appraising the boiling currents.

"No, you can't," I said, a tone of desperation creeping into my voice. "There's no discussion, Bing. We're climbing. I'll help you. Just forget about swimming."

I held on to him as we made our ascent, the color draining from my hands, my fingers aching. I was afraid he'd jump in, so the truth was I was holding on to him for all I was worth. I think he knew, too, because he held on a little tighter to me.

"It's okay, Collie," he said. "I won't do anything stupid. I could do it, though, you know, I can hold my breath forever if I have to."

"Yeah, I know."

Rosie and I were okay swimmers. And Bingo? He was the best swimmer I ever knew. He *could* hold his breath forever, started practicing breath-hold diving when he was a little kid after pretty much outgrowing the asthma that almost killed him.

Even I had to admit there was something magical about seeing him in the shallows along the beach at home, sliding beneath the water's surface, barely creating a ripple, smooth and silent as the schools of silverfish. I'd watch for the fleeting rhythmic flick of long flippers—his only concession to equipment—as he made his descent, heartbeat and respiration deliberately slowed, air packed and waiting for him. My own heartbeat and respiration accelerated, panic rising, as I waited for him to emerge, four minutes, five minutes, six minutes later.

Quite a trick; a real hit at parties, where Bingo inevitably spent half the night with his head in a bucket of water and the other half touring the hidden depths of just about every girl in the joint, each one lining up for the privilege. His magic expressed itself in many ways. I wouldn't have minded a little of what he had. There was no magic in me.

All of us were getting soaked by the silver spray assailing the rock. The water and the air were cold. Bing's teeth were chattering from the cold and the wet and the pain of his ankle.

"Are you okay?" I asked him as we inched along the narrow passage.

"No," he said.

We didn't have far to go. I nearly slipped a couple of times. I was afraid I would lose my balance. We decided it was safer for him to walk than ride.

"Once we get beyond the waterfalls, I'll piggyback you to the top to where the opening is," I said, promising him.

So it was me leading the way, followed closely by Bing, who was limping, then Erica, and Rosie reluctantly bringing up the rear.

"Whose fucking idea was this, anyway? Shit, Bingo, I could kill you for getting us into this jam. I'm fucking freezing up here. Where the hell is the way out?" Rosie had lost his enthusiasm for the whole project around the same time he got stuck.

"Lay off," I said. "You're not helping. Anyway, you were all in favor of this little adventure until you found out you might actually have to move your fat ass—speaking of which, that's what got us into this mess in the first place."

Bing looked over at me, eyebrows raised, clearly pleased that I would take his side over Rosie's.

I had hardly finished sputtering before Erica gave this tiny gasp, kind of an eek—a soft little yelp tacked on the end of a sharp inhalation of air. Her foot shot out from under her, and Bing instinctively reached over to grab her to stop her from falling. The unexpected twist and force caused him to lose his own footing. I saw what was happening. I lunged for him—too late.

"Collie . . . ," Bingo said quietly, no alarm in his voice, falling, midair, parallel to me, stopped in time, so close that I could almost reach out and touch him. Maybe I did touch him. I think so. I felt the tips of his fingers. I'm sure I did. And then he was falling, hitting the water, causing a minor sensation, blue and black and silver spray soaring skyward, the top of his chestnut-colored head disappearing beneath the gurgling surface, a roiling cauldron of jostling currents, the noise of him swallowed up by the noise of all that.

"Bingo!" I shouted, but my shouting was a whisper, pale and bloodless as I was pale and bloodless, powerless to make myself heard or felt against the tumult.

"Bingo! . . . Bing!" Erica and Rosie took up the chorus.

"Christ! Collie!" Rosie said, looking at me expectantly.

"Do something!" Erica screamed at me.

Everything was happening so fast—it was as if someone suddenly appeared with a gun. Bang, down he went. Bang, Jesus, Erica went in after him. Erica, Jesus Christ, what are you doing? Bang, followed by Rosie. Rosie, you were supposed to be a coward, remember? Everyone knows you're not worth shit. What's this? A hero, it can't be, not a goddamn hero. Rosie, come back! Bang, bang, bang, each one disappearing beneath the water's darkening swirl. Each one gone. They might as well have fallen from the top of a mountain through empty space. What were they thinking? And me, what was I thinking, pressed against the rock face?

"Collie!" There he was. I heard him.

I was clinging to the ledge; my palms were cut and bleeding from the sharp points of jagged rock. The sun from the opening ahead hit a patch of water, briefly illuminating something.

I pointed. "There he is!" I shouted, no one to hear me, just me, scrambling and falling, tripping the rest of the way down, close to a ledge overlooking the pool, where I'd last seen him go in, and I waited, knowing he could hold his breath forever. And everything was going through my head, everything but going in after him.

I knew the others were lost; they were human, after all. But Bing was different. Bingo was pure magic. I stood there shivering, threw up, pissed myself; it may have been days I stood there waiting for him, for all I remember.

I waited until my flashlight went out and I was alone in the dark with the only sound the carbonated surge of the water and the ghastly shrieks of night birds swooping round the cave, circling overhead. I couldn't hold my head up. I sank to my knees, wet and mossy, cold as river rock, a creature of hollow edges, and the sole light was the light from the moon wavering on top of the black water, blackbirds going round and round above me.

When the light went out I knew he was gone, buried at the bottom of the pool. Head tilted back. Face turned up to the light on the water's surface. Skin turning blue, lips blue, fingernail beds blue. Breathing stopped. Circulation stopped. Heart. Stop. Brain cells dying one after another.

I had to get help. Somehow I climbed back up onto the limestone ledge and worked my way toward the opening, but I couldn't bring myself to leave them there alone in the cave. The next morning, another group of day trippers found me and called for help.

They found Erica and Rosie downstream right away. Bingo took longer. I was there when the police divers spotted him and pulled him out. He was clutching the chain I wore around my neck, my holy medal in his hand, St. Francis of Assisi, patron saint of animals. He'd torn it from my neck when he fell. He must have grabbed for me as I grabbed for him. All he got for his efforts was a fistful of someone's goodness and courage, somebody else's bravery and martyrdom.

Nothing, there was nothing to do. Bingo was dead. It was plain enough. He was white, so white that he was translucent, a tinge of blue under his eyes, pure Irish blue, in the hollow of his cheeks. His hair was filled with sand and was swept back off his forehead, sleek and wet and shiny.

I'd never seen such stillness.

I'd thought dying was the same as sleeping. But nothing about

Bingo suggested that he was asleep. Silent and empty, he seemed to have gone far away, leaving a massive vacancy behind. Water trickled from the side of his mouth. He soaked the ground where he lay; water drained from every part of him onto the sand.

"He's melting," I said, and the thought terrified me.

He had a deep, narrow cut over his eye. It was shaped like a crescent moon and ran from the outer edge of his eye to the tip of his cheekbone, immaculately executed as if by skilled practitioner with precision blade. Water seeped from his wound. There was no blood. I wondered if his blood had turned to water.

I'd still be there. I swear to God, I would be, I would have waited for him forever, I never would have left him, but someone came along and found me and took me away.

He was scared, just something I knew about him. When he was small, he was scared of so many things, used to shake when he saw a bee, would tremble with fear when he had to go to the doctor or get his hair cut.

Uncle Tom taught him this limerick about a little mouse that lived in a bar and sneaked out at night to drink beer spilled on the floor.

"Then back on his haunches he sat. And all night long, you could hear the mouse roar, 'Bring on the goddamn cat!' "

After that, whenever Bingo got scared he used to say, "Bring on the goddamn cat!"

It worked. Everyone thought he was fearless, everyone but Uncle Tom and me.

I told myself he was all right. He wasn't alone. He had that goddamn cat at his side.

CHAPTER FIFTEEN

The cops drove me home; at least I thought they were cops, though they were in plain clothes, both had the traditional signifiers—the strangulated formal speech, standard-issue mustaches, and humorless demeanor, although I wasn't exactly a bundle of laughs.

Pop was waiting on the front porch.

He held me tight to his chest, and then he started to cry. In the dark, helpless and uncomfortable in his clutch, I could see Sykes in ghostly silhouette. He wagged his tail faintly in greeting, and then he jumped up and tried to comfort Pop, but there was no solace to be found anywhere in the world that night.

The screen door banged behind me and the light flooded my eyes as I walked into the kitchen, dogs barking and crushing around, the cops clearly thrown by the melee, Jackdaw and Mambo looking beyond me for Bingo. Then the dogs settled down and drifted off, dropping to the floor, one by one, thumping and banging in separate heaps of hair and bone. And then it grew quiet except for Pop crying and the cops, who kept clearing their throats and asking if we wanted a minister or a priest or maybe a glass of water.

My mother took a long time to emerge from behind the dining room door, appearing to lose her balance at first sight of me, her hands thrust awkwardly over her head, as if she were walking a tightrope suspended over the Grand Canyon. She made the most terrible sound deep in her throat, as if she were rusting, and only then did I realize that my parents had had no idea which one of us had drowned.

Windowless rooms, her eyes never wavered as she walked toward me and, raising her arm, winding up, hit me so hard that she knocked me into the wall, breaking my jaw in two places.

The dogs went crazy, growling and barking, half of them leaping at Ma, the rest charging me, pulling and chewing; a handful got so worked up that they attacked one another, so there were pockets of overwrought dogs rolling around the room in tight balls of fury.

Staggering sideways, I felt nothing at first, and then the whole world came in on me, collapsing on all sides, so excruciating was the pain. Leaning against the wall, my knees buckling, I slid slowly downward, my wet clothes a brush that left a broad, damp mark on the aging palm plaster.

"Holy shit!" the bigger cop said.

"Anais, my God!" Pop gasped, running to my side.

"Hey there! You leave him alone, you Female B!" Uncle Tom, in his long underwear, lurched into the kitchen—he'd been listening at the door, leaning against the wooden frame for support—speech slurred and glasses askew, reeking of urine, so drunk that he couldn't stand still or straight. Wobbling back and forth, he was on the third or fourth day of a bender.

"The resurrection," he said, striking a lopsided heroic pose, forefinger pointing heavenward. "O ye of little faith. He's not dead. There'll be a resurrection. He'll rise again. You'll see."

"Tom, for Christ's sake, you're not helping," Pop said, kneeling beside me, covering his face with his hands, rubbing his eyes as if he were trying to erase all that was before him.

"Nothing's changed. Nothing's changed," Tom said. "The world's the same as it was this morning. He ate breakfast with me. I made him bacon and eggs. Sunny-side up, just the way he likes them. He had two cinnamon buns. He drank freshly squeezed orange juice."

He started to sing: "Tom Flanagan's makin' Bingo some eggs and bacon . . . Tom Flanagan's makin' his boy some eggs and bacon—"

"Goddamn it, Tom, are you mad? You've been holed up in your room for days. Look at you, covered in piss, your mattress putrid, the whole house stinking of you." Pop stretched his arms up and out, making an expansive V shape, embracing the pantheon. "Is this to be our dead boy's commemorative perfume, the stench of Tom Flanagan's piss?"

For my own part, I could hardly breathe; I was gasping for air and swallowing blood with Sykes standing on all fours on my chest, licking my face, as I struggled to pull myself up. Leaning forward, I spat up a mouthful of everything I'd swallowed. My hands and face were streaked with blood and dirt.

"You must have stood and watched as he went under. Did you stare? You should have turned away. People who watch from their windows can expect a bucket of blood thrown in their faces," Uncle Tom said, suspended over me, his eyes bulging.

"Why did it have to be him?" Ma said, addressing the cops before turning to face me, her eyes fierce and burning, holding me in place with the vast unregulated power of their feeling. "Why couldn't it have been you?" She spoke so quietly, I strained to hear.

And then her eyes rolled back in her head, her arms went limp, her knees gave way, skin whitening, hair straightening, toes curling, she fell like scaffolding collapsing and hit the floor with a calamitous thud, narrowly missing Tom, who was already listing like the *Titanic*.

"Did you see that?" he said, twisting out of her way, teetering back and forth and grabbing hold of the nearest door handle to steady himself. "She tried to kill me. She always said she'd take me with her. Arrest that woman! I want her charged with attempted murder."

"Lord Jesus, it's Kristallnacht," Pop said, calling out, "Anais! Anais! Anais!" as he and the cops pulled dog after dog after dog away from her lifeless body and he dropped to his knees beside her, his hands on her shoulders.

"If you don't arrest her, I will," Tom was raving.

"She's dead, you lunatic!" Pop shouted. "I want that man taken into custody," he said irrationally to the cops, who must have wondered if they, too, were dead and didn't know it, stuck in some overlooked corner of purgatory.

"Calm down," the smaller one said finally. "You've all had a terrible shock, well, series of shocks . . . ," he added, sounding confused.

"If the Catholic Church can dig up Pope Formosas nine months after interment and charge him with perjury, prop him up in the courtroom, and convict him, then I can arrest a dead woman." Tom wouldn't quit, he didn't know how—experiencing Uncle Tom firsthand was knowing what it's like to be a sedan in one of those coin-operated car washes, water and detergent and hoses and brushes and flaps and hot air coming at you from all sides and no end in sight.

I lay there watching it all unfold from my spot on the floor, bloody hand holding my shattered jaw in place, tears like a waterfall running down my dirty face, my mother small and still, lying across from me. Her face was white, her hair a deep chestnut color, her lips parted slightly, revealing the top line of her lower teeth, as the cops struggled to fend off the dogs. Uncle Tom fell slumped into the kitchen chair and stared over at Ma. Pop rose to his feet but staggered.

Punch, one of the poodles, was trying to get me up off the floor, his front paws digging into my calves. The other dogs were crowding around, wanting me to stand up, wanting things to assume a shape they could recognize, and all the while the screen door was opening and shutting, banging intermittently in the wind.

Pop and the cops finally managed to get all but one of the dogs out of the kitchen and onto the veranda, where they barked at the latched door and pounded on the windows. Lenin hovered like Cerberus over Ma's body, threatening to murder anyone who came near, and that included Pop, who quickly gave up and lay with his head buried beneath his arms on the kitchen table, his shoulders shaking. Uncle Tom had vanished.

"What in the hell is that thing? Is it a bear?" one of the cops asked as Lenin lunged at him, snarling. He looked at me, and I shrugged and gurgled, unable to speak, trying to hold my face together. Lenin might as well have been a bear—saying that an Ovcharka is a dog is kind of like saying that a gorilla is a monkey. "An Ovcharka," as Ma loved to proclaim, "is not a Labrador retriever."

I felt as if I should do something. I dragged myself across the tile as Lenin watched, and as I drew closer, I reached up to touch his face and he wagged the tip of his tail. He relaxed a little as I positioned myself next to Ma, and growing calmer, he curled up alongside her and began to lick her face. Lenin never liked the hours that Ma kept, and he used to jump on her bed late in the afternoon and lie next to her, licking her face until she'd finally agree to wake up.

When the ambulances came to take us away, my last sight of Ma was of the attendants loading her onto the gurney and Lenin on his hind legs, licking her face in the expectation that she might wake up.

Before they closed the ambulance doors, I looked up at Bingo's room. The window was wide open. I could hear all the windows in all the rooms of the house systematically slide open, one at a time, their curtains blowing.

I heard the back door to the kitchen swing open and watched the dogs pouring in and out. The last thing I saw was Uncle Tom on the veranda, the front door wide open behind him, all the doors and all the windows in the house open wide, Ma and Bingo free to leave, neither door nor window to block their way.

CHAPTER SIXTEEN

I CAME TO A FEW HOURS LATER, MY HEAD POUNDING, THE ROOM spinning, my jaw wired in place, harsh light in the hospital corridor overhead, nurses whispering confidentially, the low-grade olfactory smear of liquor and residual anesthesia making me sick to my stomach. Pop was crazy drunk and bent over me, his hair an irregular skyline, his florid Celtic face inches from my own and sounding like a refugee from *Going My Way*.

"There, there, Collie, you've had a terrible time. You've just come out of surgery. Your mother, God bless her, she packed quite a wallop, the strength of the bereaved, she had, the madness of a corpse. But you're on the mend and your papa is here and I'll take care of everything. You haven't a worry. And Mammy and Bingo are in heaven, and I'll bet there are dogs in heaven, aren't there, Collie? Now, you must not try to talk. And you're forbidden to think. I don't want you thinking of anything, just that your papa is in charge and everything's taken care of, everything's perfect, never better," he said, slurring and choking back sobs.

I stared at him, finally aware of what people mean when they refer to a feeling of sudden terror.

"And I don't care what anyone says, you're the bravest one of them all, and I'll fight to the death anyone who says otherwise. If you'd gone in after him, you'd be dead, too."

He took my hand in his. "I've never been more proud of you, Collie. I'm bursting with pride in my son. You did the practical thing. Let no one tell you otherwise."

Pulling a deck of weathered cards from his back pocket, he swerved unsteadily from side to side. "Are you thinking of a card, Collie? Pick a card."

Drawing himself up, he swayed back and forth, complained of not feeling very well, and passed out cold and blunt on my chest, all two hundred pounds of him. He was covering my face, the cards spraying across the bed. I couldn't breathe. He was like a plastic bag over my head. I was seeing stars, resigned myself to dying right then and there, when one of the nurses spotted my predicament, and she and an orderly pulled him off me—it felt as if the whole world were shifting—and they shook their heads in disgust at his condition.

I closed my eyes and went away. Hours passed, maybe days. The next face I saw was my own, taking blurry shape in the form of the great and powerful Peregrine Lowell standing over me.

"I suppose you'd like to know what happened to your mother," he said. "It appears she died of something called stress cardiomyopathy—it typically occurs among middle-aged women who've suffered a great shock or trauma, although I pointed out to the doctors that King Lear succumbed to the same condition, an example which seemed to elude them altogether. It isn't always fatal, it doesn't need to be fatal; however, in the case of your mother, unfortunately, it proved quite deadly."

He inhaled deeply and then exhaled slowly, as if he were making an effort to control his breathing.

"Now, Collie, let me say that none of this is your fault." His gaze was slightly deflected, his focus was on the black beret he held in his hands, his fingers clenching and unclenching the fabric. He paused and stared into my eyes. "Now, I acknowledge the temptation to lay the burden of blame at your doorstep. After all, it was your idea to go caving, to take along your younger and inexperienced brother, to attempt such an ill-conceived venture with so little consideration for your safety."

Setting aside his hat, he began to smooth the sheets on my bed as he talked, straightening out the wrinkles and tucking in the edges until I was so tightly wedged in white cotton, I felt as if I'd been consigned to a pod.

"As a result, not only is Bing dead, so is your mother and so are two other young people, including Telfer Ferrell's only grandson. I have no doubt but that your mother would be alive today had she not been faced with the horrendous shock of Bing's terrible and premature death." He paused and surveyed his handiwork, his lips curving into a half smile, my immobilization somehow satisfying to him. He leaned down, his eyes trained on mine, and put his hand on my right forearm, the only limb that remained exposed, and he secured it under the sheets and pulled the blanket up around my neck.

"Considering the carnage, one might be moved to say, Thank God you didn't actually set out to do harm." He finished me off with a smile.

Covered head to toe in a dark, rich shade, he looked like a bottle of cognac, tall and slim and so well dressed, it hurt my eyes to take him in.

"That aside, I'd like you to know I don't blame you for what happened, nor do I think you were cowardly for *not* trying to rescue your brother. You made the right decision." He hesitated. "At least, let's hope it was a well-reasoned response and not the act of a coward—I give you the benefit of the doubt in that regard, although others might not be so generous. I'll leave the matter to your conscience, and you and Bing can sort it out in the afterlife, assuming, of course, that Catholics go to heaven, which is another matter entirely. So, we understand one another, then?"

My eyes watered, tears pooling, blurring my vision, an involuntary response to all the pain I was feeling. The Falcon impatiently drummed the back of a chair with his fingers.

"Good. The matter's put to rest. So it's back to school this fall. You must focus firmly on the future. There's a job for you at one of the newspapers after you finish school. I want you to learn the business from the ground up. I've arranged for you to come home with me.

Enough of this damned hospital business. . . ." Looking around the room with an expression of disgust, he waved his arms dismissively.

The Falcon despised doctors—he had never recovered from the indignity of a colonoscopy he'd had when he was fifty. In his view, the test was clinically sanctioned buggery, and he hadn't been to a doctor willingly since.

"You'll live with me." He glanced out into the corridor, speaking vaguely, seeming to be distracted, although there was no one there. "It's what your mother would want—especially now," he added, knowing that sending me to Cassowary would be my mother's way of telling me to go to hell, a fitting punishment for what had happened.

"What is it?" he said, turning back to confront me, his mouth twisting with exasperation, noting my reflexive frown.

"What about Pop? Uncle Tom?" I wrote in a shaky hand on the yellow notepad kept on the little table next to my hospital bed. My shoulders were sloping; I felt so tired, the effort to breathe brought more tears to my eyes.

He glanced down at my note, then methodically tore the paper from the pad, shredding it into small pieces that fell to the floor.

"What about them?" he asked, heading for the door, delighted by my enforced silence. We'd never had such an agreeable encounter.

There was a joint funeral for Bingo and Ma in Boston, the same church where Ma and Pop were married, their burnished coffins side by side at the front of the altar, so near that they touched. I sat in the first pew, my swollen face a deep aubergine. On one side of me, Uncle Tom was clear-eyed, well scrubbed, and sober. He smelled like cold air. My grandfather sat on the other side, gloves on his hands, silk scarf at his throat protecting him from the disease of Catholicism. Pop was nowhere to be found.

"Unforgivable," the Falcon said, dusting off his lap, scanning the pews, conducting a silent head count.

Pop showed up midway through the Mass, reeling down the center aisle of the church, leaning to the left and bending to the right, hollering at the priests and berating guests of the Falcon, stopping to attack me.

"You've stabbed me in the back for the last time, you yellow coward, leaving your dear brother to drown, and he was worth a thousand of you, and killing your mother as sure as if you'd plunged the dagger into her heart. Go on, coward, traitor, bastard, I know your dirty game."

"Pop, please . . ." I was talking to myself, my jaw clamped shut, marveling at my own ability to think things couldn't get any worse.

"Mr. Flanagan, you're obviously distraught," said one of the priests.

"Don't practice your priestly bullshit on me," Pop said. "Pederasts, the lot of you. You wouldn't recognize the will of God if it came down from heaven and bit you on the wrinkled ass."

Crimson-faced and speechless, the Jesuit abandoned his benevolent posture and signaled for the ushers at the back of the church to escort Pop from the premises.

Pop never did grasp the concept of gracious defeat. "Dignity," he used to say, "is the last refuge of scoundrels." He started swinging the moment they came near him.

The choir continued its protracted torture and murder of "Ave Maria." Pop shook his fist up at the balcony. "Catholics cannot sing! Catholics cannot sing!" he shouted in a desperate parting shot, his voice echoing from the vestibule.

I felt the eyes of the world on the back of my head. Poor Collie, what do we make of him, having recently distinguished himself as a moral and physical coward? And what of the old man, his shanty Irish father whom he obviously takes after, a raving drunken lunatic?

Back at my grandfather's house, I was subject to endless rounds of solicitous inquiries and compassionate murmuring from people who could hardly bear to look at me. I was nodding and smiling weakly, good manners my formal wear, as around me the conversational buzz grew loud and uniform, absent melody, sounding like the godless chant of cicadas deep in August.

"Poor Anais, she died of a broken heart." I overheard two women talking, friends of the Falcon. "She adored that boy. I understand her heart stopped beating on the spot."

"I heard she's the one who broke the older boy's jaw. Imagine. She must have been out of her mind with grief. What a tragedy. It makes me shudder to think about it. Her death feels like a curse. Poor Colin. . . ."

The other woman looked startled. "Aren't you being a bit melodramatic? Anais wasn't a Gypsy, after all. Oh, by the way, I think his name is Collier."

I stopped listening and wandered alone into the study, where I sat in the window seat and stared outside.

The Japanese call what happened to Ma *tako tsubo*, which means "octopus trap" in English. The left ventricle bulges and balloons—in an X-ray, the affected part of the heart looks like a traditional fishing pot for snaring octopus.

When Ma died she let the octopus out of the bag. I had already begun to feel the long strangulating reach of its tentacles.

Ingrid, the housekeeper, came looking for me and, with her arm around my shoulders, ushered me back to the main part of the house, where the Falcon's guests continued to circulate.

"This is no time for you to be alone," she said.

It was hot. The sun was bright and hard. I went and stood by the open window in the cherry-paneled dining room. The curtains were blowing, but the breeze was warm as wool. Everyone was embarrassed, discomfited—each awkward kindness a searing rebuke.

Parched and feeling as if I were about to burst into flames, I retreated to my room on the second floor, where I sat dejected on the edge of my bed, cradling my glass jaw. Eyes wide open, still I couldn't see a thing. It was dark where I was.

"Collie!" I heard a muted shout as a spray of gravel hit the bedroom window.

I drew the curtain. Pop stood below, a debauched Romeo pleading his mottled case.

"Collie," he said, clearing his throat, "I'll come to the point. Could you spare a twenty? It seems we were living a lie. Your dear mother ran through most of her fortune years ago, spending it all on the Commies. Your grandfather's been supporting us, and now he's frozen the accounts and left me practically penniless but for a meager monthly honorarium. I've got only enough for dog food."

I signaled him to wait a moment, walked over to the dresser, picked up my wallet, and withdrew the contents—three twenties. After taking a moment to fashion them into paper airplanes, I leaned out the window and let fall all three bills, watching as they drifted gently downward, an incongruous rescue flight, Pop struggling to catch them in midair.

"You're a peach, Collie. I won't forget it. I'm a broken man, but I've got my integrity. I can't be bought, and by God, they'll never own me. They can't take it away from you, try as they will, don't let the bastards get to you, promise me, Collie, you'll never surrender."

It's hard to surrender when you're not putting up much of a fight. I wasn't Pop—Pop didn't know how to give in.

"Collie," Pop said, turning to leave, pausing, not looking up at me there in the window, holding back the white curtain, crumpling the bills and folding them into his pants pocket, "it's all right. You mustn't blame yourself. It wasn't your fault."

I just looked at him, his profile outlined in a charcoal glow. I was listening to him talk, and all the while I knew that by morning it would be my fault once again, that Pop's emotional support was as unsettling as a Mafia kiss.

"Your mother loved you, Collie," he blurted out as if he were apologizing for something.

Somewhere in the distance, a dog barked. "Well"—Pop was struggling—"if it seemed sometimes she preferred your brother, it was only because she'd convinced herself he was her reincarnated Irish setter . . . and didn't she love the look of him?"

The dog's barking grew louder and more insistent. "Jesus," Pop said, suddenly fuming, turning to face the offending sound.

I stared after him as he disappeared into the amber light.

CHAPTER SEVENTEEN

THE FALCON WAS POOLSIDE, FROWNING INTO THE SUN, A SEAWALL of newspapers stacked around him like a fortress when I took up my seat across from him, a climate unto myself—the fog rolling in, gray sky as far as the eye could see. He was eating lunch beneath a huge unfurled patio umbrella. A creature of enshrined routine, the Falcon ate scrambled eggs and fruit every day at ten minutes past twelve, the table always formally set, white linens and white porcelain plates shimmering.

Lifting his eyes from his grapefruit, he took one long, wintry look at me and let me have it.

"Look here, Collie, this nonsense, this infernal silent routine of yours, has gone on long enough. Your jaw's healed. There's not a thing wrong with you. Grief is not something to be indulged; it's to be overcome. Moping is very unbecoming in a young man. Even the dogs are starting to think you're nuts."

I reached for a piece of bread, my gaze fixed on the butter, the sharp edges of all those words passing through me like rock through haze.

Impaling the summer air with his fork, his arms approximating a flail, his white cheeks deeply flushed, the Falcon was reaching new depths of lividity.

"Good God, these eggs are a culinary obscenity. Ingrid, is it possible to get a decent lunch around here, or must I make it myself?" He banged the fleshy part of his palm on the table, making the cutlery jump and inspiring the canaries in their cages to sing.

The Falcon kept a dozen canaries in a collection of antique cages in the dining room's big bay window—their cheerfulness seemed to be voice-activated; the more annoyed the Falcon got, the more loud and joyful grew their collective chorus—since I had moved in, their soaring high notes threatened to shatter glass. In summer, staff moved them outside for short periods during the day.

"They're done the way you like them. I can't imagine what would be wrong with them," Ingrid said, winking in my direction. I smiled back at her and reached for the cheese. Ingrid had been with the Falcon for years, since before I was born, since Ma was a little girl. She supervised the staff—cook, chauffeur, gardeners, a couple of housemaids, the groom—good old Ingrid knew where all the bodies were buried.

"They simply have no flavor. . . ." The Falcon was going on and on. "Is it too much to ask that an egg should taste like an egg? Never mind. Coffee and grapefruit will have to do."

"No, it won't do at all. Don't be so stubborn, and eat," Ingrid insisted. "I'll reheat them for you. Just give me a moment," she said as she absently went about deadheading long stalks of freesia in a tall vase set in the center of the table.

"By all means, Ingrid, take all the time you need. Don't rush on my account. Where was I? . . . Ah yes, Collie. Where's your fight? Have a little moxie. This other stuff, sulking like a little girl, is bloody offensive. I have a philosophy about life and it's served me well, and I'll pass it on to you at no cost." Pinning back my shoulders with the sharp edges of his tone, he leaned across the table. "Get on with it!"

I broke off a small piece of buttered bread and tossed it to Cromwell.

"Must you feed the dog at the table?" His dramatic sighs were taking deadly physical shape, rising up like mushroom clouds and hovering overhead.

"Would you mind passing the sugar?" I asked, the first words I'd said aloud in almost a month. Cromwell lifted his head and wagged his tail. Otherwise it was a pretty anticlimactic moment; despite his ranting, the Falcon never even noticed.

"Don't you think you get enough sugar? My God, you'd think you were five years old the way you eat sweets."

"It's nice to have you back, Collie," Ingrid whispered, pausing on her way to the kitchen, hugging me in the open doorway between the conservatory and the dining room.

Alexandra broke up with me a few days later. She came to Cassowary to spend the weekend and, intermittently crying and shaking, kept talking about the merit of going our separate ways. She was sorry for the timing, but given the circumstances, wouldn't it be worse for me if I were to rebuild my house on a shaky foundation?

She broke down, beige hair covering her face, and talked about how difficult this whole thing was for her, how terrible she felt about Bingo and Ma, and what an impossible spot she was in.

"I swear to God I planned to break up with you that weekend, but then Bingo died and your mother . . ."

"It's okay," I said, handing her a tissue, giving her an epicene squeeze. "I understand. Believe me, if I could figure out a way to break up with me, I'd do it."

"Oh, Collie," she wailed, face flushed and soggy.

It didn't matter. I didn't care. You could have popped a live grenade down the front of my pants and I wouldn't have reacted. I felt as if I'd been stripped of my humanity, were empty inside and inured to the concussive effects of all that was exploding around me.

Wringing out my shirt, water dripping onto the floor from her equatorial drenching, I watched from the dining room as she drove away, hand like a white glove waving proper farewell, when the Falcon appeared in soundless landing behind me.

"Well, sorry as I am for your situation, one can hardly blame her. After all, women do like a knight in shining armor, and unfortunately, Collie, given recent events, your breastplate's looking a little tarnished—at least to those who make a habit of being uncharitable in their judgments."

He put his hands on either side of my neck and tightened his grip in some bizarre burlesque of comfort, as if asphyxiation were somehow reassuring. He relaxed his hold on me, and as I turned to leave, I noticed a framed portrait of my mother, an oil painting done when she was in her teens, newly hung on the dining room wall.

"It went up this morning," the Falcon explained, seeing my expression.

"It's nice," I said. "She's not smiling."

"No," he said. "It's a good likeness."

"Ingrid told me that when Ma was a baby she used to sleep all day and that you could hear her laughing alone in her crib at night. She said that when she was six she drowned her pet crow in a rain barrel after he flew off with her charm bracelet."

"Ingrid should confine her hyperbolic color commentary to the back staircase," the Falcon said as he positioned himself directly in front of the portrait, turning his back to me. I hoisted myself onto the dining room table.

"What was Ma like when she was younger?" I asked him.

"Your mother was right-handed."

"No, she was left-handed," I said, puzzled by the remark. "She always made a big deal of it, saying that Fidel Castro was left-handed and Joan of Arc and Cole Porter."

The Falcon turned around to face me. He wore a mildly condescending expression—usually he looked at me as if he were suppressing his gag reflex. I perked up a little, thinking that his view of me had evolved from contemptuous to patronizing.

"So were John Dillinger and the Boston Strangler . . . and you, too, for that matter. I assure you, Collie, your mother was right-handed. She decided as a little girl that being right-handed was dull. She trained herself to use her left hand so that she would appear more interesting to the greater world. Anais thought being difficult was the hallmark of the artistic mind. . . ."

I nodded in recognition as he continued.

"If her criterion was accurate, then your mother died with the distinction of being the most creative intellect of her time."

He walked over to the garden doors, where something caught his attention, and he trained his focus on the canaries trilling away in the background.

"Canaries are remarkable for being uninteresting," he said, reaching into one of the cages, setting things aflutter. "They tend not to form attachments to their human caretakers and need very little interaction or stimulation to make them happy. Pretty, entertaining, and remote—a perfect pet for those who admire beauty and performance but don't want to be bothered with emotional engagement."

"Unlike Carlos," I said. Carlos was the Falcon's forty-year-old hyacinth macaw.

He laughed—laughed! I couldn't believe it. This was turning into a latter-day version of *A Christmas Carol*.

"Carlos is a damn nuisance," he said.

Encouraged by his friendliness, I persisted. "Did you and Ma ever get along?"

"No."

"Why not?"

"Genetics. Let's just say that when it came to alienation of affection, her mother, your grandmother, could have written an instruction manual."

He snapped shut the birdcage door and walked back toward the portrait, pausing in front of a large mirror in an ornate Oriental frame.

"In some ways, your mother was very much like my grandmother Lowell, who was a willful, opinionated, stubborn woman. Very stern and unyielding, though certainly she had her good qualities, too," he said, making some concession to her character while seeming a little unconvinced. "I spent a great deal of time with her when I was a child after my mother died. I lived with her until I was twelve, and I formed an attachment to her of sorts. She passed away when I was about your age. She was the most humorless person I've ever encountered. I suppose I loved her, well, yes, I did love her, but to this day, I've never shed a tear over her passing. " He paused and glanced over at the grandfather clock as it chimed in the background, and then he turned and waited for me to speak.

"I don't know why, but I haven't cried over Ma," I blurted out. "I did love her."

"Maybe you loved her in the same unkind way that she loved you," the Falcon said softly.

"Maybe . . . I don't know."

"Don't worry, Collie, your mother will extract her period of mourning from you. Some people just get buried more deeply than others. You'll find out that sorrow takes different forms, but in the end true grief is an honorific conferred on those people, however unlikely they may be, who bring us some measure of joy. Your mother was many things, but a joyful presence she was not. Unfortunately, Anais's grave is not a shallow one."

Ingrid appeared at the dining room door. "Have you forgotten the plane is waiting?" she said to the Falcon, tapping her foot.

"Please feel free to interrupt us anytime, Ingrid. Do I actually pay you to be meddlesome? If so, then you deserve a bonus for a job well done."

The Falcon reached for his leather bag looped over the back of one of the dining room chairs.

"Well, I must be going. I'm flying to Chicago, but I'll be back tomorrow morning. In the meantime, Collie, please don't sit on the table. It makes you look like a yahoo."

Hearing his footsteps on the stairway, his vigor belying his age, I slid off the table and walked through the garden doors and out onto the patio, where cages of canaries were enjoying the brilliant sun and its early morning warmth.

Ingrid followed behind me. "Would you like some tea, Collie?"

"No thanks," I said, the prosaic sound of my voice no match for the singing of the canaries and the responsive chorus of wild birds. "I'm fine."

"Of course you are," she said.

CHAPTER EIGHTEEN

THE NEXT DAY, I GOT UP AROUND DAWN. IT WAS SATURDAY MORNING. The house was still, and the air was infused with a sepia-toned light. I grabbed a bowl of cereal, cleaned up, or so I thought—Ingrid later told me that she knew something must have been wrong when she found the milk in the cupboard along with the orange juice, and the cornflakes in the fridge. I left the water running in the shower. I wore my T-shirt inside out.

I drove to the dock where my grandfather kept the *Seabird*, a fully restored forty-three-foot antique wooden sailboat, a fractional sloop made from teak and mahogany. The Falcon had insisted we take sailing lessons when we were little. Pop, on the other hand, had no experience of boats. Every time we set sail, he was convinced we'd never be seen or heard from again. As far as Pop was concerned, boats sank.

"Your father," my grandfather, referencing an old joke, once said to Bing and me, "thinks that yacht rhymes with hatchet."

"You sure you want to go sailing today, Collie?"

Gil Evans operated the marina. He was a nice enough guy—I'd known him since I was six years old—but like a lot of people, he was a little overzealous in his level of concern about my grandfather and what he knew and what he didn't know and what he should know.

Although the Falcon was preoccupied with matters of personal entitlement, he didn't need to be. Keeping Peregrine Lowell happy seemed to be a pretty big priority for just about everyone he ever encountered, even those who noisily prided themselves on pretending otherwise.

"Just thought you should know, Mr. Lowell . . ."

It was Gil's signature greeting, accompanied by muted voice and deferred glance, his perpetually doffed cap in hand. The Falcon used to parody his obsequiousness—referring to him as "trouble at the mill Gil"—but nevertheless considered it his due.

"It's okay, Gil. I'm just taking a short run home. I'll be back soon."

He shrugged, frowning. "I'm not sure. . . . Does your grandfather know about this?"

"Hey, you old guys worry too much. It'll be fine. Anyway, he's not around. He's busy terrorizing Chicago into submission. . . . Don't worry about it, I'm just kidding around," I added lamely, seeing the alarmed expression on his face.

"Oh, sure," he said, forcing a smile.

I pulled a hooded fleece over my head and steered into the choppy current, setting a course for the Vineyard, my first trip back home since Bingo and Ma died, another tentative step on the road to getting over it. I hadn't seen Pop or Uncle Tom since we'd buried Bingo and Ma.

I felt as if I hadn't eaten anything in days, as if I'd been fasting so long, I'd forgotten how to eat, and all I could think about was that big empty house on the beach.

I shielded my eyes from the golden light of the emerging sun with my hand. The deck was glowing in luminous shades of orange and peach, wavering in the dreamy first light of day. The winds brisk, the sailboat skimmed through the indigo waves, cobalt sky on the horizon, and I was gliding toward home.

I walked along Squibnocket Beach after docking the boat a couple of miles or so from the house. I needed the walk. The waves rushed in, and white foam gurgled around my ankles. Bingo and I used to hit the beach at dawn on days like this, strip down to nothing, and ride the waves into shore.

Hundreds of white seagulls lining the morning beach soared suddenly skyward. I was standing thigh-deep in the Atlantic, ocean water bubbling around me like a cauldron. I wiped my wet face and pressed the palms of both hands against my eyes. I was up to my ass in water. The mist rising like steam, undertow dragging me sideways, I was in the waves and teetering, toes shifting and digging into the loamy clay bottom. It was a wild day in the ocean, and I should have been having the time of my life with Bing; instead I was just standing there and bawling like a baby.

As I opened the unlocked door leading into the kitchen, the dogs rushed forward, nearly overpowering me, barking and spinning, dashing past me and through me, between my legs, out to the driveway, noses in the air, looking for Ma and for Bingo.

It was early afternoon. Pop's bedroom was empty, and Uncle Tom was still sleeping. I don't know quite what I expected. I didn't expect to see so many pies. There were pies everywhere—in boxes with clear cellophane windows. Pies all over the kitchen table, mounted in layers from one end of the counter to the other, stacked like books on chairs; there were pies being used as doorstops, and a pie box was turned on its side, holding open the kitchen window.

Several of the little dogs greeted me with lemon filling on their whiskers. Bachelor may have been in mourning, but still his muzzle was sticky and covered in cherry filling, crumbs decorating his deep chest. An empty vodka bottle on top of the stove presided over the pie population like a totem.

Mambo followed me up the stairs, goosing me all the way to Bingo's third-floor bedroom. I hesitated before opening the door. Bingo's room was painted ice blue, the walls, the woodwork and fireplace, the ceiling. There was an old wooden model sailboat on the dresser, its delicate sails blowing. A breeze came in through the open window. In a tall vase on the mantel, bunches of blue asters wavered.

Bingo's bedroom window was thrown wide open. There were fresh linens on his bed. His shirts, newly laundered and pressed, hung in his closet waiting for him. And everywhere in the house there was the unspoken thought that Bingo was coming home.

This oasis of neatness in an otherwise topsy-turvy household was my aunt Brigid's handiwork, the fragrance from her favorite perfume, Tweed, still lingering. She had flown in from Ireland for the funeral and stayed for a few weeks to help out Pop and Uncle Tom, but their drinking finally chased away her good intentions.

Bingo's room never looked like this when he was alive—then the floor was littered with clothes and comics, dog hair and textbooks in piles in the corner, their spines uncracked. It was never quiet the way it was that day.

I was in the middle of this unfamiliar shimmering shrine to my brother, and my heart lurched into my throat. Mambo's head next to my knee, I sat on the edge of Bing's bed for what seemed like a long time. I got up and opened the closet and removed a handful of ties. Bingo never learned how to tie a tie. I always did it for him. I tried to teach him, but he was impatient and insisted he didn't need to learn because I would always be there to do it for him. I sat on the side of the bed and made my knots, Mambo watching casually as he licked whipped cream from his front paws.

"So rumor has it that you're a little the worse for wear," Uncle Tom said, finding me stretched out on Bingo's bed, Mambo beside me, his head next to mine on the pillow. I was scratching his ear. Every time I stopped, he made this low throaty sound and then thumped me on the top of the head with his big paw. I felt as if I were an enslaved oarsman on a galley ship.

"I'm all right."

Tom sidled into the room from the doorway, giving the floor a lingering sideways glance—he had a habit of looking at you without ever looking at you.

"Say, he's bold," Uncle Tom said as Mambo gave me another whack.

"What's with all the pies?" I asked him as he sat at the end of the bed, still avoiding my eyes.

"Charlie and I are trying to buck up the baker's spirits, so we've been buying up his daily inventory."

"Mr. Peekhaus?" I sat up on my elbows and looked at Uncle Tom.

Tom nodded.

"Why?"

"His wife of twenty-four years left him for another man. Just like that. No warning at all—he came home from his deliveries one day about three weeks ago, and she was gone. Vamoosed." Uncle Tom punctuated the last word, using his hand to make a diagonal slash in the air.

"So I don't get it. What have the pies got to do with it?"

Uncle Tom frowned, exasperated by my stupidity. "A man in his position likes to feel in some demand," he said impatiently.

"What are you and Pop going to do with all of them? You can hardly get in the door. . . ."

Uncle Tom sighed with theatrical fervor and looked provoked beyond reason. "Well, I don't know," he said, drawing out each word.

"Okay, okay . . . I was just wondering," I said, lying back down and staring up at the ceiling.

"So anyway," he said, "as far as the matter of your mother goes, it's a miss, but it's a good miss."

I leaned into Mambo, his nose touching my nose; he was panting, his moist breath sweet and warm, like an apple pie.

"As to the other, well, now he's gone, I could use some help at the loft taking care of the pigeons. I've missed most of the racing season on account of all this trouble. He was helping me field a team this year, you know. You weren't much help." Uncle Tom glanced toward the open bedroom door.

"I know." I wondered if my face was as blank as my brain.

"So, as usual, I'm left in the lurch." He was staring out into the hallway.

"Yeah, well . . . he liked pigeons. . . ."

"He was all right," Uncle Tom said, eyes directed on the floor.

Neither of us spoke for a few moments.

"Where's Pop?" I finally asked.

"Oh, he's around here someplace. The way he's carrying on. . . . Well, I'm not impressed. Does the world revolve around Charlie Flanagan?" He shook my shoulder, forcing me to look up at him. "You know, he's not the only one who's suffering. What about me?"

The weather had taken a turn for the worse, but I didn't care. I hardly noticed. I took off without seeing Pop, and I left Uncle Tom in the kitchen making us something to eat—I could hear him chatting up the dogs, the refrigerator door opening and closing, the teakettle whistling in the background. He'd sometimes let that thing whistle until the kettle burned dry, he and Pop bickering about the same old things. I slipped out the front door and ran full out toward the water.

I just couldn't face all those pies.

Barefoot, I jogged along the beachfront and back to where the boat was pulling and bucking, straining at its moorings. The waves rose and the wind whirled around me, sand cutting into my skin like pellets. The sun was gone, replaced by gray clouds and bruised skyline. The wind and the waves combined to make a single deafening roar, and everything on the boat was flapping, banging, and rattling. I pulled a sweatband from my jacket pocket to keep my hair, crazy as seaweed, from blowing into my eyes, and I went about the business of setting sail for Cassowary, where I knew Ingrid would be waiting for me with a glass of iced tea.

Where the hell *was* Pop, anyway? What were they thinking, loading up the house with pies, the dogs helping themselves, and Pop and Uncle Tom wandering around indifferent to the world they'd made, their stories and opinions preceding them, announcing them like trumpets?

Ma was gone. Bingo was dead. Everything had changed and nothing had changed and all I could think about was the view of the gardens from the fragrant back veranda at Cassowary.

A deafening crack of thunder overhead jolted me back to the *Seabird* as ocean waves shot up around me like catapults. Within moments I was staggering around, struggling to keep my balance and feeling sick to my stomach from all the lurching. Slipping and sliding, I somehow managed to make my way to the cabin, where I put on a life jacket before heading back up on deck. This trip home was beginning to seem like kind of a dumb idea.

The boat was rocking uneasily back and forth, from side to side, and up and down, when it began to shake violently. I had just finished zipping up my yellow nylon jacket and pulling the hood of my fleece over my head when I was sent flying, propelled forward and up off my feet by the force of an incoming whitecap. Trounced by gallons of receding bubbling water, I rubbed my knee and checked the back of my head where it hurt. I pulled my hand away and saw blood.

I was soaking wet from the spray and the dousing. My head throbbed. I headed straight into the wind—figuring it was better to take it on the bow than abeam—sailing into tall waves at a forty-five-degree angle to minimize the pounding. I was in the middle of making a hard tack when the boom, hit by a sudden high gust of wind, swung wildly out of control and knocked me overboard and into the churning Atlantic.

I went under briefly and then bobbed up from the tumult. Disoriented and momentarily stunned, I rubbed my eyes and looked around. The *Seabird* had begun to drift away. Instinctively I tried to swim toward her, diving under the water and beneath the waves, swimming fast and for as long as I could hold my breath, surfacing for air, the boat always just out of reach. I almost caught up with her, but the waves beat me back, picked up the boat, and carried her off some distance.

It's hard to describe my feelings—horror seems too understated, terror too anemic; I'd need to invent a whole new word—as the impact of the wind and the waves flipped her over and then righted her just as quickly. The *Seabird* was quickly drifting away. I swam after her, but the waves were too strong and I had to give up and watch her disappear.

Waves hit one right after another, breakers colliding from every direction, swamping me, asphyxiating me—I was spluttering and gasping, coughing up gallons of water—where there should have been air, instead there was water. I barely had a moment to shake off the effects of one watery assault and I was sinking again and feeling pulverized, and all that kept repeating in my head was the phrase *buried at sea, buried at sea, buried at sea.*

I felt this panic rising, so overwhelming at first that it threatened to dwarf the ocean; my mind was scrambling. The waves were impossible to swim against, so I did the dead-man's float—big intake of air and then facedown in the water. And repeat. My idea was to let the waves roll over me. My plan was to live with it. I had some setbacks; it wasn't perfect, but it worked okay.

The waves finally died down after a couple of hours. As I treaded water, I took a sweeping look around. The ocean was a deep navy blue, smooth now but for the occasional indifferent ripple.

As darkness descended, there was a fitful drop in air temperature. I alternated between floating facedown, floating on my back, and bobbing with my knees to my chest. Every once in a while I ran my hand over my face, trying to read my features the way the blind interpret Braille. I was shivering from the cold. Something bumped up against me in the dark. I jumped, startled.

"Bingo!" I reached for him. My arms around him, I held him tight. Then I hoisted him on top of me, piggyback style, so he could rest, to help keep him warm, as he was keeping me warm. Deep into the night, I felt his body gently go limp and his head slide onto my shoulder.

I was sinking, falling; but slowly I fell, comfortably. Rather than resist what was drawing me downward, I relaxed into it. It was like falling asleep. I liked it. It felt good. It felt safe. It felt like something I should be doing.

To this day, I have no idea what it was that jerked me awake. I opened my eyes. Everywhere was blackness. I took a deep breath. And that's when I realized I was underwater. I reacted in sheer terror of where I was. I reached out blindly. Where was Bingo?

Propelling myself upward, I broke through the water's surface, gasping loudly. I called out for Bingo. I swam first one way and then the other. On my third attempt, I bumped into him floating aimlessly, still asleep. I took hold of him and vowed never to let him go.

It was dawn when they found me. A Coast Guard vessel picked me up. They told me how lucky I was to be alive.

"I can't die," I mumbled.

"You can stop a bullet same as the next fellow," somebody said.

I tried to tell them that Bingo was still out there, but nobody would listen.

"There he is," I said, pointing to where the first peach-colored rays of sunrise glimmered on the blue water. A kindly doctor on board gave me a sedative. And then I fell into a long, deep sleep.

When I woke up, I was back at Cassowary. The windows in my bedroom were shuttered, giving the room the obscure aspect of dusk.

"What in God's name were you thinking?" The Falcon loomed over me, a black shroud blanketing my view of the world. "You could have been killed."

"I'm sorry," I said, attempting to pull myself up into a sitting position, my back against the pillows. My head was spinning. I covered my eyes with my hands. "What happened? How long have I been sleeping?"

"Since yesterday afternoon," he said, his face gray and hard.

"What day is it? What time is it?"

"It's Monday. It's seven o'clock in the morning."

"Holy shit."

"Your eloquence is an inspiration. Now, why in God's name would you take the boat out in such threatening weather? Fortunately, Gil Evans grew concerned when you didn't show up and called to see if I knew you'd gone for a sail."

"It was all right when I left."

"What kind of an idiotic explanation—"

"I'm sorry about the boat."

"What's wrong with you? Were you trying to kill yourself? Hasn't there been enough tragedy in the last few weeks? The Coast Guard says you were insisting your brother was out there with you all night. . . . Look, if there's a screw loose, say so and we'll get it fixed—"

"I'm not crazy."

"There comes a point when crazy is preferable to stupid and

stupid is preferable to having a profoundly weak character. I'm not convinced that in your case we don't have a trifecta happening."

"What about Pop?"

"What about him?"

"He must be worried. I should call him." I threw back the covers and started to get up.

"Allow me," the Falcon said, taking me by the arm and leading me to the window. Puzzled, I looked down to see Pop sprawled out on his back on the ground below.

"Pop!" I called out reflexively, but he didn't move, not even a twitch.

"Save your breath. He showed up here last night roaring drunk and then proceeded to loudly pass out under your window, nicely fulfilling expectations, I might add."

"You can't just leave him there."

"Watch me," he said on his way out the door.

Spread-eagle on the sweating grass, Pop was the picture of discord. He was wearing a suit—on the rare occasions Pop ventured onto Cassowary, he always wore a suit and tie—putting great if inexplicable faith in formal dress.

"Pop," I said, my voice hoarse from exposure. Hesitant, kneeling next to him, I reached out and touched his shoulder. "Pop, you need to wake up."

"Look all you like, but don't touch," he said, grinning, gesturing elaborately, striking his magician's pose, waving an imaginary wand and slurring each word, settling back down into deep hibernation. His red hair gleaming in the morning light, deep blue jacket and pants covered in dew, Pop was drunk and drooling, abidingly subversive in a bespoke suit, posed inelegantly in the green garden, and around us the soft sound of sprinklers signaling a kind of soft, wary oblivion.

So this was what forever looked like. I stood up and, alone, made my way to the house.

CHAPTER NINETEEN

IT WAS THE FIRST WEEK IN AUGUST, AND THE FALCON WAS HAVING a dinner party.

I found him in the kitchen going over the menu with the cook, who had a nervous smile plastered to his face.

"You've got to be kidding," I said. "I can't believe you think that it's okay to entertain so soon."

"The faster you get on with it, the sooner you get over it," he said, putting a terse end to the obligatory tedium of mourning.

"What's that supposed to mean?"

"Oh, Lord, I'm too old for this conversation." He put both hands on his hips and, closing his eyes, tipped his head back, arching his spine, stretching conspicuously, as if he'd spent hours confined to a box.

"Well, you can count me out. What am I supposed to do? Stand around and talk about the stock market with a bunch of your friends?"

"You could do worse. I expect you to be there with bells on," he said. "There's enough talk circulating about you. You're in need of a little social rehabilitation, and the quicker we get to it the better," he said, his eyes sweeping the ceiling corners for evidence of missed cobwebs.

Earlier in the day, he'd thrown a vase at one of the servants, narrowly missing her, a young girl who had mistakenly introduced color into the all-white music room.

"Only white, idiot!" he'd said. "I told you all white. I want everything to be white!"

"I'll tell you what," I said, suddenly inspired by the opportunity to redeem myself for the New York party. "I'll show up if you agree that Pop and Uncle Tom can come."

His back to me, his shoulders stiffened and then relaxed. "All right," he said unexpectedly. "Invite them if you want to."

"Are you serious?"

"I never joke when it comes to Tom and Charlie Flanagan."

Tiny ivory candles flickered in the tree overhead—junior members of the household staff were expected to keep them lit despite a persistent extinguishing August wind. Cocktail dresses blew about like the flames from torches dipped in pitch and dug in along both sides of the driveway. The camphorated air from the roses was sweet and heavy, a fuel made for burning, as if at any moment the night might catch fire.

Little white lights illuminated the tree canopy overlooking the pool. A narrow path of moonlight led to the open garden doors of the dining room, softly awash in candlelight; deeply red roses amassed in burgeoning arrangements spilled onto the table's creamy linens. The wind lifted up the corners of the tablecloths.

A smoky trail of gray birds passed overhead as I approached the front door, back from hours spent waiting at the ferry for Pop and Uncle Tom, who never showed up, despite all of Pop's extravagant promises. I paused, my hand on the doorknob, feeling alone and unequal to the evening that loomed ahead of me.

The leaves of poplar trees made a temperate, pleasing, summery sound as I fingered my car keys and thought about running away.

"Kitty! . . . Kitty! Where are you?" an angry male voice called out from somewhere near the pond.

A woman stepped from the shadows and stood next to me. She clutched my hand and giggled. Shit.

"Mrs. Paley," I said, fumbling, trying not to swallow my tongue.

"Oh, God, that's Steven, I can't stand it. Let's run away together, shall we?" she said, not exactly surprising me with her shrill subversion. "You've no idea how dreary a middle-aged man can be. Come help me hide. Look, over there!"

A curve in the path led away from the house and into a cove made up of dense shrubbery and tall ornamental grasses. I reluctantly followed her there, and once inside she pulled me toward her like some style-minded Apache dancer. We sank to the ground, where it was crunchy and moist and covered with periwinkle.

"Collie Flanagan, I can't believe it."

Tall, with short-cropped platinum hair, she looked vaguely architectural, a contemporary structure, all glass and mirrors. Kitty Paley was married to the junior senator from New York. Steven Paley was considered the likely Democratic presidential nominee; the convention was still a few months away, and he was looking for the Falcon's endorsement.

I went to Andover with their daughter, Edie—I wasn't likely to forget Kit Paley: Her ribald laughter at graduation decorated the room like string art, wrapping itself around her husband as if it were a brightly colored garland. In public, she stuck to him like brilliant feathers.

She and Ma went to the same boarding school as kids—Ma detested her, loudly and in great detail. To Ma, who could grow a second head at the sight of a woman in stilettos, Kitty Paley was "a public washroom, a talking vagina with serrated teeth."

"Here, here, Anais, there's no need for a biology lesson. You're frightening the boys," Pop rebuked, "although I'll concede your point—that woman is s-e-x in a convertible."

"Look at you. You're all grown up! You always were a marvelous-looking boy. You look more like Peregrine every day. By the way, I think you're big enough to call me Kitty."

"What are we doing out here?" I rubbed my right temple, my unease throbbing like an awkward cliché.

"Hiding from Steven, of course. Just indulge me a moment, won't you?"

"Sure." She had a way of making me feel as if I were five years old.

"Your mother . . . I felt terrible when I heard the news. And that darling brother of yours . . . well, it's just the most horrendously cruel thing to have happened. . . . It's such a tragedy for everyone, particularly for you. I'm sure you suffer terribly. . . . poor thing. But isn't Perry lucky to have you? You must be such a comfort to him."

She turned around so that her back was facing me, and reaching behind, she put my hands on her shoulders.

"Be a doll, won't you, Collie, and rub my neck? I'm so tense—all this campaigning is such a dreadful ordeal. You've no idea."

Painful discomfort humming away like a dull headache—I'd been avoiding this woman since I was fifteen years old and she hunted me down at a school fund-raiser, plopped herself in my lap, and started blowing in my ear.

"Kitty, this isn't funny. Where are you?" Senator Paley was shouting her name. "Goddamn it."

I could see him from where we were, an irritable presence on the terrace, impatiently waving away mosquitoes.

"Fuck," she said. "What's the use? He'll never give up." She slipped from my hands and turned around to face me. "I'll take a rain check on the massage, okay?"

I looked into her eyes, understanding what I saw there, her black eyes glowing back at me and all around us the saturated scent of clover, her serrated teeth sparkling.

Slightly flustered, I was standing in the entranceway to the living room, watching the Falcon, elegantly cloaked in his dark suit, as he smoothly navigated the room, pausing to chat, to joke, to gossip, to perform the laying on of hands, convivial maestro of the incisive remark, each immaculate gesture flawlessly executed.

He was so subtly integrated into his surroundings, I was having trouble distinguishing him from all that enhanced his presence—white candles gently flickering, white linens politely enshrining each table, white gardenias and red roses making music on the softly perfumed air.

Wherever I looked I saw him there, in the gleam of reflection, the crystal clarity of the glass, the sparkle of the cutlery, the transparency of polished windows.

I was quiet, sipping my ginger ale and smiling a little, laughing a little, talking a little.

"Don't mind my grandson. He thinks it's sexy to be sullen," the Falcon explained, looking both amused and appalled at the same time—a fairly standard expression for him.

Deadening explosions of laughter greeted his most bland observation.

Members of his household staff had to sign an employment contract stipulating no eye contact with him unless he authorized an exemption.

"Where do I sign?" Bingo said, thirteen or fourteen when he heard about it for the first time. Uncle Tom called it the Medusa clause.

The Falcon sidled up to me. "So where are the Flanagan brothers? Still dressing?" He laughed and looked for a place to put his glass, his eyes focused on a conversation occurring across the room.

"You knew they'd never show up. That's why you agreed to let me invite them, because you knew they wouldn't come," I said, feeling like a very slow learner.

"I don't know what you're talking about," the Falcon said, patting me on the arm, lifting his other hand high over his head, loudly greeting a new arrival, making his way through the parting waves.

The dreaded Senator Paley caught sight of me loitering near the doorway, inching into the hallway, yearning for the sanctuary of my bedroom, looking to disappear. He snapped his fingers and pointed. I jumped, and Kitty glanced up sharply, her false eyelashes descending like an immodest veil.

"I know you. Perry's grandson Kevin, isn't it?" He walked toward me as I corrected him, his hand extended like a loaded gun, the Falcon watching attentively as the other guests took notice. He'd met me at least a dozen times before over the years but acted as if each time were the first time. The senator was a big black bird of a man, landing among us like a crow at a bird feeder, aggressive and carping—you were always waiting for him to steal your bread crumb or drown you in the birdbath. Not in the same league as the Falcon, more like a top predator's sadistic, sharp-beaked henchman.

"Your brother died a couple of months ago. Your mother, too, right? Sorry about that," he said indifferently, trampling on the niceties, rushing to his purpose. "He drowned. A surfing accident, wasn't it? Some others died that day, too. You were the only one to survive."

"Not surfing," I said. "We were in a cave. . . ."

I stopped and stood up straighter, swallowed deeper, knowing what was to come, aware that I was in the presence of someone determined to make me aware of exactly what he was thinking. Kitty was looking uncomfortable. She and Steven exchanged a swollen glance—their flushed faces and overall humidity suggested an incoming storm. I shuffled from one foot to the other, fiddling with the papery contents of my pants pocket.

"It's all coming back to me now. Your brother was in trouble. The others went in after him. They drowned trying to save him. But you were"—he paused, glanced around at the gathering crowd, the corners of his mouth curling in contempt—"different. You didn't go in."

"No. I didn't go in."

"You should have gone in after him. Your brother, I mean." He jabbed me in the arm almost playfully, as if I'd missed the big catch in the game. "What was his name?"

"Bingo. Bing."

"You and the Ferrell kid—I know his uncle, Whitney Ferrell—it was your idea to go caving that day, wasn't it?"

"Yeah, I guess. . . ."

"Well, why the hell didn't you go in after him? You might have made the difference. Now you'll never know. First response, gut response, the thing you do before you think—that's the measure of a man."

"It was aerated water. If I'd gone in, I wouldn't be here talking to you. I would have drowned, too. Even the rescue divers wouldn't search at the base of the falls."

The senator ignored me. He was gesturing broadly, looking around and nodding, trying to recruit support. Beaming, visibly proud of himself for diving in, he took a drag on his cigar and puffed smoke in my direction, hoping I'd cough. "I don't care if it was sulfuric acid. There's an old saying, kid: A brave man dies once, a coward dies a thousand deaths. Anyway, here's the thing—when you decide to do something risky, even something stupid, then it's all for one and one for all—you kiss your own ass good-bye if you need to. Is that clear enough for you?"

"Steven doesn't understand the concept of small talk," Kitty said, tittering nervously. "He likes to think life is a Charles Bronson movie."

"Kit, please, Collie's a big boy. You don't mind, do you, kid? It's just talk. I'm trying to help you wade through this mess. I'm sure you've had it up to here with everyone pussyfooting around your feelings."

He framed his reference to my feelings with a sneer, looking at me as if he suspected me of menstruating.

"Anyway"—he confronted Kit—"don't you need to fix your hair

or adjust your makeup or something?" He gestured derisively with both hands before motioning for me to sit down.

I shook my head. "No thanks."

"I'll give you a good case in point so you realize that I know what the hell I'm talking about." He was just getting warmed up, the ice cubes in his glass colliding loudly.

"When I was in my early twenties, some friends and I took a trip to Austria for backcountry skiing. Helicopter dropped us into some pretty treacherous territory and took off. We'd been there a couple of days when there was a small but deadly avalanche and my buddy was swept into a glacial lake, hundreds of feet deep and freezing cold. He was loaded down with equipment and calling for help. We immediately went in after him, regardless of the consequence. We got him out, by the way, although we almost died in the effort. I'm not telling you this to shoot my mouth off or toot my own horn. I'm no hero. It's what we signed on for. Do you get it?"

"Yeah, I get it, but it's not the same."

"It's tough. These things are hard, but the failure to act is the toughest act of all to follow. You don't strike me as a coward, but more the kind of guy who doesn't appreciate what it means to sign on. Am I right?"

"Look, I don't know what you want me to say. . . ."

"For Christ's sake, Steven . . . ," Kitty objected as the other guests, some of them nodding in agreement, most of them embarrassed and murmuring, began to move on.

The Falcon, on the other hand, was riveted—oh, he was concealing his raptness well enough, grazing and nibbling, mingling, indulging his penchant for light, insincere laughter, but I could feel his intensity from across the room.

I got the impression he was evaluating my worth somehow.

"Look, I'm not trying to put you on trial here." Having made his point, the senator was trying to reposition himself as having my best interests at heart. "You must be going through hell over this. Jesus, you look terrible. How old are you, anyway?"

"Nineteen."

"Is that all? You look like shit. You've got to stop beating yourself up over this thing. You've got a long road ahead of you. You need to ask yourself these questions for the sake of the rest of your life."

"And Steven, you need to stop this now," Kitty said, sounding firm.

"Please . . ." The note of pleading that I heard in my voice surprised me. "Try to understand. It was hopeless. No one stood a chance, and anyway . . . I didn't think he could drown—"

"Enough small talk. Shall we retire to the dining room?" the Falcon interrupted, smiling coldly, gesturing for the others to precede him. He brushed forcibly against me as he passed by, the corner of his shoulder jabbing me in the chest and briefly knocking me off balance.

"How dare you let that nincompoop speak to you that way, and in my house," he hissed into my ear.

I was astonished. "I thought you'd get mad at me . . . I didn't want to make a scene. Anyway, you could have said something. Why didn't you stick up for me?"

"For the same reason that General Patton never called on his wife to make his case to Eisenhower—stop trying to be all things to all people. I can't make up my mind whether it's cowardice or arrogance that makes you behave as you do. Now if you don't mind, my guests are waiting."

"I don't know about this," I said as the senator's wife lowered herself under me.

I was retreating to my room, walking backward, trying to make my getaway, when I ran into her on the landing of the back staircase off the kitchen.

"Ma Griff," I said, inhaling her perfume as if it were chloroform. Ma would have been horrified to know that she and Kitty Paley shared the same taste in fragrances.

"Shut up!" She put her hand across my mouth.

Somewhere in the cosmos, Bingo was splitting a gut.

Twenty minutes later, I was alone in my bedroom, throwing up into my pillowcase.

Two weeks after the party, I was sneaking into the unused side entrance of Cassowary, tiptoeing by the Falcon's bedroom at four in the morning, when Carlos, his parrot, caught sight of me.

"Son of a bitch!" he hollered, peering out into the hallway.

"Shhh . . ." I put my fingers to my lips. Carlos was a mainstay of my childhood; I felt about him the way Candice Bergen must feel about Charlie McCarthy.

"Motherfucker." He said it as if he meant it, head bobbing, showing off his spectacular four-foot wingspan and cobalt blue feathers. Bingo taught him to swear like a death row inmate, and the Falcon never forgave him for it. Jailbird, Bingo nicknamed him.

I heard my grandfather's voice preceding him around the corner. "What's the racket, Carlos. . . . Oh, I see . . . well, if it isn't the playboy of the Western world." The Falcon, in slate gray silk dressing gown and pajamas, stood in the doorway.

"Hi, Granddad."

"Hi, Granddad," Carlos mimicked as I glared over at him, and he smirked at me in return.

"How kind of you to put in an appearance," the Falcon said, pretending to examine his fingernails. He looked up. "Where have you been all this time? Entertaining the senator's wife?"

He recoiled in disgust. "Good God! Look at you. What rock did you crawl out from under before coming home?"

"I shouldn't have come here. I'll leave." My eyes were trained on the floor.

"Where will you go? That's right. Run for cover. Take flight. There's an answer," he said as I began to back away, preparing to descend the stairs, my hand on the balustrade. He reached out to stop me. I glanced down at his fingers pinching my forearm.

"Before you leave, Collie, I'm curious. Where will you go tonight?

Back to service the lovely Mrs. Paley? She's already run through the entire graduating class at Groton and Andover. Rumor has it you're seeing her daughter, Edie, as well—the possibilities are positively ill making. I've had the senator on the phone every night this week, apoplectic with rage and making threats all over the place. Seems it's a game they play—she taunts him with her young lovers, and he's willing to pimp out his wife and daughter and keep silent about it in exchange for generous support from me for his campaign." He tightened his grip.

"It's not like that. . . ."

"Oh yes, it's exactly like that. I can smell it on you. Tell me. Are you punishing yourself for what happened or are you trying to make yourself feel better? Or are you just living up to the abysmally low standard of performance you appear to have set for yourself?"

"It's not true."

"Well, prove it, then. Pull yourself together. Get over it." He released my arm and took a couple of steps back, as if he were trying to regain his perspective, looking me over as if he were assessing an unfinished painting.

"I can't." I was becoming a sheet of ice that had begun to crack, intricate ventricles spreading soundlessly across a vast and barren frozen lake.

"Don't tell me that you can't when you can," the Falcon said, sounding firm, almost angry. "For goodness' sake, Bing was a lovable boy, there's no disputing his appeal, but he was at the peak of his attractiveness, believe me. The rest of his life was going to be conducted on a downhill slide. He was cut from the same cloth as Charlie and Tom—he was destined to become just like them, eccentric, silly . . . a hopeless drunk . . . Collie, this must be said. The very things about Bing that so amused you in your youth would eventually become the same things that made him intolerable to you. I regret his passing. I do." His voice softened a little as he folded his arms across his chest, hesitating for a moment before continuing. "And it pains me to say it, but men like your brother, Bingo, come a dime a dozen. . . . Well . . . now I see I've made you cry. Good Lord." He threw up his arms in exasperation. "I'm trying to make you feel better."

Was I crying? I guess I was. I touched my hand to my face. My cheeks were wet.

My grandfather always preferred me, made it plain to everyone. His choosing me left a stain that resisted scrubbing. By picking me, he put me on the wrong side of everything—money, power, privilege, love. The Falcon seemed to have no trouble forgiving me for what happened. To him, Bingo was not worth dying for.

I couldn't sleep after my encounter with the Falcon. When the sun came up, I wandered down to the rose garden, took off my shoes, and sat beside the fishpond. The koi, orange, blue, red, and gray, some of them twenty, thirty, sixty years old, swam to the water's surface to greet me, greedy mouths gaping, heads poking out, looking for breakfast. I tossed some pellets into the water—Bingo loved to feed the fish. He gave them crazy names: the Empress of Japan, Tangerine Dreams, Huckleberry Fin. The Falcon's koi had outlived Bingo and Ma, and I was starting to think they accomplished it by swimming around in circles.

The aging koi at swim, the topiary elephants stopped in midtrot, for a moment I thought I saw him there, hiding in the grass, the breeze picking up. He smiled, wanting me to spot him and calling out for me to come catch him.

"How about having a little fun for a change? The Falcon's right, you're getting to be a drag with this grief stuff. Hell, you couldn't stand me when I was alive, and now that I'm dead all you do is moon over me. You're turning into a giant, hypocritical pain in the ass."

"I want you back, all right? You win. You're right. I can't think of you without feeling as if someone has punched me in the stomach. I'm sorry. I'm sorry for being a prick to you when you were alive. I'm sorry I didn't go in after you. Just come back. Come back. Give me another chance."

I looked for him everywhere, but he'd vanished. "Bingo, come out from where you're hiding. I said I'm sorry. I didn't want to die. Now I don't want to live anymore."

"It's okay, I forgive you, Collie."

There he was, standing under the old willow tree on the other side of the pond. I walked toward him. I could feel the tremor of his hands as he spoke. In the light cast from the early morning sun, I saw the events of the past preserved in all their original intensity, and calling out clear as a bird for me to hear was the beating of his open heart.

"Don't," I said. "I don't want you to forgive me. I can't stand it."

For the first time, I felt despair for the future because I knew that for me there was no redemption in forgiveness and so there was no redemption at all.

CHAPTER TWENTY

I WAS AT A SMALL LATE SUMMER GATHERING IN A BOSTON TOWN house that was owned by a friend of a friend. I didn't feel much like another party, but I got talked into it. Everyone agreed it would do me good to get out. Life goes on, Collie, my friend prodded gently. He didn't need to worry about being so sensitive. After the senator's wife, I was on a roll that would have made Bingo blush.

I spotted this girl right away. She had one of those stark hairstyles, graphic ear-length black bob with short bangs, red lips, and white complexion. A glossy pelt in a roomful of dull coats, her conspicuous interest in me glowed like a distant light in the mist—a very red light.

The music was loud. She asked me to repeat my name.

"Can't hear you. . . ." She shook her head and leaned in closer.

"His name's Collie Flanagan," someone shouted in her ear before I had a chance to respond. I reached out and put my hand on her upper arm to draw her even closer, but in the crush of people we got pushed apart before she had time to introduce herself.

I saw her again when she decided to escape to the second-floor balcony of the old Victorian-style brick house for a cigarette.

"Hi," she said, surprised to see me.

"Hi."

"So your grandfather is Peregrine Lowell . . . wow, you must be rolling in it."

I was smiling in an agreeable sort of way but not responding. Pop had a horror of people who ask personal questions, which he's transferred to me. Hell, I don't even ask myself personal questions.

"What do you do?" she persisted.

"Mind my own business."

"Fuck you, rich boy."

I laughed and did up my jacket. It was a cool night.

"Sorry," I said, feeling suddenly embarrassed. "I'm not usually so rude."

"You're the one whose brother died a couple of months ago. I read all about it. Wasn't he hit by a go-kart or something? Weren't you driving?"

I nodded and closed my eyes. "Yeah, something like that."

"Too bad. How old are you?" she asked between puffs.

"I'm nineteen, well, almost twenty."

"You seem younger, and you seem somehow older, too," she said, her voice lowering a few octaves, her descending voice inappropriately intimate. She was sounding like a refugee from an afternoon soap opera, but I wasn't in the market for someone to help me deconstruct Hegel. I shot her an investigative glance.

"I'm twenty-six," she said, adding in a flippant aside, "Hey, I could almost be your mother."

The rain had barely subsided. There was water on the floor of the balcony. The air was thick and moist, wet as a sponge. She'd grown quiet, practically meditative, both of us silently sifting through what was trapped dankly in the vaporous air, trying to determine how much of what was passing between us was the leftover steaminess from the rain, or was it the humid expectation of whatever she detected emanating from me? I was nineteen, so my intentions were about as subtle as a hurricane.

I didn't even bother to ask her name.

We turned the corner in the dusk of the parking garage of her building, and she grabbed me by the arm and pushed me into a corner, into the tight spot where one wall meets another wall, and she was kissing me, licking my lips. She kissed me behind the ear;

she kissed the back of my neck. She was kissing my face. She bit my lower lip. She put her hand on my thigh. I put my hand in her hair. I pulled her into me and lifted up her skirt—was this what it felt like to be Bing?

Someone in the car across from us honked the horn.

"Hey, you two, get a room," some jerk hollered as his friends hooted. I was vaguely conscious of where this was going, of it being somehow inappropriate, but I couldn't seem to apply the brakes.

Bingo did pretty much the same thing and made all the papers. I gave him hell for it. Oh, but typical Fantastic Flanagan high jinks, at least he was in a nightclub, bright lights shining, his high spirits spraying the crowd like an uncorked champagne bottle, blurring what little judgment he possessed.

I might as well have been at the mechanic's having my carburetor inspected. What with the smell of grease and oil in the surrounding air, my back against concrete, the rough edges digging into my shoulders like fingernails, drawing blood and making shallow canals from my collarbone to my waist.

I didn't feel a thing.

Whenever I think of that night, I remember it as a trail of footprints on watery glass. The wet soles of her bare feet leaving their damp imprint on the fire escape door of her apartment building, on the tabletop in the kitchen, tattooed on the inside of the shower enclosure.

It was raining. We were in front of a restaurant. I was with someone new, some girl who smelled like lilacs, someone whose name I didn't know. I called her Lilac. She didn't care what I called her. We were under the marquee, making out in the rain. I was finally able to free one hand long enough to get the attention of a taxi driver. We climbed into the squalid rear of the car, and in the ten minutes it took to get from the restaurant to her hotel, I shamelessly screwed her in the backseat of the cab.

I could feel the shredded ends of the torn fabric rubbing against my knees. I smelled the mildewing carpet. I soaked into my bones the dampness of the air. I was conscious of the driver's wide eyes reflected in the rearview mirror. We left a stain on the upholstery. I paid the cabbie a hundred bucks and told him to keep the change.

The next morning my whole body ached from what I'd done. That night I went out and did it again, only this time it was with a girl I called Lavender. Her real name was Edie Paley.

It was turning into the summer of a thousand fragrances—a perverse kind of aromatherapy. Even now, I can stand, eyes closed, among a throng of women at a summer garden party and pick out individual scents as easily as if I'm reciting the alphabet: L'Air du Temps, Chanel No. 5, Trésor, Youth Dew, Shalimar, Allure, Alliage, Le Dé, Quelques Fleurs.

Rubbing the back of my head, I found a worn spot. It was only mid-August and my skull was dented from too many recent encounters with floorboards. My fingernails were bitten to the quick— my hair was falling out, my inner organs, too, pieces of me were scattered from one end of the hotel room to the other—I couldn't pick myself up fast enough, and anyway, I couldn't figure out where anything went anymore.

Bingo, ever merry in his willingness to believe, was enamored of reconstruction, always trying to refurbish old junk he found lying around the property, refusing to throw out anything; everything had a higher purpose as far as he was concerned.

Pop had his own way of adapting and adjusting to life's little setbacks, insisted there was magic in third-person accounts. He called it *tertium quid*—a third something. He started talking to us about it when we were in our early teens.

"Boys, sometimes this I-slash-me-business just gets you down."

His voice raised an octave as he recited in singsong this confessional litany: "'I drank the Communion wine. I got drunk. I passed out and missed my own mother's funeral. I dishonored my dear wife with other women. Woe is me.' Where does it get you? Try substituting 'he' for 'I' and it sets a lovely distance in place. Not that you're trying to avoid responsibility—just you're aiming for a little breathing room.

"Put it another way: 'Charlie Flanagan stole the money his brother William had been saving for a year to purchase an old car and used it to buy drinks for everyone at the local bar instead.' Do you see the merit? You view your deeds in the cold light of day with no great loss of self-esteem. Your good opinion of yourself is very important. Well, in the end, what else have you got? If I say, 'Charlie Flanagan gave his aunt Colleen a Christmas gift of white bark chocolate, which he then took back and hid in his coat jacket as he was leaving her house—'"

"Did you really, Pop?" Bingo interrupted.

"He did indeed. But maybe he had good reason, which he's not prepared to go into for the sake of an old lady who's dead and whose memory, however complicated, deserves to be considered in respectful silence. Do you see the magic of it, boys? As a species, we tend to go easier on the other guy—at least in public. Make yourself the other guy. People will hurt you, boys. The world compels suffering. Satan is a first-person man. Be kind to yourselves, and always remember God is in the third person."

I reached for Pop's theory as if it were an analgesic; it was worth a shot if it would ease the ache. In the process I added my personal touch, discovering the merit of metaphor as an effective tool for putting distance between me and my misdeeds. My third-person version of events went something like this:

He lay back in the long grass, waiting, eyes closed, almost sleeping, arms at his side, sun on his face, the summer breeze stirring his hair. At first he thought it was the warm breath of the wind, the caress of the long grass, the burning touch of the sun. By the time he knew otherwise, knew what it was, it had him by the throat, had him, shook him violently, and carried him off. Dragged him through grass and ground, took to the air with him, landed with a thud far away, and dashed him against a flat rock. Shredded his shirt, cracked him open from stem to stern, ripped out his entrails, sucked his marrow, drained his blood, flayed his flesh, and tore strips of stringy tissue from his living body.

He opened his eyes. "What fragrance are you?"

"Shut up." Oh, that's right. No fragrance at all—just the ruthless scent of Kitty Paley, or maybe it's her daughter, Edie, or maybe it's someone whose name doesn't matter. He was beginning to suspect he wasn't built for promiscuity.

"I want to revive the dead," he thought aloud. "I want my brother back." He hesitated. "Possibly my mother as well—though that one's up for a little negotiation."

"For Christ's sake," she said, "would you keep your mind on your work?"

His mouth was full of her. He was drowning in bodily fluids, sinking to dangerous murky depths, his pulse ringing in his ears like a plunging diving bell.

"That's for what you did to your brother," she whispered in his ear before leaving.

CHAPTER TWENTY-ONE

THE PHONE WAS RINGING OFF THE HOOK. INGRID CAUGHT IT JUST as Pop was about to hang up. I'd done a pretty good job of avoiding him and Uncle Tom since my sailing debacle.

"Thanks, Ingrid," I said as she handed me the phone.

I held the receiver to my chest, closed my eyes, and took a deep breath.

"Hi, Pop."

"Oh, Collie, Mambo's dead." Pop started to cry. "He was hit by a car and killed. When he didn't come home, your uncle Tom went to look for him and found him by the side of the road. . . . Jesus, Collie, it's like losing Bingo and Mama all over . . ." Pop lost it again.

"What did you say?" For an instant, I felt as if I'd stepped into an empty elevator shaft and I was plummeting. "Oh, Pop. How could something like this happen?"

Ma was fierce about keeping the dogs away from the road, and it was a quiet road—training them as puppies never to leave the property. They all knew better than to wander down the laneway, and among all the dogs, Mambo was the smartest. We called him the Commissioner; he used to alert us when any of the other dogs started down the driveway, rushing to tattle, barking and whirling, jumping up and insisting we follow him, herding the offenders like sheep.

"He's been inconsolable without you boys, not eating, his tail dragging, he's been heartbroken missing Bingo and your mother, and he's been looking for you, too. He's gotten in the habit of waiting at the end of the laneway, checking out the cars, hoping. . . . Tom and I've been after him about it. . . . I've walked that laneway a hundred times in the last few weeks, dragging him back up to the house. You know the way some people barrel down that road and around the curve. . . ."

"I should have spent more time at home. I should have come home. I should have known." I had to fight the urge to keep on repeating the same refrain. I should have come home. I should have come home.

"Don't go blaming yourself, Collie. It's nobody's fault. These things happen. And who's to know but that seeing you all the time might have made him think that Bingo was coming home? Oh, Jesus, to think of Bingo coming home and no Mambo to greet him . . ."

"Cocksucker. Dogfucker," Carlos said as he caught sight of me heading past his perch. That damn parrot. I could hear Bingo's distinctive way of speaking in every word and inflection. Carlos laughed, and I recognized the carefree echo.

He whistled as if he were summoning a dog. "Lassie, Lassie, here, girl . . ."

He sounded like Bingo, but he thought like Ma.

"Collie?" The Falcon emerged from his office on the third floor, and leaning over the banister, he shouted down at me from the landing, "Was it you who tracked mud from the pond onto the carpet in the living room? How many times have I spoken to you about your habit of making a mess wherever you go?"

"Lassie . . . here, girl, here, girl . . ." Carlos carried on until I disappeared from his view, the bathroom door making a dull thud behind me.

"Yoo-hoo. Shit for brains," he said, his muffled final insult.

I went about the business of emptying medicine cabinets, tossing things onto the floor, pills spilling into the sink as I looked for stuff to swallow, all the while I was chugalugging cough syrup and downing vials of dated prescriptions. I even tossed in a little lawn fertilizer and splashes of the Falcon's cologne—it was expensive stuff, terse as marginalia, a redolent memo in low notes of verbena from the desk of Peregrine Lowell.

Just to make sure, I used a razor blade on my left wrist. I did such a good job slicing up one artery, I didn't have the strength to cut the other one.

Despite my finest efforts, felo-de-se eluded me somehow. It was almost funny what happened. Crazy old Cromwell sounded the alarm shortly after I passed out. Jesus, what can I say? The world is awash in unlikely heroes. He dragged me by the shoulder into the hallway and rallied the household.

I woke up a day or so later in the psych ward, and from there I was transferred to Parados House, a therapeutic hideout for privileged lunatics.

I quit talking for the second time in my life. Over the next couple of weeks, I felt myself becoming a solitary outgrowth of volcanic stone, parched rock in the still center of an eerie private universe. I kept saying Bingo's name over and over in my head. I repeated his name the same fearful way obsessive-compulsives wash their hands.

"What in heaven's name is wrong with him?"

I was faintly aware of my grandfather's raised voice, somewhere around me, doctors and nurses nervously trying to appease him. Louder than the people surrounding me was the sound of my own blood flowing through my veins. It made a *whoosh*ing noise in my ears.

I was under the impression I was sitting up until one of the nurses reached around my waist and gave me a lift up. Turns out I was slumped over, listing to the left, my forehead touching the breakfast table in front of me.

"For God's sake, what's the purpose of this pathetic performance? Get him back into bed," the Falcon ordered, thunder and lightning accompanying each word, as a pair of orderlies scrambled to lay me out on the hospital bed, fluffing my pillows, pulling the covers up to my chest, my arms at my sides, my eyes dim and lightless like broken windows. I peered out at the world through cracks in the glass.

"Granted, Mr. Lowell, this medication hasn't given us the result we were hoping for. We're planning on trying a different course of drug therapy," one of the doctors explained. "There's a promising new antidepressant we think may prove effective. . . ."

The Falcon reached down and picked up my hand, holding it limply aloft. He let go and watched in disgust as it flopped back down on the bed.

"That's the best you overeducated idiots can come up with? Another goddamn pill? I don't think my grandson's depressed. Frankly, I'd be delighted if he were despondent. Unfortunately, I think he's dead."

I dreamed about myself as a man, brave, intelligent, hair miraculously straight, confident half smile on my lips, looking faintly amused but all-knowing, as if I had access to some secret denied the rest of humanity. There were women at my feet, children and dogs, other men looked at me and felt jealous, but I was too mature and character-filled to enjoy the shortcomings of lesser men. I was the naked savage.

And then I heard Bingo. He was calling my name. And when I heard his voice, I got confused about my life. Was I a brave man dreaming that I was a coward? Or was I a coward dreaming that I was a brave man?

I couldn't move. Bingo needed me, and I couldn't move. I banged on my thighs with my fists, but my legs wouldn't budge. So many nights I woke with a start, dreaming that he needed me, feeling his hand in mine, feeling the tips of his fingers touch the tips of my fingers, scraping him off of me, thinking better of it, reaching out for him finally, only to let him go.

"Oh, Collie, that much, you hate me that much. . . ." It was so dark, but even in the dark I could see thin strands of chestnut hair hanging down over his eyes.

"Hate you? Hate you? Is that what you think?"

Somewhere outside my reverie I heard a couple of orderlies in conversation, their talk intruding on this dream of my past and future selves.

"What a little prick," the older man said as they lifted me from the bed to the chair. "And more money than God—wouldn't you know it?"

"Imagine if he actually had to deal with life same as the rest of us," said the younger one. "I'd love to see him doing our jobs. Can you imagine him changing bedpans?"

"Life stinks. I'm working for peanuts, driving a shit box, living in a dump, and I've got to bust my hump for him just because his grandfather's a big shot," the older man said as the younger one pulled a pack of cigarettes from his back pocket. For a second, I thought he was going to strike a match on my forehead. Instead, he checked his watch. "Break time. Let's finish him off fast."

He hooked his hands under my arms and signaled for the other orderly to grab my feet as they lowered me back into the bed, where I landed with a deliberate thump.

"Man, if I'd been there that day, to hell with it. They were white-water rafting, right? I read all about it. The brother got trapped under a log or something. I would have jumped in there so fast . . . I wouldn't even've thought about it," the younger guy proclaimed, pulling the covers up to my chest.

The older guy was quick to concur. "Same here, but then that's just me. You know me. You know what I'm like. I don't back down from nothing."

An hour or so later, I sat up, and after kicking off the bedcovers, I tapped the nurse on the shoulder—she almost fainted, kept staring at me as if I'd risen from the dead. I asked to use the phone.

"Uncle Tom?"

"Who's this?"

"It's me. Collie."

"Oh. I'm not speaking to you."

"Is Pop there?"

"I suppose."

"May I speak with him?"

"Oh, so now it's you who wants to talk . . ."

"Uncle Tom . . ."

"I'm not impressed."

"I'm sorry, Uncle Tom, I don't blame you for feeling the way you do . . ."

"And wasn't I the one who gave you the secret of happiness all those years ago when you were a little boy? What did I tell you to do whenever you got upset?"

"You told me to whistle."

"That's right. It's humanly impossible to whistle and feel sad at the same time. My mother taught me that, and she's right. You had the secret, but you made the conscious decision to despair. Shame on you. And what about your uncle William? Didn't he advise you about the French language?"

When I was twelve, my uncle William told me a story. He was Pop and Uncle Tom's older brother and served with the American army in the Second World War. He and a handful of surviving members of his fighting unit prepared to make a last-ditch assault on a German-held farmhouse in France. It was near the end of the war.

"We didn't expect to survive," he said. "We made our plan and put our faith in God and one another and got up and ran directly into the incoming mortar, machine-gun, and artillery fire. Suddenly our only commanding officer started to scream, '*Appel du devoir!*' I thought he had gone mad, but then we all started to holler, '*Appel du devoir!*' as we attacked the house.

"Collie," he said, "I believe that's what saved my life that day."

"You mean the moral power of duty, Uncle William?"

"No! No! Don't be such a schoolgirl, Collie. The French language. Don't you see? It has remarkable powers of inspiration. It provokes one to marvelous feats of courage. Always remember: When you're frightened bolster yourself with a French word or two. The effects are positively galvanizing."

Pop grabbed the phone away from Tom.

"Collie, is it really you?"

"It's me, Pop."

"Thank God. How could you think of taking your own life? Where did your mother and I go wrong? What did we do? How did we fail you? Didn't I always tell you when you're feeling low to say the Hail Mary? I could walk through fire as long as I've got the rosary in my hand."

"Pop, I want to come home. . . ."

"Don't move. I'm on my way. Just the small matter of my train fare and traveling expenses and I'll catch up with you tomorrow. . . ."

The next morning I got up and sneaked out of the clinic, which wasn't nearly as dramatic as it sounds. I called a cab and walked out the front door and caught my ride in the parking lot. I waited for Pop at the local train station. His train came and went. It whizzed through the station without stopping.

Pop got so drunk in the dining car that he passed out and wound up somewhere in Canada, a mining town in Ontario called Sudbury. He came to on a park bench and stumbled into a store on the main street that specialized in hunting and knitting supplies.

"I got out of there fast," he said when I finally talked to him. "This great behemoth in a toque was making plans to go hunting all right. 'You remind me of my dead husband, Squeak,' she says with a toothless grin. Squeak? Well, I ask you."

I decided against the train. I shredded my ticket, abandoned my luggage, left the station, and stepped outside onto the quiet street and into a downpour. Whistling to beat the band, singing the French national anthem, hair in my eyes, my running shoes full of water, I hoisted my thumb in the air and said the Hail Mary.

CHAPTER TWENTY-TWO

IT WAS A LONG WALK TO CASSOWARY, A FEW DAYS, AT LEAST, AND I was in no rush. I wanted some time to think, time away, free from the opinions of the living and the dead. The side of the road was the last place that anyone would ever think to look for me. I spent my first night lying on the broken and weathered floorboards of an abandoned barn.

Brotherless and motherless, but with an oozing excess of father, uncle, and grandfather, my inadequacies pulsing like stigmata, I decided that with the right attitude I could exert some influence over the rest of my life. I needed a strategy. I needed a blueprint, some kind of template that I could follow.

The moon and the stars were visible overhead; the old roof was open in a large gaping part to the black sky. It was there by the silver light of a country night that I remembered Bingo's Man Plan—despite the way I'd ridiculed him at the time, I was beginning to think that setting goals wasn't such a bad idea. In some ways, it made me feel as if he were still a vital part of my life, as if it were a project we shared.

I figured two years would do the trick, a timeline I soon realized might need a little adjusting. Waking up on the floor of my bedroom one afternoon soon after arriving back at Cassowary, I caught a glimpse of myself in the mirror, Cromwell licking my hair.

When you find yourself regularly substituting dog spit for shampoo, successful adulthood seems about as attainable as a gold medal in synchronized swimming.

The two-year plan officially became the five-to-ten-year plan.

My first thought was to approach manhood as if it were a formal design, as if I were tearing down one old building and erecting a more functional shiny new structure in its place. I was taking notes, writing things down, setting goals, and establishing timelines, but I had to face it, I was operating less on doctrine and more on impulse. Like me, the Man Plan was a work in progress, a book I could set down and then pick back up again.

According to my evolving strategy, sometime between the ages of twenty-five and thirty, finally I would be a man. It was a heartening thought.

But to start, I needed to dispose of Collie the boy, murder his memory, and bury him where no one could ever find him, including me.

I'd been back at Cassowary for about a week. First on my agenda was to tell the Falcon that I had no interest in the family business. When I was at Andover, I did a brief co-op stint at one of his papers, the *Boston Expositor*, which was enough to convince me that I wasn't interested in working as a journalist.

"So you're the golden-haired boy," said one of the editors by way of introduction. I got accustomed to their derision. The literary editor referred to me as the Rajah, and the sports department called me Peewee. The food editor called me the Little Prince, and the guys in the advertising department favored a rotating number of preferred alternatives, including Pretty Boy or Poor Little Rich Boy. On the loading dock, I was simply Dogfucker Flanagan.

The editor, Darryl Pierce, had an assistant who was the only person to call me by my real name, and she mangled the pronunciation, referring to me repeatedly as "Coaly."

Despite the Falcon's threats of reprisal, even Mr. Pierce, a reverse snob with a fetish for reminding everyone that he'd come up the hard way, had his own nickname for me.

"Nice to meet you, Shoes," he said, glancing down at my feet. "Never seen it fail. You can spot a rich kid from miles away—well-shod and manicured paws."

He sent me to cover weekly service organization luncheons, nastily making sure the club's senior officers knew in advance that the Falcon was my grandfather, which pretty much guaranteed my being variously but consistently viewed as a potential son-in-law, an investor, a talentless weasel, or the potential target of a kidnapping.

The Falcon was determined that I would one day run his empire. I was just as resolved never to set foot inside a newspaper or magazine again if I could help it. I realized that an adult would quit stalling and tell him. I kept hoping to catch him in a good mood, which might have been comical if it didn't represent such a pathetic stall. At that rate, the Man Plan was threatening to become the Old Man Plan.

I approached the dining room, humming and whistling, trying to pluck up my courage. All sensation was gone in my hands and feet by the time I reached the open doorway, where I paused, pulse racing, feeling as if I were about to inform Satan that I'd forgotten to order more barbecue fluid.

The Falcon looked up from his breakfast, mellow September sunlight filtering in through the open window behind him. He was buried up to his elbows in newsprint; all those dozens of newspapers were stacked neatly on the long dining room table every morning for his avid scrutiny. I swear to God he read every word—the air around him smelled like cordite, smoking with his continuously expressed fury.

"Good God! What kind of imbeciles do I have working for me?" he asked me, holding up the front page of one of his London papers, grease pencil marks scrawled in red all over the page. His favorite trick when he was angry was to write, "Ugh!" in huge flaming red letters, scorching the front page, and have the offending edition hand-delivered to the editor.

Obviously, this was not a happy morning—I lost count of all the "Ughs!" that were visible even from where I was standing. It was like the aftermath of a nuclear explosion, his radioactive rebukes falling through the air, covering every surface, incinerating onlookers.

A vigorous wind blew through the room—lifted the hair from my forehead and scattered newspaper pages all over the floor.

"For goodness' sake, Collie, leave them!" the old guy barked at me as I bent to retrieve the papers. "Why do you think I pay staff? Ingrid!" he shouted. "Ingrid!"

Ingrid appeared around the corner from the butler's pantry. "I'm right here. There's no need to bellow. Good morning, Collie, and how are you this beautiful fine day?" She smiled over at me, calmly ignoring his bluster.

"Never mind the nonsense. He's fine. . . . This mess is what you should be worrying about. What kind of a household are you running? Well, don't just stand there, Collie, with your thumb in your mouth. Sit down. . . . What is it, Ingrid?" His clenched fists simultaneously hit the tabletop, spilling his water.

"You called me, don't you remember?"

"Can't you put on a dab of lipstick and some rouge? Add a little bright color to that pale pudding face of yours? It starts raining every time you walk into the room. And for heaven's sake make an appointment for some hair color. I won't have gray heads in this house. How many times must I repeat myself? And for God's sake speak to the staff about the declining state of their appearance. And tell the girls in the kitchen to buy some decent support garments or I'll fire the whole unsightly lot of you. It's an aesthetic affront. No wonder Collie's lost his will to live, walking around here with that hangdog expression all the time."

"Really," Ingrid said disapprovingly before turning her attention to me as I slid into the nearest chair across from the Falcon at the dining room table. "Don't you listen to him. Collie, it's so wonderful to hear you walking around the house whistling. You're giving the canaries a run for their money. I can hardly believe it after such a terrible dark time. It's like a miracle to hear you happy."

"Thanks, Ingrid," I said, breaking my rye bread into ragged chunks.

"Personally, I find it a little offputting. So what are we to conclude from this little episode—the dramatic escape from the clinic and the contemplative journey on foot back home? Suicide in small doses will either kill or cure you?" the Falcon said, a glass of tomato juice to his lips. He took a small sip and patted the edges of his mouth with the corner of a white linen napkin.

"Such a dreadful thing to say," Ingrid said, instinctively raising her hand to her mouth.

The Falcon's napkin dropped to the floor. "Really, Ingrid, you are beyond the pale. I'm either the most tolerant employer in the world or the most foolish—my God, but you take liberties—"

"I want to talk to you." I cleared my throat, glancing over at Ingrid, who instinctively withdrew, disappearing into the kitchen.

"Why do you preface your intention with such an inane gratuitous announcement? You are already talking to me. Don't dilute your conversation with lukewarm qualifiers. Just spit it out. What is it? I've got a flight to catch." He impaled me with his eyes, sharp and metallic as spears.

I felt my resolve gasp and look around frantically for a place to hide, my brief experiment with manhood collapsing.

"Uh . . . nothing—it's nothing important . . . just . . . well, would you like me to drive you to the airport?"

CHAPTER TWENTY-THREE

POP CALLED ME AT SCHOOL. I WAS LIVING IN A TOWN HOUSE off-campus. It was November 22, my twentieth birthday.

"You're no longer a teenager, make of it what you will," Pop said.

"Well, I guess I should be taking manhood a little more seriously. Today I am a man, or is that next year?" I said, back at Brown in my third year, mumbling offhandedly, phone to my ear as I lay stretched out on my bed. I glanced at the clock on the table beside me. It was almost two in the afternoon—Jesus, what was Pop doing up so early?

"Age is the least of it, and by the way, Collie, self-declaration is immodest."

To Pop, being a good father meant never letting a lighthearted remark go unchallenged.

"I was just kidding, Pop," I said, half smiling at his predictability.

"Oh well, so you say. Just remember, the graveyards are full of people who were just kidding. . . . I know a little something about manhood, and it's not an automatic affair. There are strict time-honored criteria, which you ignore at your peril. To become a man you must undertake a quest. The arduous journey is critical if you're ever to emerge from the shadow cast by your parents, the mother being a particularly tricky business. Simply put, to become a man you must go off into the woods and take your own measure."

"Is that what you did?"

"In a manner of speaking. Think about how all through your life

I've encouraged you boys to stay home from school occasionally, call in sick, take time off work."

"You'd never let us get a job. . . ."

"There you go. Exactly. Absenteeism. Beautiful. It's a journey of self-discovery. Of course, capitalists such as your grandfather encourage attendance in all things, attach moral significance to it, make it an aspect of character in order to ensure compliance and guarantee themselves a cooperative workforce. When a man knows himself through absenteeism, he can no longer be controlled, which would put an end to the world as we know it."

I could hear Tom grousing in the background, angling for the phone and an in on the conversation.

"Tom's driving me mad to talk. Just a minute . . . for God's sake, Tom . . ."

"Collie?" It was Tom. "Do you want to know when I could call myself a man? The day I could freely admit to hating a child, that's when. Do you remember that damn kid down the road, Adam, the porky one, always dressed up like Little Lord Fauntleroy?"

I could hardly forget Adam. Uncle Tom carried on a war of attrition against him and his mother, the Conceiver, for more than a decade.

"The size of the big lump, hanging on to his mother's tit until he was three, diapers sagging in kindergarten, all the while she's telling me he was special, with an IQ bigger than Einstein's. I said to her the only thing oversize on that boy is his—"

"I remember, Uncle Tom."

"The point being that regardless of what men may say, there's no greater hatred in the world than you feel for a neighbor's kid. Cold war be damned. The bottom line is that a real man is full of passions about which he can do nothing."

"That's an interesting perspective, Uncle Tom."

"By the way, real men are never patronizing, and one more thing, a man makes himself useful."

"How do you make yourself useful?"

"Jesus Christ, Noodle. Don't they teach you anything at Brown? You learn to vacuum. . . . When I think how useless you are . . . Say, do you know that a hundred years ago cats used to deliver the mail, and presumably not one of them finished grade school? That puts someone like you in a little perspective. So I suppose your grandfather bought you the Taj Mahal for your birthday."

"No . . . not exactly. Well, he got me a car. . . ."

"A car! You've already got a car. How many cars do you need?"

"It's not as bad as you make it sound. I've got a car at home. I don't have one at school. Anyway, I didn't ask for it. He just got it for me."

"But did you take it? That's the question. You're tempting fate with the way you allow yourself to be pampered and indulged by that devil. It's an invitation to disaster."

Uncle Tom used to insist that devils walk among us. He said you could recognize them by their black hair and blue eyes, their fair skin and bundles of so-called charm. Devils were finely dressed, full of self-regard, and easily distracted by the chattering of large gatherings of birds, according to Tom, who swore that he could smell them.

"Your grandfather fairly oozes verbena," he said. "You want to watch out for him and his gifts. The only thing missing in his case is a forked tail, and how do I know what he keeps in his pants?"

I laughed.

"Look out, Collie. Watch your step. There is a great devil that's turned his interested eye toward you. It's dangerous ground to find yourself on when you're on good terms with the devil. That's just what they count on. Next thing you know, the earth's given way beneath your feet and you're a devil, too."

That night my friends took me out to celebrate my birthday. Hysteria was my drug of choice in those days—my preferred pals the kind of guys who got drunk on laughs, who thought that leaving a pile of steaming dogshit on the doorstep of a four-star restaurant was the height of comedy. Bingo's kind of guys.

It started as a joke, a dumb prank, something to do; it was just me vacillating between despondency and hilarity, finally settling on stupid. We got a little carried away. My buddy hot-wired a rickety old Impala, worth about five bucks tops, that belonged to the head of the English Department, and along with some other guys, two of them hanging bare-assed out the windows, the car swaying and swerving from lane to lane, we drove out into the country, along a dirt-and-gravel road, grinding the tires and hitting a hill so fast that we left the ground. It felt as if we were flying, the car spinning so far out of control that we landed facing in the wrong direction.

The engine smoking, we gunned it, the car lurched forward, and as it was accelerating, fifty, sixty, seventy miles an hour . . . *wham*! A young deer ran right in front of us. We tried to swerve, but it hit the windshield with a dull *thwack*, cracking the glass before being thrown several feet into the ditch at the side of the road.

I struggled a little with the passenger-side door, momentarily jammed by the impact. Reluctantly, my legs wobbly, I walked toward the fallen deer, whose shape was outlined by the light from a full moon, damp breath visibly rising, the air around me smelling of camphor and musk.

Sometimes out walking, playing in the conservation area near home, Bingo and I used to find pieces of deer strewn along the trails, fallen prey to wolves. I never did get used to the primordial jolt of seeing a deer leg minus the deer.

The deer looked up at me, eyes dimly aglow, like a mellow light in a distant room, and then it was quiet, and what happened next was so simple and common, almost a form of domestic ceremony, as if a curtain were quietly drawn, the light disappearing behind it, his view of the world forever obscured.

It was a pretty quiet drive back. I took over the wheel. The car was a mess and barely made it to the campus. I dropped the other guys off at their residence and, rolling into Professor Fuller's parking spot, didn't make any effort to conceal my identity from a couple of overly officious security guys summoned to investigate the missing clunker, their walkie-talkies crackling with self-importance.

Delighted for the opportunity to stick it to Peregrine Lowell's useless grandson, Professor Fuller, called to the scene, sputtered invective about the moral turpitude of debutantes like me, threatened to involve the police, and insisted I be expelled.

I apologized, all but volunteered a nonessential organ, but he wasn't impressed.

"You, young man—and I use the term loosely—embody everything that people rightly despise about rich kids," he said, and pretty persuasively, too. Anyway, he convinced me.

Pop figured I was on drugs. "Think of the repercussions," he said in a late night phone call. "Terry O'Neill back home was an immaculate boy until he started in with pep pills when he was thirteen, and from that point on you couldn't get within a mile of him for the body odor. Eventually, he leapt out a window—that's what they all do."

He was just getting warmed up. I could hear Uncle Tom as usual hammering away in the background, demanding to speak to me.

"Uncle Tom . . ."

"It's unseemly, that's what it is, and your brother and mother not even cold in their graves. Now, look, mourning is a type of parole, Noodle. You need to put in one year of good behavior to guarantee against a lifetime of recidivism. If you give in to all your mixed-up feelings now, you might never find your way back home."

"I'm sorry. I'm sorry. What do you want me to do, Uncle Tom? Tell me what to do."

I was practically begging him, glancing around my living room, taking in the view—my car keys were on the coffee table, my blue jeans were on the floor, my shirt was hanging over the front of the TV set, books were strewn everywhere, my jacket was flung over the back of the sofa.

"It's simple," Uncle Tom was saying somewhere in the background. "I want you to put away your dancing shoes for a while. Concentrate on walking. Just put one foot ahead of the other until it becomes automatic. Start delivering the mail."

As part of my punishment, I had to perform two hundred hours of community service. I was almost happy about the idea of doing something worthwhile for a change; making amends seemed like something I should be doing. Smashing up the car was the last straw, but I couldn't quite figure out what to do, and then I remembered that a friend of mine, working on his doctorate in psychology, ran a suicide prevention clinic at the university.

I'd never had any kind of real job—my résumé was a little thin unless you count perfume testing and the tennis club. After I aced the two-week training course, my buddy reluctantly agreed to let me volunteer as a counselor.

"Just stick to the script," he said. "No improvisation."

My first shift, I was so excited by my enforced quest for goodness that every time the phone rang I pounced as if it were a game-show buzzer and I were in competition with the other volunteers. It was a slow night. Most of the calls were wrong numbers or personal.

"Hey, don't worry about it," said the guy sitting across from me. "Cheer up. There's a full moon coming—that brings out all the crazies."

He was right. The next night, the phone ringing like an alarm bell, I took a call from this guy who was so agitated that he insisted he was going to hang himself. He was crying, panicking, he kept dropping the phone and running around in circles. I could hear his frenzied footsteps in the background, it felt like bedlam on the other end of the line. I could hardly understand him—I talked a long time on the phone with him, trying not to sound like Pop or Uncle Tom.

It was an interesting personal exercise given recent events, me finding myself in the position of persuading some stranger that life was worth living. I don't think I said much of value, but whatever I did it seemed to work. He calmed down and told me he was going to think things over.

The next night, the same guy called again, only this time he asked to speak to me. I spent two hours with him. It was pretty intense. Jerry's statistics were alarming. He was in his midthirties, had no money, no job, no girlfriend, no friends, no education, and no prospects, was overweight, was bald, had only one testicle, was living with his parents, and had accumulated thousands of dollars in credit card debt and gambling.

"The worst part is that I used my parents' credit cards. They never use them, they don't believe in credit. They just keep them around in case of an emergency. They have no idea."

"How much do you owe?" I asked him.

"Fifteen thousand dollars," he said. "Oh, my God, I'm going to kill myself. My parents will lose everything."

"If you kill yourself, then they really will lose everything," I said, wincing at my sudden appreciation for clichés.

"You don't get it. My old man will kill me anyway when he finds out what I've done. I've been hiding the bills and using one credit card to pay off another credit card. . . . What's the use? I'm going to throw myself off a cliff."

This went on for about a week—him calling and threatening to jump off the Brooklyn Bridge or swallow antifreeze. I even had to talk him out of lowering himself into the polar bear exhibit at the zoo, at which point he said he was going to douse himself in lighter fluid and strike a match. Sometimes he'd call two or three times a night, always with a new threat, another inevitably more gruesome method for disposing of himself.

I was running out of tricks and feeling increasingly desperate about Jerry's situation. I was lying awake at night trying to figure out what to tell him.

"There must be something good in your life. Is there anything you like to do? Maybe you can find a way to make your interests work for you somehow—get an entry-level job and start paying back the money."

"Well, I like history. I'm kind of an amateur historian. Ask me anything you want about the Second World War," he boasted. "And then there's sports. I like curling," he said a bit brightly, but his enthusiasm quickly disappeared. "Jeez, what am I supposed to do—get a job sweeping sidewalks? Oh God, my life is a mess."

I found myself nodding in agreement. His life was a mess. What the hell was he supposed to do? I decided to ad-lib.

"I'll give you the money," I told him.

"What?"

"I'll pay off the credit cards for you, but you can't tell anyone."

"You'll pay them off? How can you pay them off? Why would you do such a thing for me?"

"Don't worry about it. It's not a big deal."

"Who are you? You must be my guardian angel. Oh God, I can't believe it. Thank you. Thank you. Thank you." All the while, he was emitting a deep rumbling sound, like a low-grade weather disturbance. Jerry had a few distinguishing personal habits—you could hear every breath he took, and he was always loudly clearing his sinuses, tripping my gag reflex with every snort and honk.

It was embarrassing—all that misplaced gratitude. I came into some money on my twentieth birthday. I used some of it to help dig out Pop and Uncle Tom, temporarily, anyway. If Pop left the house with a million bucks, he'd find a way to come home later that afternoon having spent a million and a half—oh yeah, and he'd be drunk to boot.

The money was from a trust fund established by my maternal grandmother—it was gleefully administered by the Falcon, who could give lessons to the Mossad when it came to interrogation methods. Fortunately, he was hopelessly out of touch—I could have told him that I needed ten thousand dollars to buy a can opener and it wouldn't have raised an alarm.

There was always more money, more money to come, turn on the faucet and money would fill the sink, the rest of my life was just one big money slide and me buried in it so deeply that no search-and-rescue team would ever find me, so rich that I'm a lost civilization.

I would be ashamed to tell you what I'm worth—financially, anyway.

A few days later—so easy, so solvable—debts paid, Jerry showed up at the clinic to thank me. "Anything you want. Just name it. I'll do anything. I'm indebted to you for life."

His face was so close to mine, I could smell an unappetizing combination of churning stomach acids and partially digested hot dog relish on his breath. Jesus, was this the face of charity?

"No. No more debt. You're free. Just enjoy your life. Go curling," I managed to joke, walking him to the door, my attempt at a kind of grassroots redemption rapidly coming unmoored, fallen victim to a failed deodorant and neediness so vulgar, it was its own sandwich board.

"I'd love to, but my knees are in pretty rough shape . . . all this extra weight I'm carrying," he said, patting his stomach. Jerry, at least three or four inches taller than me, was about as big as someone could be without exploding.

"Maybe this would be a good time for you to start making some changes. Lose weight, get in shape, then you'd feel more confident about making friends and getting a job." I was leaning against the door frame, reluctant to offer advice but feeling as if I should.

"I've got the only friend I'll ever need or want," he said with such passion that I was afraid the top of his head was going to erupt and start spewing steam and ash.

I looked down. His hand gripped my forearm so tightly, he cut off the circulation. A tiny silent alarm vibrated in my stomach.

His pressing money worries taken care of, Jerry was now free to obsess about me. He was waiting for me after classes, trailing me to the cafeteria, lurking in the library, calling me at the clinic every night and at home during the day, asking me to come with him to the gym, to a club, would I introduce him to some girls, did I want to go hiking with him?

"I'd like to, Jerry, but between school and volunteer work I don't have time for much else. . . ." I was talking to him between classes, walking backward down the hall.

"Yeah, right, sure. I understand. Why would a guy like you want to spend time with someone like me? It's okay. I don't blame you. We come from two different worlds. You've got everything. I've got nothing. If I were you, I wouldn't want to hang around with me either. I mean, what can someone like me offer someone like you?"

I squeezed my eyes shut, hoping that by the time I opened them I'd surprise myself by knowing what to do.

"Did you say something about wanting to go on a hike?"

"Holy crap, would you slow down? What are you trying to prove, anyway? This isn't the Olympics," Jerry said, sweat streaming down his face as he strained for air, gasping and exhaling windily.

"I'm walking normally," I said a few feet in front of him, struggling for patience. "It's just that if we walk any slower, we'll atrophy."

"Thanks for the cheap shot," Jerry said. "Must be nice to be perfect. Where the hell are we, anyway? Is there some reason we have to set up base camp at the foot of Everest? Ever heard of a nice relaxing stroll?"

"We're in the arboretum at a conservation site. We're ten minutes from the main building. Senior citizens and little kids are leaving us in the dust. What are you talking about? You're the one who begged me to go on a hike. This is a pretty gentle interpretation of a hike."

"I didn't expect to reenact the death march to Bataan."

"Do you want to go back?" I asked him. I stopped and turned around to face him.

"Go back? Easy for you to say, yeah, right, let's go back. What have I got to go back to?"

"I think this was a mistake," I said, speaking over my shoulder as I turned away and resumed walking. A mistake, it was a goddamn catastrophe. I was beginning to think that the only reason people held ivory towers in contempt was that they'd never managed to scale one.

"No," he said, panic in his voice, picking up the pace. "No. I didn't mean it. Did you want to play tennis later?"

The next morning around two or three, I heard this roiling yowl, like a giant tomcat, and someone calling my name. I stumbled out of bed and onto the balcony, and there was Jerry, a BB gun in his hand, threatening to blow his head off if I didn't invite him in.

"Go away," I hollered. "Call me at the clinic."

"Hey!" shouted one of the neighbors, fed up with all the noise. "Can you two girls please keep it down out there?"

Someone finally called the police, and they dragged him away kicking and fighting and screaming my name, hollering something about an apology, I couldn't make it out.

CHAPTER TWENTY-FOUR

FEELING RESTLESS, WITH YET ANOTHER FAILURE UNDER MY BELT, I decided to go home for the weekend. Autumn leaves were falling and the ocean winds were blowing as I walked slowly up the long laneway leading to the house, running into Bachelor and Sykes halfway. Their barking attracted the other dogs, buoyant pack swirling around me like leaves and wind, like so much ticker tape and confetti—I felt as if I were liberating Paris instead of just going home for the weekend.

"Oh, it's you," Uncle Tom said, greeting me from the veranda steps, looking right past me.

"Hi, Uncle Tom." I smiled at him from halfway up the walkway.

"Well, there's stew," he said. "That is, if you still like stew."

"I still like stew," I said.

"May I have more stew, please, Uncle Tom?" I asked. Pop, Uncle Tom, and I were in the kitchen eating dinner.

"No, you may not. I promised the rest to Gilda," Uncle Tom said, referring to his Akita, speaking from his separate table in the corner of the kitchen, a spot he called "the bistro." A rarely extended invitation to join him there was our family's version of the Purple Heart.

"You can have mine," Pop said, preparing to offer his untouched serving.

"No, Pop, I don't want yours."

"It doesn't matter a bit." Pop wouldn't take no for an answer.

"You're not going to actually take your father's helping?" Uncle Tom asked, watching as Pop transferred his stew onto my plate. "What are you? The Dauphin?"

"You try stopping him," I said, gesturing helplessly.

Uncle Tom was shaking salt on his supper.

"Another way you're turning into your grandfather. Remember what your mother said. When she was growing up, her father always received the best cut of meat in deference to his alleged preeminence," he said. "Solipsistic devil."

Now that Ma was dead, Uncle Tom, ever the contrarian, was always finding reason to quote her.

"It was that way with all my friends," I said. "Ma made a big deal of it, but it wasn't unusual. The dad got steak and the kids got hot dogs."

"It's a travesty," Pop said. "The captain of the ship makes the sacrifices. What's happened to our concept of leadership?"

"Need I remind you people that I'm the senior member of this family, and if there's any preferential treatment to be handed out, I should be on the receiving end," Uncle Tom said.

"I think it should be the youngest and not the oldest who gets special treatment," I said, kidding him.

"Say, Tom, news from home. I heard from James today, and he says they had to pull the plug on Gerald, same age as us, imagine. Gives you pause," Pop said, referring to a former neighbor who had a heart attack.

"I don't care what the doctors say; no one is ever to pull the plug on me. Are you two listening? I don't care if it brings Con Ed to its knees, you keep that electricity humming, is that clear?"

"So you want to live like a vegetable?" I asked him.

"Vegetables do fine. Just set me out in the sun and water me," Uncle Tom said.

"Where's Pop?" I asked Uncle Tom the next day, pulling up a chair and sitting at the kitchen table as he stood at the stove and stirred porridge with a big stainless-steel ladle, a semicircle of dogs drooling at his feet. It was early afternoon, and I'd just returned from a long walk on the beach.

"He's out running errands with your new brother."

"My new brother? What's that supposed to mean?"

"You look like you've lost some weight," he said, putting a big bowl of oatmeal on the table in front of me. "You were already too skinny."

I heard the muffled rumble of a car coming up the laneway. I got up and went to the window. My old Volvo was approaching the front of the house, the dogs running alongside and barking. I could see Pop in the front passenger seat, hands waving in animation.

"Who's driving my car?" I said, moving toward the screen door and out onto the porch.

"Collie, see who's here," Pop said, slamming shut the car door, his hands full of shopping bags. "Come give us a hand."

The screen door banged shut as Uncle Tom appeared behind me, and out of the corner of my eye, I saw Jerry in the driver's seat.

"Welcome home, Collie," he said, smirking.

Pop's infamous pragmatism was in an active phase. He'd been using Jerry to drive him around and run endless errands. Leave it to Fantastic Flanagan to exploit stalking as if it were a valet service.

"If he's going to do it anyway, why not make good use of him? You might as well have the benefit of it, if you're forced to endure the headache," Pop said, shrugging, half smile on his face, when he and I were finally alone in the living room. He walked toward the fireplace.

"I don't think you get it. He's obsessed with me, Pop. He's crazy. He follows me, he monitors what I do. He followed me home! How'd he know I'd be here, anyway?" I was standing inside the doorway, a few feet from Pop. I had the sensation my arms were flailing, though when I checked they were calmly by my side.

"I told him," Pop said quite cheerfully, poking around the fire, adding another log to the flames.

"You told him? How did you get involved with him?" I slid down into a beat-up leather armchair, scratched to hell from the dogs.

"He called me a couple of weeks ago to tell me that he was worried about you, and thank God he did. He's been keeping me informed about your state of mind. How else am I to know what's going on with you?" Pop stopped the business with the fire and turned around to face me.

"Pop, you call me fifty times a day! It's not healthy for any parent to know as much about their kid as you know about me. What are you thinking? There's something wrong with him. He needs a psychiatrist." I threw up my hands.

"The only people who need psychiatrists are psychiatrists," Pop said, using his poker as if it were a pointer. "All I know is that he thinks the world of my son, and that's good enough for me. You're probably overreacting because of the recent trauma." Pop's eyes sparkled with tears, and he struggled for composure.

I averted my eyes and gulped—trying to swallow it, the thing that was always stuck in my throat. Sykes suddenly appeared from around the corner.

"What were you up to?" Pop said affectionately as Sykes smiled and wagged his tail and jumped into my lap. I gave him a squeeze, grateful for the reprieve.

Meanwhile, Uncle Tom was circling Jerry, who was sitting warily in a captain's chair in the kitchen, spinning his baseball cap in his hands.

"Say, you don't happen to know how to spell 'lugubrious,' do you?" Tom asked him.

"I beg your pardon?" Jerry said.

"Uncle Tom," I cautioned, walking through the open doorway.

"How much do you weigh, four, five hundred pounds?" Uncle Tom persisted.

"What? You need glasses. Anyway, that's none of your business."

"The day you started blocking out the light from the sun is the day your weight ceased being your private business and became a matter of public concern. By the look of Collie here, you've been stealing the food right off his plate. I knew someone like you back home when I was a boy. We called him Big Fat Liam. We went on a camping trip and got lost, and after a few hours he panicked and wanted to start eating us, beginning with the youngest and weakest. You watch out, Collie, this one's got instant cannibal written all over him. A flat tire on a dirt road would be all it would take and he'd be getting out the carving knife. What is that smell, anyway?" Uncle Tom was sniffing the air, his face contorted with disgust. He disappeared temporarily, reappearing with a can of Lysol in his hand that he began spraying in Jerry's immediate vicinity.

Uncle Tom was always spraying guests with something—he once came at the Falcon with Black Flag.

"Jerry, I'm sorry, but you need to leave," I said, choking back the cloying scent of pine.

"Fine. I can take a hint. I guess I should have expected something like this. I'm not good enough for you, is that it?" His arms were circling wildly like an unhinged helicopter blade.

"I'll answer that question," Uncle Tom said, interrupting. "No, you're not, and that's a scary proposition because God knows my nephew isn't up to much."

"Say, Jerry," Pop said, following me into the kitchen, his tone almost wistful, "before you head out, would you mind picking up the dry cleaning and maybe bring us home a nice pizza pie while you're at it? What do you think, Collie? How does that sound?"

"Great, Pop," I said, so weary suddenly that my bones were dissolving, powder and fragments swimming in my bloodstream, blocking the flow of oxygen to my brain.

"Hold the anchovies, okay?"

Jerry was waiting for me at the front door when I resumed my shift at the clinic later that week.

"I thought you were different, but you're not. You're just like everyone else," he said, using his bulk to maneuver me into the corner of the building, so uncomfortably close that I was being barbecued, marinated in garlic every time he exhaled, his purple face looking as if it were a balloon about to pop.

"It's too bad you feel that way, but you've got a bigger problem than I can handle," I said, squeezing by him as he attempted to block my way into the building.

"It's because I'm not your kind, isn't it? You won't give me a chance because of my appearance and because I'm not your idea of classy."

"I don't even know what you're talking about. What does 'classy' mean? Your appearance doesn't have anything to do with it. Your appearance isn't what offends people, believe me."

"Don't worry, Mr. High-and-Mighty, Mr. Pretty Boy, Mr. Money Bags, you won't have to think about me anymore because I'm going to kill myself. I'm going to drink a quart of bleach—"

"Yeah, right, sure you are. Until they start making bleach that tastes like chocolate milk, I figure you're safe from harm," I said, turning to walk away.

He reached out and grabbed my arm. "Safe from harm—what a joke coming from a chickenshit like you. After all, you're the same guy who stood by and did nothing while your brother died on the train track right in front of you. You just left him with his foot stuck and saved yourself."

"That's not what happened. . . ."

"Whatever. All the more money for you, is that it? Did you enjoy it, you little weasel? Maybe you'd like to come and watch while I throw myself in front of a subway so you can carry on with your perfect little world undisturbed by dirt like me."

"That's not going to be necessary," I said to him.

"Why not? Give me one good reason why I shouldn't kill myself?"

"Because I'm going to do it for you," I said.

It took two guys to pull me off him.

CHAPTER TWENTY-FIVE

JERRY PRESSED CHARGES, WHICH WERE EVENTUALLY DROPPED. He filed a lawsuit claiming millions of dollars in damages, and then he called every reporter in the country to tell them I'd been harassing him for weeks, I'd lavished money on him, tried to buy his "friendship," and when that didn't work I set out to ruin his life.

Looking for refuge from the publicity, I went back to Boston for a few days, but only after getting the all-clear signal from Ingrid—the Falcon was in the United Kingdom on business. He showed up unexpectedly on Saturday in the middle of the night.

I'd fallen asleep watching TV on the sofa in the study, Cromwell on his back stretched out next to me, paws in the air and snoring softly, keeping me nice and warm and compressed, when I heard the Falcon come in. I felt as if someone struck a match on the sole of my shoe, panic crackling through me as if I were a live fuse. Cromwell's tail thumped in recognition.

"Quiet," I whispered, practically begging him to be silent, my hand on his muzzle.

After shrugging off his coat, signature white gardenia boutonniere coming loose and landing just outside the study door, the Falcon twisted off his tie and tossed it over the banister, where it immediately became a matter for someone else's concern. He headed up the staircase and began pounding on my bedroom door and shouting my name.

"What on earth?" Ingrid's door opened.

"Where the hell is Collie?" the Falcon asked.

"Isn't he in his room?"

"Is everyone around me totally useless?" he shouted.

"Collie!" My name his favorite profanity, he turned around and kicked over an antique cupboard in a surprise attack that sent its priceless contents sailing, iridescent cranberry, cobalt, and amethyst exploding into shards of glass like needle teeth to cover the carpet.

Terrified members of the staff crept from their rooms on the third floor, pausing to stop and gasp when they saw what he'd done.

Oh, but he was only getting started.

Cromwell licked my face and curled up alongside me on the sofa, ears pricked, listening to the sounds of dishes smashing in the kitchen. The Falcon was breaking every dish in the house, every plate, every bowl, every saucer, and then he headed up the back staircase to the second floor. I was calling him, but he didn't hear me. He tore apart my closets, emptied the drawers, threw all of my clothes down the stairs, and then he started in on the furniture, pitching dressers, nightstands, chairs, desks, lamps, stereo equipment, even my mountain bike, for Christ's sake—he was murdering every inanimate object he could get his hands on, and frankly, I didn't like the way he was looking at me.

"I guess you heard what happened," I said, ducking as he pitched one of the rival New York papers at me, the story about the lawsuit on the front page. All I could see was the name "Peregrine Lowell" in huge bold type.

"Erotomania? Who is this fat fuck, anyway? Are you insane? Is there no end to the embarrassment you're prepared to cause me?"

I looked up at him from my place on the sofa, stunned to hear him use an expression like "fat fuck"—Jesus, it felt like the start of Armageddon. I was half expecting him to hit me or piss on me or both; he was spinning like a funnel cloud, his skin radiating a color that doesn't exist in the natural world. My hand on Cromwell's broad back, I pushed myself to my feet, recognizing a unique opportunity.

"I guess now is as good a time as any to tell you that I won't be coming to work for you at the newspapers."

Like a giant cobra, he recoiled and struck—my hair blew back off my forehead, he was spitting fury, coating me head to toe in a venomous glaze, shellacking me in his personal poison.

"You're my only living heir, God help me. You've never given me any reason to take you the least bit seriously, so why would I start now? You're Charlie Flanagan's son through and through. Collie Flanagan . . ." He hissed my name, and it made a scalding sound like acid hitting pavement. "And please, spare me the pathetic show of independence. The only way you'll ever amount to anything is if it's handed to you on a silver platter. I'm all that stands between you and a lifetime spent in a padded room fashioning a giant ball out of tinfoil."

Like flames deprived of oxygen, he suddenly vanished, the air still sizzling and sending out sparks, snapping with the improvised electricity of his rage. I put my arms around Cromwell's neck and gave him a hug.

"It's a good thing you're his favorite," Uncle Tom said when I told him what happened.

CHAPTER TWENTY-SIX

By early December, Pop was on the phone and insisting that I come home for the Christmas holidays. I figured it was the least I could do, though I wasn't feeling too festive. My other plan for the holidays was to sit in a chair and stare.

"Where's Uncle Tom?" I asked Pop shortly after he got up. I looked over at the kitchen clock. It was two p.m. on Saturday. I had arrived late the night before and still hadn't seen Tom.

"He's taken Gilda and Nuala," Pop said, withdrawing without further explanation behind his beloved *New York Times*, engrossed in his reading and oblivious, as if it were the most natural thing in the world for someone to disappear for twelve hours at a time while out walking an Akita and a Boston bull terrier.

Tom once vanished for a day and a half trailing his crabby old cocker spaniel Fagan around the island—I was well into adolescence before I realized that other people actually made the decision for their dog about when to end the walk and not the other way around.

Finally, the light from the late afternoon sun burning through the cracks in the blinds, the side door banged open and then shut, and Uncle Tom began hollering out complaints from the kitchen.

"Gilda had no interest in coming home," Tom said, turning on the tap and running fresh water for their bowls. "If it weren't for Nuala finally prevailing upon her to turn around, why, we'd still be out there."

"It's a good thing you're home, Uncle Tom, there's supposed to be a big storm," I said as wind gusts whistled through the brittle windowpanes.

"A storm, did you say?" Pop set aside his newspaper and looked over at me. "Where did you hear about this?"

"Pop, all the weather guys are talking about it."

"Well, there's reason enough to ignore it. Whenever there's a consensus about anything, you can count on it being wrong," Uncle Tom said as he buttered stacks of bread slices for the dogs that surrounded him in anticipation of their daily treat. "I prefer to rely on Gilda. She has an infallible sense of weather, and she doesn't seem particularly alarmed."

"Couldn't we at least take a few precautions just in case she's mistaken?" I asked, knowing better than to challenge the basic assumption concerning Gilda's meteorological insights.

"If you're that scared, there's an umbrella in the front closet," Uncle Tom said.

"Pop . . . ," I implored him to intercede. You know you're truly desperate when you're depending on Fantastic Flanagan for a show of common sense.

"Do we have a fully stocked larder, Tom?" Pop asked, using code to make sure they had enough booze to see them through a nuclear winter.

"Say, what do you think?"

"You see, Collie, everything's taken care of. My, you're becoming a worrier. You get that from your grandmother McMullen. She'd work herself into a frothing fit anytime she had visitors to the house, going mad about every little detail. She was in her eighties and rushing about trying to make everything perfect for company when she lost her balance, tripped, and fell in the bathroom, and they found her with her head in the toilet, drowned, " Pop said, and resumed his reading.

"And don't forget she was only wearing her underclothes when she was discovered," Uncle Tom said, staring over at me, making it clear that I could expect a similar fate.

The bishop of all things great and small, Pop frowned, ministerial crease forming on his forehead. "Collie doesn't need to hear about that," he intoned.

"I'm going out for some fresh air," I said, shaking my head, heading for the porch.

"Watch out for the rain," Uncle Tom said.

The storm struck a few hours later as gale-force winds overturned boats, downed power lines, and bent trees at the waist, leaves blowing like streamers.

"So much for Gilda," I said, unable to resist, sitting next to Tom on the sofa in the living room.

"Oh, she knew all right. I underestimated her capacity for mischief. She's got a perverse sense of humor, but that's what makes her such a challenging companion," Uncle Tom said as the lights flickered out, replaced by candles that lined the coffee table and the fireplace mantel.

"Pop, what are you doing?" I asked as he appeared a few moments later, illuminated by candlelight, an ax in his hands and heading for the door.

"I'm going to chop down the garage," he said, wearing a fierce expression.

"Chop down the garage!"

"Collie, think. We've got an emergency situation here. No power. No heat. We're going to need firewood if we don't want to die from the elements. We need to boil water."

"Pop, don't you think you might be overreacting a bit? Just put on some extra clothes. Things should be cleared up by tomorrow morning. It's pretty drastic to start tearing down buildings and setting fire to them because of a power outage."

"Collie, how many times must I tell you? A man acts—he doesn't react. Is that warm blood you've got circulating through your veins or cold pablum?"

"Neither is fancy enough for the royal Noodle—he's got vintage champagne bubbling through his veins," Uncle Tom said. "Say, will you look at Gilda, grinning ear to ear. She's getting quite a kick out of this. I never knew a dog to enjoy a good laugh the way this one does. She'd tell jokes at her father's funeral."

Fortunately, the wind drove Pop back into the house before he could dismantle the garage. "Jesus, it's mad as the moon out there," he said, cheeks red as his hair, his clothes dripping sheets of water onto the kitchen floor. "I can't feel my hands or my feet. That's not a good sign. Your great-uncle Patrick lost the feeling in his hands and feet and was dead two hours later. Tom, do we have anything in the house that might get the circulation up and running again?"

Within no time Pop and Uncle Tom were going at it, fighting about something Walter Cronkite once said, brawling in the living room, furniture flying, the dogs in an uproar, books sliding off shelves and onto the floor. I rushed in to pull them apart, and hollering louder than the wind, the two of them staggered off into different parts of the house, Pop heading upstairs, Tom reeling off into the TV room, and me left to survey and repair the damage.

Early in the morning, around three o'clock, I woke up with a jolt, instantly alert, the sudden smell of booze making its invisible incursion, rolling in like an early morning fog. Pop was standing over me in fragrant silhouette. A startled yelp and Nuala went sailing off the bed. The toy poodles were hissing and growling, nipping ineffectively at Pop as he bent down, kissed me on the forehead, and then staggered wordlessly out into the hallway.

A few seconds passed, and then I was jarred by the noise of a thump and a crash and a series of descending bumps outside my room. I rushed from my room to find Pop lying at the bottom of the stairs, passed out and bleeding from a bad cut to his forehead.

"He'll be all right," the doctor said. "He's lucky. But one of these days he's not going to be so lucky. Your father's going to kill himself if he doesn't stop drinking. You've got to talk to him about it. Find some way to get him to quit."

I nodded agreeably. I was being polite. Pop's drinking was like an embarrassing relative. We delivered food trays to the attic and occasionally we made a place for it at the table, but we never talked about it. Even Ma had kept her thoughts to herself on that particular subject.

Pop, who never met a subject he didn't like, considered it unmanly, a sign of weakness, practically sacrilegious to talk about highly personal matters, which in his idiosyncratic view included drinking, death, and family planning. His brother William died of cancer, and on his last visit to the Vineyard, the matter of his imminent demise never came up. Meanwhile, he and Pop spent their remaining few hours together arguing to the point of a fistfight about who was a better musical stylist, Rosemary Clooney or Perry Como.

"This nonsense about 'getting your affairs in order,'" Pop used to say. "You can't plan for death any more than you can plan for life, and why would you want to? Uncertainty is what keeps us sharp. And anyway, it's an insult to God. If He wanted us to plan, He would have provided us with an itinerary at birth."

I was alone in the emergency room lounge, waiting for the doctor to stitch up the hole in Pop's head. The early morning sun cast a smoky golden light, visible dust particles floating all around me. I sat on the sofa, my eyes slowly shutting, head tilted back, resting against a grimy industrial green wall. I could feel the warmth of the sun on my face.

My body ached with phantom pain—something was missing, and I knew who he was. Bingo would have found a way to make this mess with Pop funny. I didn't know how to make things funny anymore.

I settled back into the pillows, was sinking into myself, and I was bottomless like a crevasse, but lost in plain sight, same as the frozen dead interred on the slopes of Everest, the sun on their faces, the sun on my face. I wanted to walk right past my frozen remains, leave myself behind as a warning to others.

I must have fallen asleep—I awoke to the light touch of a hand on my shoulder.

"Collie Flanagan, I can hardly believe it. I would have recognized you anywhere. You haven't changed, the same sweet face, the same distinctive expression. You look just as you did when you were in my grade six class at St. Basil's. There always was something different about you."

"Sister Mary Ellen?" I stood up and ran my fingers like a comb through my hair. "What a surprise."

"For me, too! I'm visiting a friend in the hospital, Sister Mary Aquinas—she runs the emergency ward. I heard about your father's accident and I wondered if you'd be here, and . . . well, here you are. It's wonderful to see you again."

"You too," I said.

"Oh, Collie, I was so sorry to hear about what happened to Bingo—he was a pistol—and your poor mother. What a terrible time you've had these last few months, and now this worry with your dad. Shall we sit down?"

"Sure. Yes, please, have a seat."

"And how are you?" she asked, sitting across from me, pulling her chair close to mine, taking my hand in her hand. She was wearing a habit, her medium brown hair visible on her forehead and temples. Her eyes were the same color as her hair. She appeared to be in her forties, although I couldn't be sure.

"I'm all right, really I am."

"Someone told me you were at Brown. I'm so happy to hear you're pursuing your studies. You were the best student I ever taught. What are your plans, Collie?"

"Oh, I don't know. I don't think I have any plans." I was conscious of not looking at her.

"But that's what people your age are supposed to do. Make design on the future."

"I'm just hoping to do better than I have so far, I guess. So pretty modest ambitions, you might say."

"I have a feeling that no one can meet the standards you set for yourself, Collie."

I laughed mostly because I could think of no other response.

"My gosh, you're only what? Twenty years old. Stop being so hard on yourself." She was smiling at me in a kindly way, admonishing me in maternal fashion. "You were so helpful when you were small, such a good little fellow. You always did have a pale and sober and serious heart, even as a little boy."

"I . . ." I stopped. I didn't have a clue how to react.

"Yes. And now you're consumed with the dead, I can see it in your eyes. You need to make them go away if you want to carry on the practical matters of your life."

"I'm okay, Sister." Leaning forward, elbows on my knees, hands clasped in front of me, I concentrated on my shoes. I was trying to deflect her searing intensity. She was determined to get to the heart of the matter. My foot tapped nervously, my knee bobbing up and down. Whatever happened to pleasant chitchat? It seemed as if everyone was determined to take a power saw to my rib cage.

I could feel her appraising me in the momentary silence that followed.

"Well . . ." She hesitated and then plunged in. "I might have an idea for you if you're interested." She gave me a sideways glance.

"Oh?" I was wearing what I thought was a polite expression.

"We have a mission in El Salvador, and we could do with some secular volunteers—in fact, I have a group of college students coming to help out during the Christmas holidays. I could make a spot for you if you'd like. It would do you a world of good. Take your mind off your troubles." She was speaking so fast, I could hardly track her words.

"Me? What could I do? I don't have any skills . . . I'd just get in the way."

"You've a very nice manner, Collie, a pleasing way about you," Sister Mary Ellen said, her voice softening as she fingered the black rosary beads that hung at her waist. "And you're easy on the eyes—"

Her voice cracked, and she dropped her beads and put her hand to her chest like a fan. "I suppose I shouldn't notice, but, too late, I've discovered chastity's not all it's cracked up to be—oh, I'm sorry, I've made you blush—the cure's half-done just by you walking into the room. And you know how to listen. That's a rare thing. Can you drive?"

"Yeah, I can drive."

"Well, there you go," she said victoriously, as if the matter were settled. "We're always looking for drivers. Believe me, if you're able-bodied and willing, you're an asset."

"I'd be happy to make a donation if that would help," I said uneasily, trying to put a little distance between myself and her zeal.

"That would be very nice," she said evenly, clearly unsatisfied and wanting a commitment from me. She put her hand on my knee. "But why don't you try donating yourself? You know, Collie, when I was young and upset about something, my mother used to tell me to scrub the floor. I resented it at the time, but guess what? She was right. Hard work is the answer to most of the world's ills. It takes your mind right off yourself."

"I'll think about it," I said, watching as she wrote down her contact information on a scrap of paper and pressed it into my hand.

"I think you should do more than think about it," she said firmly, almost disapprovingly, as I stared up at her blankly, feeling a bit ashamed to find myself focusing less on her words and more on the vacant territory on her forehead where her eyebrows should have been. "You're a person of rare privilege. You've been given the whole world. Don't you think maybe it's time you started to give a little bit back? You don't want God to regret His generosity, do you? And wouldn't your grandfather be proud of you? Do you think he might be persuaded to take an interest in our work?" Her eyes widened, and she was smiling brightly. It was a look I'd seen many times before.

"Anything's possible," I lied. I wasn't angry or disappointed—well, maybe I was a little bit disappointed, but the feeling didn't last.

I never wanted to be one of those rich guys who spend their lives second-guessing everyone's interest in them.

"So"—she rose to leave—"I'll hear from you, then. Don't let me down, Collie."

I stood up and shook her hand and smiled and said I'd give it some serious thought, and then I popped the scrap of paper into my back pocket without looking at it. I don't think I ever intended to look at it again. I wasn't much of a Catholic.

Pop had a headache but was otherwise okay, chatting animatedly in the car about the doctors, the nurses, other patients, strangers he'd encountered in the corridor. Jesus, he even made a dinner date with the night supervisor. "Sadly, Collie," he said, "life goes on."

When I didn't respond, he said: "No one will ever replace your mother in my heart. I swear to you I will never remarry, if that's what's worrying you."

"I want you to be happy, Pop. It's just that . . ." It was just that I *didn't* want to think of Pop with another wife.

"I know what it is," he said.

His drunken header down the stairs never came up.

"Uncle Tom?" I called out for him when we walked through the kitchen door. Receiving no answer, I dropped my car keys on the table and asked Pop if he'd like some tea.

"Where are all the dogs?" I asked, struck by the ease with which we'd navigated our entrance.

"Tom must have taken the lot of them down to the beach to check out the damage from the storm," Pop said.

The kettle on the stove was whistling when the phone rang. It was one of the neighbors. Located about half a mile down the road, he was calling to report that Uncle Tom was passed out facedown on the beach in front of his house and surrounded by epidemic numbers of dogs and overhead a flock of pigeons circling like vultures.

"Can you come and get him?" the guy asked, annoyance registering loud and clear.

Later that evening, the hospital a distant memory, Pop patched up, not quite as ruddy but characteristically undaunted, Uncle Tom, retrieved by me, out cold in bed, and then Pop and the dogs all finally sleeping, the house quiet and remote, scrap of paper in one hand, the phone clutched in the other, I sat that way for an hour before I finally called Sister Mary Ellen and told her I thought maybe I'd like to spend Christmas in El Salvador.

"Isn't there the small matter of a civil war going on down there?" I asked her.

"Don't worry, Collie. We're in a reasonably protected area. There's a great deal of poverty, of course, but only sporadic violence. The people are wonderful, warm and welcoming. We'll take good care of you. You'll be nowhere near the fray. We haven't lost a student yet," she added cheerfully, "and we've been doing this for a long time. Think of it as a cultural exchange program with dishwashing."

I hung up and leaned back, the old leather chair heaving a peaceful sigh as I contemplated my vacation in a war zone with something akin to relief.

CHAPTER TWENTY-SEVEN

I LIED TO POP AND UNCLE TOM ABOUT CHRISTMAS. I TOLD THEM I was going to spend the holidays with some friends in the Caribbean. They weren't impressed.

"Tell them to check under your mattress for errant peas," Uncle Tom said.

The Falcon was equally disgusted by the truth. I hadn't planned to tell him anything at all, but he overheard me on the phone talking to Sister Mary Ellen.

"So this is some obscure Catholic missionary effort . . . good grief! Don't tell me. Let me guess. They operate a modeling agency on the side. How reputable can these nuns be when they blithely take you on to do what, exactly? Look good on camera and provide them with the highly exploitable resource of my name? You know there is a war going on, don't you? Or has it escaped your notice? This Catholic organization of yours . . . they'd like nothing better than to see you killed so they can wring every last bit of publicity from your battered corpse. Oh well, suit yourself, I'll tell Ingrid to make a spot for your ashes over the fireplace."

He carried on like that for the rest of the morning. For maybe the first time, I realized that despite all the conversations over many years, we had really ever had only one conversation.

The day I was scheduled to leave I went to see him at his office in Boston—I was hoping the impersonal setting might ease our farewell scene. The *Expositor* was his first North American paper, and he still maintained an office at the historic Winthrop building, which he had bought in the forties and where Thought-Fox Inc. was still headquartered.

The building retained a lot of old-fashioned charm, and you could still open and close the windows. "Last time I checked, this was not the moon," the Falcon said about why he resisted modernization. "There is no need to be protected from the earth's atmosphere."

I ran into my old nemesis the editor, Darryl Pierce, when he intercepted me on the way to the Falcon's office. Accompanied by a group of editors, he was on his way to see my grandfather.

"Well, if it isn't Shoes. So are you here to take over? Is today the big day?" he asked me as the others laughed.

"No, nothing so exciting, just here to speak to my grandfather," I said, striving to appear good-natured as half the group fell all over me and the other half ignored me, each faction's conditioned behavior arising out of their own particular set of prejudices.

The Falcon had an assistant whose office acted as a guardpost to his own. I had my hand on the door to her office when Pierce took the opportunity to remind me that I was a parasite.

"And one more thing, Shoes, all this"—he gestured expansively with both arms outstretched, like an evangelical contemplating the gates to heaven—"my entrée into the upper echelons of journalism, wasn't handed to me on a silver platter, you know. I climbed the ladder—every goddamn rung—the hard way. There were no rich benefactors to carry me around on a satin pillow before handing me the keys to the universe. . . ." He furrowed his brow, furry point forming, as I smiled anemically in polite concession to his intended insult.

"What is it, Pierce?" My grandfather unexpectedly appeared at the door, looking austere.

"We had an editorial meeting scheduled today with all the section heads." Mr. Pierce wanly turned to indicate the others, all of them visibly ill at ease, assembled around him. An epidemic of throat clearing and nervous coughing erupted.

"Well, it will have to wait. As you can see, my grandson is here. Marie will let you know when I'm free," the Falcon said. "And by the way, Pierce, straighten your tie. Your position doesn't entitle you to ignore the dress code."

The Falcon's office was modest but attractive. The walls were exposed brick and board and batten and lined with books, including many of his own scholarly analyses of Dickens's work. The original wooden floor creaked as we walked together, and he sat at his antique desk, more typical of a university or a library than a business office. There were two lovebirds in a brass cage, Dennis and Beryl. They were a Christmas present from Bing and me when we were kids.

"So how may I help you?" he asked, folding his hands in front of him on the desktop.

I sat across from him. "I'm not happy about how things went the other day at the house, and I wanted to say good-bye. I'm leaving tonight."

"I prefer that you not go," he said, picking imaginary lint from his lapel.

"I know, but I'm going."

"Why?" He raised his voice—his imperial voice. The one that was used to issuing commands and having them obeyed. "You've never demonstrated the slightest interest in politics or world affairs or the plight of your fellow man. Is this some sort of misguided tribute to your mother, who, by the way, was not a serious student of the world?"

"Don't you think I know that? I don't pretend to be Albert Schweitzer."

"I think the appropriate comparison is to Michael Rockefeller."

"Look—" I leaned forward in my chair. "Nothing bad is going to happen. It's all being supervised. It's just like a foreign exchange program. I would think you'd be happy that I'm doing something serious for a change."

"There is a considerable difference between making an informed choice to undertake a difficult journey and stumbling into a war zone as if you were some sort of privileged pop star on an adventure holiday."

"Is it so wrong to want to see what I'm capable of? Maybe I just want to do something good for a change."

"Oh Lord, that's what I was afraid of," he said, sitting back in his chair and looking skyward, his arms folded at his chest. He was getting angry. He picked up a paperweight and banged it back down again on the desk, making a loud boom. "You're obviously being manipulated by this nun. Ask her to show you some evidence of God's interest in good works—and don't settle for some damn quote from the Bible. From what I've observed, He's just like the rest of us, preoccupied with sports and Hollywood and keeping Elton John happy."

"I'm not here to argue with you. What do you want me to be? Some useless rich kid who everyone thinks is a coward? Maybe they're right. I've got to do something. I don't want to wind up thinking of myself as one of those guys on the *Titanic* who wouldn't give up his seat on the life raft for some little kid." I was sounding a little desperate, my veneer of calm rapidly cracking.

"Collie, stop romanticizing things—you're embarrassing yourself. These are not legitimate questions. Most people won't even surrender their seats on the bus to a paraplegic, let alone sacrifice their lives in an emergency at sea."

"What's the use? I don't know why I thought I could talk to you. You're not listening to me. You never have and you never will." I stood up to leave. "I'll see you when I get back."

"Sit down. This discussion is far from finished. You have no experience, no knowledge, no insight into the culture, nothing to offer, no way to protect yourself. You can't speak the language. . . . You don't know a thing about what's going on down there." He stood up and leaned across the desk, waving his hand in front of my face. "These supposedly disinterested Catholic organizations are up to their eyeballs in it—"

"I know enough. I'm not going to be on the front lines. I'm just helping out around the convent for a couple of weeks. Take it down. You're way overreacting." I was getting a little hot under the collar myself.

"For your information, there are no front lines. Pardon me if I'm a little intense. We're dealing in absolutes here. Do you get that? I'm trying to preserve your life, you know, that tenuous ephemeral thing that can be snatched away in an instant, never to be retrieved . . . the thing you're so anxious to throw away. The thing that Bingo lost in a similar lapse of judgment. How badly do you want the infinite to kick in, Collie? How many miracles do you think you get?"

The Falcon's long-term assistant, Marie, appeared in the doorway.

"Mr. Lowell, I can hear you down the hall," she said. "The others are starting to take notice. Is everything all right?"

"Let's run this past Marie, shall we?" the Falcon said. "Collie has decided he's going to jump on a jet and go to El Salvador for the Christmas holidays."

"Oh no, Collie, you can't be serious," Marie said. "What does your father say?"

"He's okay about it," I said, feeling uncomfortable about lying. Withering a little under the attack, I was aware of sounding adolescent and defensive.

The Falcon threw up his hands. "Oh well, then, that's different. Why didn't you say that in the first place? That would have been a hard-fought and -won endorsement, because as you know, your father is always so thoughtful in his decision making. What did you do? Leave a message taped to the fridge? 'I'm off to El Salvador to get killed. Don't worry, I won't embarrass the family. I plan to die with my Oxfords on.' "

Sensing emotions were escalating beyond the scope of her pay grade, Marie made a discreet exit, scurrying back into her office.

"I'm not looking for your permission. I'm telling you what I'm doing. Take it or leave it. As for me, good-bye, I'm going away now," I said, searching distractedly for my jacket. "I'll call you in a few days."

"Collie, you haven't a clue what's awaiting you. You think because you've had a rough time of it these last few months that you're equal to whatever happens. You can't even defend yourself against the critical views of others. You're a babe in the woods, and the woods are full of nasty surprises that make your losses seem like a walk in the park." He paused to regroup and try a different tack.

"Do you understand human nature? Are you in any way prepared for the evil that men do? Nothing surprises me. Nothing anyone does will ever surprise me. I worked for a time as a war correspondent for one of my father's papers. I once saw a ten-year-old girl shot dead deliberately by an Allied sniper as she drew water from a well in a French village. And we were the good guys. Tell me that Mother Teresa has been eating orphans in Calcutta and my only response is to wonder if she prefers them poached or scrambled."

"But can't you understand, I need to find out these things for myself. What am I supposed to do, piggyback on your experiences and live off your wealth?"

"It sounds like a reasonable choice to me—why else accumulate money and power except to insulate your children from the world's evils? If I'd wanted my grandsons to see war, I would have relinquished my fortune and taken a job in the press room."

"For the last time, I'm not going to war. I'm just driving some nuns around a village for a couple of weeks. I'll be fine."

"Please, Collie, don't go." The Falcon sounded almost pleading. He walked toward me. He reached for my arm. "Don't do it. It's no place for amateurs. If you go, there is a good likelihood that you won't come home."

He made a unique supplicant. I almost gave in. I wanted to give in.

"I'm sorry," I said.

He let go of me and rubbed his face with his hands, dropping his arms suddenly to his sides. He walked over to the window and sat in an armchair next to the birdcage.

"All right, I can't stop you, but you must listen to me. Promise me you will trust no one. Remember, Collie, you can't trust anyone." He leaned forward in his chair, lending emphasis to his admonition.

"Except friends and family," I qualified, confident in my response.

"No one!" he repeated. He wasn't kidding.

"But your family . . ."

"Especially not your family." He was reacting with spectacular annoyance to my naiveté.

"What about you?"

"Not even me," he said, sinking back into the chair.

I thought he was exaggerating to make a point. I assumed it was his way of urging caution. That was before I realized I couldn't be trusted, I couldn't even trust myself. I didn't understand that life consists in hidden possibilities and unknowable motives and that steadfastness of character exists, if at all, between episodes of private discord.

"Well . . ." I was hemming and hawing at this point. "I should get going."

"All right," he said, rising back up to his feet, decorous and formal, as if he were extending courtesies to a junior officer.

He extended his hand. We exchanged a brief glance, and something that I saw in his eyes made me come in closer. I kind of extended my arm around his shoulder—call it a half hug as opposed to a halfhearted hug. His forehead flushed crimson.

"Yes, well," he said. "You don't want to be late."

"I'll see you again soon," I said as he sat down and picked up his reading glasses and began to examine the documents he'd set aside.

"Hmmm . . . ," he muttered in acknowledgment, head bent over, not looking at me as I walked away, backpack thrown over my shoulder.

I don't know which was more memorable—the day I realized that Ma didn't love me or the moment I realized the Falcon did.

Outside on the street, the air was cold. The snow mirrored the sun, and the snow was everywhere. There was so much light, I could hardly see. The rush of the winter wind filtered through the thin, loose layers of my clothing, wedging itself like an ice pick deep in my bones.

The Falcon's words terrified me, but I was going. I didn't know why I was going. I didn't know what I was thinking. I was just going. I wanted a change of scenery, but that wasn't it. It was nothing I could explain even to myself. It was something I needed to do, take a hatchet to my life and hack away at it. Maybe if I went away, when I came back it would all be somehow different. I would be different. In those days, I thought that life was a point system, and occasional planned acts of goodness would somehow help balance my wildly skewed scorecard.

Each step I took away from the Falcon's building was accompanied by an urgent crunching sound, another perilous crack in the glass. I don't like the cold. I have this indelible image in my mind, left over from when I was a kid in a grocery store. I saw a little boy about my age, his tongue stuck to the bottom of a can of frozen orange juice, and I just stood there, not knowing what to do, just waiting for something to happen.

I wondered what the temperature was like in El Salvador.

"Excuse me, sir." The stewardess touched me on the shoulder. "Sorry to wake you."

"That's all right," I said, straightening up in my seat, glancing out the window to the gathering lights below.

"Please fasten your seat belt. We'll be landing soon."

"Okay. Thanks." I smiled and watched her walk down the aisle toward the cockpit, her perfume a thin trail of scent wavering in the air like the surrounding white cirrus clouds.

I turned my attention to the glimmering ground below, my first luminous sight of El Salvador. It was 1983—the year of my so-called revolution.

CHAPTER TWENTY-EIGHT

A YOUNG GUY, BETO CRUZ, OLDER THAN ME—IN HIS THIRTIES, I guessed—met me at the airport in San Salvador. He had dark hair and eyes and was emanating intensity from across the scuffed miles of linoleum that separated us, holding up a makeshift sign with CALY FLANAGUN written in black Magic Marker.

His English was fluid, and he spoke with almost no accent—turned out he had lived most of his life in Canada with his mother. He'd been home for only a few years.

"You'll be staying in a hotel tonight here in San Salvador, and then tomorrow we'll drive to the Pacific coast. I've got something I want to show you," he said as we drove, me riding shotgun in an old VW van, his arm stretched across the top of the seat, fingers almost touching my shoulders.

"Oh, I thought we were going to . . . Where's the convent? In the north?" I said.

"Yeah, yeah, it's on the way. I'm taking the scenic route," he said, smiling, lighting up a cigarette, the tips of his fingers stained with nicotine, looking away from the road and over at me. "Well . . ." He laughed nervously. "We're going to go north, but first we're going south—just a few hours out of the way. I'm a documentary filmmaker, and I figured you might be interested in my work concerning child labor. The nuns are into it big-time, and Sister Mary Ellen thought it would be good for you to see what's going on here. And who knows? Maybe you get a little interested yourself. Maybe you want to help. We could use all the help we can get."

"Sure," I said, chewing my bottom lip, trying to be upbeat, though I was feeling less certain than I sounded.

The car pulled up in front of the hotel, and even though it was nighttime there were hundreds of people on the street, crisscrossing our path. I was looking for a gap in the steady flow and stepping away from the curb, luggage in my hand, when I was stopped in my tracks.

A stranger approached me, came out of nowhere, walked right into me, bumped my chest with his chest, then took two quick steps back so we were facing each other. He raised his hand to my forehead, his hand took the shape of a gun, his forefinger touched the spot directly between my eyes, and he made a muffled sound, a popping noise, what kids do when they pretend to shoot someone. Lowering his arm to his side, he disappeared into the steamy surge of human traffic.

"What was that all about?" Beto said, catching up to me. "Hey, let's go. You can make friends later."

"Yeah, okay, that guy surprised me, that's all." My heart was pounding, gut churning—I felt all these miniexplosions going off inside me.

"Good thing it wasn't real," Beto said as we stood inside the elevator on the way to the top floor.

I nodded, marveling that in a country where guns were as common as fingers, I had encountered the only pretend pistol. The adrenaline rush finally subsided, but for the first time in my life, I was conscious that a silent bang and an imaginary gun, made of human thumb and forefinger, can be almost as terrifying as the real thing.

Trundling along in our beat-up van early the next morning, I was looking around, trying to acclimatize myself to all the brilliant colors—the trees, the houses, the sky overhead. We'd traveled about thirty miles when Beto pointed to a rocky field, a body dump where the government routinely abandoned the corpses of murdered citizens. By midmorning, deeper into the mountainous countryside, I was shocked to see dead bodies along the side of the road, rotting under the sun, hands tied behind their backs, the stench filling the car. There was a young man wearing blue jeans. He was bare-chested, and his arms were extended out from his sides. His head was missing. I wasn't able to figure out whether he was lying on his back or his stomach. I couldn't help but look and look and look. I was repulsed, but at the same time I wanted to see as much of death as I could. The only other bodies I had ever seen were Ma and Bingo, and their deaths hadn't looked like these.

Pulling my shirt collar over my nose, I signaled Beto to pull over. He stopped the car, and I leaned out the open door and retched onto the side of the road.

Beto waited patiently and then restarted the engine. "Anyone caught burying the dead risks getting killed himself."

"Is this a good idea?" I asked, sitting on my hands to conceal their shaking. "Should we be traveling around like this?"

"Sure. Why not?" he answered me, his eyes on the road ahead as an oncoming car, swerving dangerously, deliberately veered to hit a duck in the middle of the road. It was chaos on the roads, and every once in a while we'd encounter a group of people walking and Beto would dutifully roll to a stop and offer them a ride, all of them piling into the back of the van, some reaching over into the front seat, offering their firm handshakes in greeting.

Wet and hot, it was early afternoon, I was sweating, hair pasted to my forehead, the fabric of my shirt catching on the car's torn vinyl upholstery as we bumped along rugged dirt roads, passing coffee farms and sugarcane fields, stopping occasionally to let the overheated van cool, a Baltimore oriole, reassuringly familiar, singing in the trees overhead, a nice change from the clucking of chickens. I was hearing roosters crow in my sleep.

"Where are we going?" I finally summoned the nerve to ask.

"Don't worry. Everything's okay." He sipped water from a thermos as I eyed him with suspicion. He grinned back at me and slapped me on the upper back. "Hey, man, where's your sense of adventure?"

We both looked in the direction of the mountains, distracted by the muffled exchange of automatic gunfire not so far away.

"I don't have a sense of adventure," I said.

"Jesus Christ, I hope you can swim! Hold on."

I was sitting alongside Beto, both of us soaking, huddled together on a wooden bench in an aging fiberglass outboard. I nodded and wrapped my arms around my chest, my knees jumping as I tried to stop my teeth from chattering.

"Yeah, I can swim," I said, taking a look around—surrounded on all sides by the Pacific Ocean.

It was a little past dawn. After spending three sleepless nights in the van in a tiny fishing village, the locals scrupulously avoiding eye contact, we were heading out to a fishing platform where kids from the area villages were forced to net fish eighteen hours a day, seven days a week. Starved, bullied, threatened, and even sexually abused, they were at the mercy of thieves, storms, and natural predators. For respite, there was the war.

By using my money to bribe foremen over the last few days we were able to do some limited filming aboard the leaky platforms, as they wavered back and forth on shaky stilts battered by the wind and the waves.

But now we were on a different mission. Beto and I and a handful of foreign Catholic aid workers were making the journey by boat to film the rescue of some of these underage child workers.

"Don't worry, Collie," Beto said in a reassuring manner I'd come to distrust. "It's all arranged. It will be smooth as silk."

The shore birds circled noisily overhead, blurry and overexposed, banking in the strong west wind. Waves were washing over the boat, and I was on my knees, clinging to the sides. I leaned over the side of the rickety boat and threw up into the water.

"Are you sure you're not pregnant? Pull yourself together, Collie, or what the hell good are you?" Beto said as another ten-foot wave washed over us. He looked like a pillar of salt, his hair white and stiff and standing on end.

I was in over my head, the executive part of my brain relinquishing power to a terrified intern. The water smelled briny, the boat reeked of fish and gasoline, my clothes stank—I was experiencing El Salvador as if it were an olfactory hallucination, minus the hallucination. The aid workers' boats had already pulled up alongside the platform, and they were shouting out their intention to come aboard. Beto was filming, and I was handing him equipment as the fishermen waved their arms and screamed threats and swore.

Some of the younger kids were crying. One of the platform workers grabbed a small boy by the hair and dragged him to the edge of the wooden deck; the boy was maybe eleven or twelve years old, skinny, his arms and legs covered in bruises and sores.

The man picked up the boy, arm around his waist, bent him almost in half, and lifted him two or three feet off the ground. The boy was crying loudly, and the man was threatening to throw him overboard if we didn't leave.

We moved our boat closer—I maneuvered until we were positioned right next to the man and the boy, just beneath the corner of the platform. All around was shouting, screaming, crying, when the platform worker made a sudden violent move and threw the boy in the water, and two of the aid workers jumped in after him, all three of them disappearing below the water's surface.

I heard a low laugh, almost a growl, and looking up caught sight of a platform worker appearing like a toothless grin just above me. He made a wind-up motion with his right arm, hurtled something my way, and I felt a heavy wet thud in my lap.

"Holy shit!" I leapt to my feet, jumping backward, colliding with Beto, who kept right on filming. A sea snake slid from my lap onto the floor of the boat, recoiled, and struck out at the air, curled back in on himself, and shot forward, biting the camera's strobe arm. I was so scared that I couldn't even close my eyes.

"For chrissakes, Collie, dump that thing overboard!" Beto yelled as the adult workers on the platform pointed and laughed.

I intuitively reached for one of the oars and used it to poke and prod the snake until he wrapped himself around the end of the paddle. He kept biting into the wood, his mouth open wide enough to swallow a soup bowl, and I tossed the snake and the oar over the side and into the water. A warm, thin trickle of piss ran down my inner leg.

"Let's get out of here!" the cry went up among the aid workers in the other boats, the little boy safely aboard.

A mournful wail ensued as a handful of older boys—sixteen, maybe seventeen years old—clapped and waved over at me, calling for help. It was clear they wanted to come away with us. I sank to my knees in the bottom of the boat.

Shaking so much I felt as if I were coming apart, I forced myself to take one last look behind as our boat churned away.

"Well, we got one of them out of there, anyway. Too bad about the others," Beto was saying as he fiddled around with different camera lenses. "The sea snake was a nice touch, don't you think? . . . Hey, are you all right? You look as if you've seen a ghost. You've got to toughen up, Collie, or you'll be no use to anyone."

I shook my head and pawed at my ears. His words were muffled—it was as if I were listening to him from beneath a waterfall.

"When are we going to the convent?" I asked.

He appraised me for a moment and sighed. "Tomorrow," he said. "We'll leave in the morning."

"I'm sorry," I said. I was nodding gratefully, thinking that if I could only get to the convent, everything would be okay.

"Quit apologizing," Beto said, registering a mix of contempt and pity. "Where the hell do you think you are, anyway, at a fucking dance recital?"

Ma once accused me of treating life as if it were a dance recital.

Six nuns, four of them Americans including Sister Mary Ellen and two Canadians, came out to greet us when we arrived in the tiny village of Adora a couple of days later.

"Hello, hello!" They were very happy and hugged and kissed us—I remembered something that Pop once said: "Nothing like squalor and suffering to cheer up a nun."

The sisters, along with a couple of secular aid workers, lived in a pink-and-tan house made of adobe and mud. Tin sheets and cardboard covered the roof. Everything was makeshift. Most of the people in Adora lived in shacks constructed of wood and plastic.

"So has Beto been a good travel guide? Showing you all the sights?" Sister Mary Ellen asked me, as if we'd arrived for a long weekend in Palm Beach, linking her arm in mine as she led us inside the house. There were three rooms, including a bedroom and a rudimentary kitchen, along with one big living area that had a worn sofa with springs poking through polyester fabric and a couple of metal chairs. Dishes and books were stacked on a long table with a bright green shiny top.

"Where's the bathroom?" I asked.

"Outside," Sister Mary Ellen said. "I'm sorry it's not what you're used to, Collie."

"It's what I'm getting used to," I said, not meaning a word of it.

"If you want to get cleaned up, then you should head down the road to the spring where there's a plunge pool. But be careful not to swallow any of the water. You might want to plug your nose, too, as an added precaution. Lots of little thingies that could cause you problems," she said, laughing.

"Here's where you'll sleep—" A young nun pointed to a hammock in the main living area.

"Thanks," I said as Beto put his stuff in the corner and caught my backpack as I tossed it to him. I could hear tropical birds calling to one another outside the open windows.

"It seems pretty quiet around here," I said.

"What did I tell you?" Sister Mary Ellen said, offering me a glass of lemonade.

"Where are the other students?" I asked her. "You said there was going to be a group of volunteers."

"Oh, they're in different places. Most of them are with the priests in the south and a couple of them are with us, but they're a couple of miles out, living with a farmer and his family, helping to dig a new well."

The next morning, Beto and I met some of the villagers—everyone was friendly, and all the little kids followed us as we walked among their homes, tiny one- or two-room shacks without plumbing or electricity or appliances. Whole families slept on plastic sheets laid out on the floor.

One girl, maybe nine or ten years old, with black hair and black eyes, followed me around most of the morning. I gave her a twenty-dollar bill. Her eyes widened, and tears ran down her cheeks. She hugged me and ran, crying out for her parents. I made up an excuse and went back to the little house where the nuns lived, knowing it was empty. It took me a while to pull myself together. I never want anyone to look at me that way again.

After lunch, Beto and I drove Sister Mary Ellen and one of the aid workers, a girl named Sandy from Philadelphia, out to the farmer's house. We joined the other volunteers, two engineering students from Northwestern who were helping dig the well. They handed us a hammer and nails along with some flimsy wood and a roll of chicken wire. I caught them exchanging a look—their skepticism about my abilities was obvious.

"Nice manicure," one of them said as Beto laughed.

I spent the next few days helping to design and build a chicken coop and did such a good job that I won them over. I got lucky those first few days getting the chicken coop assignment. When I was a kid, I helped Uncle Tom build an elaborate loft for the pigeons—this was a snap by comparison.

When it was finished, the farmer and his wife and kids gave me an egg laid by one of the hens. I held the brown egg in the palm of my hand, and its warmth spread throughout my entire body. So this was what it was like to be good, to feel goodness in every part of you—for those few days, I thought I had found what I was looking for in the rough shape of an El Salvadorean egg.

Five days later, the village and the mission were attacked by government militia wanting to teach the nuns a lesson. Sister Mary Ellen and the two Canadians had flown to Bolivia for a conference. They were due back the day of the attack. I was getting ready to go to the airport to pick them up when we got hit with the shrapnel from a mortar shell that exploded near the car.

Beto jumped into the jeep alongside me, and we sped away, abandoning the car when it ran out of gas.

We walked for two days, when I again heard the sounds of helicopters overhead strafing the fields and villages, and we were back up and running. Some guy I didn't know had a hold of one of my arms. Beto grasped my shirtsleeve. Sandwiched between them and along with hundreds of villagers, I fell to the ground and started to climb the steep mountainside on my hands and knees.

Volcanic rock crumbled and gave way; my fingers were stained the same caramel color of the rock, blood beneath my nails. The sky overhead was a brilliant blue and cloudless. There was a warm breeze, lime and orange trees waving on the surrounding green hills, bodies like tumulus beneath them.

"Keep moving. Keep moving. Don't stop," Beto said as guns from the helicopter raked the ground in front of us, behind us, to either side of us. A chicken appeared from nowhere and landed on the stranger's shoulder, pecked the top of his head. He was trying to swat it away, but he couldn't budge it; the two of us and Beto were laughing like crazy, tears streaming down our cheeks.

Seems like all I did was laugh, I was aching from laughter, couldn't breathe, it hurt to laugh.

"Stop, you're killing me," I said.

The chicken abruptly lifted off, clucking, wings flapping, and the stranger was on his stomach, not moving, he was perfectly still. He looked like laundry, like clothes left out in the sun to dry.

"Don't stop, Collie," Beto said.

"Laughing?" I said as I kept moving up the mountain.

A few days later, on Christmas Eve, we were able to connect with another group of Catholic aid workers, when five government militia types wearing identical mirrored sunglasses stopped us at a checkpoint outside of a small village in Chalatenango, which was mostly under guerrilla control.

They pulled me off the back of the open truck, wanting to do a visa check. The others were ordered on their way—Beto put up polite but vigorous argument, but nobody wanted to listen. I was struggling to understand what was being said. After some discussion, they emptied my pockets, took the money from my wallet, and when I objected they shoved me, pushed me around a bit, and tossed me in the backseat of an old Chevy, locked the doors, and sped off. I looked behind me and saw Beto standing in the middle of the road, watching. I never saw him again.

"What are you doing with me?" I tried to speak with more confidence than I felt.

"We're taking you to the airport. You're going home today," the guy who appeared to be in charge answered me in heavily accented English.

"Why?"

"Visa's expired."

"No, it hasn't—" I stopped myself. I wanted to go home, but I wasn't sure they were telling me the truth about going to the airport.

"Expired visa or you expired. Makes no difference to me. You choose."

Pleased with his wit, he turned and translated for the others, who laughed. I laughed, too—inappropriate laughter had become my stock-in-trade, though I wasn't feeling very funny. It wasn't good to disappear in El Salvador.

Twenty minutes later, we spotted a burning bus on its side stretched across the narrow dirt road. Our driver scratched his head and asked what he should do.

"Well, what else can you do? Stop," said the wit. He ordered me to stay put as the car came to a slow halt and he and the others, weapons drawn, got out to assess the situation.

I heard a series of loud bangs, and the militia guys went down like bowling pins, some wounded and the others dead. I felt a fiery pain in my left thigh—glass from the window of the car. Guerrillas, too many to count, emerged in waves from the surrounding jungle and converged on the car. Shooting the sky, they jumped on the hood, kicked the doors, and some enormous guy picked up a huge rock and tossed it into the center of the windshield. Glass shattered as the rock landed next to me in the backseat.

I was dragged from the car, knocked to the ground, and struck in the head with the butt of a semiautomatic weapon. For a minute I saw stars, then my vision gradually cleared. A young guy about my age stood on top of me, grinning.

He nudged me in the hip with the muddied tip of his boot. "So what are you doing here? Saving the world?"

"You're an American," I said.

"No, but I grew up in Los Angeles, lived there with my grandparents. I got sent home when they died. What are you doing with these guys?"

"I got picked up at the last checkpoint. They were taking me to the airport, sending me back home. . . ."

"Why?"

"They said my visa had expired."

"Sounds like a bullshit story to me."

"I'm telling you the truth."

"You an American?"

I nodded, squeezed shut my eyes, and held my breath.

"What are you doing in El Salvador? You with the CIA?'

"No. I'm a volunteer at the Catholic mission. I'm supposed to go home in a few days."

"The mission that got attacked?"

There was a crowd of angry faces staring down at me. It was quiet but for the moaning of the wounded and a long, low hiss, the sound of steam escaping the bus's ruptured radiator. One of the insurgents put his rifle against my heart, cocked the trigger, and, shrugging, looked at the young guy who was asking me all the questions. My interrogator—his name was Aura—chewed on his thumb for a moment and then, seeming indifferent, gestured to the others to bring me along.

"*Merci*," I said, whispering, recruiting the power of the French language.

"Don't you mean *gracias*?" Aura asked in a civil fashion, as if we were in some bizarro-world language lab.

Force-marched along with two wounded policemen through miles of swamp and dense jungle for the next three days—right away I lost my hiking boots in the deep, sticky mud—and continuing on barefoot, I developed these god-awful oozing sores from dozens of burrowing foot worms.

My leg, already in rough shape, caused me a lot of grief and stopped working altogether on the second day. I sank to my knees. I think I may have passed out. One of the guerrillas dragged me up onto my feet, handed me a big stick, and gave me a push just to get me started. Enormous leafy canopies of twelve-foot-high prayer plants and knifelike thorny vegetation blocked every step as a haze of encircling sweat bugs and mosquitoes covered me like a second skin.

We finally got to an area of some relief where the rain forest was intersected by a wide, flattened swath, a rudimentary road made by local wildlife. We came to a semiabandoned village, where we were greeted by a handful of hooting and jeering men and a few villagers who had set up camp among the burned-out huts.

After a brief conference, one of the men ran to get shovels. When he returned he handed them out among a small group, who took us to a remote end of the village, where they began digging in the ground. Somebody pushed a handmade shovel into my chest and ordered me to start digging. Shovels were in short supply, so the two wounded soldiers were pushed down onto all fours and made to scoop out the dirt with their hands.

Standing barefoot in the moist, loose dirt and hacking away at the buried roots of resistant palms, I dug until the edge of the hole was so high that it touched my waist. Behind me, without warning, I heard loud voices, a sudden great commotion, and truncated shrill pleas for mercy.

Two gunshots were fired one right after the other. Gripping the shovel's handle, my arms trembling from the effort, I shut my eyes tightly, anticipating a third.

Instead, coarse hands reached down and yanked me up by the shirt collar, lifting me from where I stood inside the hole. My legs buckled, and I fell on my knees and watched as the lifeless bodies of the executed policemen were tossed into the freshly dug grave, one on top of the other. Aura looked over and laughed at me, the sharp edges of his pleasure slicing through me like a knife.

"It's okay," he said. "You might come in handy."

Some guy came up from behind me, grabbed me by the arm, and dragged me on my stomach for several yards, paused, and threw me into a deep trench dug into the earth sometime earlier. A thick cover of branches and palm leaves concealed it.

I fell asleep. I was afraid to wake up.

It was raining, the pit filling several inches with water along the bottom where I was lying on the ground, soaked to the skin. I was pulling glass and maggots from the random pattern of holes in my thigh. I heard a rustling overhead; the air was filled with the feral odor of wet pelt and, looking up, my head spinning, vision blurred, I was amazed to see several monkeys peering down at me through the twigs and the leaves.

Curious and unafraid, they watched me for a long while, chattering to one another, and then one of the monkeys picked up a loose rock and lobbed it at me, hitting me in the leg. It stung. A few of the others picked up scattered sticks and threw them at me, striking me to no great effect, but I stayed still, and soon they got bored and left. For some reason, the monkeys' attack had the strange effect of cheering me up.

The sticky musk of flowers clung to the air like night sweat. Staring up into the black sky, sedated by the meditative drone of insects, I saw the ghostly shapes of blackbirds circling overhead. Their wings softly fluttering, they called out to one another.

"Ma says she's proud of you, Coll." It was Bingo, even if it was only in my head.

"Now I know you're not real," I said to him. "Even if she were proud of me, she'd never admit it. She'd die first."

"She did, don't you remember?"

The next day, the village was attacked by militia, who were going systematically from village to village in the area. Some local guy, after nearly falling into the hole with me, took strange pity and pulled me from the pit as he ran for his life. We were hiding in the forest, in flight from men who were thrashing through the deep tropical undergrowth, hunting for human prey, slashing away at stubborn, spiny plant fronds.

I was shaking uncontrollably, my teeth chattering violently, and my noisy terror threatened to give us away. My savior pushed me down and clamped his hand around my mouth, nearly suffocating me, pinning my face in the mud until I passed out.

"You speak English?" I asked him finally when I came to.

He looked at me and shrugged.

"Are you a Catholic?" I asked him, thinking it was a safe question even if he couldn't understand a word I was saying. "I'm a Catholic, too," I said. I was having trouble standing.

"You're probably wondering what I'm doing here," I said, feeling practically delirious as we walked along together, his arm around my waist, my arm thrown over his shoulder, my left foot dragging along the ground, him not saying a word. And then I told him the whole story, about lying to Pop and Uncle Tom about the holidays, about how the Falcon had tried to keep me from making the trip, about how I'd built the chicken coop for the farmer and his family.

"I'm here helping," I said as he looked at me as if I were out of my mind. My knees buckled—there was a lot of that going around.

My leg was chewed up and pulsing. It was infected, and I kept passing in and out of consciousness. The man from the village talked someone into driving us to a makeshift clinic—a converted chicken coop—full of young kids being treated for injuries they'd suffered as soldiers after being kidnapped and conscripted by rebel forces. The man who dragged me out of the hole was scanning the beds, obviously looking for someone. He left disappointed without saying good-bye. I never knew his name.

There was only one doctor, assisted by a handful of nurses. He was French. The nurses were Belgian. One of them, named Madeleine, seemed to be in charge. She had a nice way of being bossy as hell. They were going crazy trying to treat all the kids, and they just kept pouring in—it was like using your thumb to try to stem the flow from a breached levee—and it was the middle of the night and there was nowhere to put them, no one to take care of them.

They treated me and my leg, and after a few days I started to come around. Madeleine offered me the use of a primitive cane and asked me to help her take care of the kids. I had my shirt collar pulled up over my face—the smell—I was slipping and sliding among the dross of a charnel-house floor. One little boy, he seemed dead to me, needed a transfusion—there were no blood supplies, no electricity. The French doctor pointed at me and called me over and told me he was going to take 500 cc of blood from me for this boy.

"But what if I'm not a match?" I asked, thinking it was a reasonable question.

He wound up and hit me in the face, knocking me into the wall. He hit me again when I straightened up. I put up my hands, the cane went clattering to the floor, and I was saying, "It's okay, just do it, take my blood if it will help."

He calmed down a bit, not much, but by now I was feeling pretty upset. He hit me one more time, open-handed, a slap upside the head, for good measure. Then, his hands shaking, he and Madeleine set up to do the transfusion.

Lightning illuminated the black sky. The night was a cold and shining lake. A flame from a single white candle fluttered, creating the illusion of quietness where there was none.

The French doctor was like an unvisited place, his solitariness so thorough that it was as though I were seeing him from a distance. The dead and dying were all around him, hanging overhead, unsightly as flypaper, part of the architecture of his calling. He finished with me, and then he just got up from where he was sitting, didn't say a word to me, pushed me aside, bumped me with the edge of his shoulder, and went on to the next kid and then the next one after that. I tried to stand up, but I started to black out. I fell back onto the cot and closed my eyes.

After it was over, Madeleine sank down beside the little boy on the floor to comfort him, easing into all that percolating effluvium as if it were a Hot Springs. Her hands were stained with blood.

The next batch of kids came in and the next after that, and I was nothing more than a turnstile, people pushing past me, going forward and back, in and out, and I wasn't exactly in the way but just someone from whom nothing much was expected.

The next day, the little boy seemed better, brighter; the general consensus was that he was going to make it. I couldn't stop staring at him. He used to be dead.

One of the hospital workers, his name was Santo, bravely offered to help me get back to San Salvador, to the airport and home. He asked me if I could walk. I was okay with the help of the cane, which was little more than a T-shaped stick. I felt like hell, but all I could think about was getting back home. We set out while it was still light, hoping to avoid the insurgents and the militia that prowled in the night—the area was crawling with both. We had been traveling for hours when we heard screams and shouting and saw the lick of flames shooting above the tree line.

Glowering billows of smoke obliterated the sky, choking the field, as, curled up and facedown, swallowing petrol fumes, I pressed my hands against my ears.

Rain was falling gently on giant lobelias, making a *pat-pat* sound against the leaves of young trees that were bending back and forth in the humid night breeze. My heart was beating, bumping erratically against my rib cage.

It was the last thing I heard. I turned and tried to speak to Santo, but I couldn't hear the sound of my own voice. He dragged me around in the dark, his hand wrapped around my wrist, pulling me along, stumbling and fumbling, the night a world without boundaries. With every step, I felt as if I were walking off the edge of the earth.

Santo somehow got word to Sister Mary Ellen. She arranged for me to stay with an American priest, who got in touch with the Falcon, who organized a flight back home.

Santo left me with the priest. I hugged him in gratitude for what he had done for me. He hugged me in return, and then he turned and left. He was going back up north, back to the hospital. I don't know if he made it or not.

I was in El Salvador for one month. During that time, I saw brave people do things that defied logic and circumstance to save my life, a stranger to them—Beto, who spoke up for me with the militia; the villager who could have kept running but instead pulled me from the pit and took me to the hospital; Santo, who brought me to the priest.

I thought about the French doctor, who could have been home in Paris, drinking champagne.

I told myself I did the right thing when I didn't jump in after Bing. Sensible people everywhere would say I did the right thing. But that logic didn't square with what was done for me in El Salvador, where every minute of every day people confronted with the same kind of decision I faced chose to make the leap of faith—Santo had faith he would make it to the airport and back alive.

They all jumped and would jump again and again. I wanted to believe that only an extraordinary person, knowing the dangers, would have jumped in after Bing that day in the cave. But ordinary people did brave things every day in El Salvador in 1983.

I was an ordinary person. Why didn't I jump in?

I went to El Salvador to excavate a little personal courage.

Courage exists—even if it doesn't exist in me.

CHAPTER TWENTY-NINE

THE FALCON ARRANGED WITH THE PRIEST TO FLY ME HOME IN a private plane, accompanied by a Catholic aid worker who was scheduled to come back to the United States around the same time. I don't remember much about the return journey. I couldn't hear a thing. I was back at Cassowary for two weeks before I heard another sound.

"They don't call it hysterical deafness anymore—too stigmatizing, apparently." The Falcon was sitting beside me, writing on a long yellow pad of paper. "It's a conversion disorder. The doctors insist it happened as a result of the trauma. I tried to tell them as far as I'm concerned you've suffered from a conversion disorder all your life. It won't affect our relationship at all."

The aid worker delivered me personally to Cassowary. He brought me home and dumped me onto the living room floor like so much sand from an upturned shoe. For weeks after there was sand everywhere I looked and wherever I turned, and there were grains of sand in my eyes, in my hair, beneath my fingernails. There was sand in my food and in the sheets of my bed. I went to draw my bath and I turned on the tap and sand flowed like water from the faucet.

This wasn't sand from Squibnocket Beach—this was drought.

Sometimes you don't need to hear to know what's being said.

"My best guess is post-traumatic stress," the aid worker was saying to Ingrid. "I know a bit about what he's going through. It's rough. He deserves a lot of credit. You must be proud of him."

"Yes, we are very proud of him," Ingrid said. "Why, I couldn't be more proud of Collie than if he—"

The Falcon, elusive main attraction, appeared without warning, slicing through the nebulae, stepping up and extending his hand in greeting. The aid worker's face flushed in sporadic crimson patches, physiological acknowledgment of a certain nectarous kind of star power.

"Oh, hello . . . ," he stammered, so nonplussed that he introduced himself as Peregrine Lowell.

"It's all right," the Falcon reassured him, smiling and gracious, visibly pleased at wielding such a disconcerting effect. "I know who I am. Most of the time, anyway . . . and yes, Brian, yes, Ingrid is quite right. Allow me to finish the thought—we couldn't be more proud of Collie than if you told us he had drug-resistant gonorrhea."

"I beg your pardon?" The aid worker was confused. "I'm sorry. I must be missing something. Presumably there are things about which I am unaware." Resorting to tact, he continued:

"Collie has been through a terrible time. It's perfectly natural to feel and react the way that he has. I don't think he needs a psychiatrist. He needs some time and the love and support of his family."

"And that's what he shall have—in abundance."

The Falcon was taking over.

"I appreciate your efforts and your input. You've provided marvelous assistance when your help was really needed. And I intend to take your recommendations under serious advisement. I'll think things over, and I'll make the best decision for Collie."

"Well, I think that's wonderful. I'm sure whatever decision you make will be the right one. Collie is very lucky to have such a devoted grandfather. . . ." Brian was nervously applying obsequiousness like a poultice.

The Falcon laughed as he ushered the aid worker out of the room. "Our dear Ingrid will see you out. Thanks so much for your expertise. We'll be in touch. . . ."

"Presumptuous son of a bitch," the Falcon said, watching as my escort disappeared into the hallway with Ingrid at his arm.

I got quite a jolt the first time I looked into a mirror. My skin was the color and texture of ancient newsprint. My eyes were dark and recessed. My hair was dull and wild, so indiscriminately chopped up and sun-bleached—short, long, dark, light, shaved in spots, plucked in others—I looked like a man with a thousand frantic haircuts.

I was always pacing, trying to walk it off, needed a cane to walk, would always need a cane to walk, according to doctors, couldn't sit still, the pounding of mortars sneaking up behind me, I was scrambling in and out of devastated buildings, and jumping aside for careening pickup trucks.

My sleep disrupted daily by nightmares, I had picked up some nuisance virus of unknown origin—my guts, soggy and bitter, felt as if they were marinating in bleach.

My hearing came back, returning as mysteriously as it had disappeared. Deafness kind of agreed with me—I actually pretended deafness for a couple of weeks after my hearing was restored. I wasn't trying to be a jerk—I just needed a little more time, needed to get stronger to face the barrage of words I knew was coming my way.

School was out of the question; the second semester was pretty much a write-off. Pop was bugging me to come home for a visit, so he could take care of me, he said. Finally I agreed. I always liked the Vineyard in winter. In the winter, the beach was deserted, made up of crystal and craters, remote as a moonscape.

Pop was so worked up about what happened that he was ready to sue the Catholic Church and the governments of the United States and El Salvador.

Uncle Tom had smaller goals—he was lying in wait for me. We were alone near the pigeon loft. Sneaking up alongside me, he blew a whistle next to my ear to confirm his theory that I was a fraud.

"Jesus, Uncle Tom . . ." I covered my ear against the blast.

"I knew it, you conniving bastard. I never took you for a professional victim, but here you are playing us like a saxophone."

"It's not like that, Uncle Tom." I felt my shoulders sag and decline into an inverted Y shape.

"No, well, so you say. Look here, Noodle, it takes a certain type to do what you set out to do, and that's not you. God knows you tried, and that means something. But it's no good. . . . Time for some plain talk—you're too soft. I knew you weren't up to much right from the start. When you were six you were crying in the garden, begging me not to kill the potato bugs. No one cares about potato bugs. No one, that is, except you. Do you understand?"

The whole time Uncle Tom was speaking, I was sitting on the edge of an empty limestone urn, freezing, wind whistling through my torn jeans, my head down and fiddling with a ballpoint pen, twisting off the plastic cap, clicking it back on again.

"Here, here, stop that distraction," Uncle Tom ordered. "You're acting like a child. Now, are you listening to me? Have you heard a word I've said?"

"I hear you."

"But are you taking it in? Are you paying attention?"

"Yeah."

"Well, have you learned anything?"

"Maybe I'm trying to make the world a safer place for potato bugs."

"That's enough smart talk. Being a wise aleck is what got you into this mess in the first place. You come inside before you expire out here in the cold. And quit thinking so much about yourself and how you're feeling."

"I'll be there in a minute," I said, watching as he headed into the house, my finger running along the rough topography of the urn.

I kept thinking about the little boy in El Salvador, the one the French doctor brought back to life. I couldn't get him out of my head. I thought about the French doctor, too. I wanted to learn his language, wanted to absorb its magic.

It should have been a grown-up decision, my way of being useful—my first meaningful formal step on the road to manhood—but it was freighted with delusion and wishful thinking.

Does anyone ever actually make a sensible decision? Do the stories we present to the world ever correspond to the stories we tell ourselves?

How could I tell Pop or Uncle Tom or anyone else, for that matter, what I was up to? The truth was, I was trying to make some Fantastic Flanagan magic.

How could I admit even to myself that by deciding to become a doctor, I was trying to pull the ultimate rabbit from a hat and return my brother from the dead?

CHAPTER THIRTY

I WASN'T BRAVE, BUT I WAS SMART—IF ACADEMIC ACHIEVEMENT is any indicator, which Pop and Uncle Tom repeatedly told me it wasn't. Fortunately, courage wasn't a prerequisite for medical school. For inspiration, I kept the image of the French doctor active in my mind through all my years of study.

It was spring 1991, and I was in the final year of my fellowship. Pediatric oncology was my specialty; it was the one that least appealed to Collie the boy—he lusted after gynecology—but it would be a feather in the cap of my glowing, fine young manhood.

I was doing okay. I decided to study medicine at Harvard, despite Uncle Tom's everlasting disdain. All my life I'd been made daily aware of my privilege by others—*You've been given the whole world, Collie,* being everyone's favorite refrain. By everyone, I mean everyone except Pop and Uncle Tom, who never could be bothered with received wisdom, and the Falcon, who considered the world to be his and saw no reason to pretend otherwise.

But as far as the rest, it seemed all anyone ever really wanted from me was the appearance of gratitude and seriousness, and a simple set of scrubs took care of all that—the world was happier with me than before. The limp didn't hurt; the ubiquitous presence of an old cane cemented my image as penitent. And although he was not entirely reconciled to my becoming a doctor—I might as well have declared my intention to become a bedbug—the Falcon wasn't oblivious to my rising-star status at Harvard.

Boston magazine named me the city's most eligible bachelor; actually, they said I was one of the best catches in the world, which is quite a declaration when you think about it. An anonymous source supplied them with a shot of me at some hospital party, my hair so black and curly that it looked as if I were wearing a French poodle. I found myself holding up the page, looking at it upside down and sideways and seeing something different every time—I was becoming my own Rorschach test.

"Can you see the monkey?" I asked my grandfather, playfully extending the photo across the table for him to view.

"Every time you open your mouth," he said, barely looking up.

Bam! Talking with the Falcon was still a labyrinth of shut doors. I made a point of seeing him a couple of times a month. He was in his eighties but seemed ageless, was still working with no intention of stopping. But for my visits and the odd dinner party, he ate his meals alone at the dining room table, except for Cromwell, who sat at his elbow, awaiting dessert.

"Aren't you cute and proud?" the old man flattered away, commandeering me in the hospital corridor during morning rounds.

"Yeah, yeah . . . what do you want, Pop?"

"If it isn't Dr. Collie Flanagan, the flower of them all. . . ."

Impatiently—I had stuff waiting, important stuff—I reached into my back pocket, pulled out my wallet, and handed over the contents, peeling off bills like so much scorn. I felt a dull thump delivered to the back of my head.

"Keep your dirty Lowell lucre," Pop said, stinking of whiskey.

"Jesus, Pop." I felt an anti-WASP diatribe swarming like so many angry bees.

"You think it's money I'm after, at the expense of being treated like shite beneath your feet? You bloody Baptist, you damned Methodist circuit rider, you Presbyterian bastard . . ."

I gave him all the cash I had, I gave him my credit cards in a vain attempt to stop him before he uttered the final familiar insult—

"Dirty-legged Protestant prince . . ."

I was sagging even as the stinging swarm was receding; Pop was beginning to glory in his swag.

"May I keep bus fare?" I asked. "My car's in the shop."

"Jesus, take a cab, for Christ's sake," he said with some tenderness, returning a twenty. Immediately, he thought better of things, took back the twenty, and gave me a ten-dollar bill.

I watched him weave down the hall, shouting out happy greetings to all the good-looking nurses—homely women continued to dismay him; he viewed them as a personal affront.

Sometimes it's a blessing to be blind, he'd say. "Did you see the sourpuss on that one? Why God in His infinite wisdom created the female gargoyle is a matter between Him and Satan. I'm persuaded they struck a deal about time served here on earth, and ugly women are a big part of the penance."

He disappeared to the sound of feminine laughter, through the exit and down the stairwell, and I prepared to walk into the room of a nine-year-old girl in the last stages of dying, and it was a curious form of relief.

So, you can imagine the situation for yourself: twenty-eight years old, unexpectedly groomed to glistening by medicine, the Man Plan visibly progressing, here and there a rough patch, but it was mostly still water. I had made the calm choice, though I didn't know it at the time. I thought I was okay, maybe not fully alive but not dead, either, no ocean to drown me, no wave to tip my boat.

I had this growing thought that catastrophe strikes but once and then you're off the hook for life. The monstrous event and its sticky aftermath were behind me. I had every intention of letting convention take hold, tightening its pleasant grip around my neck until I no longer felt the need to breathe, until I became implacably mild.

Dr. Collie Flanagan, my decency a belt to hold my pants in place, incandescently ordinary but for all that money, a glimmer of bland pride, shining and uneventful as a weedless lawn.

CHAPTER THIRTY-ONE

LOOKING AROUND, I SAW THAT EVERYONE WAS THERE—THE BOY, tall and slim and ill; the boy's shaken parents, pale mom, dad unsmiling; an intern; and a nurse. The nurse had a run in her stocking; I know because I was checking out her legs. Thick ankles, Jesus, ankles like a cart horse, as Pop would say, whatever the hell a cart horse is. Something you don't want to rub up against in the night, Collie, I was thinking.

The boy's name was Gary. He was seventeen years old. His leukemia had reappeared after a long remission. I was treating him for the first time. His regular doctor was sick at home. I was annoyed because we weren't on the oncology ward. There weren't any available beds. Instead we were on a surgical ward, and it was seven o'clock in the morning.

The official inquiry would eventually refer to the cumulative effect of small factors.

Geography was small factor number one.

I was new to St. Agnes-Marie Hospital and still learning their protocols.

Small factor number two.

Gary was prepped to receive the first round in a chemotherapy regimen of spinal canal injections of methotrexate, cytarabine, and hydrocortisone. I gave my head a shake and focused. Later in the day he was scheduled to receive an intravenous treatment with a drug called vincristine.

I was accustomed to protocols on the oncology ward at my

previous hospital, where intravenous medications were stored separately for safety reasons. In oncology, they weren't allowed in the same room together. And they were packaged differently. Drugs such as vincristine were double-bagged and wrapped in a towel. On other wards, on this ward, they weren't so meticulous. Hospital rules didn't oblige them to be—small factor number three. I wasn't thinking about that, of course. Somewhere in my unconscious, I was making the assumption that standards of risk management with regard to drug handling were the same on all wards.

But even on oncology I always double-checked the medications—that's how thorough I was; that's how seriously I took my responsibilities. I always checked the labeling first. I was strangling, all that virtue a lump in my throat. I could hardly breathe for my determination to do it right, follow through, be better than I was, elusive maturity choking the life out of me.

So when a nurse brought a bag containing what I thought were the three syringes into the room, I checked just to make sure. But I didn't remove the syringes from the bag. I never touched the bag—small factor number four.

The nurse was unfamiliar with chemotherapy procedures. She didn't know anything about the drugs and how they should be administered. That would never have happened at my old hospital.

Small factor number five.

Viewing the syringes through the transparent plastic, I visually confirmed the contents and the labeling. But there was a fourth syringe. I didn't see it. It was concealed by the other three.

Small factor number six.

I was chatting with Gary about football. He was a bright, likable kid, cheerful as an accordion. He was making fun of me for not looking like a doctor, and he was right. You look like a skater, he said, and I was shrugging because I knew it was true.

"How'd you get that limp?" he asked me.

"Heliskiing in Nepal," I told him. I'd told the story so many times, I'd come to believe it myself.

We were laughing and talking. It felt like fun, what was going on between us. I liked the way we were ignoring the crisis, our levity a nice counterpoint to the gravity of the situation.

Ever since medical school I couldn't help myself: If it looked like fun—and joking with this kid was fun—I was running it down, dog after cat, just for the hell of it, for the sheer pleasure of chasing and catching.

Why didn't I pull the syringes from the bag and check? Was it because I was having too much fun?

The intern automatically withdrew the syringes from the bag and put all four syringes onto the tray. Small factor number seven. And why wouldn't he? He had watched me approve the contents. He knew my reputation for thoroughness. I was so confident in my abilities and judgments, I instilled the same assurance in others. Everyone knew I was a star. Unlike Collie the boyish fuck-up, I didn't make mistakes. That was behind me.

I sat down and began the procedure. The tray stand was at shoulder level when I was in a seated position. Because I was looking across, rather than looking down, I still didn't see that there were four rather than three syringes. Now there were eight small factors at play.

At that moment, a fire alarm sounded out in the hallway. The boy's mother looked anxiously over at the door, as did Gary. I was mildly distracted by the noise and was focused on trying to ensure that Gary remained perfectly still. Small factors nine and ten.

The nurse handed me the syringes one by one, and one by one I injected the methotrexate, the cytarabine, and the hydrocortisone, and then I injected the fourth syringe.

That's when I killed him.

The second I withdrew the syringe I knew. A fourth syringe. Why did I know the second after and not the second before? I looked down at the syringe. The label was clear: vincristine, written in black letters.

I made immediate efforts to flush out his central nervous system, but vincristine injected into the spinal canal is fatal. It was certainly fatal for Gary.

It took him three agonizing days to die. I have no memory of those three days.

An inquiry exonerated me. There was persuasive testimony as to my competence, my academic standing, my impeccable training and credentials, my reputation for caring and conscientiousness, the conspiracy of circumstance. The hospital decided the matter should end there.

Gary's parents heroically supported their decision. I found out later both the hospital and the parents accepted large sums of money from the Falcon.

CHAPTER THIRTY-TWO

GARY'S FAMILY WASN'T AFFLUENT. HARDWORKING, INDUSTRIOUS, thrifty—their clothes were wash-and-wear, off-the-rack. My clothes were all wrong. My suit, my shoes, my shirt, my tie, everything about me was wrong. I shouldn't have gone. I don't know what I was thinking, showing up at the funeral in those clothes and with my shoes shining.

I was standing alone at the back of the church, and I dipped my fingers in holy water and made the sign of the cross. I genuflected, and then I heard someone gasp; there was this long, low moan, and from the front of the church Gary's father looked up and around. "Jesus!" he said as his wife began sobbing loudly at first sight of me.

Crying, everyone was crying, the church was swaying, and the volume grew in intensity and fervor with every step I took until it became one long wail without end.

When Mambo died, Bachelor howled every night for weeks. Pop told me about it, and then I heard him myself; he woke me up, making this purely mournful sound that rose and fell and resonated throughout the house. To listen, it felt as if I were dying and being born at the same time.

"You heard it, did you?" Uncle Tom asked me the next morning. "Now, you tell me there's no God."

I watched from far away, from beneath an old oak tree, as Gary was interred, and then I drove to the caves where Bingo died, the first time I'd been back since he and Rosie and Erica drowned. I sat amid the rocks in the dark; it was cold, early spring, and I listened to the rush of the waterfall. Nothing had changed—the waning light of day shone through the gap in the rock overhead. Nothing had changed—the spray of the waterfall was like rain against the wet mossy stone, jagged rock, so sharp that I cut my hands, the black water shining and churning under the moon and the stars, blackbirds going round and round above me. Nothing changes.

It didn't matter. Everywhere I looked, inside and outside, inner eye and outer eye, in crowds and in solitude, I saw him there, in the familiar faces of dogs, in the circling of blackbirds at dusk, reflected in the eyes of those who looked back at me. Even now, all these years later, behind every tree, there he is. Hiding, following me, I turn to look and there he is, persistent and inextinguishable, holding his breath waiting for me to say yes, to nod, to give him leave, there he is, there he is, there he is.

He'd been dead for almost nine years, and sometimes deep in my heart was this terrible ache, acute and fleeting, this feeling that haunted me, a recognition, not that I didn't miss him, I missed him, but that I didn't miss him as much as I once did.

I was holding an ivory-colored candle from the church. I lit it, and I sat in the barely illuminated darkness, watching the candle flicker, warm wax rolling down all sides, melting onto my fingers, until my fingers looked like candles and the candle faltered and went out, leaving me invisible to the night and indistinct, and knowing as I had always known that he would have jumped in after me.

I had my own place in Boston, but I couldn't face going back there. I didn't want to walk in the door and be met by myself—my choices everywhere—the stuff I owned, my things, my life hanging on the walls and crowding the cupboards.

I drove to Cassowary. It was the middle of the night. Cromwell barked from the upper hallway, where he slept in front of my grandfather's bedroom, but he wagged his tail when he recognized who it was, giving me a sloppy greeting. The light in my grandfather's room flickered briefly on and then shut off when he realized it was me coming home.

The next day, groggy and giving in to the panacea of sedation, I could hear a commotion outside my bedroom door, the vague sound of raised voices, not so muffled that I didn't recognize Pop in all his fury. The door opened and banged shut and then opened a crack, Pop's big rubber overshoe acting as doorstop.

"What do you think you're doing?" Ingrid was trying to prevent him from entering the room.

I lifted my head off the pillow, propped myself up on my elbows, and saw Pop's intruding shoulder form a wedge against the open crack of door.

"I'm here to get my son."

"Well, I'm going to speak to his grandfather about that—"

"The hell you will!" Pop shouted, pushing hard against the door.

"Pop!" I said as he charged toward the bed. "What are you doing?"

He took me by the arm. "Come on, Collie, you're coming with me."

"Now, Collie, your grandfather will want to talk to you before you go anywhere," Ingrid said, appealing to me. "We're worried about you."

"This hasn't a thing to do with his grandfather. Collie's my son. Peregrine Lowell has nothing to say about what happens to him."

Neither, apparently, did I. It didn't seem to occur to anyone that I wasn't a kid anymore.

"But Pop . . ." I was struggling to clear my head, trying to shake off the residual effects of too much Valium.

"Collie's exhausted. Let him rest here for a day or so. . . . Be reasonable, Charlie, for heaven's sake," Ingrid was sputtering as the futility of her protest became evident to her.

But Pop wasn't listening; his aggressive indifference had a gangster's edge—he might as well have mashed a grapefruit in her face. He threw off my blankets, pitched them onto the floor, and pulled me up so I was standing, pathetic in my pajamas and bare feet. He reached for my cane and threw his raincoat over my shoulders.

"What the devil?" The Falcon stepped out of his bedroom, dressed for an early flight to Vancouver, turned to the left, and walked right into us.

"Out of my way, Perry," Pop said, tightening his grip on my elbow.

"What's going on here?" the Falcon demanded.

"Call the police!" someone was shouting.

"Don't call the police," I said. "Why would you call the police?"

"Collie, you're not going anywhere," the Falcon said as he reached out and hooked his fingers in a tight grip around my forearm.

"Get your lousy hands off him," Pop said, pulling me toward him.

The Falcon yanked back. My cane clattered to the floor. I felt like the main course at a feast of jackals.

"You drunken maniac. What do you think you're doing?" The Falcon raised his voice as he and Pop tugged away at me.

"Settle down, you guys, this is crazy. Just give me a moment to think," I said, but no one was listening to me.

"He's my son. Let him go!!" Pop was shouting, and then with one great heave-ho he pulled me free, so I was standing behind him as the yanking force propelled him into the Falcon, who was forced to take several steps backward. He was chest to chest with Pop, who struggled to keep his balance by hanging on to the Falcon's outstretched arm—the collective gasp of anguish from the staff could be heard throughout the universe.

"Run, Collie, run!" Pop was hollering, pushing free of the Falcon. "Head for the stairs, I'm right behind you."

"Jesus," I said, stunned as I watched the Falcon stagger backward, disbelief in his eyes, hands to his face, fury like blood spurting between the cracks in his fingers.

"Well, see what I've got," Pop said, chortling, as we emerged into the sunlight from the front door. He was holding up the Falcon's antique money clip, containing several inches of cash.

"You picked his pocket!" I couldn't believe it.

"I did not. It's just a bit of magic. A little sleight of hand. I should have done it years ago. When your mother and I first got married and we stayed at the house, he used to leave great wads of money lying around in the hope I'd steal it and confirm his worst suspicions about me. I fixed him—I blew my nose on his dressing gown."

"Pop, it's stealing. . . ."

"The hell it is. I earned every cent. Jesus, Collie, you need to put finances in some perspective. It's only money," he admonished as we descended the front steps in silence. "Do you think he'll put a stop to the monthly checks?"

"Pop! You humiliated him in front of his employees. You stole his money clip! The Falcon! What do you think?"

"It's a sin to lose hope, Collie," he said solemnly. "And anyway, a little humiliation never hurt anyone. I guarantee you your grandfather will be thanking me for this before he's through. You don't want to be proud, Collie. Is there a greater sin than pride? Not from where I sit there isn't."

We reached the driveway—why the hell was I going along with this? The waiting taxi driver looked up, stunned to see me in my pajamas, and hesitated; his fingers fluttering on the top of the steering wheel, his feet tapping nervously, he reacted as if he were the driver in a kidnapping.

"I don't know about this," he said, swallowing deeply. "Is this allowed?"

"For goodness' sake, man, he's my son," Pop said, climbing into the passenger seat. "It's not a prison break."

"It's okay," I said, sliding into the rear seat behind the cabbie.

"If you say so," the cabbie said, shaking his head resignedly.

"Now, I want you to drive us back to the ferry, and we'll need you to cross over to the island with your car and drive us home. Whatever you charge is fine. Spare no expense. And don't you worry," Pop said to the cabbie, leaning forward confidentially, peeling off several large bills, part of the Falcon's stash, "there's a big fat bonus in it for you."

Pop was chattering away from the front seat, enlisting the increasingly involved cabbie's support for his plan to take me abroad with him the next day. "You've got a touch of the aristocrat about you, Collie. Just a tincture, mind you, no reason to sharpen the guillotine, but you're a tiny bit rarefied, prone to 'the nerves,' as my aunt Margaret used to say. She was a great believer in the curative powers of the beach for people such as you.

"Marrying into a nervous family like the Lowells, I've come to see she was right. The beach calmed your mother down, not much, but without it, she would have soared way beyond the earth's atmosphere, like some sort of mad kite. A mouthful of sand is the only antibiotic old money needs. You and I are going home to Ireland—now there are beaches! And then you'll come and spend the summer with Tom and me, and we'll have you right as rain by the fall."

I took an extended leave of absence. For months, the last word I said to myself each evening was the first word in my head when I woke up the next morning—*vincristine.*

I think I will never be free of the power of that word.

And in my mind, I carried on the brutish practice of scattering quicklime over the dead.

CHAPTER THIRTY-THREE

IRELAND IS A FUNNY PLACE TO VISIT IF YOU'RE LOOKING FOR peace and quiet or a reason to go on living. It's a pretty argumentative culture; I got the impression my limits were being tested constantly and I was usually found wanting, which meant that I felt right at home from the moment I stepped off the plane and onto the tarmac at Shannon.

The countryside was spectacular, wild and remote, at least in north Clare, where Pop and Uncle Tom were from. We were staying with Aunt Brigid in the house where they grew up, a weathered old cottage, white plaster walls peeling under a thatched roof with a sky blue door, located on a windy bluff above the ocean overlooking the Burren, with shrouded views of the Cliffs of Moher and the Aran Islands.

We were minutes away from a couple of small villages populated mostly by old bachelors and incomprehensible farmers who were either backward in a toothless-grin sort of way or weirdly refined, almost statesmenlike in their rubber-booted gentility.

There were a handful of cottages nearby, but I rarely saw any of the people who lived in them—at least not their faces, anyway. For me, Ireland will always be a country of shifting curtains, neighbors taking up their positions in the shadows, lurking behind window frames, peering around lace and muslin, stealing furtive peeks as I went for long solitary walks every morning. Being surrounded by all that active misanthropy was like a tonic—I didn't need to worry about making friends or being sociable, chatting up strangers.

The locals viewed me with a combination of distrust and distaste. The Falcon's aggressive Protestantism was well-known, the IRA once threatening to bomb his London office. Meanwhile, it took Pop two hours to travel a hundred yards.

"I swear your father would talk the ear off a cob of corn," Aunt Brigid said, watching as he waved his hands animatedly in the air, gesturing to make his point, arguing with people he'd known since childhood, taking up right where he'd left off decades earlier.

"It's too bad Uncle Tom didn't come with us. He said he wasn't interested in seeing Ireland again. I don't get it," I said one day to Aunt Brigid as I sat on the back steps and watched her hang clothes on the line.

"Oh, well, that's easily explained," Aunt Brigid said, talking as she worked. "He made himself very unpopular here after what happened to Ellen O'Connor. She lived down the road. She was a bit of a neighborhood sensation, for having survived more than twenty suicide attempts. . . . Oh . . ." Aunt Brigid's face turned bright red, and she clapped her hand to her mouth.

"It's okay, Aunt Brigid, go on," I reassured her. "It was a long time ago. I think I'm cured of that problem."

"Well, in her case it was hard to take it seriously. We began to think of it as something she did as a matter of routine, a behavior, like getting a perm or washing your car," Aunt Brigid told me. "She didn't want to die. She liked a fuss made over her."

According to Aunt Brigid, she timed her pill swallowing to coincide with her husband's return from work. "It was a religion with that man to be on time. Every day for thirty years he'd walk in the door at exactly five-twenty on the dot. So she'd dress herself nicely, fix her hair, and she'd take her bottle of pills, one by one, comfortable knowing he'd be in time to rush her to hospital."

On this particular evening, he crossed Uncle Tom's path at five-fifteen and was kept talking in the shared driveway for a full two hours.

"Rigor mortis had set in by the time he found her in the bedroom."

"She died! What was Uncle Tom's reaction?" I asked.

"Oh well, he always hated her."

"Why?"

"Well, you know your uncle Tom. She was a big woman. He used to tell her that she should be ashamed of herself. He became quite preoccupied with the sight of her trying to fit behind the wheel of her tiny car. He used to go out every morning just to watch. He'd sip his coffee and stare and shout out rude remarks. She drove a Mini Minor, and he'd make a point of telling her it was the height of vanity, like a woman with a size ten foot trying to squeeze into a size four shoe. She hollered back that she was only eating salad, and he said, 'Well, then you're eating it the way a cow eats hay.'"

"I see." Sometimes I used to think I'd die during one of Pop's or Uncle Tom's diatribes and neither one of them would notice but just carry on talking.

"Oh, I know it's terrible. But he used to say she hurt his eyes to look at her, and there must have been some truth to it. I never knew him to have headaches, but his head was always hurting that summer, so with that in mind, you can't hold him entirely to blame."

"Collie, come over here!"

I looked up. Pop was next door at the neighbor's house. He was calling for me, wanting me to join in, but I just smiled and waved and got up from the stoop to go walking. It's all I did, walk, and all I wanted to do, go for long walks, not thinking about what I was constantly thinking about.

The velveteen cows were beautiful and the only friends I made in Ireland, and even they barely tolerated my presence—watching as I walked, monitoring every step, less with interest than suspicion, every bit as *Irish* as the people. Sometimes I imagined them whispering to one another as I passed by: "There he goes like clockwork, the moody stranger."

I once walked for seven hours, walked until even my cane was tired, my gimpy leg throbbing with pain, navigating the rocky disposition of the desolate Burren in my knee-high rubber boots, hobbling along, never saw another soul, though Aunt Brigid complained that the place had become a zoo what with all the American tourists.

Gray and green, the Burren was vacant as an empty planet, so vast and monochromatic that it was hard to judge distance, faraway destinations seeming within arm's reach. The air was cool and fresh and full of moisture, and it rained almost every day, a light rain, almost a mist, like a spray, so gentle that you'd barely feel it, but it had this way of soaking you to the bone so I always was a little chilled.

I liked forcing myself out into the cold and wet, walking for hours in the pouring rain and feeling chilled for hours afterward, trying to warm up in front of the fireplace. It was good to feel cold and damp—it gave me a banal concern on which to focus, and for that I was grateful.

But I wasn't entirely alone. The dogs followed me. Ownerless dogs ran free in the Irish countryside— gaunt and carefree in a wiry sort of way. A little mutt I called Jack joined me almost every day. One day he sprang out of a field carrying a cat's skeleton, its mouth open and fixed in a snarl.

I was an anomaly in the nearest village, with my long curly hair and my white shirt, getting stared down by the street-corner wolf packs, growling over at me, graphically unhinged, with their shaved heads and stinking overalls, missing their teeth and smoking their cigarettes, hostility dangling from their lower lips. They'd skin me alive with their sharp glares, smashing empty beer cans on their foreheads, saying "feck" this and "feck" that, snarling like the cat corpse and as wiry as the stray dogs.

Sometimes I wished they'd just pounce and get it over with, I was that low.

Aunt Brigid, unable to conceal her concern about my mental state—she was too polite to mention Ma and Bing or the mess in El Salvador and the tragedy of Gary—devised her own remedy, setting me up with a girl called Mary Margaret Fanore, whose main claim to fame was that she had won the local beauty contest.

"Oh, not just beautiful, Collie—this one has talent pouring out of her like she was a spigot," she said. "She came first in the talent competition."

"What was her talent?" I asked, the two of us alone in the large open kitchen, me sitting across from her as she ironed, dipping her fingers in a container of water, which she sprinkled on the fabric. Clean laundry was like a religion to her.

"Well . . ." She paused, holding her finger to her lips. "I believe she's double-jointed," she replied, continuing to iron her tablecloth, steam rising.

Again she paused, deep in thought, but wanting to tell me something. I sat waiting patiently, averting my eyes. "Isn't it funny, Collie, how it's not the sorrow that consumes a person, nor even the pain of loss? I'll tell you what it is—it's the trauma. Your grandmother was in her eighties when she passed away from throat cancer. I found her in the bathroom, dead on the floor. She'd bled out. Well, it was quite a sight, as you might imagine."

She started quietly to cry. "It's the pictures that haunt you, Collie, the snapshots you carry around in your head that never fade." Quickly recovering, she pushed her hair off her forehead with the palm of her hand, smoothing it into place at the temple. "So, here's my advice to you, for whatever it's worth." She leaned forward, her hand outstretched, almost touching my knee. "Pack away all those pictures, lock them up, and whatever you do, resist the temptation to look."

I couldn't think of how to get out of meeting Mary Margaret without offending Aunt Brigid, so I agreed to accompany her on a ferry ride to the Aran Islands, where her mother lived. Aunt Brigid had arranged for her to give me a tour.

The first thing I realized on meeting Mary Margaret by the ferry in Doolin was that Aunt Brigid and I did not share the same definition of beautiful. In fact, I'd go so far as to say that when Aunt Brigid used the term *beautiful*, she was referring quite specifically to someone who compensated in forehead for what was missing in chin.

I introduced myself, but she seemed barely to notice. Her lips were chapped, and she kept chewing them nervously. Her face was raw and peeling, as if it had been washed once too often in harsh detergents. Her hands were twisting frantically as she fingered a small wrapped package in a cloth sack.

"It's my mam's birthday," she explained.

"Oh, that's nice," I said, offering to carry her bag.

"Um, yes, I guess. Will you excuse me while I use the telephone for a moment?" she asked, pointing to the booth next to us.

"Go ahead," I said as she took her place inside the open booth and started loudly dialing.

"Mam, it's me. . . . Yes, Mam, we're running a bit late. . . . Running a bit late. About thirty minutes."

There was silence, then she resumed, her voice growing more emotional and tense, soaring skyward until its sustained pitch circled overhead like the flocks of marine birds.

"Mam, please try to understand, it's a question of petrol. The boat's refueling and we can't get aboard just yet. . . ." She started sniffling as she was apparently listening, suddenly interrupting with a wail, "Mam, do I have your faith? Do I, Mam? If I don't have your faith, I have nothing, Mam."

She hung up the phone and, weeping, came and stood next to me, dabbing at her eyes, tears streaming down her cheeks.

"Are you all right?" I asked dumbly, feeling at a total loss. Everyone around us was ignoring her obvious distress. The Irish have a high tolerance for hysteria.

"I'm fine. Will you please excuse me again?" Her manner was awkwardly formal.

She went back to the phone and redialed her mother.

"Mam, I have your birthday gift, and I will bring it to the back door and then leave." She was shaking her head vigorously. "No, I won't come in. I will bring your gift and your papers to the back door, and I will lay them down gently, then I will turn around and leave."

Now she really started crying, and *loud*. "Mam, if you had any idea what I've been through . . ."

I was standing with my arm around her as she cried, waiting as the drizzle became a torrential downpour and a rusty fishing boat called the *Old Fart* docked not far from us. I looked on astonished as people began to board.

"This can't be the ferry?" I said as Mary Margaret, clutching her bag, nodded and wailed anew.

I walked along the solitary beach at Inisheer, leaving Mary Margaret at her sister's house—my last sight of her, the two of them were sobbing in each other's arms in the front yard—and all the while I was asking myself, Whose faith do I have?

When I got back to the cottage, Aunt Brigid was waiting with dinner. Pop never showed up. "Oh, don't give it a second thought, Collie," she said later that night, taking a knowing sip of tea, sitting in her rocking chair in front of the fireplace, overweight calico cat called Dorothy purring in her lap. "He's no doubt gone into Dublin to seek the company of a hotel. You know how your father loves a good hotel. He learned it from my father, who used to run away to the Gresham Hotel whenever he got upset. When your aunt Rosalie announced her engagement, he took an ax to the shed, smashed it to the ground, and then vanished for a week, eventually coming home loaded down with monogrammed towels. Why, we're still using them today."

She had an experienced laugh, and it made me feel reassured—both of us choosing to believe that "hotel" in this case was an actual location and not a synonym for Guinness.

The next day, there was a note from Aunt Brigid taped to the door when I got back late that night from my day trip to Galway. Pop had called and wanted me to join him in Dublin. He was staying at the Gresham and "enjoying it very much by the sound of it," Aunt Brigid wrote in expansive script punctuated with multiple exclamation points, followed by a cartoonish ellipsis—three oversize circles. My heart palpitated, tapping out its own Morse code, each beat signifying growing alarm.

When it came to Pop, even punctuation had the power to terrify.

Navigating rural Ireland's narrow roads wasn't my idea of fun, so I hopped the bus in Lisdoonvarna and settled in for the six-hour journey to Dublin, with stops along the way at Ennis, Shannon, and Limerick. The bus filled with a mix of locals and a bunch of buoyant American tourists who immediately engaged the bus driver, who was doing his best impersonation of Pat O'Brien: "Good morning, girls." He tipped his cap to the visibly middle-aged women, who giggled delightedly, instantly charmed.

He was chatting away, brogue so preposterous that it would make a leprechaun blush, answering questions, volunteering quaint folklore, pointing out the local fairy bush, and they loved every moment of it. By the time we got to Ennis, which is about twenty miles from the cottage, his voice betrayed a bit of strain, as if the burden of his Irish charm were rubbing up against the sandpaper of his truer nature. The tourists seemed clueless, ignoring the deepening of his sighs, but I sat up and took interest as his attention was diverted by a group of drunken teens who noisily clambered aboard in Shannon.

Ten miles later, the kids were fighting with him because he

wouldn't let them off to pee. Within moments it had turned into a full-out rumble, the bus driver shouting out profanities, the kids laughing and goading him on—the tourists exchanging worried glances, stunned into silence by the sudden turn of events. One of the boys hit the bus driver in the back of the head with an empty beer can, and the bus screeched to a sudden jolting halt; some people were thrown into the aisle, and my backpack tumbled from the overhead carriage and landed in my lap.

"Get out, the lot of you! Get out! Now, before I throw you off!" The bus driver was standing up and shouting at us, his hands doubled into fists, his mouth twisted into a cudgel.

"You can't be serious!" One of the American men stood up to try to negotiate with him as the locals unemotionally gathered up their stuff and prepared to disembark. "Be reasonable. We're in the middle of nowhere."

"Oh, say, don't waste your breath on that one. He's a right bastard, and doesn't he do this whenever the mood strikes? Pay him no mind," one of the Irish ladies said to the Americans. "There'll be another bus coming along soon enough."

Those of us who weren't natives watched in disbelief from the side of the isolated country road as the bus driver, flipping us the bird, drove off, wheels spinning, gravel churning. After about an hour or so, another bus finally lumbered along and we climbed aboard.

This driver, who stank of stale body odor, which I'd come to think of as Irish country cologne, made no pretense of charm. When I asked him how many more stops before we reached Dublin, he waved me off angrily. "Go on," he snarled. I sat next to an Irish woman, who rolled her eyes and shook her head and immediately started in on the bus driver. She was being helpful in the Irish way—she wanted to start shit.

"Oh, that one's a menace. And doesn't he beat up his poor wife on a regular basis and the children, too, if the truth were known. You shouldn't put up with that treatment for one second. And you a paying customer and a visitor to this country!" She pursed her lips, and her head wobbled on her thin, wrinkled neck. "It's a bloody shame, and he should be reported. If more people were to take action against such tyrants, well, then the world would be a better place. You're not going to just sit and take it, are you? But then maybe people are different in America. It's none of my business, after all."

She carried on like that for the rest of the trip—the bus broke down midway, and what should have been a six-hour journey turned into a ten-hour ordeal, the bus driver, Cerberus in an Ike jacket, refusing to give up any information. I was pretty worked up with miles yet to go by the time the bus rolled into Limerick. Sensing victory, my companion encouraged me to go and speak to the inspector.

There was a twenty-minute wait in Limerick, so I got off the bus and immediately encountered the inspector. I approached him in friendly fashion, polite, not looking to complain; I'd decided to take a cab the rest of the way to Dublin. At that point, I would have gladly bought a car and driven to Dublin myself.

"Excuse me," I said, and he looked at me, clearly annoyed, and waved his hand.

"I don't need to hear it. Just tell me where you are going."

"Dublin," I replied, feeling a flash of anger. "Just wondering, when you get a moment, will you please order me a taxi?"

"Go over there and wait," he said, flushed with irritation, pointing to a stand of chairs. Livid, I marched into the office to complain about him and the two bus drivers. The people inside were just as surly and reacted with considerable alarm, not at me being mistreated, but that I had the nerve to dare complain. They obviously thought I was a touchy-feely North American looking for deferential treatment, which engendered in them an instant hatred for me.

"Yes, well, we'll take your complaints under advisement," said the woman in charge, sniffing the air, not looking up from her paperwork. I turned to leave and heard her mumble something about the "arrogant Diaspora." I headed back out to the seating area, and a few moments later the inspector came out of the office like an angry hornet—obviously they couldn't wait to tattle—flying over at me, wagging his finger, and in a high-pitched nasal whine hollering at me to apologize.

"What are you talking about? Are you asking me to apologize *to you*?" I asked him incredulously, throwing my hands in the air.

"I certainly am," he declared, folding his arms and waiting.

"That's ridiculous. I asked you a simple question and you totally dismissed me. I have every right to complain about your attitude."

"Oh, well, excuse me for not dropping everything to take care of Your Majesty. I was busy taking care of people who really needed my help, but obviously I'm guilty of not paying proper heed to someone as important as you appear to be." He twisted around and poked me in the chest.

"Apologize, apologize!" he was railing, flipping right out.

Disbelieving what I was hearing, I was focused on his bushy eyebrows and his shoulders like ledges designed to catch falling dandruff. He was shorter than me and leaned into me. He gazed upward, staring at me; his eyes, yellow where they should have been white, were inches from my own.

"Apologize, apologize!" His voice lowered to a hiss.

Jesus, I couldn't believe I was actually entertaining the idea, thinking about apologizing just to put an end to the madness, a part of me wanting to scream a thousand pardons to the universe, another part of me wanting to knock him into the next life. Instead, deceptively calm, I interrupted to say that I was not going to apologize so he might as well forget it.

"Well," he said, drawing himself up, making grand sweeping gestures with his arms, glancing around at the crowd that had gathered in appreciation of his performance, "I will order you a cab this one time and this one time only, but I will never order another cab for you again in my lifetime."

Applause greeted his announcement—an older man in a cap stepped forward and said, "No man should consider himself above saying he's sorry. Do you think your expensive luggage grants you some sort of special entitlement from those of us in steerage?" He pointed to my leather backpack.

"Apologize? Apologize?" I said, refusing to be sidetracked, speaking to the group of onlookers, who surrounded the inspector protectively and looked back at me, their lips compressed in judgment and expectation. "Why? What did I do? Tell me what I did?" I persisted.

"Well," said one middle-aged woman, wearing a transparent plastic raincoat and a kerchief on her head that was tied under her chin, "why involve all of us? What have we to do with it? Say you're sorry and be done with it. I'm sure you know what you did."

CHAPTER THIRTY-FOUR

For Pop, spending three weeks in Ireland, where there was a pub under every rock, was like being hooked up to a Budweiser drip—between his unabated reeling drunkenness, Aunt Brigid's clueless matchmaking, and Uncle Tom's haranguing phone calls, I decided to quit the trip and come back home earlier than we'd originally planned.

On the flight back to the United States, the plane, bucking and pitching, wrestled with turbulence as I struggled to keep Pop from turning into a human liquor balloon. By the time we landed, he was both bombed and belligerent, immediately refusing to obey an order to remain in our seats while some British VIP was escorted off the plane.

"I will not!" Pop stormed, standing and reaching up for his overhead bag.

"Sir, please sit down," the flight attendant ordered calmly but firmly.

"Sit down yourself! I'll be goddamned if I'm going to wait like some sort of serf while some third-rate pasha is carried out of here on a sedan chair." He looked around at the other passengers, who were clearly stunned by his outburst. "What's wrong with you people? Putting up with this feudal nonsense—are you all card-carrying colonials?"

A handful of others began to express agreement as the stewardess, recognizing a minor mutiny in the making, went into the cockpit looking for reinforcements.

My first instinct was to try to get him to settle down, forget about it, let it pass, but watching him there in the aisle, up on his feet and raging—Pop never would take anything sitting down—well, it had a certain appeal. I stood up, hooked my bag over my shoulder, and took my place alongside him. "Come on, let's go," I said.

Several other passengers followed us as we headed toward the exit, where the decision was reluctantly made to let us off as Pop punched the air triumphantly with his fists.

"So," he said, opening the cab door as the driver loaded his luggage, "I suppose you'll be going to your grandfather's house."

"No, I think I'll come home for a while," I said, lifting my bags into the backseat of the car and sliding in next to them while Pop took up his preferred spot next to the cabbie.

We'd been home for a couple of days. It was mid-May, late at night, around eleven o'clock, and Uncle Tom and I were at the northernmost tip of the island, listening for areas of low-frequency sound generated by the earth's magnetic field.

"There it is. Do you hear it?"

"I don't hear anything, Uncle Tom."

"And why am I not surprised? You've no facility for listening—it's an art form, you know. When it comes to listening, you're a paint-by-number proposition, Noodle. Shhh . . . quiet . . ."

He froze, cupped hand midway between his shoulder and ear. He was next to me in the passenger seat of the car—neither he nor Pop drove; Uncle Tom never learned to drive, and Pop had lost his license years earlier, driving drunk. I can still see him nodding off behind the steering wheel, eyes rolling, and me under orders to pinch him whenever he fell asleep.

"Clear as a tuning fork. Perfect. Here's where we'll do our first training toss in the morning," he said.

"What do you mean, we?"

"I need your help if we're to be in shape for the race. We haven't much time, only a month, but I have a feeling we've got a tiptop team."

"Uncle Tom, I'm not interested in racing pigeons."

"Is it the money? Is that what this is about? Do you want me to say I'll split the purse with you? Ten thousand dollars, fine, I won't give you half, but I'll give you a third of ten percent."

"Give me a break. It's not the money. I just can't get that excited about training pigeons. . . ."

"Oh, I'm sorry. I forgot who you are. Dr. Collie Flanagan is too good for the likes of a band of pigeons. It's canaries all the way for you, isn't it? Just like when you were a boy and you wouldn't help me plant vegetables because you thought gardens were only for growing flowers, do you remember that?"

"Kind of."

"And you'd still plant a tulip over a potato, wouldn't you?"

"Yeah, I guess I might."

"Well, if it will appease your snobbery, then think about this. At one time, the common man was prevented by law from owning pigeons; it was an honor reserved for the high and the mighty. And here's another fact that may appeal to your discerning mind and fragile temperament: Racing pigeons are more properly termed racing doves. Is that balm enough to your gentility?"

"I don't care about all that. I just can't get that worked up about a bunch of birds. . . ."

"And what does inspire your interest, Noodle? Brooding? Moping? Creating great dramas in your head with yourself as the main actor?"

"Uncle Tom, for crying out loud, would you respect me more if I just shrugged off what I've done? A kid is dead because of me. What am I supposed to do? Roll my eyes and say, 'Shit happens,' and forget about it?"

"Say, keep your Alans on! All I know is that the dead have no currency among the living. You might just as well be devoting all your thoughts to leprechauns as moon over the dead. You owe me, the person sitting next to you, more than you owe the dearly departed. And by the way, while we're on the subject, you owe me plenty. It's time you started paying me back for all I've done, and instead there you sit, gnashing your teeth over a stranger and not showing even the tiniest whit of gratitude for all I've done. But I suppose you'll cry buckets at my funeral and get me a fancy coffin. Is that it?"

"It's not so easy, Uncle Tom. My negligence cost a seventeen-year-old boy his life."

"It's a sorry business all right, but there's no need to compound the tragedy by making my life more difficult."

We turned off the road and slowly drove up the long laneway leading to the house. Brendan and Kerry, two Irish wolfhounds, appeared out of the darkness, Pop and Tom's dogs, their favorite breed, the only breed Ma never liked. Barking and racing from door to door, they banged their front paws on the car windows, towering over the roof. I turned off the ignition and opened the door. Tom tapped me on the shoulder.

"Anyway, enough about you—you know, Collie, the world wasn't made just for you. Be sure to get a good sleep. I'll be shaking you awake at five-thirty. We'll want to toss the birds at seven on the dot."

At five o'clock the next morning, Uncle Tom woke me up the same way he used to when I was a kid: He threw a glass of ice cold water in my face.

"Holy shit!" I said.

"Hey, hey, language, Collie, language. That type of talk is as old as Adam and Eve," Pop yelled from his room directly across the hall from mine.

"Did you learn that cursing from Brown, or was it Harvard?" Uncle Tom asked before disappearing into the dusk, his footsteps sounding heavy on the stairs.

"All right. Time for you to meet the team. Let's see what they think of you. Here's Francis, and then there's Patsy, Raymond, Joe, Martin. Further down is Kevin, then Kieran, Thomas, and Michael and—"

"I know. Bobby Sands," I said with a sly glance.

Uncle Tom wouldn't look at me. "I suppose you think you're very intelligent right about now."

"I just happened to recognize the names of the hunger strikers."

"Just remember, you're never so smart that you can't learn something from a pigeon—it's a philosophy that's served me well my whole life. You think about that, Noodle, when you're congratulating yourself on your cleverness."

"Who's this?" I said, stopping in front of a solid red bird, russet feathers sleek and shining in the early morning sunlight that streamed into the loft.

"Here's the champ. He's one in a million. I call him Bingo. . . ."

"Oh, I guess Bing would like that, I think he would. Don't you?"

Uncle Tom rolled his eyes. "Well, say, use your head. How would I know? And anyway, what difference does it make?"

"Well, none, when you put it that way. . . ."

"He's named for the game, not the nephew. I have more in my life than you two nitwits, you know. If I'd named him Collie, would you assume it was in your honor?"

"Not any more I wouldn't."

"You could use a few lessons in subtlety—and while you're at it, stop drawing the obvious conclusion," Uncle Tom said, rumbling with annoyance.

Tom's pigeons were bred from a strain imported from Holland years ago. They could trace their lineage back to the frequently mentioned legendary Michael Collins, the pigeon who walked home after breaking his wing. Uncle Tom had plans to enter them in the prestigious Chilmark Classic, a five-hundred-mile race from Rogue Bluffs, Maine, to Martha's Vineyard. Since I was the only one who could drive and help him safely transport the birds, he named me assistant coach, introducing me to his fellow pigeon racers as Barney Fife, which somehow mutated into Harvard Barney, my official pigeon-coaching name.

My Ivy League education was always good for a laugh among Uncle Tom's cronies.

My principal practical duties seemed to be cleaning out the loft twice a day while listening to endless lectures about the care, feeding, and handling of racing pigeons, along with complicated sermons concerning the aerodynamics of flight.

Uncle Tom was always pulling pop quizzes, just the way he did when I was a kid.

"What is the name of the pigeon awarded the French Croix de Guerre for bravely continuing his mission for the American Army signal corps despite being shot twice?" he asked one early morning as he sipped his coffee while I scraped pigeon shit from the loft's wooden floor.

"Cher Ami."

"Can pigeons read?"

"No."

"Oh, is that so? Explain then why they can distinguish all twenty-six letters of the alphabet?"

"How do I know?"

"The answer is obvious—to read directions and the occasional biography. They also enjoy limerick books and how-to manuals."

Uncle Tom drew up a twenty-eight-day training schedule. The first day, we drove to the farthest tip of Vineyard Haven and tossed them skyward—it took them about two hours to make the twenty-mile flight home. Bingo was the first back at the loft, followed by Bobby and then Patsy. Within a week of training, which included a couple of days off, they were able to find their way home in less than thirty minutes.

Bobby, Patsy, and Bingo were the consistent front-runners.

"We've got our three top competitors," Uncle Tom said as we traveled by boat out into the ocean, where we were getting ready to release them for a longer flight—forty miles.

"Lovely birds, Tom," Pop said, accompanying us on the trip, reaching for Patsy, cupping him in the canoe of his hands. "Collie tells me you expect great things from them in the race."

"I do indeed. This is an exceptional group—the finest birds I've ever bred."

Pop and Uncle Tom could be inexplicably formal with each other. I was holding Bingo in my hands and leaning against the deck, listening as they talked— sharing their mutual love for birds and animals, they were practically cooing.

"Six hundred heartbeats per minute for up to sixteen hours . . . their wings beating up to ten times per second." Uncle Tom was reciting his favorite statistics to Pop, who was listening avidly.

"Who is the fastest bird?" he asked.

"Bingo," I said.

"What's his fastest time?"

I said, "Ninety miles an hour—"

"Look here, Noodle, quit interrupting, that's for me to say," Uncle Tom said. "I'm the senior coach."

"Sorry," I said as Bingo gently pecked the knuckles of my other hand.

"Has Collie been a big help? I'll bet he has," Pop said to Uncle Tom, who looked sorely put out.

"No, he has not. Every moment I feel the effects of dealing with a listening-impaired amateur."

"So, Collie, you seem to be enjoying your stint as a pigeon coach," Pop said.

"Not really," I said as I tossed Bingo high into the sky, watching as he powered straight up into the air, followed closely by Patsy and Bobby, all three beginning their mysterious journey home.

CHAPTER THIRTY-FIVE

It was my first visit to Cassowary since the trip to Ireland, and I found the Falcon down at the stable checking out a new foal, born the night before. He seemed mildly surprised to see me, gave me an awkward hug, and then took a few steps in reverse, his back coming to rest against the stall door.

"You're looking well, Collie. Nice shirt," he said. "You can't go wrong with a good white shirt. Where did you get it? Brown and Thomas?"

I nodded. "How did you know?"

"I have an unerring instinct for such things."

I reached into my back pocket. "Here's your money clip," I said sheepishly. "I'm sorry about Pop."

"That makes two of us," he said, popping the clip into his jacket pocket. "So, how did you find the old country? Was it suitably challenging and charming?"

I laughed. "Yeah, you might say that."

"I hope you don't nurture any sort of sentimental desire to live there," he said, looking faintly concerned.

"Oh no. No chance of that happening."

"And you're feeling better, are you?" he asked, averting his eyes.

"Yeah, I'm okay, Granddad."

"I understand from Ingrid that you've taken up pigeon racing with Tom Flanagan," the Falcon said, relaxing a little and folding his arms in front of his chest, his head cocked to one side.

"I'm just helping him out. It's no big deal. He wants to enter some of his birds in one of the big races coming up."

"You could do worse things with your time," he said. "The racing pigeon is a remarkable creature."

"You sound like Uncle Tom," I said, unable to resist.

"Yes, well, oh, dear," he said, momentarily set back. "Come and look at our newest addition to the family." He opened the door to the stall and gestured for me to follow him inside.

"What's his name?" I asked, reaching down to pet the baby horse, a deep sorrel color.

"Mr. Guppy," the Falcon said, rubbing the mother's forehead and offering her a carrot from inside his jacket pocket. "You must bring some of your pigeons to Cassowary. I'd like to see them," he said.

"Sure. I'll bring Bobby Sands sometime next week, if I can sneak him past Uncle Tom."

"Bobby Sands? Of course, what else would he be called? Your mother would appreciate that, wouldn't she? Poor Mr. Sands, I understand he loved birds. Oh well, maybe there are birds in heaven—there must be. It wouldn't be heaven, would it, if there weren't any birds?"

"That's what Ma used to say about dogs," I said.

"Really? Did she say that? I had no idea." He reached into his pocket for another carrot. "Will you stay for dinner?" he asked me.

"Yes, thanks, I'd like that," I said.

"All right," he said. "Let's hope that after three weeks in Ireland you haven't begun eating your peas with a knife."

I woke up early the next morning, the day before the pigeon race. Uncle Tom and I were scheduled to make the drive to Maine.

"Pop, have you seen Uncle Tom?" I stepped from the hallway into the open door leading to his bedroom—the same one he shared with Ma for so many years.

"Pop?"

"Good heavens, Collie, you woke me from a dead sleep. What time is it?" He was buried under a mountain of blankets even though it was warm.

"Seven o'clock. Uncle Tom's not in his bedroom. I can't find him in the house. I checked the loft and he's not there, either—"

"Seven o'clock! What are you thinking? It's the middle of the night." He rubbed his eyes and patted his chest before lifting himself onto his elbows. "Wait a minute while I collect my thoughts."

"Pop, come on, it's important. . . ." I could see him deliberately stalling, relishing the chaos he knew would ensue from what he was about to say.

"Now I remember . . . I'm afraid I've some bad news for you. Swayze came calling after you'd gone to bed—"

"Oh no. No! No! Jesus." The news blew me off my feet and into the nearest armchair. "You've got to be kidding. That's just great. We're supposed to leave for Maine today. . . ."

"Well, if history's any teacher, your uncle Tom will be AWOL for the foreseeable future."

"I don't believe it." I hopped back up onto my feet. "The race is tomorrow. What an idiot I am to get involved. I really thought this time would be different." I was pacing. I didn't know whether I was sad or angry or both. At the same time, I was trying to figure out why I was so upset when I should have been relieved. I'd been resisting the idea of the race since the beginning, and now I had a perfect out.

"Settle down, Collie. Why all the emotion? Where's this coming from? Panic isn't a becoming trait in a man." Pop never missed an opening for a sermon. "What did you expect? You know your uncle Tom." Transparently thrilled by Tom's truancy, he pulled the pillows up around his head, making himself comfortable, settling into the disarray as if it were a featherbed. "What will you do now?"

"What do you mean, what will I do? What can I do? This was his stupid project. All I can do is hope that he shows up sometime today before it's too late. . . . Does Swayze still live in Chilmark?"

"No, he's in Edgartown with his sister and her husband. . . ."

"Okay. I'll see if Uncle Tom is there . . . or maybe they know where the two of them are. Fuck . . ."

"Please, must you swear, Collie? I've told you since you were a boy, bad language makes a man ordinary."

"I am ordinary, Pop."

Swayze was passed out in the living room of his sister's Edgartown cottage. She helped me roust him into temporary lucidity.

"Last time I saw your uncle Tom, he was headed to Victoria Park to feed the pigeons," he said, his eyes like slits.

"When was that?" I asked him.

"I haven't a clue," Swayze answered, collapsing like a hollow suit.

I found him in a heap, familiar position, facedown on the ground, two pigeons perched on his shoulders and one nesting in the small of his back—Uncle Tom finally had become a living monument. They reluctantly lifted off as I approached.

"Uncle Tom . . ." I squeezed his arm. "Wake up. . . . Uncle Tom."

He opened his eyes and mumbled something unintelligible. Bending down, I reached for his arms and tried hoisting him to his feet. He was a dead weight. I couldn't carry him or drag him, either. Finally, I managed to revive him enough to get him vertical, my arms around his waist, his back against my abdomen, his feet positioned on top of my feet, as I tried to walk him to the car, struggling with my cane and my bum leg.

He lurched forward and I went over with him; he was sprawled out over the ground, face forward, me on top of him and struggling to get free. I pulled him back up on his feet, and this time we fell backward, him landing on top of me with a thud.

He weighed a ton; I could feel my lungs collapsing under the weight of him. For a moment, I thought about just staying there forever beneath him, crushed by the rock slide of Tom Flanagan, buried under an avalanche of booze and blarney.

I wriggled out from underneath him and grabbed his ankles, dragging him over to the car, where I coaxed some reluctant Good Samaritan into helping me lift him into the backseat.

"Pop! . . . Hey, Pop!" I called out from the kitchen, the midafternoon June breeze rippling in waves of sound through the open and unscreened window next to me. "Where are you? Can you give me a hand with Uncle Tom? I need your help."

I followed Brendan and Kerry into the living room, where I saw Pop splayed in the shape of a cross, stretched out on his back on the pine floor—the dogs licking his face and covering him in a thin veneer of saliva.

"How's about another kiss, Miriam, my love?" he said, grinning, making smacking sounds, wrapping his arms around Brendan.

Slowly I sagged into the closest chair. Wagging his tail, Kerry came over and put his wiry head in my lap. He smiled up at me. I looked down at him looking up at me.

"Pray for me, Kerry," I said.

A few minutes later, I stood up and went outside, and after a ludicrous struggle, I managed to get Uncle Tom into the house and lined up alongside Pop on the floor. I went upstairs and got a couple of blankets, covered them up, and went back upstairs to get washed and dressed.

Uncle Tom was sitting up on the floor, had dragged himself up, his shoulders against the sofa, eyes closed and head leaning back, when I came back down to the living room.

"Thanks," I said to him from just inside the doorway. "I didn't want to do this. I don't care about racing pigeons. You're the one that talked me into it. I was just doing this for you. It was all you. You asked me. You wanted me. Even if you won't admit it, you know you did. You needed my help. You wanted my help. So I gave in and spent weeks training the birds with you and taking care of them and listening to you talk about nothing but this big weekend, and this is how it ends? Now what am I supposed to do?"

"What's all the fuss?" Pop said from his spot where he lay next to Tom, drawing himself up on his elbows and squinting elaborately in my direction.

"You're hopeless, both of you, you'll never change. You know, I look at you two and I wonder. What would it take to stop you from doing this? Jesus, why did I let myself think this time would be different? How could I be so stupid? What's wrong with me?"

For probably the first time in their lives, both Pop and Uncle Tom were speechless, and in Pop's eyes there was a look I took to be something almost like shame flickering briefly.

"Well," Pop said finally, rubbing his hand over his face the way he always did when he was trying to pull himself together, "that stings."

"Oh no, you're not going to make me the villain in this," I said, though I had already begun to feel the part.

"It's one thing to tell a man off, Collie," Pop said. "It's another to strip him of all that he is and leave him with nothing. Are we nothing? Do our lapses make us nothing? All right . . ." He shrugged, an improbable dignity hovering over his head, and Uncle Tom's, too, appearing like a muted rainbow. "Maybe it's so."

The whole time, Uncle Tom kept uncharacteristically silent—drunk or sober, he always had plenty to say—just sat there with his back resting against the legs of the sofa, his chin in his hand, his hand cupped around his cheek, his elbow on his chest, his eyes averted.

When Pop finished, Uncle Tom's gaze finally met mine, and something passed between us—it didn't last long, but it lasted long enough.

An hour or so later, I was on the road heading for Maine with Patsy and Bobby in a release cage in the backseat. Bingo sat perched on my shoulder, cooing the whole five hundred miles that it took to get to Rogue Bluffs.

By the time I got to the race site, I was pretty much at a loss to explain why I was there at all. I seemed to be under the influence of the earth's magnetic field myself, following a prescribed route, keeping to this unyielding linear journey for reasons I didn't understand and decided not to explore.

I tormented myself with thoughts about Bingo being torn apart by a hawk or a falcon. They're so vulnerable, pigeons, when they're on their own. Racing season must be for predators a kind of avian carnival; Patsy, Bobby, and Bingo were looking more and more like cotton candy and corn dogs.

I argued with myself right up until the moment of release, but in the end I let them go.

I held on to Bingo a second longer than I should have. I tossed him into the air above my head. I watched as he disappeared into a moving gray cloud that temporarily obliterated the sun, hundreds of birds surging forward as a single unit, driven by the same purpose but ultimately destined to make their own individual journey, separate and alone.

"You must be Harvard Barney," said someone in a pair of overalls, sidling up alongside me, his baseball cap spattered in birdshit, both of us beneath the shifting sky of birds.

"Yeah, that's me. How did you know?"

He laughed. "You got the look. How go the hieroglyphics?"

I suppressed the urge to lop off my head with my Swiss army knife. "Fine. Thanks for asking."

"Good. Where's Tom?"

"He was feeling a little under the weather."

"Too bad. I hear he's got quite a bird this year, a real contender, a little red fella. . . ."

I nodded in agreement, all the while staring skyward, the two of us focusing on the birds, not talking but looking, watching until you couldn't see them anymore. It has a name, the moment when a pigeon disappears from sight—it's called "vanishing bearings."

Two weeks passed with no sign of little Bingo.

"It's no use, he's not coming home," I said to Uncle Tom as I walked into the kitchen after checking the loft for the hundredth time over the course of the morning. Bobby and Patsy made it back to the loft the day of the release, placing fourth and fifth.

"What kind of talk is that?" Uncle Tom demanded. "You never know. Remember the story of Michael Collins. He walked home."

"Uncle Tom, please, enough with the Michael Collins fable. Bingo's fallen victim to the perils of the flight home, we've got to face it."

"And why is that, exactly?" Uncle Tom stuck out his chin, a wedge between himself and my pessimism. "Because you say so? You're never right about anything, Noodle. What makes you think you're right about this all of a sudden? Anyway, he was my bird. I'm the one who's suffering the loss. What about me? You're always trying to steal my thunder. Why don't you make yourself useful for a change, think of someone other than yourself and get out there and look for him?"

"Look for him? Where in the hell am I going to look for him between here and Maine?"

"You're so smart, you tell me. You've got so many years of high-priced education stored up in your little pea brain that you can't think anymore. If you were half as intelligent as a pigeon, you might be worth having around."

"Jesus," I said, slumping into the kitchen chair, burying my head in my hands.

"You can start by following all the major highways, for sure that's what Bingo is doing. Let the mountains be your guide. Use your olfactory senses and open yourself up to the sun and the earth's magnetic forces—in other words, aspire to a higher intellectual plane and try to think like a pigeon, if it doesn't hurt your head too much."

I was looking at him now the way you might look at a termite infestation or mosquitoes, fleas, bedbugs—what the hell was God thinking?

"I'll pack you a lunch," Uncle Tom said, opening the refrigerator door and viewing the contents. "Nice fresh soda bread, thick-sliced, tuna fish, and sweet gherkins. How many sandwiches would you like?"

"Uncle Tom, I don't care. . . ."

"Well, say, that's a fine attitude," he said.

"All right, three or four, I guess."

"Three or four! What do I look like, a short-order cook? And not even a 'please' or a 'thank you'? Two will do just fine. Say, what gluttony. When are you ever going to learn to grow up and forage for yourself?"

CHAPTER THIRTY-SIX

"Noodle, one last thing . . . ," Uncle Tom said when I was halfway out the kitchen door.

"Yeah?" Pausing, one foot on the veranda, I turned around to face him.

"Don't forget to whistle the way I taught you to. Bingo's very partial to that tune."

"I won't," I said.

I drove myself nuts singing "Bye, Bye, Blackbird" over and over again as I toured the island looking in vain for Bingo, retracing the route I used for the race. I was clipping along the back roads and main roads, looking everywhere for a little pumpkin-colored bird. It seemed like such a dumb thing to be doing, I didn't even know why I was doing it, I felt like the patron saint of futility, but I was responsible for what happened to him. I let him go, and I shouldn't have. He was happy in his little world. The greater world isn't always what it's cracked up to be.

The windows in the front seat were sealed, the air-conditioning was on, it was hot for June, more like July. I was driving slowly, the Vineyard was loaded with tourists, people behind me honking and passing in disgust. I was scanning both sides of the road as I drove, and I wondered how it had ever come to this.

Earlier, I had argued with Uncle Tom about searching for Bingo. "For Pete's sake, Uncle Tom, it's only a pigeon."

"Only a pigeon?" He looked at me in disbelief, hands gripping either side of the armrest in the chair where he sat, staring up at me. "Is that what you said? Only a pigeon? Why, I'll have you know that pigeons can hear the wind blowing a thousand miles away. They can see over a twenty-six-mile expanse. Compete with that, why don't you?"

Nobody knows how pigeons find their way home. How do they do it? Why do they do it? Why the hell does anybody do anything?

"Everybody's looking for a little magic, Collie," Pop used to say, polishing his framed Karl Malden autograph.

"Except for Collie," Bingo would answer back. "He doesn't believe in magic."

I wouldn't be driving around looking, would I, if I didn't believe in magic?

After a couple of hours driving in and around the shoreline, I was feeling a little discouraged and tired, and then I remembered that Uncle Tom had packed me a lunch. So I turned into a conservation area bordering the ocean and kept going until I came to a clearing in the dunes on the beach that had three or four picnic tables set up for day trippers.

After parking under the shade of an enormous tree, I undid the laces of my running shoes, slid them off, and walked barefoot to the beach with my homemade lunch.

Within moments, the seagulls arrived and shouted out demands. Sitting at the picnic table, I tossed out thick pieces of crusty white bread and watched them bicker over who got what.

Uncle Tom only ever made three kinds of sandwiches—white tuna fish, red sockeye salmon, and egg salad—and he always made them exactly the same way. I bit into my two pieces of fresh bread, buttered lightly and then filled an inch thick with a combination of tuna fish, mayonnaise, sweet gherkins, and slivered scallions, and it tasted the same then as it had when I was a little kid. He made great chocolate fudge, too. I started going over in my mind some of my other favorites. I was thinking that maybe when I got home I could talk him into making what Bingo and I reverentially dubbed his "green salad" when it occurred to me that food was probably the only thing in life that never disappoints.

"And that," I said to one of the seagulls poised tentatively on the tabletop within striking distance of what was left of my sandwich, "is pretty damn disappointing."

Something on the shoreline caught my eye; squinting, I decided to get a better look. The seagulls scattered as I stood up and jogged up to the waterline, where a huge rock sturgeon had washed up on shore and was dying in the sun. Three or four feet long, the olive brown fish was struggling for air, rubbery elongated mouth frantically opening and closing. Grabbing him by the tail fin—he was heavy, about forty pounds—I dragged him back into the water to ease his passing. He floated on top. He was being carried away by the undertow; there was no struggle left in him.

I hadn't seen such a big sturgeon in years. He must have been fifty years old. Sturgeons are bottom-feeders. Pop told me that sturgeons can live to be one hundred years old—some may even live to be two hundred. I watched as the giant fish settled in for the inevitable, rocked by the water's gentle motion.

Dogs go into decline after a decade. Bingo was only eighteen when he died. Ma was fifty years old. Eighty years is considered the top end of a human life. Yet for some reason, God thought it was important to confer virtual immortality on sturgeons.

Thinking about it had the odd effect of buoying my spirits—looking for a lost homing pigeon didn't seem quite so crazy when you consider some of the ways that God chooses to entertain Himself.

Back at the car, I pulled on my running shoes, swung the car into reverse, and decided to devote a little more time to the search for Bingo.

I boarded the ferry and thought about what I was going to do—retrace the whole trip to Maine, hoping to spot him somewhere en route? Chances were he was dead, a raptor got him, a cat, maybe a car. He could've flown into a store window, or some creepy kid probably nailed him with a BB gun.

The more sorry fates I conjured up for Bingo, the more motivated I was to keep looking.

I drove around on the mainland for a couple of hours. At one point, a mourning dove flew up in front of the windshield and I slammed on the brakes, thinking it was him, trying to reconcile my conflicting feelings of hope and futility.

I'd been driving for most of the day, the sun was beginning to set, and I was considering calling it quits—but then, Jesus, there he was. Over there, it was him, Bingo, there was no mistake about who it was. I couldn't believe what I was seeing.

I almost missed him. I was on this narrow country road, quiet, sweet, overgrown, smelling like clover. I couldn't even say what made me take this offbeat side road, but I spotted him: There he was, walking, full of purpose and looking straight ahead, pausing occasionally to peck the ground but steadily making his way on the train tracks, his wing a half-extended fan and dragging on the ground.

We were about twenty-five miles from home. He was hoofing it on this defunct railway line, overgrown tracks surrounded by cornfields and open pasture—the only sounds the buzz and whir of insects and the chirping of birds. He couldn't have chosen a safer route; those tracks hadn't seen a train in years.

The sun burned down on the top of my head as I stepped onto

the grass at the side of the gravel road and softly shut the car door—I didn't want to scare him. I didn't feel like chasing a bird through a field of weeds and rock. I walked slowly toward him, calling his name and whistling "Bye, Bye Blackbird" to attract his attention.

He paused at the familiar tune and, cooing, continued pecking along the track, looking up finally as I came toward him. After pausing for a moment, I bent and scooped him up in my hands, where he relaxed. As I was walking back toward the car, I was hoping there was no one around, no one watching and wondering what the hell I was doing.

Sliding in behind the wheel with little Bingo in my hands, I couldn't believe how lucky he was that I found him. His wing was obviously broken, but it was easy enough to repair a broken wing.

I set him beside me in the passenger seat and then lifted open the carrying case Uncle Tom had made me bring just in case I found him.

I put him inside, and his contented cooing grew stronger. He was safe. He knew he was going home. I turned onto the narrow two-lane highway, shut off the air conditioner, and rolled down the window, the air warm as a blanket; I took a moment, half laughing, half crying, to breathe in the consoling aroma of a perfect day in June.

"Maybe we should change your name to Karl Malden," I said.

Overhead it was dusk, the blackbirds circling above me in feral benediction.

CHAPTER THIRTY-SEVEN

"Uncle Tom, I think I can figure out how to set a broken wing on a pigeon."

"Pride goeth before a fall," Uncle Tom said. "Remember, no man's a hero to his uncle."

We were on the veranda, early morning sun glimmering on the water, Uncle Tom holding on to Bingo, who was cooing mildly and pecking, and I was checking to see that the broken part of his wing felt warm.

"Circulation seems okay," I said. "I think there's a good chance his wing will heal."

"What would you know about it? When's the last time you treated a bird?"

"It's applied knowledge, Uncle Tom," I said.

"Say, you're patronizing," he said. "I liked you better when you were a deep disappointment."

Uncle Tom continued chatting away to Bingo as I lined up each fragile bone and then taped the wing so it folded in a natural resting position next to his body.

I went to see the Falcon that Sunday. Our Sunday suppers were becoming a routine occurrence. The Falcon had finally set some limits on his practice of flying the globe to terrorize his employees. He rarely entertained anymore, and although he kept up social contacts via the phone, I was his only regular visitor.

He was older. I was older. The strains that characterized our relationship, while still present, were more reassuring than infuriating. Learning to cope with Pop, Uncle Tom, and the Falcon was my greatest struggle and achievement—I finally realized that the Man Plan was more about adapting to their various manifestations of manhood than carving out my own dilute impersonation.

The Falcon and I were sitting in our usual spots at the end of the long dining room table, the grandfather clock keeping noisy time in the background, the canaries tittering in response to each loud tick-tock.

"So what do you intend to do with your life?" the Falcon persisted. It was the same question he asked me every time he saw me. He had probably asked me that question a thousand times, and a thousand times I avoided answering him.

"I don't know." I reached for a glass of water and took a sip.

"Will you go back to medicine?"

"Honestly, I don't know."

"Well, don't you think you should be thinking about it?"

"Have some faith in me," I said. I laughed. "Do I have your faith, Granddad? What about you, Cromwell?" He looked back expectantly. "Do I have your faith?"

"Collie, what *are* you talking about?" The Falcon put down his fork and knife and stared at me. For once he didn't seem thoroughly annoyed—just annoyed. He seemed honestly perplexed.

I laughed. "Oh, never mind. It's nothing. It's a joke. Just something I once overheard."

"Well, it helps in one's life to make some sense, and last time I checked, jokes were supposed to be humorous. Good Lord, you're not becoming whimsical, are you? You must get a hold of yourself. I mean, do you intend to marry? It seems to me you've been engaged half a dozen times, most of them suitable girls. And yet nothing sticks. You're threatening to become some sort of perverse version of Porfirio Rubirosa. Do you want to have a family? Devote yourself to something worthwhile? Or do you plan to simply knock around the beach picking up beer bottles with the Flanagan brothers?" He took a sip of water as if he needed to cleanse his palate after invoking the specter of Pop and Tom.

"First of all, I've been engaged twice. Things don't always work out according to plans. They were great girls, but I want to feel as if—"

"You can't live without her," the Falcon finished my thought. He stared up at the ceiling. "Lord, grant me the serenity."

"Don't worry, I'll figure out something. I just don't know what it will be yet. Life doesn't always run on schedule. Anyway, what do you care? I obviously annoy the hell out of you. Why are you so interested in my life?" I really didn't mind his inquiries—I just couldn't understand their origin. I thought by asking, finally I might find out.

"Because you're my grandson," he said, straightening out the napkin on his lap. I stared down at my plate. Cromwell's heavy panting was the only sound.

I reached for another helping of salad. "How's your leg?" I asked.

"Bloody arthritis," he said, rubbing the top of his thigh. "They want me to have knee surgery, but I'm resisting their best efforts. It looks as though I may need a cane."

"We'll be twins," I said cheerfully.

"Don't get carried away, Collie," he said. "Is it ever painful?" He pointed to my leg.

I glanced down. "I hardly notice anymore. It's amazing what you can get used to."

He considered for a moment. "I suppose that's true. Do you ever think about it? What happened in El Salvador?"

I smoothed the tablecloth with the palm of my hand. "Yeah, I think about it now and again."

"We'd like some coffee," he said to Ruby, a longtime member of his household staff. She was serving dinner.

"Thanks," I said as she poured me a cup. I reached for the cream and sugar.

"Young men have pursued glory and heroism, testing themselves and their characters, since the beginning of time," the Falcon said, watching me. He took a sip of his coffee. "If they're lucky, they live through it. Did I ever tell you that I was in Africa during the recolonization period in the fifties?"

I looked over at him, surprised not that he was there, but that he assumed he'd told me about it. I was even more surprised that he was telling me about it now.

"No," I said. "But then there is a lot I don't know about you."

"I wasn't always an old man, Collie," he said wryly. "You and I aren't as different as you might imagine."

I tried not to look startled, which isn't easy when you've just swallowed your tongue.

"I once saw a man try to intervene to prevent a group of terrified girls from being taken away from his village by rebels. They were being loaded into the back of a truck. The girls were screaming and pleading for help. It was a terrible scene. Everyone stood and watched. All of us knew what was going to happen to them even if we couldn't admit it at the time." He paused and cleared his throat. He reached for a glass of water and drank before resuming his story.

"They were going to be raped and then murdered. And no one could stop it." He shook his head and shrugged. I nodded in acknowledgment.

"This madman suddenly appeared from the back of the crowd. In terms of his looks and manner, he was a most unremarkable fellow. He may have been in his early forties. He must have known he didn't have a prayer, but he came out of the crowd and attacked one of the militia who was helping to load another girl onto the truck, and bang! They shot him. He fell forward, and still he didn't give up. He dug his nails into the mud and dragged himself to the back of the truck where the girls were. His fingers made deep furrows in the mud." The Falcon gestured with his hands, extending his fingers and dragging them along the top of the table.

"He pulled himself along that way for a few feet, and then someone—one of the rebels—stepped forward and shot him in the back of the head. The truck drove away with the girls, and their parents were crying, a terrible wailing went up as the crowd slowly dispersed. When the sun came out later in the day, it baked the mud and preserved the grooves he'd made in the ground. The dried mud was like cement, and for a long time afterward you could see those claw marks on the ground, a memorial to him and a rebuke to the rest of us who did nothing."

He snapped his fingers softly. Cromwell looked up from his place on the floor near the door and wagged his tail.

"What happened to the girls?"

"I haven't a clue," he said, reaching down to pet Cromwell, who rose from the floor to meet his hand.

Just then Ingrid walked in. "Smile," she said, grinning as she snapped a photo of the Falcon and Cromwell.

"See what your grandfather got me for my birthday," she said, showing me her new camera.

"I've regretted it ever since," he said, shaking his head. "Wait a minute—" He gestured in my direction. "Collie, come stand beside me. Ingrid, take a picture of the two of us together, and make sure to focus."

He was sitting in his chair at the head of the table. I took up a spot behind him and waited while Ingrid fidgeted around.

The Falcon started to stand up and signaled the place next to him.

"Stand beside me," he said.

"Okay," I said, moving into place. He reached down and slipped his hand in mine as Ingrid ordered us to smile and the camera clicked.

"Have Ruby bring us some more coffee," the Falcon said to

Ingrid as he withdrew his hand and motioned for me to join him in the living room.

The conversation shifted to other things, to Mr. Guppy, to the state of the London office, to the pigeon race, to the unfortunate length of my hair, to the way my mother looked on her bicycle as she rode around the circular drive at Cassowary in her teens, beloved pet dogs chasing after her. As we talked, the Westminster chime resonated, marking time in the same old way that it had since I was a little boy.

I can still feel the warmth of my grandfather's hand in mine.

"Tom tells me Bingo's thriving," Pop said over lunch a few days later.

"I hope so," I said.

"I said no such thing," Uncle Tom objected from the bistro. "I said that he didn't appear to be getting worse, which is a far cry from thriving."

"Is there any more chicken, Uncle Tom?" I asked, hoping to change the subject.

"No, there isn't."

"Here, take mine," Pop said, offering his plate. "Nothing's too good for the man of the hour."

"No, Pop, no thanks. I'm fine."

He just kept on insisting and I kept on refusing, but you know, you couldn't fight Pop and win, so I finally gave in.

"I've been meaning to speak to you," Uncle Tom spoke up. "Swayze's got a sore throat and an earache. . . ."

"That's too bad," I said. "He should have it looked at."

"Good of you to offer," he said sarcastically.

I stopped eating. "You want me to treat Swayze?"

"Well, I don't know. Are you equal to it? I don't want to give him a bum steer."

"I'm not a GP, but I think I can handle an uncomplicated sore ear and throat."

"I have my doubts. Seems to me by declaring it uncomplicated you've already made a diagnosis. . . ."

"It's not a diagnosis, Uncle Tom. I was putting forth a feeble defense."

"Maybe instead of getting defensive and hoarding your alleged skills, you should apply your energies to thinking about others for a change."

Pop, looking thoughtful, sat back in his chair. "I've got to agree with Tom on this one, Collie. What's the point of training to become an astronaut if you never plan to travel farther than Decatur?"

My hands gripping the edge of the table, I focused my attention on a spot on the wall directly across from me. "I'll be happy to have a look at Swayze."

"Gratis?" Uncle Tom asked.

"Of course. Cripes, Uncle Tom, you think I'd ask Swayze for money?"

"How should I know? I wouldn't put anything past you."

It turned out Swayze had a simple infection. I prescribed an antibiotic—actually, I wound up driving him and Uncle Tom to a drugstore in Edgartown, where I bought the medication and then chauffeured them around for the day.

"Swayze says to tell you he's all better," Uncle Tom said after a week or so.

"Good."

"I don't know. I'm thinking about letting you treat me, but then again I'm not sure you're up to the task."

I shrugged.

He narrowed his eyes and gave me the once-over. "How do you spell 'malpractice suit'?"

Three weeks later, Pop and Uncle Tom and I were together at the East Chop Lighthouse. The late afternoon sun disappeared behind a cloud. I was holding on to Bingo, clutching him close to my chest.

"Time to release, Collie, let's see how he fares," Pop said, rubbing his hands in anticipation.

"Well, what are you waiting for?" Uncle Tom asked, nudging the tip of my cane with his foot.

"Okay, here goes," I said, tossing Bingo skyward, all three of us holding our collective breath, watching as he flapped his wings, the air lifting him higher and higher as he headed for home.

"Say, you should be a doctor," Uncle Tom said.

"Good man!" Pop said.

Back at the house I looked out over the open water, the sun shimmering at the surface, all around me so silent that I could hear the earth humming.

I once read that some geologists think that the earth hums loudest late in the afternoon, vibrating in response to ocean waves or distant windstorms. Frequencies are low enough so that when the earth hums it sounds like a garbage bin lid banging on the road.

As I turned and walked up the path leading to the back door of the house, the wind and the waves picked up, a loose edge of the stable's metal roof clanged methodically against the old barn beams, the world and all the living banging bin-lids so loudly, it was enough to wake the dead.

Later that night, I was lying in bed listening to the familiar music of my childhood, Pop's records playing gently below, Pop singing along, but quietly, the back-and-forth rhythm of water lapping on the rocks and the sand, offshore breeze whistling softly, insistent tapping on my window.

"Bingo!" I opened the window wide and stroked his silky feathers, watching as he pecked away at insects and grit all along the wooden sill. Seeming to ignore me—pigeons have a careless way of giving their full attention—he hopped into the room and onto the arm of an aging wicker chair and made himself at home.

Bing used to swim way out into the ocean. One time I was on a sail with friends and we came across him floating on his back in the middle of the choppy Atlantic. One of my buddies from Andover got all excited thinking we'd discovered someone lost at sea and in dire need of rescue. "Collie!" he shouted, pointing. "Look! Over there!"

I was standing on the deck, and I was shaking my head seeing that unceremonious glint of chestnut hair bobbing up and down. Pulling up alongside him, I extended my hand.

"If you try to pull me in . . . ," I warned him.

"I promise," he said, lifting his eyebrows and grinning up at me.

"Come on," I said to him. "Don't be an asshole. Climb in." But he dove deep beneath the water's surface and disappeared.

"Oh, my God, where is he?" My friends were in a panic, pulling off their shoes, getting ready to jump in after him.

"Forget it," I said to them. "He's fine."

"How do you know?" someone asked me.

"He's my brother. He was born with gills—and shit for brains." I couldn't resist.

"What's he doing out here? Aren't you worried? He's been underwater all this time. . . ."

Three minutes, then four, five minutes passed, and up he popped. Waving, he slid onto his side, blowing bubbles, and then he glided away from the boat, heading with smooth, rhythmic strokes toward home.

"Holy mackerel," said my friend.

"I guess," I said.

I shut my eyes, and all these pictures appeared: the Falcon alone among his newspapers, feeding shortbread to Cromwell, talking to him about the state of the world as the edge of daylight recedes. Back at home, Bingo is running from the porch, pale and shining under the summer moonlight, stripping away his clothes as he runs, kicking off his shoes and hollering, the dogs following after him as he hits the water with a splash, and Pop's singing along with his favorite songs, and Bingo's back from his midnight swim, hair slicked away from his forehead, Uncle Tom's making scrambled eggs, and Ma and Bingo are dancing to Pop's music, drifting apart from us in ever widening circles, laughing in the kitchen, the dogs sweetly spinning.

Through the window, I caught sight of shifting shapes going from dark to light and light to dark and moving in slow motion and formal as they made their way to the beach. Down on my knees, the window open to the ocean, I leaned forward on my elbows for a better look, squinting gently, trying to focus on what was quietly out there among the gray shadows.

Gazing into the night, by the pure white light of a crescent moon, tiny blackbirds darting and moths and fireflies, I could see Uncle Tom, bareheaded and undistinguished at the heart of a solemn procession.

Gilda was in front and Nuala fanned out to the side, the stately Irish wolfhounds, long muzzles like tapers, Brendan and Kerry followed along like acolytes, the odor of early summer rolling in on violet waves. It was getting darker, the blackness lit by the moon and the stars, Uncle Tom's old red cardigan glowing like a ruby and fringed with starlight, his gray hair like silver now, the dogs in golden shadow and silent.

I can hear the wind blowing in the mountains a thousand miles away.

ACKNOWLEDGMENTS

Apologize, Apologize! would not exist in its current form were it not for the marvelous contributions of many people, starting with Emily Heckman, wonderful first reader, editor, and friend, and my fabulous agent, the unsinkable Molly Friedrich, who made the whole process entertaining, educational, and fun. Special thanks to Paul Cirone and Jacobia Dahm. Enormous thanks as well to my editor, Jonathan Karp, at Twelve for his intelligence, insights, and generosity of spirit, and to Angelika Glover, Diane Martin, Susan Traxel, Michelle MacAleese, and Louise Dennys at Knopf Canada for their superb editorial suggestions, support, and enthusiasm. They and the hardworking, talented members of their teams have made this experience a pleasure.

I would also like to recognize help and interest extended to me along the way by James D. Hornfischer, Jeff Gerecke, and Leigh Feldman. Thanks, too, to Deone Roberts, of the American Racing Pigeon Union, for her aid with research and for contributing anecdotal evidence concerning those pigeons who may, indeed, have walked home. I'm also indebted to "The Planet that Hums," which appeared in *New Scientist*, September 1999.

I want to express my love and gratitude to my mother, Doris Nightingale Kelly, who always kept the ship afloat regardless of the weather; to my siblings, Virginia, Susan, Arthur, and Rooney; and to my dear children, Caitlin, Rory, and Connor; with special thanks to my brothers-in-law, Andrew Judge and Robert Armstrong, my sister-in-law, Marilyn Pettitt, and my friend Debora Kortlandt.

I am forever indebted to the Kellys, the Monahans, and the Nightingales, who enriched my life in typically complicated fashion and who taught me that we love people as much for their weaknesses as for their strengths—the world is a quieter place without them.

This book honors the heart and mind and remarkable editorial skills of my daughter Flannery Dean, my toughest critic and greatest supporter. And to my husband, George Dean, the largely unsung hero of my life, thank you.

Finally, I want to pay tribute to my beloved little dog Marty, who kept me company as I wrote.

ABOUT THE AUTHOR

Elizabeth Kelly was born in Brantford, Ontario, Canada. She is an award-winning magazine journalist and editor and lives in a little village in eastern Ontario with her husband, four dogs, and three cats.

Reading Group Guide

DISCUSSION QUESTIONS

1) Throughout this account of Collie Flanagan's life (so far), he appears to be the only conventional—or perhaps even sane—member of his family. However, the novel is told from his perspective. Do you feel like you can trust what he's saying?

2) What do you think of Collie's mother? Does she seem to have lived a life of passion, or is she defined only by her rebellion against her aristocratic roots?

3) Should Collie have gone in after Bingo and the others, knowing as he did that there was no hope?

4) In one interview, Elizabeth Kelly referred to Bingo as "representative of full-blown adolescence, but in all its glory," and as something of a heroic character as well. What do you make of him?

5) Elizabeth Kelly has clearly had a lot of fun creating the hilarious and often manic characters at the heart of this novel. How did you react to the various Flanagan family blowouts? Did you more often cringe or laugh out loud?

6) Talk about the role of money in this novel: who has it and who doesn't; how it can be a motivator, or stunt one's ambitions; how it insulates the Flanagans, yet forces them into the limelight; and so on.

7) "Dignity is the last refuge of scoundrels," Collie's father was known to say, and he certainly was one to put himself into undignified positions, despite his charm and sharp clothes. What do you make of him as a man, and as a father?

8) Who is your favorite character in this novel, and why?

9) Collie and Bingo have a relationship that's not always straightforward, yet at its heart is a strong sibling love. What does each expect, and receive (or not), from the other?

10) What was Collie hoping to achieve in El Salvador? Did he change as a result of his experiences there?

11) What are Collie Flanagan's personal strengths? Were there small events that stood out for you as monumental in terms of proving his character?

12) More than any other member of the Flanagans, Collie has a close—if complex—relationship with his grandfather, Peregrine Lowell. Why is that so? How has their relationship developed by the end of the novel?

13) The Flanagans inhabit a world of elite privilege, yet are so self-absorbed you can't help but wonder whether they'd even notice if the rest of humanity ceased to exist. Does Collie rise above all that, or is he just like the rest of them?

14) Collie's father has a knack for showing up wildly drunk for even the most staid of events, including the funerals held for his wife and son. Talk about how his disappearances and arrivals function in the novel.

15) Whenever anyone talks to Collie about the events of the day Bingo and his mother died, they always get the details wrong. What is Kelly saying about living up to the expectations of others in this novel? Should Collie have stood up for himself more often?

16) The Flanagans are a wild and wildly humorous bunch, and even their seemingly unwarranted jabs at Collie are terrific. Discuss the role of cutting humor and over-the-top judgment in the novel.

17) At the end of the novel, Collie appears to have come to terms with his family, or at least seems to have achieved some measure of peace. What does the future hold for Collie Flanagan?

AN INTERVIEW WITH AUTHOR ELIZABETH KELLY

1) Can you tell us how you became a writer?

From the time I was little I wanted to be a writer; in fact, I thought of myself as a writer long before I had any legitimate claim on the title. If you can envision a seven-year-old swaggering around, imagining herself on literary par with Dylan Thomas, then you get the picture in all its Ted-Baxterish glory. As with everything in my life, it wasn't until my delusions collided with daily reality that I began to understand the significance of discipline, hard work, applied knowledge, and *humility.*

2) What inspired you to write this particular novel? What is it that you're exploring? Is there a story about the writing of *Apologize, Apologize!* that begs to be told?

Apologize, Apologize! has its origins in my admiration of personal courage, especially when paired against my own failings in that regard. Although the book has generated much discussion about family, the dynamics of family emerged as a byproduct of the central exploration of the story—which, at its core, is an examination of what it means to be brave.

As to some of the particulars: I grew up in Brantford, Ontario, within blocks of a deadly site on the Grand River, called Wilkes Dam—the great bogeyman of my childhood. Wilkes Dam has claimed many lives. Despite its dangers, it was common practice to cross the dam on foot. I was too terrified to make the journey but wound up doing so to impress my fearless boyfriend—now my husband, George—when I was eighteen or nineteen. I fell in! Had it not been for my fashionably wide belt and his strong grip—he was able to hoist me back on top of the dam—the local newspaper would have recorded yet another adolescent death in the aerated waters off Wilkes Dam.

I also wanted the book, both in style and content, to replicate the natural rhythms of life. In my experience, life is not a calm, sedate, organized affair, nor is it an easy fix—Collie Flanagan is charged with trying to learn the art of navigation.

3) Who is your favorite character in the novel, and why?

I like all the characters, each one for different reasons. They were fun to write. Ultimately, I suppose Collie is my favorite. When you write a novel in the first person, you develop a God-like understanding of the narrator, which tends to engender a certain amount of sympathy and empathy.

Collie is a good person struggling to be better.

4) Are there any tips you would give a book club to better navigate its discussion of your novel?

Although it may be presumptuous to tell readers how to read my book, I can't resist trying. So, here goes: Read with a sense of humor and bear in mind that the Flanagans value the performance of conversation over and above the actual substance of conversation. They entertain themselves with talk—they prize their opinions and the clever wordplay that characterizes their expression.

They love one another and they torture one another—they live for the "big" moments and operate like firecrackers, full of explosive energy; they're vivid and colorful, generating little lasting impact on their surroundings, but having enormous permanent effect on one another.

5) Do you have a favorite story to tell about being interviewed about your book?

As someone accustomed to being the interviewer, I was absolutely horrified at the thought of being interviewed. I spent a lot of advance time focusing on my leaden tongue and dull wit and my inability to come up with an engaging or thoughtful answer to questions. Of course, once the anxiety loop was set in motion, I tortured myself on a daily basis about the thought of being photographed and even resorted to giving myself a temporary facelift using green-and-red veterinary tape, only to discover that my overweight geriatric Lab, for whom it was intended, looked better than I did.

So asking me if I have a favorite story about being interviewed is akin to inquiring about my special memories of prepping for a colonoscopy.

6) What question are you never asked in interviews but wish you were?

Has anyone ever told you how much you look like Annette Bening?

7) Has a review or profile ever changed your perspective on your work?

While it's always interesting to read what others say about the book, I would never allow the views of strangers, no matter how seemingly insightful, to influence my view of myself or my writing. I think working as a journalist for many years helped inure me, to a large extent, to both good and bad responses to my writing. When you're writing to an audience (aside from the obvious practical considerations) I believe you're under professional obligation to focus only on the work; everything else is an indulgence. It's pretty effortless for me to accept criticism and accolade in the same spirit—benign indifference—though when I was younger, such equanimity eluded me!

Which is not to say that I'm not tremendously grateful to anyone who takes the time and makes the effort to read my work and comment.

8) Which authors have been most influential to your own writing?

When I was very young I loved Albert Payson Terhune, who wrote about his beloved Sunnybank Collies. I read *Rebecca* a million times and was an avid reader of fairy tales and animal stories—*Beautiful Joe, Black Beauty.* As an adolescent I read Dylan Thomas and T. S. Eliot. I admire Yeats, Joyce, Dickens, Bruce Chatwin, Kazuo Ishiguro, and Kingsley and Martin Amis, among others including Donna Tartt, Dave Eggers, and William Maxwell.

I love the nonfiction work of writers such as the late Marjorie Williams. I read newspapers and magazines compulsively and indiscriminately—including *Soap Opera Digest* and *Bark*, a magazine for dog lovers. When it comes to writers, I don't date; I fall in love and get married. It's an all-or-nothing-at-all proposition.

9) If you weren't writing, what would you want to be doing for a living? What are some of your other passions in life?

I'm a big proponent of doing nothing. I think if I wasn't a writer I would sit in a chair and stare. I love dogs but only as companions. I don't want to turn them into work. I would have loved to be a musical theater performer, but I think that makes me delusional, so better to sit and stare.

10) If you could have written one book in history, what book would that be?

Diary of a Nobody by George and Weedon Grossmith.

The Irish Connection

By Elizabeth Kelly

A friend of mine once confessed that she felt sorry for people who aren't Americans. "I know it's wrong," she admitted, "but somewhere deep inside of me, I feel as if we really are the most special people on earth."

I suspect she isn't alone in her narcissism. I mean, I think my Shih Tzu is the best Shih Tzu in the world, just because he's mine. In truth, many of us harbor the secret conviction that anyone who is not *us*, or *ours*, is, well, second best.

So how then do we explain the mystery of St. Patrick's Day? And why for one day each year do millions of people want to be Irish?

Just about everyone, everywhere, sets aside a day in March to celebrate Ireland and being Irish, as if it were a highly desirable state of mind rather than a distinct nationality with some unfortunate associations to a hand soap whose scent evokes nostalgia for BO.

As secularists, we're not in the habit of saluting saints, especially other people's saints. After all, every country has national holidays worth celebrating. Like many of you, I can't wait for Turkmen Melon Day, held in Turkmenistan on the second Sunday in August, and I already have a flight booked to Latvia in September—think of me in your little cubicles while I'm at the head of a conga line rejoicing in the Day of the Workers in the Oil, Gas, Power, and Geological Industry.

I know what you're thinking. It's the party-on factor that makes everyone so excited about St. Patrick's Day, but nobody likes beer that much—except maybe Canadians.

Oktoberfest is all about beer—many countries celebrate Oktoberfest, too—but I don't know anyone who, outwardly at least, wants to be German, even for a day.

There's just something about Ireland that makes it seem like the right place on earth to take the human temperature and still get an authentic reading.

Maybe it's because, with its love of language and ideas, Ireland creates the impression of a country that might still prefer James Joyce to James Bond, a place where people might still look for insights in the poetry of Yeats rather than the placebo of self-help.

Or maybe the rest of us, caught up in a romantic notion, only imagine an island in an ocean inhabited by an imperfect people, opinionated, resilient, irreverent, funny, and fierce, a place that could cause a man to write *The Importance of Being Earnest* and *De Profundis* in the same lifetime.

Maybe we all want to be Irish for even a little while because Ireland takes the best and worst of what makes us human and turns it into poetry.

Oscar Wilde had his faults—thank God—but he gave rebellion eloquence and eloquence rebellion. He shrugged off every authority—church, state, social, and sexual—and he did it with authority. He made art of private pain and comedy out of morality. He served hard time and he never let the bastards get him down.

As Bobby Sands slowly starved to death, he smuggled out tiny scraps of paper containing his final thoughts, hopes, and disappointments.

"I am awaiting the lark for spring is all but upon us," he wrote in his diary. "Now lying on what indeed is my death bed, I still listen even to the black crows."

I don't know why the world celebrates St. Patrick's Day. But I know why I do. I want to be Irish because for just a moment I would like to feel what it's like to be brave.

A young woman I know recently visited Dublin. She explored the streets during the day and in the evening she went to visit a pub with a girlfriend. As she was leaving she spotted a man she recognized from earlier in the day. When she'd seen him then he was conservatively dressed, walking to work, wearing a suit and a tie.

Now it was midnight and he was standing outside the pub naked from the waist down.

"Don't worry," one of the regulars reassured her, "it's just Francie."

Or maybe it's the beer after all.